# SON OF STEEL

## CHILDREN OF ASH
### BOOK TWO

# ALLISON ANDERSON

Published by Oliver-Heber Books

0 9 8 7 6 5 4 3 2 1

*For Lindsay Hiller*
*You sat down next to me at that table, and my life hasn't been the same since.*

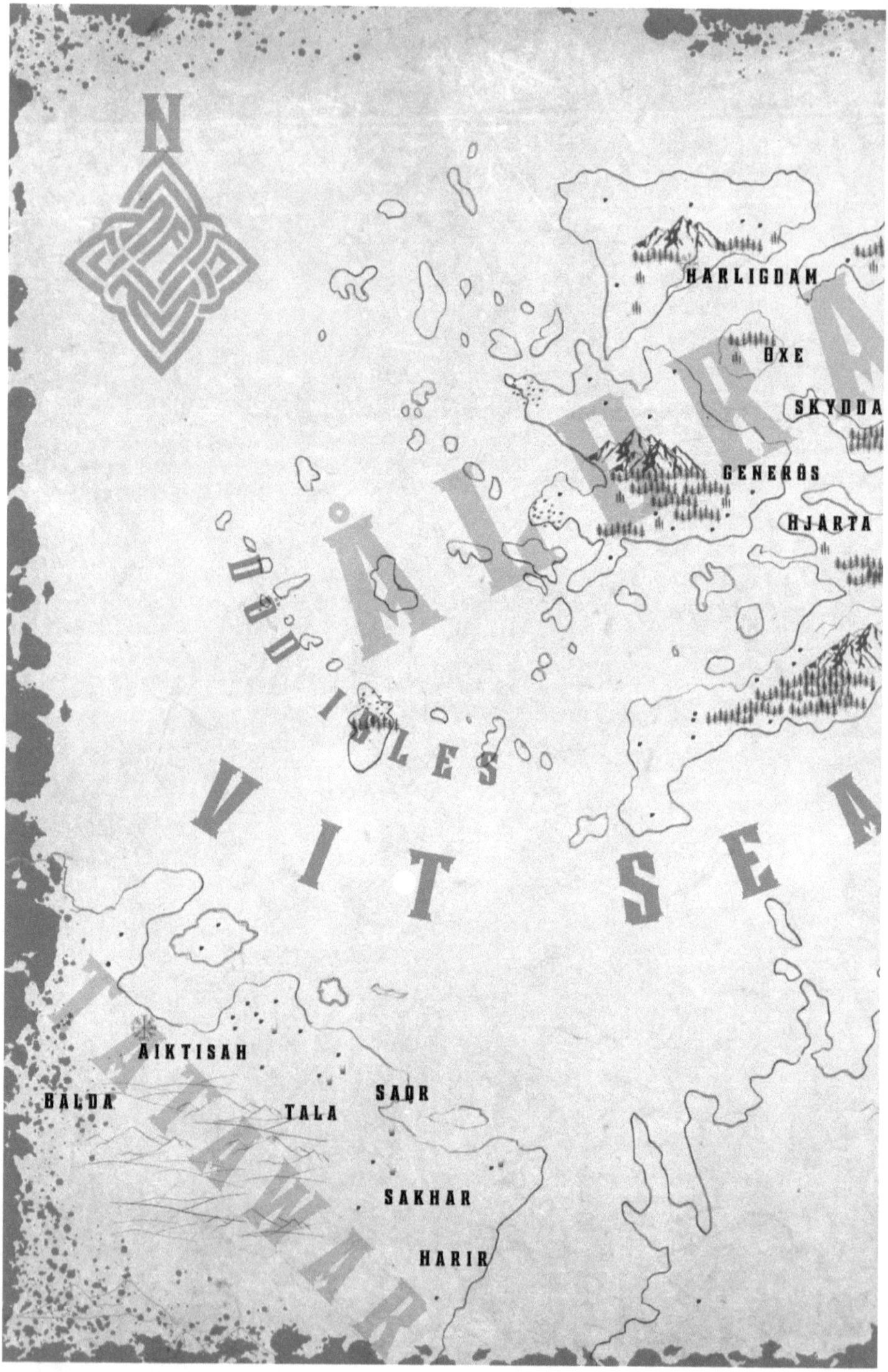

N
ÅLERA
ISLES
VIT SEA
HARLIGDAM
ÖXE
SKYDDA
GENERÖS
HJÄRTA
AIKTISAH
BALDA
TALA
SAQR
SAKHAR
HARIR

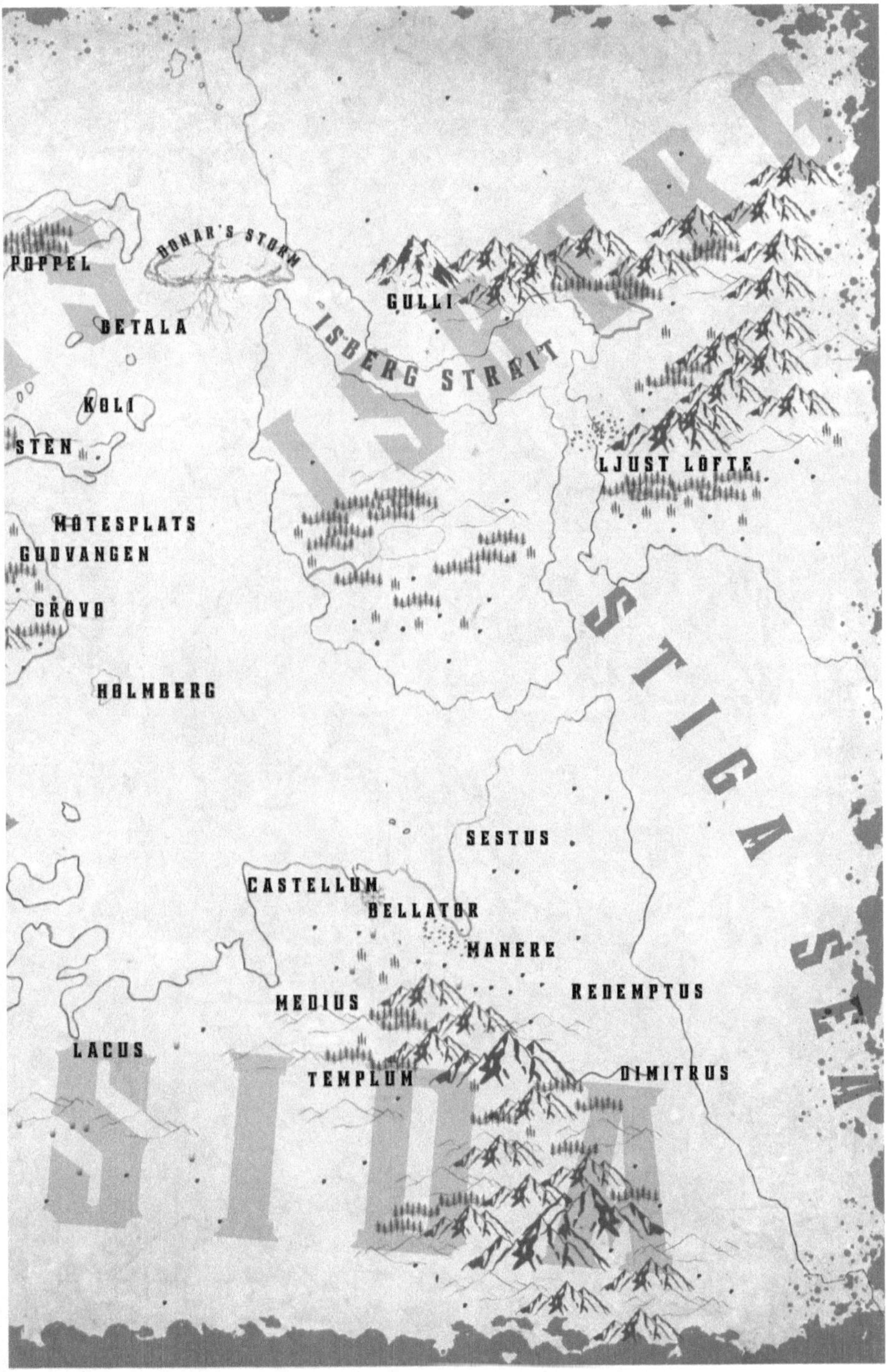

POPPEL
DONAR'S STORM
GULLI
BETALA
"ISBERG STRAIT
KØLI
STEN
LJUST LÖFTE
MÖTESPLATS
GUDVANGEN
GRÖVØ
HOLMBERG
SESTUS
CASTELLUM
BELLATOR
MANERE
REDEMPTUS
MEDIUS
LACUS
TEMPLUM
DIMITRUS
STIGA SEA

# GLOSSARY

**Häxa Terms:**
Häxa—women gifted with power over elements of nature
Animal Shifters—shift into other animals, communicate with animals
Air Whisperers—manipulate the weather, use the air to communicate long distances
Fire Charmers—manipulate fire, self-healing
Plant Healers—grow plants without aid, heal other people's infirmities
Spirit Walkers—walk without their body, commune with the dead
Stone Carvers—manipulate rock, imbue stone with magic
Water Wielders—wield water, see into the future
Ekte—Häxa killers, men who have carved their skin with runes to negate magic
Förändra—the catalyst for a Häxa's gift

**Magical Beings:**
Dragon—a winged beast of legend
Draugr—undead beings whose bite will kill even the strongest of warriors
Dwarf—creatures with perfect craftsmanship who can enchant the things they create

Elf—a creature of great magic who can wield shadow or light
Fossegrim—a fiddle-playing creature that lures women and children to their deaths
Giant—a humongous creature known to dwell in the most frozen parts of the world
Hafgufa—a ship-eating creature; known for looking like an island and luring desperate sailors to their gaping maws
Hamingja—benevolent spirits that will bestow luck upon those they deem worthy
Huldra—a forest-dwelling creature that takes the form of a woman, distinguished by an animal-like appendage and a large, hollow cavity between her shoulder blades
Jörmungandrson—spawn of Jörmungandr, the Great Serpent, known for dragging ships down into the water depths
Jötunn—another name for the gods who dwell over all of Yggdrasil
Marbendill—a creature with the torso and head of a woman and the tail of a seal
Nixie—water-bound creatures who drag sailors to their doom
Phoenix—a bird that rises from the ashes with new life
Valkyrie—servants of the gods, usher the souls of warriors to Valhalla
Vätte—small creatures often found in the midst of cattle, wear furred hats, and known for killing an entire herd of cattle if displeased

**Gods:**
Baldr—god of beauty, light, and peace
Donar—god of thunder
Freyja—goddess of beauty, love, death, war, and magic
Freyr—god of the harvest
Frigg—goddess of motherhood, marriage, and prophecy
Fulla—goddess of service
Hel—goddess over the dead
Hermod—messenger god
Hrimthursar—frost giant
Logi—god of fire
Loki—god of mischief and disguise
Máni—goddess of the moon
Njord—god of the wind and sea

Sol—god of the sun
Three Norns—goddesses of fate
Wōden/Allfather—god of all Yggdrasil, father of the gods

**Ships:**
Langship—Sidan longships, known for their speed and maneuverability over the water
Karve—longship used for both war and cargo, known for its broad hull
Knörr—merchant ship, used for long voyages for trade
Skeid—large longships used to transport soldiers over far distances
Snekkja—small ships, used in battle

# Chapter 1

## Fools

*Praise the Allfather Axel and Petyr—I still don't know how else to refer to Mallory's child—made it out of the city before Firmin learned of the escape of the girl he'd taken to dangle over Axel's head. She'd killed eleven guards to get away. I'm not at all surprised. Firmin was in an uproar once the discovery was made. It took me all day to convince the High King not to send a fleet of ships after The Phoenix and her crew. I pray he doesn't discover the truth.*

*— From the writings of Doran Finnsson, the last King of Grovö*

If Axel Ashersson wasn't such a hero, he wouldn't be hanging off the neck of a two-ton jörmungandrson in the middle of the bloody Vit Sea.

"Hold the lines!" Erik yelled from below. The skipper practically hung over the side of *The Phoenix,* the harness strapping him into the ship the only thing keeping him on his perch next to the tiller.

The beast beneath Axel swiveled through the water, its sinuous body gliding over the surface of the water. Lines of rope tied around large hooks kept it from diving under the sea and coming up under the ship. Water ran down its silvery back in rivulets, making any footholds Axel could find on the beast's back slick. He'd lose his footing and crash into the sea below if he wasn't careful.

Axel stabbed down and sank his sword between the jörmungandrson's soft scales. *At least it isn't a hafgufa this time.* Those things were twice the size with four times the jaw mobility. A jörmungandrson would use its snakelike body and large snout to shoot upwards through the water, breaking apart ships. The sailors that fell into the water didn't last long.

The jörmungandrson writhed under Axel, roaring at the pain from its wounds. Fans on either side of the beast's head flared out, shaking with its rage. If only the Great Serpent that gave the beast its namesake would have kept its spawn out of Midgard. Then Axel wouldn't have to worry about his ship getting eaten while he was in the midst of a suicide mission.

Freyja's golden tears, if he wasn't such a hero, he wouldn't be sailing through enemy waters undetected to fetch Lady Idalia after she left her husband for Prince Roman. The Sidan Prince had been foolish enough to insult High King Firmin and King Anders when he'd stolen the lady out from under King Anders's bulbous nose. Not that the man didn't deserve it. Anders was a blubbering idiot who couldn't tell his wife from his pigs. If Axel hadn't been tasked with retrieving the wayward lady, he might have cheered for Lady Idalia. He might have even prayed for the gods to help her flee. But hanging onto slimy scales by the tips of his fingers while he fought a giant sea beast exhausted any of his good humor. While the lady would find peace if he let her escape, Åldras would be the one to pay for her choice. Frigg's all-seeing eye, he had to take his crew through monster-infested waters because of her. Hadn't they faced enough? Hadn't his crew done enough for Åldras in the name of a war that should never have been?

But Queen Eva had pleaded with him to go after Lady Idalia. The Åldran queen had practically sacrificed herself to save Axel from Firmin's machinations in the name of saving Åldras from the war that had already taken so much from them. She'd taken the blame for Princess Ella's disappearance after Firmin had convinced everyone that Axel had kidnapped the girl to break the armistice between Sida and Åldras, when in reality Axel had been entrusted with the princess's life after it was discovered that she was a Häxa. A girl gifted with magic over plants and healing.

Magic that was outlawed in Åldras due to prejudice and malice.

Magic that ran through both Axel and Petra's veins.

A harpoon sank into the scaly beast's neck only an ell from Axel's leg.

He glanced back over his shoulder.

Petra stood at the stem, tying down the line she'd just sank into the jörmungandrson's neck.

If Axel wasn't such a hero, he definitely wouldn't be so confused about Petra.

He didn't know what to do with her. Didn't know if he was furious or grief-stricken or relieved to finally have the truth after all these years. She'd lied to him. Lied about what she was. About what had happened the night their village had burned to the ground. About who had really started this war. About everything.

And now they were on this godsforsaken mission neither of them wanted to be on. Even if bringing Lady Idalia back to Anders didn't feel like a betrayal to everything Axel believed, trying to come up with how to do it without getting their crew killed was a nightmare. Every time Axel even attempted to seek Petra out, it turned into a fight rather than a strategy meeting.

Which was absolutely not Axel's fault. He hadn't been the one who lied. He wasn't the one snapping at every sideways glance or hint of a frown.

Petra's gaze cut to him, but before she could even narrow her eyes, Big Hal shoved her to the side and took the rope she'd been tying down. The idiot didn't even glance her way as her expression flashed with fury directed at him.

Axel wasn't the only one confused about Petra.

While none of the crew knew the true extent of her deception, they knew she'd been hiding her gender for eight years. That she'd been acting as a soldier in Åldras's army, an occupation not granted to Åldran women. Axel could imagine they felt just as disoriented and betrayed as he did.

He turned away, grabbing the handle of the harpoon and twisting it further into the jörmungandrson's neck. The beast bucked, and it took all of Axel's strength to keep his grip on both the harpoon and his sword as the beast writhed under him. With its distraction, the crew of *The Phoenix* struck. The ropes all grew taught, each crewmember using the pulleys bolted to the ship to pull in the lines attached to the beast's hide.

The crew wrenched its head down.

Close enough for Axel to jump in the water.

He yanked his sword from the sea monster's neck and dove to the side, away from the falling beast. The water embraced him within its cold arms, hugging him tightly as it pulled him away from Sol's glare above. He let the thrashing sea tug him from the beast until it grew calm. His lungs ached for the want of air, but little else. There was no spasm. No real pain. Just the lack of air inside him.

He sheathed his sword and kicked to the surface.

Water sprayed in every direction from where the beast writhed next to the ship. But the jörmungandrson couldn't dive back under the surface, the lines against the sides of the ship preventing it from disappearing into the watery depths.

Erik's voice rang out over the ship, though Axel couldn't tell what he said over the crash of the water. Axel cut around the serpent, aiming for the rear of the ship to clamber back on board.

He didn't see the jörmungandrson's tail until it caught him in the stomach.

The tail pushed him out over the water, sending him flying toward the ship.

"Incoming!" Little Hal hollered.

Axel tucked in his limbs and attempted to relax his body as he crashed onto the deck. The landing knocked the air out of him, but besides the pressure of the hit, his skin didn't split, his bones didn't break, and his organs didn't more than spasm. The magic running through his body made him as impenetrable as Valhalla's gates and as strong as the giant Hrungnir. He groaned as he flopped onto his front. Thank the Allfather he'd had his sword strapped to him. It would have been miserable to fetch if he'd dropped it in the water.

"Axel!" Erik barked. "Stop lying about and get your sad excuse for a carcass to the side of the ship!" The skipper sat at his perch, both hands gripping the tiller with white knuckles. At least he would keep the ship upright. He continued shouting orders to the other crewmembers as Axel pushed himself to his feet.

Big Hal still stood at the stern, teeth gritted as he tied off another rope. While the man was just younger than Axel, his strength made up for his youthful idiocy in spades. Ulf and Ludvig stood at the side of the ship, their faces lined with concentration as they sank large hooks into the beast's underbelly, doing their best to weaken it. Little Hal stood at the center of the ship, wading through the hold and throwing hooks, ropes, and nets onto the deck. All of them wore the leather harnesses strapping them to the mast in case the beast tried to knock them overboard. Axel's gaze darted over every inch of *The Phoenix*.

No Petra.

He stepped back to where he'd clambered over the gunwale. Had she fallen in the water? She wasn't stupid. Axel shook his head. She would have tied a harness to the mast like everyone else. He wove his way over the deck toward the cargo hold. She'd likely gone for more rope.

A shadow passed overhead.

Axel's gaze flew upward. Petra perched at the very top of the mast, her jaw-length hair whipping into her face as she adjusted her hold on a long spear. Before he could even take a full breath, she leaped from the mast. *Without* a harness.

Little Hal called out for her, his eyes wide with terror. He'd watched Olav, the last surviving member of his family, get lost to the sea only a few weeks ago, and now Petra was forcing him to watch her leap into the turbulent water.

*Hel's bloody halls.* Axel stormed to the side of the ship.

She raised the spear overhead, her face grim with determination as she hurtled toward the jörmungandrson. Erik hissed obscenities as she plunged the spear into the sea monster's head.

The beast jerked, coiling up as the life drained out and the muscle memory kicked in.

Petra lost her footing on the slick scales of the jörmungandrson's neck and slipped down into the water.

Without a single thought, Axel dove back into the sea.

He swam around the beast, his eyes scanning the dark water around him. The serpent's body still thrashed even in death, stirring the ocean around the ship.

How could she be so reckless? Since they left Harligdam, she'd been throwing herself around and getting in fights with Big Hal every chance she got. Her eyes were constantly narrowed into sharp slits, and her fingers hadn't strayed from her axes much. She was building up walls, as she always did when she experienced a moment of vulnerability. But Axel had finally seen what was behind those walls, and he wouldn't let her retreat behind them again. When he figured out how to do it without losing the semblance of control he had—or without her trying to stab him—they would talk. One of the few times he'd attempted to broach the subject, he'd gotten too angry to even breathe and she'd ruined his third favorite tunic.

He found her floundering a few feet under the writhing beast, trying to swim against the water that continued to shove her farther down. Only her right arm paddled through the water, her left tucked against her chest. She'd likely dislocated it. Again. She claimed she'd been injured during her time with Firmin and his goons when he'd taken her, believing her to be a simple Häxa girl from Ljust Löfte.

How wrong they'd all been.

When Axel reached her, he wrapped an arm around her waist and pushed toward the surface. Petra's head came up first, and she gulped in a lungful, coughing up the water that had made it down her throat.

Axel wiped his hair out of his face. He could kill her. Or shake her. Or kiss her.

But he wouldn't do any of those things.

"What on Frigg's bloody lands were you thinking?" he said, still holding onto her as he shoved them through the water.

She tried to wriggle herself out of his grip, but he wasn't going to let her go. Not when she would just get herself killed.

"I can get back to the ship on my own," she insisted.

He scoffed. "Right, because you were doing so well a minute ago when you were *drowning*."

Her eyes narrowed, and he could perfectly read her thoughts in the steel of her blue-green irises. *I don't need your help.*

He shook his head but kept his mouth shut. It was as if now that the secrets between them had been brought to light, she was doing everything in her power to drive him to insanity. And it was working.

He didn't know whether to run away with her and find a secluded mountain somewhere to live out the rest of their days in hiding or to throw her over the side of the bloody boat and let the killer whales eat her.

When she'd told him a week ago that the past he knew was a lie, something between them had broken. It wasn't the fact that she was a Häxa or that she had magic not seen in Midgard in generations that made his stomach twist into hundreds of knots. It wasn't even the fact that her magic had been the reason their island burned to nothing but ash that made his gut tighten.

No, it was that she'd made him believe a lie.

That for nearly nine years, she'd let him believe in a war built on the bones of their families.

She let him believe the Sidans had been the ones who destroyed their home.

When they'd been just as innocent as the Åldrans were.

He couldn't deny they had been there for something. Petra's retelling of that night's events was proof of that. While Sida had been poking at Åldras for decades before—trying to renegotiate borders and making stingy trade deals—they hadn't stormed any islands until that night. Axel had fought them beside Father and the rest of Holmberg. Had stood with Mallory and Petra's brothers as the Sidans had stormed the beach like thieves in the dark of night. But why?

Petra finally stopped trying to wriggle out of his grasp, allowing herself to float on her back as he dragged her through the water.

They reached the side of the ship and Axel finally let her go.

When she reached up to haul herself onto the boat, Ulf and Ludvig grabbed her wrists. She winced when they pulled on her left arm.

"Let her go," Axel said, more bite to his voice than was necessary.

The men released Petra's arms, and she finally hauled herself onto the ship. Axel followed right behind her, vaulting over the side just in time to watch her stomp toward her trunk, her steps splashing across the puddled deck. She practically threw herself onto the lid and stripped her boots from her feet as if skinning a wolf.

Little Hal watched her from his place at the pulleys; eyes filled with relief.

*Freyja's golden tears, she'll be the death of me.*

The thought brought on more memories, making his heart drum rapidly against his ribs. Petra's lips on his. His fingers in her hair. Her hands pressed to his chest.

He shook his head. He couldn't think about that day. Couldn't think about the one moment where he'd allowed himself to believe he could have everything he wanted. It wasn't just the fact that she pushed him away after their kiss that proved she didn't feel the same way that he did. It was the fact that his magic hadn't even budged that proved it all the more.

The prophecy his absent mother left him with had been clear.

> *In war's dark fray, steadfast, unharmed*
> *Until one day by love disarmed*
> *When, with a maid his heart is traded*
> *By gods betrayed—in war unaided*
> *The hero's strength in battle fails him*
> *At last, at length, his foe impales him*
> *The reaper calls from deathly hollows*
> *The hero falls, the she-bear follows.*

If Petra cared about him as much as he cared about her, his magic would be faltering.

And it wasn't.

They couldn't fall in love anyway. Not when their kingdom stood on the brink of resuming this bloody war. Not when Firmin knew where the Häxa were and the Great Mother lay on her death bed. Axel scrubbed a hand down his face. He'd had no news of the Great Mother's death, though she'd likely passed through the gates of Valhalla already. The wound she'd been dealt by Firmin's hand had been grave, and sometimes the gods' wills were stronger than any magic, Häxa or otherwise.

He grabbed the edge of his tunic, wringing as much water as he could from the thick wool. With Sol's light high above them, he would dry out before nightfall.

Free of her boots, Petra strode toward Erik. She'd lingered back there over the last several days. Avoiding the whole crew certainly wasn't endearing her to anyone. Even Erik was peevish having her hovering about him. The skipper locked the tiller in place and grabbed her arm.

"Well?" Erik demanded, his gaze full of challenge. "Prove what you wanted?"

Her shoulders bunched next to her ears, but she kept whatever thoughts had her hackles rising to herself.

The skipper shoved Petra's arm back into place before she could even gasp. The pop of the joint made Axel's stomach twist, and he took a step toward her as she grimaced.

"Put your bloody arm in a sling and keep it there." Erik shook his head and turned away from her. "All right, you lot! Let's get this jörmungandrson unhooked and head to Bellator before the bloody Sidans see us or someone else tries to get themselves killed."

ᚠᚾᚲᛟᚠᛁᛚ

THE LIGHTS of Bellator glowed along Sida's shore like a million stars, the city as wide as the sky over their heads. Small towns peppered the hills outside the capital city, only increasing the magnitude of the population. While Axel had fought the Sidans many times over the years, he'd never been so close to their capital city. Most of their battles had been on the sea or in outlying villages around Åldras. He'd been on one scouting mission to a Sidan outpost on an island near Holmberg, but that had been nothing compared to this.

Frigg's all-seeing eye, how had Åldras never fallen to this kind of might? Harligdam was the largest city in all of Åldras, and most would sail right by it if they didn't know to look for it. Axel couldn't even see past Bellator's city wall and it already surpassed Harligdam three times over.

How would they get in? He and Petra had infiltrated many a city over the years. Once, they'd even strapped themselves to the bottom of a cart and snuck into King Amund's own walled fortress. But that might not have been the wisest option this time.

Freyja's golden tears, Axel was not a strategist.

They were practically at Sida's front door, and he barely had an inkling of a plan.

"Quite a sight," said Ulf from beside him.

Petra, standing next to Erik at his perch, gave a sharp nod. Her eyes were shadowed by the hooded cloak stretched over her shoulders, but he could see the guarded expression that hardened the set of her mouth and hollowed out her cheeks. Could see the way she stared down at the glow of Erik's pipe.

Axel pulled his gaze away from her to look at Ulf. "You don't have to come with us, you know. If you or Ludvig want us to drop you off somewhere along the coast so you can go back to Åldras, we'll understand." The two of them weren't technically part of *The Phoenix*'s crew, having joined them to go to Ljust Löfte with Doran to take Princess Ella there. He'd honestly been surprised the two of them hadn't stayed with their steersman in Harligdam when they left on this fool's errand.

Ulf shook his head. "Wouldn't be right. Besides, Doran would tan my hide if I left you and Pet to yourselves. Said you needed Ludvig and me. We won't go against our king and steersman."

Axel nodded. Doran had always been able to instill a loyalty in others that Axel had never found possible. Even he and Petra found allegiance to the man important beyond measure. Perhaps it was because Doran was a true king. He listened to those around him and cared about peoples' stories. He knew more about their kingdom than the entire Council of Kings combined, and yet he was satisfied being a warrior instead of a reigning lord.

If only he could have come with them. If he hadn't had to stay with Firmin, perhaps he could have helped Axel figure out what to do. Where to go. How to get Idalia back to Åldras without betraying every particle of honor Father instilled in him during his youth. How to talk to Petra without losing his head. But Doran had stayed behind to clean up the mess left by Axel and Petra thwarting Firmin's plan to frame them for the disappearance of Princess Ella. There was no way *The Phoenix* wouldn't have been pursued. Not when Firmin had lost the one thing he'd been able to dangle over Axel's head.

Petra.

Though Firmin had thought her little else than a simple Häxa girl, he'd captured her in hopes of controlling Axel. But she'd escaped, likely leaving a trail of bodies in her wake—if the still healing bruises under her eyes and her newly broken nose said anything. Axel had watched their stern for three days before he really believed no one was coming after them. Doran's raven had found them, delivering a missive that he'd been able to redirect the High King's attention. Whatever that meant. If Doran hadn't smoothed things over or found a way to make Firmin believe Axel hadn't been involved, *The Phoenix* would have never made it out of Åldras. Whatever magic Doran had performed worked.

Ludvig called to Ulf from where he sat next to a pile of weapons, and the large man left the three of them staring at the glittering city. How long until they were discovered? How long until the Sidan langships surrounded them?

Axel cleared his throat. "We need to come up with a plan."

Petra's head whipped up, her eyes wide. *You don't have a bloody plan?*

He certainly hadn't been able to come up with anything viable. Not one to get Lady Idalia out with an entire city of bloodthirsty Sidans waiting for them.

Petra shook her head, turning to Erik. "Are you ready for us to make a run for it?"

"Are you going to help come up with a plan?" Erik let out a lazy puff of smoke, but his eyes studied her. As if the question he posed was more about what was in store for the future of the crew than how they were going to accomplish this suicidal quest.

She ignored both questions.

Axel folded his arms over his chest. "I'm certainly ready to come up with a plan."

The comment was just as loaded as Erik's question. He knew it and he knew that she knew it. But it slipped out, and he couldn't feel sorry for it. Not when the chasm between them remained.

Petra glared up at him. "Are you so impatient to take Lady Idalia back to Harligdam and show Firmin what a good pet you are? I'm sure he'll commend you for your fetching skills."

Axel's spine stiffened. "Are you bloody serious right now?"

She shrugged. "What in Hel's rocking halls have we been doing this entire time if we're going to bring Lady Idalia back to Anders for her to find a horrible end at his hands? No point in pretending otherwise. We're nothing but Firmin's dogs."

"*Pet*," Erik warned.

"Just because you don't like the truth doesn't make it any less true."

Axel growled. "Now that's definitely not fair, and you bloody know it. You know *exactly* why we had to take this mission. If you'd stop acting like everyone here is trying to attack you, you'd realize you're being an idiot."

Petra bared her teeth. "You think I'm being an idiot? You're the one fooling yourself thinking we're going to make it out of this unscathed. Anders was an idiot to lose his wife, and we're idiots for going after her. We should abandon this entire bloody mess while we have the chance."

"And abandon everyone we left behind? The good people of Åldras who need this armistice to last? The Häxa who are even now being hunted by the Ekte? Everyone who's counting on us? It would be just as bad as strapping them to the bloody pyres ourselves."

"Like that won't happen anyway." She rolled her eyes. "All this work is only prolonging the inevitable."

"And I think you're being a selfish brat," he snapped. "It's far easier to allow yourself to wallow when you need to get over yourself and help us get through this mission. You're endangering yourself and the rest of us because you think you deserve to throw a tantrum now that everyone knows you're a woman."

Erik glared. "*Axel*."

Petra snorted, looking away from him. "I'll do my best to keep my gender from killing anyone."

Something smacked into the back of her head. Erik's pipe clattered onto the deck.

She spun back to him. "What was that for?"

"For being a bloody rockhead." Erik grunted. "Not a single one of us cares that you're a woman, Pet. We care about *you*. So stop this bloody nonsense and get your act together, or the rest of us are going to find our heads on the ends of pikes the moment we step on Sidan soil."

With a growl under her breath, she stormed off.

Axel held back a groan and scrubbed a hand over his face. "Hel's bloody halls."

Erik shook his head. "The two of you need to get this figured out. Fast."

Axel could only nod, the boiling in his gut leaving no room for more words. Since she couldn't speak to him for longer than five seconds without trying to bite his bloody head off, it was up to him to figure out how to get into Bellator. Alone.

With one last glance toward the coast, Axel spun back to the rest of the ship. "Gather 'round! We've got two hours until we beach, and a two hour walk after that. We need to figure out how to get past that bloody wall without losing our heads."

Every member of the crew assembled in the center of the ship. Petra stayed at the edge of the group, but even she wouldn't ignore a summons. The only crewmember exempt from meeting them at the center was Erik, but he was needed at the tiller more than in the planning. He'd lob advice from his perch as he saw fit anyhow.

Every plan Petra or Doran had ever enacted flew through Axel's head. There was the time Doran had started a fire down a beach to distract an encampment and take it from the other side. Petra had once come up with the idea to cover *The Phoenix* in flotsam and jetsam to make it look like it had been floating the sea for months unattended, drawing a ship or two in before the crew attacked. There had been disguises, demolished buildings, and even spiked drinks to add to their many strategies. But what would work to get them into Bellator?

Axel set his hands to his hips. "We've got a giant wall, probably a slew of guards who would rather stab us than talk, and an entire city between us and Lady Idalia."

"Not to mention a prince or two," Ulf helpfully added.

Enzo and Roman weren't fools. They'd know to keep anyone from coming and snatching Lady Idalia back from them. In fact, they'd be expecting someone to come. The element of surprise had become pretty much void even before *The Phoenix* had come in sight of the city. But would they be expecting *The Phoenix* to be the ship to come for the lady? The last time Axel had laid eyes on Enzo, they'd been in that bloody draugr bog. It would likely throw Bellator into a tizzy to find out Mighty Axel had come for the lady himself.

They could make a huge ruckus.

Axel straightened. They could do a "Gone to Goat."

He glanced up at Petra. Her chin tilted down, the shadows around her eyes darkening. Oh, it would be so great to pull this trick again.

Her eyes narrowed. "Don't even suggest it."

A grin pulled the corners of his mouth wide.

"I believe," he drawled, "we'll be pulling a Gone to Goat."

## CHAPTER 2

---

# A PLAN

If Petra didn't have bloody lockpicks in her mouth, she would have been spewing curses at Axel's back as she raced after him through the moonlit field. Torches bobbed behind them, casting light over the grass whipping against their legs. She could almost feel the flames sing to her. Feel their feather-soft brush of light against her skin as they begged her to reach for them.

The ground around Bellator was lush with thick grasses and short trees, perfect for hiding in but not running through. Especially not in the blasted Sidan heat. Drops of sweat ran down her back as she wove through the thick brush.

"Gone to Goat" had been named after the time Axel had finally tracked down the Great Mother in order to save other Häxa still trapped in Åldras. Once he'd finally been given permission to form his own crew after their years under Doran's tutelage, he'd immediately set to getting in touch with the Great Mother. Ljust Löfte was in its early years, and everyone they'd spoken to believed it was still in Åldras somewhere. They'd searched the kingdom for months but found nothing. It had been Petra who came up with the plan to draw the Häxa out.

They'd started wreaking a little havoc. Found some of the Häxa readying to travel to the colony and followed them. Every time, the women had used their magic to throw Axel and Petra off their trail.

Three months of chasing the fleeing women and showing up in their camps or their safe houses finally drew the Great Mother out.

When they found out the matriarch would be coming herself, they made it rather easy for them to be captured by the Häxa and brought before the Great Mother. Petra had carried a small blade in her mouth that time, but the concept was the same. Before the Häxa could drag them before the Great Mother, Petra had gotten both Axel and her out of the ropes they'd been bound with. The Great Mother had arrived right when Petra had cut the last of Axel's bonds. When she'd seen them, she'd turned back to her companions and said, "Well, your plans to throw them out to sea have gone to goat."

The name stuck, even if Petra had done everything in her power to make Axel forget about the idiotic strategy. Getting captured, having all their weapons taken away, and making her walk around with sharp objects in her mouth was stupid.

But no matter how much she'd hated the idea to sneak lockpicks into Bellator, her opinion had not been considered.

At least, not by the rest of the crew.

Big Hal nearly stomped on the heels of her boots, and Ludvig followed behind him. They'd left Little Hal, Erik, and Ulf to watch over the ship while they enacted Axel's harebrained plan. She'd nearly thrown herself over the side of the ship when Axel made the assignments. Perhaps if she had, she would have been able to leave Axel behind and fade into the night. Not likely, especially with the grin he'd been sporting since he made the suggestion. But if she was gone, none of this would be a problem. Axel could be free of her and all the pain she caused him and the rest of the crew.

It had been ten days since they'd left Harligdam and every single moment had been filled with side eyes and fumbled words. While some of the crew had been fine with her return to the ship—Erik had known the truth long before the rest of the crew—there were still problems. Like the fact that Little Hal had grown protective of her. And Ludvig kept trying to speak to her about women he knew around Åldras. And Big Hal. Hel's bloody halls, Big Hal was the worst of the bunch. It was as if the moment he'd found out she was a woman a shutter had closed over his eyes and all he saw was a stupid girl who didn't know which end of a sword was the dangerous one.

It was exactly why she hadn't wanted anyone to know who she was. She'd seen the way women were treated in Åldras. They were property to be managed, trophies to be paraded about, or bodies to warm a bed. While there were exceptions to the rule—Mama and Da being two—they were a minority. Ever since the kingdoms decided the Häxa were a threat, women were treated differently. Callously. Warily.

It had been the best decision Petra ever made to pretend to be a man, and that her façade had been ripped away made her want to stab something.

"Halt!" someone called from behind her. Instead, Axel turned back toward the road they'd been running parallel to. Petra reacted to his shift immediately and was rewarded with Big Hal nearly bowling her over.

The itch to gut him then and there flashed through her, but she'd left her good axes back on the ship. She'd have to settle for infiltrating a bloody Sidan city filled with people that wanted to kill her. She shifted the picks in her mouth, the tang of the metal making her stomach sour. Maybe she wouldn't even need to leave the crew. The Sidans would take care of her for them.

Axel's boots hit the road hard enough to send up dust behind him. He ran for the wall surrounding the city, the shouts of the Sidans on their tail ringing against the white stone.

Petra stepped one foot on the road.

A Sidan leaped out from the brush and barreled into her.

His shoulder met her gut.

The lockpicks went flying from her mouth.

Her injured shoulder slammed into the road, and she couldn't even breathe as stars blinded her.

Instinct overcame everything else. She pulled the blade from her hip and stabbed the Sidan in the side.

The man howled, rolling off her before she could get in another strike.

"Pet!" Axel yelled from somewhere.

Petra ignored him, shaking the stars from her vision as she scrabbled over the ground. *Where are they?*

Her fingers wrapped around a thin piece of metal when she heard the crack of dry foliage behind her. She stuffed the tension pick in her mouth and rolled to the side, narrowly dodging a swipe of a Sidan's sword.

*Rocks.*

She got her feet under her into a crouch and drew another blade.

The Sidan with the sword went flying.

Axel's hair shone bright in the moonlight, his expression nearly feral as he stalked toward the man he'd just thrown.

Petra stood and gritted her teeth. Dirt and grass filled her mouth along with the one pick she'd recovered. If everything was going to go according to plan, she needed the other pick. Her eyes scanned the area where she'd found the tension pick. Most locking mechanisms needed two picks in order to open, one to hold the tension and one to hook the discs into place. If she didn't find the bloody hook, there was no way she was going to work any locks.

A hand wrapped around her arm.

Before she could stab him, Big Hal turned her.

"Keep to the plan!" he barked, pointing in Axel's direction. "You're supposed to be following him, remember?"

Petra sheathed her blade and punched him square in the nose.

He let go of her arm and staggered back. "Hel's bloody halls, Pet!"

She spat the pick out of her mouth and bared her teeth. "Don't tell me what to do."

His face blanched slightly. Good. At least he still had a modicum of survival instinct somewhat active in that thick skull of his.

She stuck the pick back in her mouth and scanned the area once more.

The other lockpick was nowhere in sight.

A horn bellowed from the direction of the city. The steady beat of horse hooves drew closer.

"Pet! We've got to go!" Axel called over the cacophony of fighting.

She threw up her hands. *Just a minute!*

Dropping to her knees, she searched through the brush.

"Pet!" Big Hal yelled. The pitch of his voice had her head whipping in his direction.

A Sidan soldier held a blade to his throat. A Sidan *woman*.

Her light hair was braided away from her face, her bright eyes focused on Big Hal. From the way she held the sword in her hand steady, she very obviously knew what to do with it. If Petra hadn't been holding a pick in her mouth, she would have cackled. *Serves the bloody idiot right to be taken down by a girl.*

"Drop your weapons!" the female soldier barked. "Comply peacefully and no one gets hurt."

Petra dropped the blade in her hand to the ground.

Axel stood a few paces away, his eyes already on her. A mischievous spark settled there as a Sidan took the sword he'd borrowed from Ulf and shoved him to the ground.

Rocks, if he didn't keep his amusement to himself, he'd get them all killed.

The soldier at his side finally came around to face him. When Axel looked up, the man retreated a step.

"Captain!" the soldier hollered, taking another step back. "Is this who I think it is?"

The woman holding Big Hal at sword point looked over at them, her eyes widening. She kept her blade straight as she nodded. "Mighty Axel. You're in direct violation of the armistice between Sida and Åldras."

Axel gave a longwinded sigh. He met Petra's gaze. "Hear that, Pet? Direct violation. How quaint."

She rolled her eyes as one of the Sidans kicked her blade out of reach and pushed her to the ground. Gritting her teeth to keep the pick in her mouth, she let the Sidans clap her wrists in irons. Her shoulder ached at the wrenching, but she ignored it.

The Sidans gathered them up, swords poised as they herded the crew toward the gate. They hadn't reached the outlying town between Bellator's northern gate and the shore before the Sidans had been on them. Petra could just make out the shadows of buildings in the moonlight. A spark of firelight here or there. Axel walked next to Pet, his expression growing grimmer the closer they got to the walled city. She wouldn't be surprised to find a similar expression on her own face. Walking into this city surrounded by Sidans wasn't how she would have preferred this mission to go, but she hadn't had much say about it.

She hadn't had much say in regard to anything since they left Åldras.

Axel blew his hair out of his face, the space between them farther than the foot of air between their arms. Her skin prickled as she felt his eyes turn to her, his anger still burning from her antics earlier in the day. She hadn't ever realized how heavy his attention was on her. Probably because he'd been doing his best not to let his feelings show all these years. Even she hadn't known how much he felt for her. At least, not until he'd kissed her outside Ljust Löfte the night Firmin showed up. Before she'd been taken by the High King and the Ekte and imprisoned to act as incentive for Axel to follow orders. Firmin had even gone so far as to charge her for being a Häxa—which they had been unable to prove. Fire charmers hadn't walked on Midgard for centuries. There'd been no reason for them to ever guess she'd been given such a curse.

Cursed to watch everything she loved burn to ash in front of her.

How much longer would she have until even Axel was taken from her?

When his lips had met hers in the forest outside of Ljust Lofte, she'd known she would be the one to destroy him. That what was between them would burn down every good thing they'd built. That it would destroy Axel's magic and make him weak. That it would bring death and destruction to Åldras.

So, she would forget. She would push down the memory of his hungry gaze. His fingers in her hair. His lips against hers.

It was obvious she no longer belonged on *The Phoenix*. It was better if she simply left, but she'd help Axel with this last mission. They would find Lady Idalia and take her back to her absolute brute of a husband all in the name of saving the people they'd given the last ten years to protect.

Freyja's golden tears, she was so sick of this war.

They reached the gate. Technically, there were two gates set into the stone wall, both heavily guarded. In the dark of night, neither gate opened to any travelers. Only glowing windows welcomed them, the sharp silhouettes of guards flashing past the flicker of firelight from within. The Sidan captain called for the group to stop as the guards on the wall stared down at them, their faces concealed by the shadows of their helmets. The gate on the left swung outward, opening wide enough to let out another dozen guards.

"Another welcome party?" Axel teased. "Do you Sidans treat all your guests with such welcome? I'm surprised we've all been at war for so long if you're this hospitable."

Petra resisted the urge to spit her lockpick at him.

The guards didn't even bat an eye as they pushed forward, the new additions blending smoothly into the host around them. Like gulls gathering to circle chum. The only words exchanged were those between the female captain and one of the men standing nearest the gate as the rest of them shuffled through the opening.

The air left Petra's lungs when they stepped through.

Buildings two times taller than *The Phoenix*'s mast soared over her head. They were made of white stone that glittered when a torch passed by them, sending a shiver down Petra's spine. No thatch covered the roofs. Instead, the houses were boxy, flat on every side. Shutters were painted in a variety of colors, but most boasted the green and gold standard of their kingdom. Across one alleyway, ropes connected buildings, stringing up colorful fabrics like dozens of banners. The main road was paved in what looked like the same stone the buildings were built with. It curved all the way up the large hill, leading toward the glittering palace on top. The royal household likely took up the same space as Firmin's entire walled fortress. It stood atop the hill, protected by two more stone walls. The Sidans were taking no chances it seemed.

They certainly weren't in Åldras anymore.

"Move it!" one of the guards barked.

Petra pressed her lips tightly together as she was herded toward a long pair of buildings. While the rest of the city seemed to be sleeping, this section wasn't. Men and women strode back and forth between the buildings, swords strapped to their hips and bronze helmets tucked under their arms.

The captain caught up to their group. "Take them to the lower cells. We don't need them escaping before the prince returns from checking in on Lady Idalia at the palace."

Petra narrowed her eyes. At least they didn't have Lady Idalia put up in a dungeon somewhere.

Not a single armed guard questioned the captain, instead taking her command and veering away from the path to follow their orders. Rather than going in the direction of the large buildings, they headed toward the wall.

Axel stiffened beside her, his eyes focused ahead. Petra followed his gaze. A single building stood apart from the others. Instead of windows, there were barred slits between the stone. Half a dozen guards stood at attention near the thick, metal door.

Hel's halls, they wouldn't get out of there without a bloodbath.

Petra gritted her teeth around the pick in her mouth. She met Axel's gaze.

He quirked a brow. *Now?*

She dipped her chin slightly. *Now.*

Axel exploded into motion. Without consideration for anyone else, he barreled into the three guards stationed in front of him. The last one had his sword drawn, but it only bounced off Axel's impenetrable forearm.

The guard next to Petra reached for her. She dodged his clawing fingers and jumped up, tucking her legs close to her chest so she could bring her bound hands in front of her. Her shoulder screamed at the jarring motion. She spat the lockpick into her hand just as another guard stabbed a sword at her midsection. Petra barely missed being skewered by the bloody thing and stabbed the lockpick into the guard's leg. The guard let out a yelp and staggered away with the pick sticking out of her thigh, a faint jingle at her hip drawing Petra's eye. With a grin, Petra punched the guard in the jaw, knocking her to the ground. Petra skidded to her knees beside the guard, her fingers quickly checking inside pockets. Her fingers wrapped around a set of keys.

An arm wrapped around her middle.

"Time to go," Axel whispered in her ear.

Petra rolled her eyes as he lifted her from the ground as if she weighed nothing and sprinted in the opposite direction of the guarded building. Ludvig and Big Hal followed quickly behind them. The guards hollered after them, the green uniforms multiplying by the second. But Axel darted between the buildings, getting out of view. Once they were far enough out of reach of the guards, Axel set her back on her feet.

The Sidans rallied, giving chase.

Darting between the buildings, Petra picked through the keys she'd snatched from the Sidan guard and fitted one into the hole in her manacle. It clicked open on the first try. She got the other cuff unlocked and tossed the keys to Ludvig, who had his hands locked in front of him. He caught the keys and quickly set to freeing Big Hal.

They ran down the stone street, the flames casting their shadows onto the buildings around them.

Petra's pulse beat with every flicker.

"Split up!" Axel said. "Get the city on alert and meet us at the palace."

Ludvig and Big Hal raced down a side street, a dozen Sidans chasing after them, as Axel and Petra sprinted the other way.

# CHAPTER 3

## LADIES

*Many don't understand how foolish this war with Sida is. As a king from the southern part of the kingdom, I was one of the few kings to have dealings with the Sidans before the war began. I was a young, foolish man when my father passed and left me his title. I did not understand then what I do now. I saw the Sidans as a bully, when in fact, they have been a slumbering bear. If we continue to poke it, there will be no saving anyone from her claws.*

*— FROM THE WRITINGS OF DORAN FINNSSON, THE LAST KING OF GROVÖ*

Axel hung back at an intersection, the soft click of steps on the streets bouncing around him. Even the noises were different in Sida than they were in Åldras. There wasn't the skitter of rats or the creak of the wind against log houses. Only the chirp of crickets and the hush of a sleeping city met his ears.

And the guards of course.

He signaled for Petra to move ahead. She brushed past him on silent feet, slipping between long stretches of fabric strung between buildings.

Axel stepped forward to follow her.

The dirt under his feet erupted.

It flew into his eyes, up his nose, into his mouth. He shoved himself backward as the bloody wall of dirt solidified. Too close. That had been too close. He spun around.

The female captain stood at the mouth of the alleyway, one hand outstretched and the other curled around a stone hanging from her neck. A förändra. A catalyst for elemental magic.

The bloody captain was a Häxa.

The fabric above their heads fluttered as he ran a finger along the thick dirt wall behind him. It crumbled at his touch. He didn't look up but glanced back at the captain, his lips pulling up at the corners.

"Hello, sister."

"I'm no sister of yours." She narrowed her eyes.

He shrugged settling his hands at his hips. "I guess that'll make this easier for me then."

She blinked. "What?"

He charged forward. While she attempted to use her magic to stop him, every clod of dirt or fist-sized stone she threw his way glanced off his skin. When he reached her, he grabbed the hand wrapped around the stone hanging from her neck.

"There's no need to get violent," he said.

The captain gritted her teeth, using her magic to lift every stone from the ground under their feet.

Axel let out a sigh. "Well, if you insist."

Carefully, he knocked her in the temple.

She slumped to the ground, the rocks falling with her.

Petra stepped silently out from around the building behind the captain. "Häxa are going to make this complicated."

Axel nearly chuckled at the irony. Even if no other Häxa were involved, he and Petra would be more than enough to brew up some complications. He turned away from the unconscious captain and approached the wall of dirt she'd summoned.

"I don't know that the wall is stable enough to hold your big arse," Petra drawled.

He grinned and punched a fist through the dirt.

The entire thing crumbled in on itself.

Petra puffed up like a spooked cat. "Great. Now the entire city knows we're here."

Axel stepped over the pile of dirt. "You say that as if they didn't already know."

She opened her mouth to retort, but whatever she was going to say was swallowed up by the sound of horns. The drone reverberated through the buildings, shaking the stones under Axel's boots. The sound rang in his skull, and he covered his ears. Sometimes, his enhanced hearing was more detrimental than not. The bellow seemed to come from everywhere, as if the white stone itself were crying out at them.

At least Big Hal and Ludvig were doing their job.

Petra grabbed his arm and pulled him forward.

They sprinted toward the palace sitting atop the hill. The cramped streets gave way to lush gardens and decorated buildings. There was a large fountain in the middle of a square. Flower boxes hung in windows and chimes made of metal tinkled in the salty breeze.

It was like stalking through a completely different world.

Axel slowed his steps as they reached the edge of a cream-colored building. Peeking around the corner, he spotted the gate. The lower gate. There were two walls they had to get through before they could get into the palace. Who on Midgard put two walls between a king and his people?

The gate here was different from the one on the outer wall of the city. Instead of two gates, there was only one patrolled by a pair of guards.

Two very attentive and alert guards.

Petra slipped away, and Axel counted each beat of his heart, trying to slow it as he waited.

The torch next to the guard on the left flared slightly.

The man disappeared.

The woman standing on the right whipped around, her sword drawn.

A shadow slipped behind her, knocking her to the ground.

Axel stepped out into the light cast by the torches. "That was fast."

Petra grabbed the now unconscious guard and dragged her back out of view.

Axel took the sword off the other guard, who was also uncon-scious. "How long until they wake up?"

Petra grabbed the other sword that had fallen from the second guard's grasp. "Minutes."

With a nod, Axel jogged up the road. He did his best to stay out of the torchlight that seemed to glow around every corner this high up into the city. How many people tended to these fires throughout the night? In Harligdam, there were a few men on feasting nights who stayed up to keep the fires burning, but if there wasn't a feast, most of the fires went out hours before dawn.

The torches weren't the only unsettling feature.

As they drew closer to the palace, something in his gut stirred. It wasn't until they passed through a large section of canopied garden that he realized what it was. In the middle of the canopy stood a rock, covered with runes.

"This entire section of the city is riddled with magic," he whispered.

Petra nodded. "I can feel it."

Of course she could. Axel's fingers tightened around the hilt of the borrowed sword. She was as much Häxa as he was. Maybe even more so. How much magic did she have? He knew some Häxa were stronger than others. Even if she did have control over fire, what could she do with it?

The memory of the walls of flame through Holmberg flashed through his mind. He'd never had a förändra, at least not one that had come with the violent reactions other förändras did. Not like Petra's. What would it have been like? Watching something that was so intrinsically attached to his soul destroy everything he loved?

Freyja's golden tears, hadn't he seen it already? He'd been aban-doned by his mother. Because of his strength, he'd been forced to fight in a war that should have never happened. Left with a prophecy that would likely kill him. There was no doubt in his mind Petra would eventually let him back behind that wall of hers. No doubt that she felt something for him. Their kiss had told him more than enough.

When Petra tapped on his arm, every hair on his body rose.

He turned back to her, and she pointed to the left.

They'd reached the next gate.

He glided forward, his ears and eyes open to their surroundings. However, no guards stood next to the torches under the single archway. No helmets glinted at the towers. If there weren't lit torches, he'd believe the place abandoned.

Petra slinked through the shadows at his side, stepping from one to the other as light as smoke. Why hadn't he noticed before? She was fire in every sense of the word. Even the way her eyes lit spoke of flame rather than the stars he saw in other girls' eyes.

Hel's halls, he was getting distracted.

He pulled his gaze from her, looking back toward the palace.

Movement at the western side caught his attention.

Standing in a pale-colored dress, Lady Idalia appeared on one of the balconies.

Petra slowed next to him. "You think it's a trap?"

He shook his head. "Couldn't tell you. She could be haunting the balcony as she waits for Anders, or she could be trying to lure us to her so the Sidans can ambush us."

Petra snorted but didn't respond. She didn't need to. They both knew what the answer was.

"What's the plan?" he asked.

She pursed her lips. "Same as before. Get in, grab the lady, get out."

"What about the guards?"

She shrugged. "You think you can't take care of some guards?"

"I think we try to get in and out without letting anyone know."

Petra gave a sigh. "You're going to have to throw me then."

ᚠᚢᚲᛟᚠᛁᛚ

It didn't take long to reach the courtyards around the palace. There were enough plants to sneak behind to keep out of sight, and Petra only had to take out three guards before they stood beneath the balcony Lady Idalia had stood on, though she was gone now.

Axel threaded his fingers together in a sling and Petra placed her boot in his hands.

"Don't you dare throw me onto the roof," she hissed.

He rolled his eyes. "I only did that once."

She crouched low, pulling as much tension into her legs as she could. She bounced once, twice, then shot up. Axel pushed her boot up and over his head. Petra flew toward the balcony, her arms outstretched as she reached for the railing.

Her sternum hit the edge of the banister.

Axel winced. That was going to leave a bruise.

Petra swung one leg up onto the banister.

With Petra up, Axel crept toward the palace wall. Unlike the thick logs making up the great halls in Åldras, the palace in Bellator was made of the same white stone as the buildings in the city. Instead of thick walls, pillars held up the roof over his head and the archways that led deeper into the palace. If someone were to get past the three walls between the sea and the palace, there would be no defense for anyone inside.

Best not to leave Petra waiting in case there was a trap ready for them up there. He slid the sword he'd borrowed from the captain into the back of his tunic. The pillar in front of him had to be twice as thick as *The Phoenix*'s mast, though just as tall. With gritted teeth, Axel carefully climbed the stone pillar. There weren't any good handholds, so he pressed his fingers into the carved grooves lining the entire thing. He was sure there would be marks where he'd dug his grip into the mortar.

When he reached the top, he used one arm to take hold of the railing and grabbed his sword with the other. He swung himself over, expecting to find Petra hidden in the shadows near the door. Instead, he was met with complete silence. Not a sound permeated the night. Not crickets. Not the crackle of torches. Not even Axel's own breath.

He found Petra in the middle of the balcony, eyes flashing, with four guards on the ground in pools of their own blood around her and six more with swords pointed down at where she knelt.

And Enzo the Scourge with a gash along his forehead and a sword to her throat.

The prince looked to the side and gave a nod. A woman stepped out from the doorway leading to the balcony. With a wave of her hand, sound returned to the space.

Prince Enzo grinned, blood staining his teeth.

"Welcome to Bellator, Mighty Axel."

Petra's teeth gritted as she lowered her head just the smallest bit.

Axel rolled his shoulders back. "Thank you for your hospitality. Unfortunately, we can't stay."

Petra slammed her head back, hitting the prince in the groin.

The sword at her throat dropped as he gasped in pain.

The guard closest to her moved to protect his prince, but Axel was there. He grabbed the man by the shiny helmet and shoved him hard enough that he ran straight into the guard next to him.

A gust of air swiped past his face, keeping the second guard from toppling over the side of the balcony. The Häxa needed to be taken out.

Axel grabbed the closest guard's wrist, twisting it until he released his hold on his sword. Axel caught it by the blade as it fell and pulled himself back as another sword tried to skewer him. No use getting his tunic shredded if he didn't have to. A guard put himself between him and Enzo.

But the guard meant little to him. If he couldn't take out the air whisperer, there was no way they would get off this balcony before reinforcements arrived.

The closest body near his feet had one of the shiny helmets. He picked it up and tossed it at the Häxa who had raised her hands to use her gift. The shiny helmet caught her eye, and she used the air she'd summoned to knock the helmet away.

Axel used the distraction to charge forward. He lifted the blade, using the end of the pommel to knock her in the head. He didn't want to kill any Häxa, but he couldn't risk her stopping them. The woman dropped to the ground with the other guards.

He spun back around, ready to join Petra. She'd gotten her hands on the Crown Prince's own sword, swinging it at its owner. Working with a sword didn't come as naturally as her axes did, but she kept pace with each jab the prince made. Enzo had picked up another sword from somewhere and parried Petra's swing. While she held her own, she wouldn't last long against the skilled prince. Not many could.

A shiny-helmeted guard stood between Axel and the dueling pair, his face pale as he slowly raised his sword.

Axel engaged him, the sword he'd taken clashing against the sword of the guard. When he caught the opening on his left side, he took it, slicing through his thigh. The guard yelped and staggered back a step.

The ring of Petra's blade crashed through the still night. She'd parried a blow from the prince, but she staggered back as Enzo came at her again.

Axel stepped forward, sword raised.

The door to the balcony behind him sprang open, crashing against the stone wall.

"Stop!" Lady Idalia cried. "Stop this instant!"

# Chapter 4

## A Failure

Petra froze, turning her head just enough to glance over her shoulder. Lady Idalia looked unchanged from the last time she'd seen her. The angles of her face still held that rebellious tilt, her skin tawny from days under Tatawar's sun during her childhood. Petra had never been able to guess her age. She looked young but held herself as if she'd walked Midgard for decades. She held the collar of her robe closed at her throat, her dark eyes wide as they flicked from person to person.

Both Axel and Enzo had frozen on the balcony, surprise rippling through their features.

Petra sprang forward. She ducked down, using her good shoulder to scoop Lady Idalia up, and raced through the door.

The sound of hurried footsteps chased after her.

Lady Idalia's fists pummeled into her back. "Put me *down*! Lord Petyr, *please*! Please don't take me back!"

Petra's grip slackened slightly. She knew that cry. The want of something more. The torture of having to pretend not to. Wōden's one good eye, it was going to kill Axel to take her back to Åldras.

If she hadn't slowed slightly, she would have missed the sword coming toward her head.

Petra jumped back, nearly stumbling with Lady Idalia squirming in her arms.

Prince Roman stepped out from the other side of the door to her left, his sword pointed at her neck. "I won't let you take her."

Hel's halls, the bloody idiot was lucky he hadn't stabbed the lady he was trying to protect. Petra adjusted her hold on Lady Idalia and took a step back.

The footsteps behind Petra stopped as they finally caught up. Axel's warmth heated her shoulders.

"Halt!" Roman commanded. "I'm not afraid to skewer this man or your friends if he attempts to take another step."

Behind him, lights bloomed. Four guards dragged in a rather bloodied Ludvig. He looked at Petra through his one unswollen eye. His right leg dragged behind him at an unnatural angle.

Where was Big Hal?

"If you don't want to lose some of your crew," Prince Enzo called from behind her, "I suggest you drop your weapons and unhand Lady Idalia."

Petra kept her sword at the ready. They needed to get out of the palace. If she could just get past Roman without getting herself or Lady Idalia skewered, Axel could probably get to Ludvig. But without knowing where Big Hal was, it would be difficult to get them all out without getting themselves killed. They even might have to leave Big Hal behind. A pity. Axel would definitely hate it, but they needed to get the lady to the ship and off to Anders before everyone decided to ignore the armistice and go back to all-out war again. And they would.

Marriage in Åldras was no laughing matter and what most people forgot was that Anders didn't marry an Åldran lass. He'd married a Tatawarie princess. There were contracts on top of contracts, bride prices and treaties between kingdoms signed and sealed. With Lady Idalia's abandonment, Anders's contracts with Tatawar would be put under scrutiny. Anders would likely put up a fuss and insult the Tatawarie king with his injured pride. If the Tatawarie were bothered, who knew how they would react? They had benefitted from the war thus far, being the only kingdom with open trade between Åldras and Sida, but if they got dragged into this war because of their princess's mistake, it was likely they would choose to ally with Sida over Åldras.

A sword clattered to the floor next to Petra's feet. "We'll surrender," Axel rumbled, "but if you kill any one of my men, I won't hesitate to tear every single limb from every man in this palace."

*Rocks.* Petra dropped her sword as well.

Roman didn't waver, his attention solely on Petra. "Put her down, Lord Petyr."

Petra's grip on the lady's legs tightened.

"Please, Lord Petyr," Lady Idalia whispered. "Please don't kill anyone else."

*Hel's bloody halls.* Slowly, Petra crouched low enough for Lady Idalia to find her feet. The moment Petra let her go, she sprang forward, wrapping her arms around Prince Roman's neck. The prince did well to not allow the embrace to knock him back. He kept his gaze securely on Petra.

"About time you showed up," Enzo said from behind. He shoved his way past Petra, knocking into her injured shoulder. She did her best not to wince. He stopped next to his brother, turning to face them. "You've been caught within the boundaries of Sida. You have threatened the armistice between our nations and are guilty of acts of war."

Petra's ribcage squeezed. She felt Axel draw closer to her. Could feel the anger radiating off him.

"You are thieves," he hissed over her head. "You've stolen away what is not yours and we've come to reclaim it. To keep the armistice we have all fought so long for in place."

"I was not *stolen*," Lady Idalia snapped. "I'm not an item to be taken or a jewel to be envied. I came of my own free will."

No woman should ever feel like a piece of property. Petra's stomach twisted. Lady Idalia's words resounded in Petra's soul, but just like Lady Idalia, they had no choice in their future. If she didn't come back to Åldras, more people were going to die for Firmin and Anders's rocking pride.

Axel leaned forward, still at Petra's back. "You would abandon your kingdom to war? You would join your husband's enemy and bring his wrath upon all of you?"

Lady Idalia's expression darkened. "Is a man who buys a woman a husband? Is a woman who is bought a wife or simply an animal, a toy to be played with until the child grows weary of it? I was not Anders's wife any more than his hounds. In fact, he treated the dogs more his equal than he ever did me. No, I was not his wife. I was simply his bed warmer, and I refuse to do that particular job any longer."

Prince Roman wrapped a hand around her shoulders, tucking her closely next to him.

The urge to roll her eyes stole through Petra. She'd seen the way these two had acted with one another when they'd been at the feast in Harligdam. The way they touched each other. The way they looked at one another. She'd suspected a familiarity between them then. She should have known the charismatic prince would sweep the lady right off her feet.

The two of them were going to get people killed.

"So you abandoned the rest of Åldras to face the consequences?" Axel snapped. "Do you know what you've done? The only reason your husband and his brother aren't storming the beaches of Sida this very instant is because Queen Eva was wise enough to convince them that sending us to sneak you out of here was better than resuming this bloody war."

Lady Idalia's face grew pale, her eyes pulling wide. She met Petra's gaze, tears pooling at the edges of her dark lashes. Whatever comfort she was searching for, she certainly wouldn't find it with Petra. If it was possible to get past everyone, free Ludvig, and find Big Hal without getting anyone killed, Petra would haul her all the way to *The Phoenix* kicking and screaming.

"Enough," Prince Roman commanded. "Idalia is an honored guest in our home. I won't have you distressing her. Not after everything she's been through."

"You think this is distressing?" Axel scoffed. "Imagine how distressing it will be when Firmin arrives on these shores. Imagine what it will feel like to watch hundreds of your people be slaughtered against these city walls. You say returning to Åldras would be *distressing*, yet you would send men, women, and children to their deaths because of your selfishness."

Lady Idalia broke down, her expression crumpling.

Petra's throat grew tight. The lady wasn't the only one to hold the weight of others' lives in her hands. At least she had a choice. At least she could make amends before it was too late.

"No one is going anywhere," Enzo said. He turned to the guards. "Take these intruders to the dungeons."

One of the guard's grabbed Petra's arm.

Axel growled. "You will release Pet's arm unless you wish to lose your own."

With a smirk, the guard yanked her forward.

Petra twisted out of his hold and punched him in the throat.

The guard gagged, stumbling back a step.

Every guard raised their sword, circling her.

"Maker above," Enzo cursed. He lifted his own sword and pointed it at Petra's stomach. "Don't make me repeat what happened outside of Grovö, Petyr Mallorysson. I would hate to anger the queen by bloodying the carpets, but I will if you don't behave."

Petra met his gaze without blinking. She knew he wouldn't hesitate to gut her like he tried to on the battlefield just north of Grovö years ago. He was Enzo the Scourge after all.

Enzo didn't flinch away. Instead, he turned to the guard next to him and gave a sharp nod.

The guards pushed them forward down the hall, Ludvig dragged ahead of them. Four guards kept their swords trained on Petra's back, but none of them got too close.

Petra glanced back at Axel, one brow quirked. *Do we fight?*

He glanced ahead of them to where Ludvig hung between the guards. His brows lowered slightly. *Not yet.*

"I say you hang all of them from the city wall this very instant," Prince Roman muttered from behind.

Petra tilted her head, doing her best not to seem like she was listening.

"Shut up, Roman," Enzo hissed.

"You know I'm right."

"We aren't doing *anything* until we speak with Father."

"I thought you were in charge of this city's safety. Do you think these brutes will simply sit in the dungeons awaiting Father's verdict? Just take care of them before he wakes and we can be done with this mess."

"We wouldn't be in this *mess* if you had just left things alone. Now take Idalia back to her room and let me do my job."

Petra glanced back. All was not harmonious in Bellator's palace. Roman shot a glare at Enzo but didn't turn to take Lady Idalia back the way they'd come. Enzo stopped Roman, his voice too low for Petra to hear, but she could see the fury in the younger prince's face.

She rolled her sore shoulder, making the guard next to her flinch. If the brothers were divided in this, it could be possible to use the two of them against one another. They might be able to convince Enzo to let them take Lady Idalia back without any bloodshed. The Crown Prince wasn't a fool. He obviously knew having Lady Idalia here put his people in jeopardy. He might be reasoned with.

At the front of the group, the guards jostled a bit past a long table and Ludvig groaned in pain. Wōden's one good eye, if his leg was that bad, he wouldn't make it back to the ship no matter if Axel carried him.

And where on Midgard was Big Hal?

"What's going on up there?" Enzo barked. The prince jogged to catch up, leaving Prince Roman and Lady Idalia standing in the hall. Hel's halls, she was so close. If only they could just grab her.

Axel leaned down near her ear. When had he gotten so close? "You have that look," he said.

The scheming look. Petra turned away from the jogging prince back to the guards still trying to right Ludvig's groaning form.

Ducking her head, she whispered, "If Big Hal's locked up somewhere, we may need to take Ludvig and run. Come back for the big pain in the arse after we get Ludvig to Erik. Create a distraction. You grab Ludvig and I'll clear the path."

She didn't turn to look at him, but she knew he was thinking it over. Looking over every possibility. If they didn't get out of the palace now, they would have to try to escape heavily fortified dungeon cells instead.

"You good, Ludvig?" Axel called over Petra's head.

Ludvig groaned again but shook himself a bit, trying to straighten his better leg. "Just need a bit of Little Hal's good mead. I'm sure I'll be good then."

A couple of the guards chuckled. The ones holding him up readjusted their grip, making him yelp.

"Now," Petra said.

Axel sprang into motion. He barreled through the guards, acting as a shield for Petra as she glided behind him. She snatched a sword from one guard and a long dagger from another.

"Stop them!" Enzo shouted.

Axel reached Ludvig and Petra swept past them. She used the sword to cut down one of the guards.

A flicker of candlelight caught her eye, and she turned as someone stepped out from behind a pillar.

Water rushed from an open window.

Petra jumped up, wrapping herself around one of the pillars. *Bloody water wielders.* She glanced up at Axel who withstood the flood with gritted teeth, holding Ludvig to him as the guards were barraged with water.

The water reached Axel's waist and turned a frosted white. The rush of water completely froze, immobilizing everyone.

Petra's fingers ached from holding herself out of the water's reach, but she shimmied up the pillar. If she could get high enough, she might find something up at the top—

Something struck her side, knocking her from the pillar.

"Pet!" Axel hollered.

Petra smacked into the ground, her shoulder popping again at the impact. *Hel's rocking halls.* She gasped in pain but rolled to her feet, the long dagger in her fist. She could still move her arm, praise the Allfather.

Axel roared, the sound of shattering ice splitting the air. Chunks of ice skittered over the frozen floor as he freed himself.

Petra spun toward the water seer, getting a good glance at the woman. She was dressed in lavender, from the top of her head to the tips of her toes peeking out from under her skirts. A long veil covered her face, and Petra could only glimpse a hint of a profile through the thin fabric concealing her identity.

Petra charged forward, keeping her feet on the slippery ice.

A glob of water sailed toward her, but she dodged it, rolling to the side. When her injured shoulder hit the ice under her feet, she stumbled.

The next barrage of water hit its mark.

It wrapped around her, pinning her arms to her sides. When her entire torso was covered, it froze. She fell to her knees, the weight of the ice pulling her down.

"Pet!" Axel skidded to a stop in front of her, one of his arms fully encased in ice. With a growl, he smashed his arm onto the ground and broke the casing.

Petra tried to push herself to her feet, but ice shot out from the ground and attached to the ice wrapped around her.

Guards swept around them, swords pointed in their direction. At least a dozen more had joined the number.

Prince Enzo stepped up behind Axel, dusting ice from his dark hair. "If you would like to live through the night, I suggest you cease."

Petra turned to Axel, who was already watching her. His green eyes flared with fury as he met her gaze. Waiting.

If she wanted him to tear through every person here, he would.

But Ludvig sat slumped against a pillar, his face creased in pain. They'd lost their chance for a clean getaway.

She gave an infinitesimal shake of her head.

He blew out a small breath. Slowly, he turned back to Enzo. "Can you blame a man for trying?"

Enzo's eyes narrowed as he took a step back. The guards took his place, reaching for Axel's arms.

"Allow me," a silky voice said.

The guards parted as the veiled woman swept toward them. With a flick of her wrist, the ice melted from Petra's shoulders. She sagged forward, only for her hands to be wrapped in ice. Axel's were the same as he glared up at the water wielder.

The patter of steps sounded from outside the ring of guards. Petra could see the tips of Prince Roman's boots through the legs of the guards around them.

Idalia was nowhere to be seen.

*Rocks.*

"Mother, it's good you came," Prince Roman's voice echoed.

*Mother?* The water seer was the bloody Queen of Sida? Petra met Axel's gaze, his eyes widened in surprise. How on Midgard had a Häxa become the Sidan's queen, and how had they not known?

"Of course I came," the queen said. She shifted away from Petra and Axel still kneeling on the ground. "I want Idalia to be safe as much as you do."

The guards pulled Axel and Petra to their feet.

Prince Enzo remained with his men, not once looking toward his brother even as Prince Roman and the queen stepped up beside him. The Crown Prince didn't take his eyes off Axel.

"Get these bloody prisoners to the dungeons before the entire palace wakes up," he ordered the guards.

The queen settled a hand on Prince Enzo's shoulder. "It seems you are too late. His Majesty has already summoned the council to the throne room."

Prince Enzo finally looked away, his head snapping in the queen's direction. "What?"

She gave a dip of her head. "I came to fetch you to bring the Åldrans straight away."

The words froze the blood in Petra's veins as much as the ice around her hands did. She glanced up at Axel, who was studying the queen with narrowed eyes.

Prince Enzo pinched the bridge of his nose. "Of course. We'll go immediately." He gestured for the guards to pick up Ludvig once again, and the guards quickly fell into formation around them, twice the number they were when this little tour through the palace started.

Petra gritted her teeth as two of the guards grabbed her arms, their swords poised at her middle as they ushered her forward. The ice in her veins made the hairs on her arms stand on end.

She looked back toward the members of the royal family.

The queen's head tilted, her attention trained on a spot on the floor. A pool of blood stained the thick carpet from where Petra had cut down the guard.

"Is that blood on the carpet?"

## CHAPTER 5

---

## ROYALS

Being herded through the palace like a pack of sheep wasn't how the plan was supposed to play out. Axel's shoulders shook with the urge to break the bands of ice around his wrists and run. The guard next to him adjusted the grip he had on the sword at his hip. No words passed between the group, but everyone was having some kind of conversation with someone.

The princes shot looks at one another behind the queen's back.

Ludvig tapped at his thigh every time they passed a doorway.

The guards sent furtive glances to one another.

And Petra kept tilting her head. She didn't turn to meet his eye, but he could feel the question she asked in her steps.

*How long until one of us gets stabbed?*

Axel withheld a sigh. With every step they took toward the throne room, they walked farther away from Lady Idalia and their ticket home. It would be nearly impossible to figure out where the prince had sequestered her when this entire place was a maze.

While the palace still mostly slept, the moonlight and Axel's heightened sight revealed every crack of the hall ahead. Unlike the great halls in Åldras, Bellator's Palace was almost entirely open, many of the walkways leading out to balconies and even some of the ceilings opened to the sky. Rather than shields and furs, there were tapestries and mosaics. The carpet under Axel's boots was soft, woven in colorful patterns. He passed by a painting of some kind of fruit, the outside a hard shell and the inside glistening with seeds like drops of blood held together by white flesh.

A warm breeze blew through one of the windows, cooling the sweat coating the back of his tunic. It fluttered Petra's short hair in front of him. She didn't glance back at him as they followed the Sidan Queen to what could spell their doom.

At least he'd gotten to kiss Petra before he died. Or was buried in some dark, dank hole where no one would ever find him.

The hall opened into a wide courtyard. A bubbling fountain stood in the center, surrounded by boxes of spindly trees with thin leaves. Even the plants looked overheated in this place. On the other side of the courtyard, two guards framed a doorway. With a nod from the queen, each guard grabbed the large rings on either door and pulled them open.

Light and voices flooded into the courtyard.

Petra's entire spine stiffened as they passed through the doorway. Axel's fists clenched as he walked through. If they were going to have to fight, he would be ready.

It wasn't until he noticed the two granite bowls filled with fire on either side of the door that he realized Petra was fighting against an entirely different urge. The flames seemed to grow slightly as she passed by them, her shoulders hunched up next to her ears.

The doors closed with a deep groan behind Axel's back, and every face in the room turned to them. Men and women in long green robes stared as Ludvig had to be dragged across the gleaming floor.

Axel's gaze caught on the lump in the middle of the room.

Big Hal lay in a heap, his clothing torn and disheveled. Blood streaked across his fingers and bruises marred his face. Axel strained to hear the man's breathing—anything to signify life.

Petra shoved forward, kneeling at Big Hal's side. She used her bound hands to search for his heartbeat. Her shoulders sagged and she turned back to Axel, the crease in her brow melting away.

Big Hal's eyes opened slightly, and he gave Axel a wink.

Axel blew out a breath. *Praise the Allfather.* If Big Hal was only faking unconsciousness, he could help them get Ludvig out of here.

There were three rows of benches on either side of the room, each row a step higher than the one below it. A large mosaic of what looked like the world tree Yggdrasil covered the floor between the rows, leading up to a short dais on the other side. A wide throne took up a good portion of the dais, as did the man sitting on it.

The similarities to Enzo and Roman were immediately apparent. King Leonardo's straight mouth reflected his oldest son's exactly, and the quirk of his dark brow matched his younger son. His hawkish nose was even larger than Enzo's and could likely balance a pitcher of mead on its bridge. A gleam struck the king's eye when he met Axel's gaze. The hairs on Axel's arms stood on end. This was not a man Axel ever wanted to face on a battlefield.

The princes found places to stand at the foot of the dais.

As the queen passed by, she gently touched the shoulder of the guard closest to Petra. In a voice no one else in the room could likely hear, she said, "Please keep an eye out. The Åldrans are known for turning a man's sword on him in the blink of an eye."

The guard stepped closer to Petra, knuckles white around the hilt of his sword.

The king's gaze left Axel to take in the queen. "Any trouble?" he asked, his voice booming around the room. He hadn't yelled or projected his words so everyone could hear him. The deepness of his voice simply thundered across the space as if an air whisperer had carried it about.

The queen stepped up the dais to stand next to the king. "Nothing I couldn't handle." The queen's voice was in direct contrast to her husband's. It was likely only because of Axel's sharp hearing that he could make out her words at all.

Something about the queen set Axel's hackles raising. The ice around his wrists felt like it grew tighter with every second, the cold bleeding into his bones. It didn't hurt so much as chafed. It almost tingled, as if the magic were trying to permeate his skin and found the resistance something to overcome. That same testing feeling came whenever the queen's veiled face was turned his way. He could practically feel her eyes on him, searching. If only he could see her face, read her expression. Having the faceless woman stare at him made his skin crawl.

The king's gaze returned to Axel. "I'm very eager to hear why Mighty Axel has decided to infiltrate my palace, attempted to kidnap a guest of my household, and attacked my family."

Axel's mouth went completely dry. Thunder's beard, his limbs hadn't shaken this badly since Father and Mallory had cornered him when he'd been nine and had stolen the sword Dane, Petra's oldest brother, had been gifted to celebrate his graduating from squire. Even Ludvig cringed, his head hanging low.

The king's slightly quirked eyebrow rose. "Well?"

Axel cleared his throat. "We have come to retrieve Lady Idalia and return her home."

"They came to steal her away like thugs!" Prince Roman exclaimed, striding toward the king. "Even though she commanded them to cease, Lord Petyr threw her over his shoulder as if she meant nothing to him."

"You exaggerate," Axel snapped. "Pet has the highest regard for our lady. We have been commanded to bring Lady Idalia home by any means necessary to ensure the peace between our kingdoms is maintained. None of us wish to break the armistice our leaders have worked so hard to put into place. We hoped to return the lady to her husband before someone did something they regretted."

The king leaned back in his throne. "Then why send you? Does King Firmin wish for us to attack first? To treat this as an act of war and walk into a trap he has set for us?"

*I hope not.* If Firmin did something so bloody stupid, Axel would kill the High King himself.

"I'm not privy to the thoughts of my king," he answered carefully. "I can only claim to be here to maintain peace between our two kingdoms."

"You expect me to believe the man who has been fighting this war from the very first spark of conflict wishes for peace? That the Häxa son who was left in the ashes of his home and trained to kill any Sidan that came into view wants to cease fighting? I've heard the songs sung on your ships as they bob on the waves of the Vit Sea. Of Mighty Axel, the hero of Åldras. I've seen the scars of my men that our Maker has spared from the death blow of your lysande sword. If you want me to believe you've only come for Lady Idalia, I will take more convincing than just your word."

Freyja's golden tears, if only Doran were with them. He would use that silver tongue of his and have this entire council eating out of his palm with some story about how they came to save everyone and make it sound like it was everyone's idea.

Axel looked to Petra in front of him. She kept her full attention on the king. Did she have a plan to get them out of there? He was sure she did, but it had to have been a bloody one.

Axel stepped forward. He ignored when the guards lifted their swords. Ignored the jolt of the council around him. He stopped next to Petra. The brush of her shoulder against his centered him, and he took a deep breath of her scent. Of steel and smoke.

Straightening his shoulders, he broke the ice around his wrists.

A few council members yelped, and the guards rushed toward him.

"Halt," the king said.

The guards stopped a few steps away, their eyes on Axel.

He held out his hands. "I have no other words to convince you of my intentions or the intentions of my men. It's up to you to decide whether to trust the word of your enemy. I have come to bring Lady Idalia back to her husband so that my kingdom and yours don't have to return to this bloody war before either of us has the time to prepare our men to kiss their families goodbye. Before we have to convince fathers to abandon their children for the hope of something that seems so far away. Before we have to convince sons to leave their mothers to pray every night to whatever gods may be listening that their boys will return home to them."

"I think we should listen, Father," Prince Enzo said.

"You can't be serious," Prince Roman hissed. "You know what Idalia will face if she returns to that barbarian."

The king lifted his hand, silencing his sons. He turned to the queen. "Do you have any wisdom to share with us, Queen Kelda?"

Axel couldn't ever remember hearing the queen's name. It only made sense that the King of Sida would have a water seer close at hand. Having a Häxa to watch the future would be immeasurably useful in this long war. But a queen? Did Firmin know and keep it from the rest of Åldras? There would be many ready to go to war just for fear of a Häxa queen coming for them. For the sole idea of taking out a gifted woman in a position of power. It was likely the same reason Firmin had sent his daughter to Ljust Löfte. People with fanatic beliefs made overzealous decisions.

The queen, who had stood silently at her husband's shoulder, stepped forward. "The waters of fate are murky, but sending her back would certainly result in her death."

"Thank you, Mother," Prince Roman said.

Prince Enzo stepped up next to his brother. "Which was why we never should have allowed her to come in the first place."

Prince Roman glared. "So, you would rather I have left her behind to continue living under the foot of that brute?"

"I would rather you have used whatever brains you might have in that thick head of yours and *thought* about the consequences of simply taking her. There's more than one way to smuggle a person out of a terrible situation. You didn't have to put our entire kingdom in danger because a pretty girl gave you a sob story and batted her eyelashes at you."

"How dare—"

"Enough, both of you," the king said. He stood and strode down the three steps separating him from the princes. "While I agree that Prince Roman ought to have thought through his actions before bringing Lady Idalia here, what's done is done and now we must move forward. Arguing will only divide us when we must face the enemy as a united front."

Petra's pinky tapped the back of Axel's hand. Her eyes were trained on the guard closest to her. The man's sword wobbled slightly as he pointed it in her direction. He was either tired or not used to the weight of his weapon. The end of his blade was only a hairsbreadth from Petra's side.

If the guard made one wrong move, Petra would be on him before he could even blink.

Axel pressed his pinky against her wrist. *Hold.*

King Leonardo turned to the robed men and women sitting on the benches. "We have been infiltrated by one of the greatest soldiers ever to walk our planet, a man of both skill and strength. Our enemies will likely be shortly behind him no matter what choice we make. If you were in my situation, what actions would you take next?"

One of the women stood. "Kill them all and send back their heads."

A man scoffed. "Have you not been listening? Mighty Axel is unkillable. It would be simpler to lock them in a dungeon and throw away the key."

A few nodded at that suggestion.

Axel's mouth grew dry.

"If we allow him to take Lady Idalia," another said, "we will find ourselves in the same spot we've been in since we signed the armistice. Tatawar might have been persuaded to our side with her coming here, but if she returns, they will revert to their neutral stance."

Axel hadn't even considered the Tatawarie in all this. If the treaty between Tatawar and Åldras was in jeopardy because of Lady Idalia's abandonment, this was worse than he'd thought.

He met Petra's gaze.

The corner of her mouth twitched. *Finally catching on, are you?*

"I believe Prince Enzo is wise in saying that we return the lady," said an older woman with pinched lips. "She isn't worth the trouble."

Queen Kelda shook her head, and the king's gaze flicked to her. "That is no longer an option," he said. "Lady Idalia will be staying."

Axel's jaw clenched. Didn't they understand what would happen if Lady Idalia stayed here? While he might have hated the idea of taking the lady back to Anders, he hated condemning his people to the fight Firmin's pride would bring them to—especially if the Tatawarie decided to get involved. Perhaps there would be a way to help the lady escape from her husband once they returned to Åldras. Perhaps there was a way to fix this. But he couldn't stop Firmin from storming these shores without her coming back with them.

A man from the back of the group stood. He wasn't in the same robes as the others. He wore a swath of green fabric wrapped around his shoulders, but his arms were clad in bracers and a sword hung at his hip. Several scars marred his face, and the tip of his right ear was completely gone.

*General Caeso.*

Axel had seen the man once or twice over the years, riding at the front of his forces. He was a savage on the battlefield. While Prince Enzo might have led the military campaigns in the name of Sida, Caeso was the one who made them happen.

"Your Majesties," Caeso said, "this war is inevitable. Whether we send Lady Idalia back or not, we can expect the Åldrans to load their boats and attack within the year. I believe preparing for that fight—whether it be before or after the end of the armistice—is where our priorities lie."

Prince Enzo turned to the general. "You don't believe the Åldrans will accept our terms of the peace treaty?"

Caeso shrugged. "If they haven't already, I don't think they will. We were more than generous in our first proposal and have only been more so in the negotiations. Maker above, we offered to give them back half the land we already claimed and give an entire year's worth of grain to supplement their harvest. Yet they still wouldn't bend. All High King Firmin and his Council of Kings are doing is attempting to lengthen their time to put themselves in a better position to defend themselves when the war resumes. But both sides know this war will end with Sida the victor."

Axel clenched his fingers into fists. If these hook-nosed fools thought Åldras wouldn't tear them limb from limb, they were wrong. While Sida might be the bigger foe, Axel would never let his kingdom fall to the hands of the Sidans while he still drew breath.

Petra edged closer to him.

When he met her gaze, her mouth was set in a tight white line.

The guard at her side shifted closer, face pale as his sword hovered right next to Petra's hip.

They needed to get out of here before one of them did something foolish.

"If I may?" Axel asked the council. When the king gave a small nod, he stepped away from Petra. "I know most on the Council of Kings would rather find a peaceful end to this war than a bloody one.

Many of them hope to work with Sida on a peace treaty rather than take up their swords once more."

"Then why have they rejected our offers thus far?" a councilor piped.

Axel held out his hands. "I cannot say, as I'm not included on their council." Not that he didn't deserve a seat at that table. Firmin just didn't want him to have any more power than he already did.

"Yet you speak for them as if you were," the pinch-lipped councilor said.

The king folded his arms over his broad chest. "We need a solution."

"Keep the girl, fight the Åldrans, and let us all go back to sleep," one of the elder councilors said.

Axel waited for someone to throw a punch, but the others around him chuckled. Even the king only sent a mirthful glare.

"If you are so tired, Albano," the king said, "I'll call for someone to fetch you a cot."

The old man huffed but settled back in his chair.

"Perhaps our queen already has an answer?" someone asked.

Every head turned to the queen, seeking the water wielder's wisdom. But she remained turned toward Axel's group.

The brush of air against Axel's bare arm was the only warning he had before Petra attacked.

Apparently, the guard had done something foolish.

She used her iced hands like a club, smashing her fists into the guard's head. The ice shattered, freeing her hands. One of the councilors screamed as the guard slumped to the ground. Petra grabbed the sword. The guard standing beside him moved to attack, and Axel grabbed him by the shoulder, yanking him back so he ran into the guard closest to him.

Petra hefted the short sword over her head and flung it in the direction of Queen Kelda.

A pillar of ice shot up from the ground, freezing the sword before it even passed over the first step of the dais.

Axel's breath caught in his throat. Hel's bloody halls, this queen was far more powerful than they were prepared to face. He spun to search for Big Hal and Ludvig. Big Hal had gotten to his feet next to

Ludvig, his large hands wrapped around a sword he'd taken from one of the guards. Axel shoved Sidans aside, allowing their sharpened blades to slice through his clothing as he strode toward them. He kicked a sword toward Ludvig. The man could defend himself from the floor while Axel took care of the queen.

He turned back to the dais.

But Queen Kelda was gone.

The guards surrounded the king as Prince Enzo barked orders.

A flash of lavender slipped through the guards.

Axel whirled.

The queen stepped up right behind Petra, a pool of water around her ankles.

Ice shot up from the ground, swallowing Petra whole.

"Pet!" Axel hollered. He raced through the guards and slammed his fists against the ice. Cracks splintered out from where he'd hit, but they repaired themselves in seconds.

Axel spun toward Queen Kelda, but she had slipped back through the fight and glided back to her husband's side.

The king's stoic expression stopped Axel dead.

Big Hal still stood next to Ludvig, the two of them holding their swords at the ready as the guards circled them.

Axel glanced back at the king. "You will release Pet this instant."

The king's brows furrowed. "And allow Åldras's demon to take another swing at my wife? While I have no doubt my queen could handle herself, I'm not usually in the habit of allowing attackers to run amok in my palace."

He glanced back at Petra. Could she breathe? How long could someone live like that? Was she hurt?

Axel pointed his sword toward the king, drawing the guards' attention right to him. He nearly bared his teeth to remind them their swords could do nothing. To remind them that nothing except his own avarice could stand between him and the king.

But he didn't. He kept the sword steady as he met the king's gaze. "You will release Pet, or your entire council will see exactly why the men of Åldras sing my name as they take the lives of your men."

The king pushed forward. "You ask for mercy for a man who would kill innocents? I know the things they say about your shadow.

You would have me spare a man who threatened my queen in her own home? A man known for being a murderer and a thief?"

"Woman."

The queen's voice was more a whisper than a statement, but everyone in the room turned at her words.

"What?" Prince Enzo asked.

The queen pointed at where Petra had stood. "Petra Mallorysdottir is a woman."

*How...*

Axel's stomach fell to his feet.

Queen Kelda was a water seer. Nothing would be hidden from her view if she was watching, and what queen would not seek the future of her enemies? If she sought Åldras's future, then she watched Axel. If she watched him, she saw Petra.

The king's eyes widened a fraction. "All the same, *she* attacked without provocation and will face the consequences."

Prince Enzo barked out a laugh. Then another. Soon, he was bent over, red in the face. "Of course she's a woman. Oh, Hildi is going to die when she hears about this." His laugh cut off as his brother shoved him.

# Chapter 6

## A Deal

Petra fell to her knees as the ice around her melted and disappeared.

Wōden's one good eye, she was going to kill the bloody queen.

Her entire body shuddered as warmth brushed against her skin. Her blood felt colder than Hrimthursar's rocking toes. The fires in the room wailed their fury, as if they would cast the cold from her if she let them. She had to bury the feeling. Bury the desire to reach for the closest brazier and let the flames consume her.

"Pet," Axel whispered, skidding to his knees beside her. His touch on her arm centered her, quieting the cries of the flames around her. "You good?"

She nodded and pushed herself to her feet. Being encased in a block of ice wasn't something she ever wanted to experience again. While she'd been able to breathe, her body had been completely immobilized. The urge to scream had built in her lungs, but she'd done her best to keep her calm even as she felt the ice around her cling to her skin. The cold had practically seeped into her bones, and she was having trouble not shivering like a drenched kitten even though the water had disappeared with the ice.

The sword she'd held earlier had disappeared, so she clenched her fists and turned back to the crowd gathered near the dais. King Leonardo's bright gaze took her in. The princes studied her as if they hadn't seen her before. Queen Kelda's face was turned toward her, but her veil concealed everything else.

Petra glanced at Axel and quirked the edge of her brow. *What happened?*

He swallowed. "They know who you are. The seer knew and blurted it out to the entire council."

*Hel's bloody halls, not again.* With her fists still clenched at her sides, she widened her stance. They needed to get out of here. If Big Hal and Ludvig remained behind, they could save them later, but if they all stayed, someone would end up dead.

The king took a step toward her. "A woman taking up Åldras's banner in spite of the laws of your kingdom is no small thing. Are you a fool or a hero?"

That was the bloody question, wasn't it? Petra glanced about the room. While the Sidans seemed to be of the more tolerant sort— nearly half of their council was made up of women—it likely meant they didn't have any qualms about stabbing her even though she was a woman.

She kept her face blank. "Both."

A twitch at the corner of King Leonardo's mouth was the only sign of his mirth. At least the giant man had a sense of humor. He turned to his sons. "A foreign enemy has just threatened the life of my queen. What would you do in my situation?"

Was everything a teaching opportunity to this brute? Petra took a step back, but the closest guard raised their sword. Wōden's one good eye, if another guard stabbed her, she was going to actually kill someone.

"We kill her," Prince Roman said. "She nearly killed the queen. It's not only against the rules of the armistice but an act of war. We make an example of her and maintain order."

Axel grew very still next to Petra.

She nearly rolled her eyes. If she was in Prince Roman's shoes, she likely would have chosen to kill her too.

Prince Enzo shook his head. "But we have to think of the conse-quences. If we even attempt to kill her, we lose any bargaining power we have over Axel. Just look at him."

Everyone in the room turned to where they stood.

Petra couldn't even look at Axel. If she looked at him, all she would see was the protectiveness. The urge to save her. The burning desire he still held for her.

None of which she deserved.

"Besides, Petyr—I mean *Petra*—is not some simple assassin," Prince Enzo continued. "She's a hero of Åldras. If we kill her, it will only make a martyr of her. High King Firmin is already sending ships to our shores. Adding the death of the most infamous warrior in their kingdom would only give him more fuel for the fire. Our shores would be swarming with Åldran ships in a fortnight."

Enzo wasn't wrong. While Firmin was a fool, he'd gotten Åldras through ten years of war without falling to the enemy. Half of the lesser kings worshipped the very ground he walked on while the other half gave their grudging respect. Even the people praised their warrior of a High King. It was one of the reasons he could get away with his campaign against the Häxa. No one wanted to go up against the king that had kept his entire kingdom alive for a decade.

"But we can't simply let her walk out of here as if she didn't just attempt to murder Mother," Prince Roman continued.

The king set his hands behind his back. "So, what is the right answer?"

Prince Roman furrowed his brows and looked down at his boots.

Prince Enzo looked to the king. "I don't know that there is one."

The king nodded gravely. "It's wisdom when a man sees there are not any right choices in a situation. However, a king must decide on the best choice and convince others it's the right one. You must also be ready to face the consequences of that decision."

King Leonardo walked back to his throne and settled his large frame back into it. "As my queen was the one targeted, I would like to hear what she has in mind."

The king was really going to ask the queen? While she might be a water seer, the question felt more like an inquiry to the queen's conscience rather than the future she could see.

Petra turned once again to the Häxa queen standing like a statue next to the king's throne. The woman's gaze penetrated through the veil, raising the hairs on the back of Petra's neck. Whatever Queen

Kelda would decide, it would likely spell Petra's death in one way or another.

The queen turned to her husband, clasping her hands in front of her. "I have a proposition, one that would not require an execution or a dungeon cell."

Prince Roman scoffed and Prince Enzo frowned.

Queen Kelda ignored them, gliding down the dais. The edges of her skirt rippled like water down the steps. "If Petra and Mighty Axel agree, I would have Petra serve as one of my attendants."

*That's it?* Petra glanced to the king, who sat in his throne with a contemplative look on his face. As if he were actually considering the queen's proposition. If it wasn't her bloody life on the line, Petra might have let an inkling of respect for the king grow between her ribs.

"No." Axel's voice was the strike of a sword on stone. It reverberated around the room.

Prince Enzo folded his arms over his chest. "What the queen is offering is a mercy no one else would even consider."

Axel took a step forward, but Petra grabbed the back of his tunic, yanking him back.

He looked back to her, his green eyes narrowed. *You can't be serious.*

She bit her lips between her teeth. *I don't think we have a choice.*

If they didn't take Queen Kelda up on this deal, they were looking at a blood bath. Hel's halls, they were looking at one no matter which way Petra turned the situation over in her head. This scenario simply gave Axel enough time to save Big Hal and Ludvig like he wanted. It wouldn't be difficult for her to escape the palace once they were ready to head back to Åldras. They could figure out this bloody palace, gain the trust of the Sidans, and snatch Lady Idalia out from under their noses.

"What are the conditions?" Petra asked. "Would you have me abandon my kin entirely? Act as your slave for the rest of my life?" If the queen expected her to give her life over in servitude, Petra would let one of the guards skewer her.

The king turned to the queen but said nothing.

Queen Kelda shook her head. "The terms are simple. You will act as my companion from sunup until high noon. During that time, you will join me for whatever I deem appropriate for Åldran ears, or you will be left to whatever task I leave for you. After high noon, you are welcome to join your kinsmen—whether they are here in the palace or elsewhere. As you are now bound to two kingdoms, you will be permitted to dwell with both. But you will return by sunup the next day, or your life will be forfeit."

The arrangement could be worse. Being here in the palace might actually be a benefit. Petra could gather information as she hovered about the queen and report back to Axel and the crew in the evenings. If they couldn't get Lady Idalia to return to Åldras, perhaps they could return to Firmin with information more valuable to him than Anders's pride.

"And how long would this sentence be?" she asked.

The queen gave a delicate shrug. "Either until High King Firmin steps onto these shores, or the original expiration of the armistice is past. Do you accept?"

The bigger question was *why*. Why did the queen propose such an underwhelming price? Why did she want Petra to herself? Would it actually be to torture her outside of Axel's sight? Was she trying to win Petra over so they could control Axel? Was the queen actually that soft and the king that tenderhearted?

There was only one way to find out what was behind that veil and get the crew out of this mess.

Petra dropped her hand from Axel's tunic, his warmth bleeding from her fingers. "I accept."

The council around them let out a collective breath, as if the fight that had been brewing had just dissipated at her acceptance. Fools, the lot of them.

"What are you doing?" Axel hissed.

Petra widened her eyes. *I have this under control.*

Axel gritted his teeth and spun toward the king. "And what of the rest of us? Will you have my crew serve as bootlickers? Wall ornaments? Perhaps there's a harem here for the queen's use? I'm sure there are many men in this kingdom who would love to get a look under that veil."

Prince Roman drew his sword. "How dare you insult Her Majesty!"

The hotheaded prince pulled away from the guards. Petra stepped away from Axel as the prince approached, his teeth bared.

Axel didn't even flinch as the younger prince swung his sword. The blade slammed into Axel's side and shattered. The top half of the sword clattered to the ground as Prince Roman staggered forward.

Petra couldn't see Axel's face, but the set of his shoulders and the stillness of his lungs told her enough. Slowly, he leaned down as the prince stared at him as if he hadn't realized a monster lurked under Axel's golden skin. Axel picked up the shard of sword, twirling it in his fingers. His voice was cold as the ice the Häxa queen wielded.

"I thought my demonstration in Harligdam would be enough to convince you, but apparently you need a reminder." His arm was a blur as he moved.

Blood welled up on the prince's arm, right where he'd attempted to cut Axel all those weeks ago in Harligdam.

The guards shifted forward, but the king called for them to stop.

Petra kept her eyes on Axel.

He practically loomed over the prince. "You're the one in this fight who can bleed."

Prince Enzo finally strode forward and pulled his brother back. "Don't be an idiot, Roman. You know this isn't a battle worth waging. You got your justice. Walk away."

Prince Roman finally spun away, but not toward the dais. He stormed out of the room. He'd likely have slammed the door if one of the guards hadn't opened it for him.

The king stood from his throne. "As for your men, Mighty Axel, perhaps a similar arrangement could be made." He gestured to General Caeso. "What do you think about having Mighty Axel join in on drills in the morning? Perhaps we could convince him and his men that we aren't the brutes Åldras has painted us to be all these years."

The general huffed. "I suspect you'll get more than just the young prince swinging a sword at them."

King Leonardo met Petra's gaze, then Axel's. "What say you, Mighty Axel? Care to have a few more swords swung at you?"

"Would it convince you to allow Petra to rescind her acceptance of your queen's terms?"

Petra glared at the back of his neck. Who was he to make that kind of offer? *Bloody rockhead.* He needed to get Big Hal and Ludvig out of here, not throw them to the hawk-nosed wolves.

"No, but it would certainly help her cause. She owes my queen penance for her attack, but you agreeing to join our men in the training yard would endear us all to you. Instead of keeping your warrior until the time my queen has dictated, we could lessen her sentence."

The king wasn't just a wolf, but a fox as well. Petra grabbed Axel's shoulder, trying to get him to look at her. King Leonardo had wanted this all along. He knew he couldn't get Axel to give her up without a fight. He'd quickly figured out Axel wouldn't go anywhere without her. So he used it to his advantage. He'd given Axel a way to stay and just enough hope that by working with them, her punishment wouldn't be as trying. And in doing so, he'd be able to parade Axel around like a prized trophy. *Mighty Axel, a Sidan dog.*

Axel let her pull him back, but he didn't turn. "I accept."

*Hel's bloody halls.*

She yanked him hard enough that he finally met her eye.

His brows furrowed with a mixture of worry and anger. *If they take you, they take me with you.*

Her eyes narrowed. *You're an idiot.* Freyja's golden tears, he was going to get someone killed.

His eyes glowed with determination. There weren't necessarily words in the expression, but there was definitely feeling.

A loud clap shot through the room.

Petra jumped away from Axel, the green of his eyes too close. Too warm. Too deep.

The king's voice boomed once again. "Now that we have all that settled, we can return to our beds."

The council all stood, relief evident in the slant of their shoulders. Both men and women spoke to one another. As equals. The entire crowd gave all of them a wide berth. Big Hal had gotten

Ludvig to his feet, though both of them looked like they would topple at the slightest breeze.

"Enzo," King Leonardo called, "please escort our visitors to some of the guest chambers. There are only a few hours left until dawn, and I suspect they'd like to get a bit of rest before their duties begin in the morning."

Axel stepped forward to wrap Ludvig's other arm over his shoulder. Petra picked up his legs from where they hung on the floor and tucked his ankles under her armpits. It would at least lessen some of the load on Big Hal's bruised shoulders and keep his energy up in case they needed to make a run for it.

Axel readjusted his hold on Ludvig and turned toward the king and the prince. "Is there a place I can purchase supplies for my men?"

The king waved a hand. "I'll send a surgeon to your rooms. It will be an honor to serve such an honored guest in my palace."

Petra gritted her teeth. Honored, were they? The bruises all over Big Hal's face told a different story. Hopefully, the cost of a surgeon wouldn't be added to the tab slowly increasing every second they stood on Sidan soil.

King Leonardo wasn't a man to be trifled with.

The prince guided them out into the hall; his hand settled lazily over the pommel of his sword. A squad of guards followed behind them, their hands ready to rip their swords from their scabbards the moment anyone sneezed. Prince Enzo cleared his throat.

"We will have four rooms readied for you."

"Two will do," Axel said.

Prince Enzo looked over his shoulder at Axel, then turned to Petra. "Apologies, but there is only one bed per room. I'm sure all of you would like to get rest."

Petra narrowed her eyes. The prince was a fool if he thought he could separate them so easily. Axel gave quite the show of trust by even requesting two rooms instead of one. The Sidans could pick them off a bit easier if they were only in pairs, but at least they couldn't attack all of them one by one.

"As I said," Axel replied, "two rooms will be fine."

Prince Enzo spun around, walking backward as if they were

going for a pleasant tour through the palace. He pointed between Petra and Axel. "Are the two of you married then?"

Big Hal choked behind Petra, making the lot of them stumble and Ludvig hiss in pain.

Petra met the prince's humored expression. "We honeymooned in Tatawar."

Prince Enzo's lips twitched. "I would believe you if your steersman didn't look like he was trying to break my skull open with his glare."

She glanced back at Axel, widening her eyes. *Calm down.*

His nostrils flared. *I'll kill him.*

"So," the prince continued, "if the two of you aren't married, your big brute is in danger."

"Why?" she asked.

The prince's mouth stretched into a grin. "Because I haven't met a woman able to resist a Sidan man's charm."

Petra pulled any emotion from her expression. Did he really think charming her in the middle of the hallway after she'd just sold herself to his mother and was covered in the blood of his men was a good idea? Or did he have a death wish? Based on the way Axel had gone very quiet behind her, he was already plotting the prince's murder. She allowed a touch of Åldras's demon to leak through, just in the tilt of her eyebrow.

The prince's idiotic smirk faltered just a bit as Petra stared at him.

Her head tilted to the side. "There's a fallacy in your logic, prince. I've met many a Sidan man over the years, and it was my brand of charm they succumbed to."

It only took a moment, but the Scourge revealed himself in the slight narrowing of his eyes. He remembered what she did to Sidans on a battlefield, and it would be best if he didn't forget it.

"Your rooms," Prince Enzo said, gesturing to a collection of doors. "Help yourselves to whatever accommodations you prefer, but there will be four rooms, and there will be guards stationed outside of each of them. If you wish for the rest of your stay to go smoothly, I suggest you all get some sleep. I'm sure the surgeon will be here shortly to attend to your injuries." With a stiff bow, he marched off.

"Way to show him, Pet," Ludvig whispered.

She shook her head. *Stupid princes.* Tucking both of Ludvig's boots in her armpits, she pushed open the door to the first room.

Why anyone believed they would need more than just this one room was foolish. A large bed lay in the middle of the room, fabric draping across the ceiling in bright reds and golds. Small flames caressed the magic in Petra's veins from the two lanterns on either side of the bed and the candles dripping on the shelf next to a small table and set of chairs. A plush fur rug covered most of the floor, and a polished chest sat at the end of the bed. Petra carefully positioned Ludvig's legs so Axel and Big Hal could get him onto the bed without jostling him too much.

"How bad is it?" Axel asked.

Ludvig sighed as he laid back on the pillow. "I reckon my leg's shattered, and I've got at least two cracked ribs."

"Bloody rockhead tried fighting a whole squad on his own," Big Hal groused. He ran fingers through his wavy hair, trying to smooth it out. "Took two or three out before an air whisperer got the better of him and smashed him into a stone wall."

A lopsided grin stretched over Ludvig's face. "At least she was a looker. Hate to get pummeled by someone uglier than myself. Not good for my pride."

Petra shook her head. "It doesn't bode well that there are so many Häxa here."

"No," Axel agreed, "it doesn't."

Based on the amount of Häxa they'd smuggled out to the Great Mother, it had made sense most Häxa had gone to Ljust Löfte to join the community there. However, in a single night, they'd faced four Häxa in high-standing positions. How many more were there? From what little Petra knew about the gifts, Åldras had the highest density of magic. There was speculation everywhere about why, but no one doubted that more women in Åldras were gifted with magic than any other kingdom.

Which meant that at least some of these Häxa had come from Åldras.

Firmin's accusations against the Häxa of Ljust Löfte—when he had threatened them if they went to Sida—didn't feel so unfounded.

The guards outside began speaking, their voices bouncing off the stone walls until they became indiscernible.

Axel took up a post between Ludvig and the door. "Sounds like the healer."

A woman, likely no older than Petra, appeared at the door. Mousy brown hair was pulled back from a pair of blue eyes and what looked like a million freckles dotted the skin beneath a pair of spectacles perched on her nose. Those blue eyes scanned the room, taking in every drop of blood and bruised eye between the four of them.

She cleared her throat and readjusted the large satchel weighing down her shoulder. "Which one of you is in the most need?"

Axel folded his arms over his chest. "Are you the surgeon?"

"Yes." The woman straightened her shoulders. "I'm Iris, and I'm here to tend to any major wounds."

They even let women be surgeons?

Big Hal stepped up next to Axel, his eyes narrowed. "How much poison do you have in that sack there?"

Iris frowned, looking down at her bag. "I suppose most of the ointments in my supply could be considered poison if used incorrectly. However, if the royal family wished to dispose of you, there are certainly more efficient and cost-effective ways to do so."

Axel chuckled. "Aye, she's a surgeon all right."

"Praise the Allfather," Ludvig groaned. "The king was quick to send her. And if she really is an assassin, she'll kill me and I won't have to deal with this bloody pain in my leg anymore."

Iris charged forward and set her bag down next to Ludvig's bed. "Which leg?"

He jabbed a thumb at his left leg. "Swelling started already. You'll probably have to cut my boot. They're my favorite too."

With a small shake of her head, Iris reached into her satchel. "I'll probably not need to cut it off." She unclasped one of the buckles and a trail of foliage popped out of the bag. She rummaged around in the sack until she found a strip of leather, a pot of dirt, and a poultice. She held out the leather to Ludvig.

"Bite down on this would you?"

With shaking fingers Ludvig took the scrap of leather and stuck it between his teeth.

Petra stepped toward Iris, standing at the foot of Ludvig's bed. She'd seen enough broken bones treated she knew what came next. It wouldn't be pretty, watching the physician reset the bone if it came to that. From the grim look on the woman's face, it just might.

Iris grabbed the leaves in one hand and took Ludvig's not-swollen ankle in her other.

*Thunder's beard.* Not only was she a female surgeon, she was a plant healer.

Ludvig sagged against the pillows, unconscious.

Petra grabbed Iris's wrist, her skin warming the moment her touch met the surgeon's arm. "What did you do?"

Iris met Petra's gaze over her spectacles. "Relax. I know you Åldrans aren't used to seeing Häxa magic out in the open, but all I did is put him to..." The surgeon's words trailed off, and her eyes widened as she studied Petra. "What are you?" she asked in a whisper.

Petra's chest seized. What did Iris see? Was she shocked that Petra was a woman? Did she see the scars that had been washed away? Did she see the magic boiling under Petra's skin?

Axel pulled Petra's grip away from Iris's wrist. "We know plenty about Häxa healers, Lady Iris. Please, allow us to leave you to your work. We know Ludvig will appreciate finding his leg whole when he wakes."

While her attention remained on Petra, she nodded. "Yes, thank you."

Axel pulled Petra toward the door. Over his shoulder, he said, "Big Hal, stay with Ludvig."

Big Hal grunted his acquiescence, though he likely hadn't even moved from his spot at the head of Ludvig's bed. None of them would be going anywhere alone. At least, not until Petra went to whatever torture she would find at the queen's hand in the morning.

Two guards stood on either end of the hallway, giving the illusion of privacy. It wouldn't be surprising to discover there were ears listening in the walls and eyes watching from every shadow.

Axel pulled her into the room right beside Ludvig's, leaving the door open a crack in case Big Hal called for help. The room was much the same as the one next door, though this rug was white rather than brown. The small flames dotted about the room brightened at Petra's presence. Ignoring them wouldn't be too difficult so long as she didn't get too close.

She glided around the room, running her fingers along the walls. She found a gap halfway down the wall separating them from Ludvig's room and another two steps after it. Turning back to Axel, who was looking through the window next to the bed, she set a finger to her lips and signaled to the wall. *Hidden door.* They wouldn't want any listening ears to hear anything they didn't want them to.

Axel nodded. "I hope Ludvig's leg heals quickly." He stepped back from the window, his fingers counting six guards.

Thunder's beard, if there were six in plain view, how many more waited out of sight? Escaping would be miserable if they attempted it tonight. They would need to lure the Sidans into complacency if they were going to get out of the palace without a battle.

Petra stepped away from the wall and lifted the edge of the rug with the toe of her boot. "Do you think Big Hal will need much attention? His black eye looked pretty swollen."

"The physician seemed competent." Axel picked up the trunk next to the bed, making it look like the thing weighed no more than a sack of wool. He placed the trunk quietly next to the wall, blocking anyone who would attempt to sneak through the cut-out door there. Gently, he pressed his ear to the wall. "If anyone was using this door, they're not there now," he said.

Petra knelt next to the bed. Even the wood underneath looked like it had been swept clean. The mattress on the bed was held up by a frame and a collection of ropes and leather straps.

Axel's face appeared on the other side; his eyes narrowed in the faint light coming from the lantern above his head.

*Don't think I'm not angry*, those eyes said.

Petra sat up. This conversation wasn't one she wished to have with sharp glares and thin lips. "What else did you want me to do?" she asked.

Axel mirrored her across the bed. "You didn't even give us a chance to come up with something else. Now, they're going to expect you to show up who knows where with that bloody queen of theirs and do the gods only know what."

"Like you didn't do exactly the same thing by agreeing to help Caeso." He'd practically thrown himself at the bloody king's feet the moment Petra had agreed to Queen Kelda's punishment. She stood, coming around the bed. "You think they aren't going to use you for information? What are Ludvig and Big Hal supposed to do while you're traipsing around with some of our greatest enemies?"

"It's definitely not the same, and you know it." Shaking his head, he stalked away from her. A washbasin with a pitcher of water sat against the wall, a candle flickering a greeting next to it. He set to washing the blood from his hands.

He seriously was going to walk away from her right now?

Petra stalked toward him, reared her fist back, and punched him right in the kidney.

It was like hitting a brick wall, but she swung again before he snatched her bloodied knuckles in his wet hands.

"I'm not going to leave you here," he hissed.

"You're an idiot," she snapped back. He'd walked right into the king's trap like it was a bloody favor. "The Sidans aren't going to let me or you go now. You know that, right? If you would have just taken the crew and gone, I could have escaped on my own. You just told them you're willing to sacrifice yourself for me, and they're going to dangle it over your head."

He threw his hands up. "The second you accepted the queen's offer, they knew they had me. There's no way they didn't. If I hadn't agreed, they would have gone to other measures to make me work with them. But they haven't taken one very important fact into consideration."

Axel stepped close enough that she could feel the air move around him with his angry breaths. "If one of them harms a single hair on your head, I'll kill them all."

Some of the fire in her veins cooled. The candle next to the washbasin settled. This whole thing was a mess.

Axel's cheeks puffed with air before he let it out in an aggravated growl. "At least with Caeso I know what to expect. Something about that queen isn't right, Pet. Why the veil? Why all the mystery?"

There hadn't been much time to think at all since Prince Enzo grabbed them. The evening went completely awry one moment after the next. "She's Queen of Sida," Petra said. "Of course there's something off about her."

Axel shook his head. "How did we not know the queen was Häxa? And the way she was able to summon water...that woman is dangerous, and I don't like the thought of you going to face whatever she has planned alone."

"It doesn't matter what you like." Petra folded her arms across her chest. "If you'd just kept your mouth shut and gotten Big Hal and Ludvig back to the ship, I'd probably be halfway out of the city with no one the wiser. We could have come up with a plan for how to keep Firmin off our backs, but now we're all prisoners in this bloody tomb of a palace."

"How was I supposed to know what you were planning? I have no idea what's been going through your head since we got back on *The Phoenix* in Harligdam. Since you showed up with your Petyr mask fully back in place. You keep throwing yourself into danger and doing stupid things."

Petra gritted her teeth. "You and the rest of the crew just can't get past the fact that I'm not Petyr anymore. Now that everyone knows about me, they think I'm fragile."

"What?" Axel's face scrunched up. "Why would that have changed anything? I've always known, and you've never been fragile."

"Then why are you snipping at me all the bloody time?"

"Because I can't bloody *trust you*."

The words clanged in Petra's ears. They were so wrong her brain couldn't even wrap around them until they settled in her chest.

He couldn't trust her. Of course he couldn't. She'd lied to him for years. Lied to everyone. She'd hidden what she was from him. Let him believe the Sidans had killed Asher and all of her family in Holmberg.

She swallowed back the fight burning in her chest.

"You're right. You can't trust me."

Axel pinched the bridge of his nose. "Pet, I didn't mean—"

"Save it," she snapped. "You'll need all the niceties you can muster when you suck up to the bloody Sidans tomorrow."

"Fine." He snatched one of the pillows from the bed and threw it against the wall next to the door. With quick steps, he crossed the room and laid down, facing away from her.

Petra stared at his back as he settled his head on the pillow. If he wanted to throw another fit, she wouldn't stop him. Marching over to the washbasin, she quickly scrubbed the dried blood from her skin, mixing the blood she'd taken with Axel's. There wasn't anything she could do about her clothes. She slipped into the bed, boots and all. If they needed to make a run for it in the middle of the night, she'd be ready. The small flame of the lantern next to the bed flickered. The bright light bobbed back to a steady ripple, matching the rise and fall of Petra's chest.

She glared at Axel's back one last time and quickly blew out the lanterns on either side of the bed.

Perhaps going to the queen tomorrow for whatever torture awaited would be the best thing Petra had done since the moment Axel had unburied her from the ruins of her home.

# CHAPTER 7

## REFUGEES

*The pair of ravens Little Hal trained have likely traveled thousands of miles across the kingdoms between our two ships. The lad raised them from chicks, and I sometimes wonder how much they take after their namesakes, whispering news from their travels into Little Hal's ear. It would answer how the lad knows so much at such a young age. Little Hal is a gatherer of stories, much like his grandfather had been, though I have a feeling Little Hal keeps those stories close to his vest. Perhaps I can convince him to join my crew once he reaches adulthood.*

*— FROM THE WRITINGS OF DORAN FINNSSON, THE LAST KING OF GROVÖ*

Though Axel had listened to Petra leave before sunup, he only moved from the floor when he couldn't hear her footsteps any longer. This deal with Queen Kelda would be the death of their entire crew. Getting to his feet, he shrugged on his still bloodied shirt and set an ear to the door. No guards stood right outside, but the murmur of voices could be heard down the hall.

If following after Petra would have actually helped their cause, he would race after her. He swallowed. If he didn't see her the moment she was released from her bargained time, he would tear through the palace. If there was a single scratch on her, he'd kill them all.

Though, if someone did scratch her, they likely wouldn't make it out of the encounter with their hands.

Petra could take care of herself.

Stepping lightly over the floor, he made his way across the room to the window. There hadn't been much to see the night before, but with dawn arriving soon, he could make out the details of the city below much easier. Their room sat on the southern side of the palace. This side of the city didn't have as many buildings, so he had a full view of the Sidan plains stretching toward the mountains.

A spot of black darted between a pair of trees decorating the palace gardens.

Axel's eyes didn't move from the tree until the spot of black leapt from the branches, coming right for him.

He moved away from the window as the flurry of feathers alighted on the windowsill.

"Good boy, Huggin."

The raven stuck out his leg, offering Axel the small bit of parchment attached by a metal bead.

Axel snagged the paper and let out a breath of relief when he found Little Hal's messy scrawl stretched across the page.

*P waiting outside the inlet. Huggin will report in city.*

A smile tugged at the edges of Axel's mouth. The little scamp had weaseled his way into the city after their capture. He took after Petra a little too much sometimes.

Axel tore the parchment to bits, tossing it out the window. No need for the Sidans to know they had a spy in their midst. He grabbed his boots and carefully slid out into the hall and through the door to the room where Ludvig and Big Hal had slept.

Big Hal lay sprawled on the floor at the foot of Ludvig's bed. Axel would need to see about getting them all beds between the two rooms. Ludvig was already sitting up, his left leg elevated by a stack of blankets and his hair sticking out from his usually tight braids. His gaze was sharp when he met Axel's and a lazy smile curled at the edges of his mouth.

"Pet gone already?" he asked.

Axel nodded. "How's your leg?"

"Could be better." He shrugged. "The healer said the bone completely shattered."

Axel settled on the edge of the bed to slip on his boots, glancing down at a still drooling Big Hal. The man's face looked far less purple than it should have. "What happened to the two of you last night?"

Ludvig brushed a hand over his frizzed hair. "It wasn't long after we separated that they found us."

They had gone in the opposite direction as Axel and Petra, hoping to take a more circuitous route to distract the bulk of the city and use the other gate into the palace. They'd made it into the lower districts of the city, where the buildings were tighter together and offered more places to hide. What they hadn't counted on was the patrol shift change. A group of guards were making their way home from the front gate when they stumbled upon Ludvig and Big Hal. The guards chasing them only had to alert the others to the threat and Ludvig and Big Hal were taken down.

"Big Hal put up a good fight, but once the Häxa guard took me up with her air magic and slammed me into a bloody wall, I was done. I could barely keep from passing out as they trussed us up and hurried us to the palace. Prince Roman greeted us at the gate. I think he knew you were coming and ordered the guards to get us into the palace as quickly as possible. I wish I could say I was sad to see you captured, but I knew I was a goner if you left me here on my own."

Axel rubbed a hand over his face. Petra had been right to take the queen's deal. With a wound like that, Ludvig might not have even made it to the ship. Men died from shattered bones, if not just from the inability to fight the infection.

"Did the healer fix your leg?"

The crease between Ludvig's brows smoothed. "She said it'll take a few days for a full recovery, but I should be able to run by this time next week."

Axel blew out a breath. "Good. That's good."

Häxa healing was nothing to scoff at. If he could have done it without getting anyone killed, Axel would have employed a plant healer on *The Phoenix* years ago. After seeing Petra healed from the draugr bite in Ljust Löfte, he'd thought about concealing one on the ship, but he wouldn't put a Häxa at risk even if it could protect his crew.

Besides, two Häxa on the ship was more than enough.

"What are we going to do?" Ludvig asked. "You can't seriously be thinking about helping these rockheads."

"We're going to do what we agreed to," Axel answered. He nudged Big Hal with the toe of his boot. "You two need to watch each other's backs today. I'll meet with the general and see if we can get the rest of the crew into the palace. I'll feel much better with a few more eyes and ears in this place." Erik would likely hate it, but having more numbers would help keep everyone safe. Besides, without Olav, Little Hal would need someone to direct him, and Erik knew how to gather information almost as good as Doran.

"You think they'll let that many Åldrans into the palace?" Big Hal mumbled.

"You think they'd rather let us run around without supervision?" Axel asked.

"Good point."

Axel nudged Big Hal's arm again with his boot. Big Hal groaned but lifted his head. Axel crouched next to him. "Stay here with Ludvig. Make sure nothing happens to him. If anything goes wrong, haul him back to the ship. I'm sure we could get another healer to look him over once we get out of this bloody kingdom if it comes to that."

Big Hal nodded and pushed himself up off the pallet. A few yellow bruises colored his jaw, but the healer had done quite the work on him as well. He pulled a small comb from a pocket in his tunic and set to unsnarling his head of strawberry blond hair. The vain idiot. "You sure you don't want backup with the general?"

Axel gave a feral grin. "When have I ever needed backup?"

ᚡᚺ᚜ᛟᚠᚤᛁ

GENERAL CAESO'S command center wasn't at all what Axel had pictured in his head. Not that he'd thought too hard about it, but he certainly hadn't pictured the small room with the single desk and only a simple shelf of scrolls in one corner.

Command centers in Åldras were temporary things, usually made of canvas tents that could be attached to whatever ship the generals sailed on. They were moved over and over as the commanders journeyed from isle to isle or battle to battle. In all honesty, the ships themselves were the only permanent structures the leaders of Åldras's army could call command centers other than a king's fortress or a town's great hall.

The general sat at a desk with two doors on either side of him. In the span of five minutes, three different messengers had come in one and gone out the other. The general had kept up his stream of words even as he'd read through the missives he received and sent replies back with the lads.

"Now, Mighty Axel," he said once the last lad scurried out, "I don't expect you to simply lay all your king's plans at my feet—though if you feel so tempted I certainly won't stop you—but I do hope the two of us can come to a truce. Though I may be the general of an army, I believe it's part of my job to keep my warriors alive which means that if I have the chance to keep them out of a fight altogether, I'll take it."

The candidness was nothing short of refreshing. Axel leaned back against the wall next to the doorway the messenger had left through. He could appreciate a leader who didn't care to twist words about and keep people in the shadows.

"You'll find an ally in me if that's true, General. If I could snap my fingers and end this war, I would."

Caeso's lips pursed. "If that were true, you could have simply snapped the neck of that brute you call a king, and we could have all gone home happy."

"You and I both know you only say that because Sida would have swept in and taken hold of Åldras in the aftermath. There still would have been war."

A glint flashed across the general's gaze, whether it was from greed or amusement, Axel couldn't tell. He'd have to be careful not to let anything he didn't want the Sidans to have slip when in this man's presence. Not that he'd be giving any of these men anything. He'd rather carve his own heart from his chest and feed it to a draugr.

Caeso chuckled. "You're probably right. But we do need to figure out how to prepare for whatever the next few steps are."

Right to business then. Axel folded his arms over his chest. "If it were up to me, I'd tell you to stick Lady Idalia on my ship and wave goodbye from the docks. I don't know that there will be any way to avoid bloodshed unless she is returned to Anders."

"He'd really end the treaty?"

Axel shrugged. "As far as him and Firmin are concerned, you did that by taking Lady Idalia. You all had the right of it last night when you spoke of the marriage agreements. Having her taken was a blow not only to Anders's pride, but to Firmin's as well. Firmin won't like the idea of Tatawar getting involved in this war. If we aren't the ones to return with her, Firmin will send more than just one ship next time."

Caeso leaned back into his chair. "If I asked about the state of Åldras, would you tell me?"

"What do you already know?"

Caeso studied him, his keen gaze taking in Axel's measure. There had been many times over the years where Axel had received such consideration. He was young. He knew it as well as these older men who generally wielded such power. But Axel hadn't been found wanting. Not in all the years he'd been riding the waves of the Vit Sea.

Axel smirked. Caeso wouldn't be any different.

With a chuckle, the general pulled one of the scrolls from his shelf, a large one with multiple layers of paper. He laid out the pages, pointing toward the accounts of some of his men but also the reports of land taken by the Sidans as well as the number of towns destroyed. There were maps showing the sheer mass of Sida's kingdom in comparison to Åldras. While Åldras was a mass of islands, Sida was all one humongous chunk of land, starting at the southern edge of the Vit Sea and stretching down to a mountain range far to the south. Honestly, the continental kingdom could swallow the entirety of Åldras three times over. And that wasn't even touching the amount of people. Axel had traveled most of Åldras over the years and Sida boasted twice as many villages throughout their lands. They spread through Sida like stars across the sky.

Caeso listed the Åldran hideouts he knew about, watching Axel for any hints that his claims were true or false. Most of his guesses to where the men were allocated were correct, but Axel kept any revealing expression from his face.

*Wōden's eye.* Axel's fingers trembled as the general succinctly laid out all the information they had. If his tone had contained even an ounce of smugness, Axel might have thrown him through a wall. But his voice was all clinical as if the numbers in front of him were nothing but scratches on parchment instead of people's livelihoods. The last paper he drew from the pile had a list of towns within Åldras with numbers in the columns next to it.

"What's this?" Axel said, tapping the page on the desk.

The general's face brightened slightly. "It's the Häxa."

Axel carefully drew the paper from the pile. Beside each town name three columns trailed down the page. At the top, it listed the subjects of each column. The first was a date, the earliest reaching back to thirteen years ago, listed next to the town of Betala. The second was the number of Häxa found within the town. The third was the number brought to Sida.

Axel's eyes trailed down the page, instantly finding the name his tongue had sung so many times over the years. Faded letters tattooed the paper halfway down.

*Holmberg.*

Next to the name was a date. Nearly nine years ago. Only a week before the Sidans had arrived on the pebbled shores. His eyes trailed to the next column where a similarly faded number had been scratched onto the page.

*Three.*

His stomach dropped. Had they known about Petra? About Mila? Based on Petra's recounting of the night of the attack, there was no doubt Mila had been a Häxa. Not if she'd known about förändra. Not if she'd used runed stones. But not even Mila had known about Petra's gifts. Had there been another Häxa on the isle?

The number in the last column hit him in the gut.

*Zero.*

He laid the paper back down. "Why do the number of Häxa not always match the number brought to Sida?"

Caeso spun it around and slid it into his pile. "Some of the Häxa don't wish to join us once we free them from Åldras. Some ask to be dropped off on other isles to start in a new village. Others wish to find their own way to the Great Mother and her people. Not many go to Tatawar, but there have been one or two over the years. And a few are discovered by the Ekte before we can reach them."

"How do you know about them?"

Caeso deliberated over answering for several seconds. "If you must know, most of the numbers on that page have come from Queen Kelda. Several others would come to us with news of one or two others in other towns, but for the most part, the queen herself has led the charge to gather Häxa from Åldras and help them escape the tyranny of King Firmin's Ekte."

Why would a Sidan queen care about Åldran Häxa? Of course, Queen Kelda was a Häxa herself, but it didn't account for this sort of operation. Axel frowned down at the pile of papers once again. Was she gathering an army for the Sidans by saving the Häxa in Åldras? It was what Firmin feared. Why he'd gone to Ljust Löfte. He'd wanted the Häxa to cease joining the Sidan forces, but if the Sidans themselves were saving the witches, how many had actually come from Ljust Löfte? Axel's jaw clenched. Firmin's bloody threats at Ljust Löfte likely weren't even necessary. The Sidans were enlisting their Häxa warriors all on their own.

"Is that why you attacked Åldras?" Axel asked. "Attacked Holmberg?"

The general gave a slow nod. "The fighters on the beach were to act as a distraction while another team went to speak with the Häxa. The fighters were supposed to retreat as soon as the Häxa had made it off the isle. They were sent with orders to simply draw fire so the other team could sneak in undetected."

The fight on the beach wasn't even a fight. With the general's words, the foggy memories of that night cleared slightly, a new ray of knowledge shedding light on the events. The Sidans had come with several ships, but few men actually ventured to the beach and those men had done little damage. At least, it was far less than could have been done. Had there even been a single fallen Åldran before Petra's fire?

He blinked. "Was I one of the three to be extracted?"

"As I wasn't general by then, I don't know if the group sent to extract the Häxa knew you were there as well. If you were one of the three on this sheet. I didn't hear word of Asher's son until a few years later, but by then we were already embroiled in the conflict. Holmberg was only the sixth extraction to take place, though it was one of the most brazen. We've become much more cautious since then. We lost a lot of good men on those shores. We didn't even know they were gone until several weeks later. We sent a party out to investigate, and they came back with reports of Holmberg's destruction and the carcasses of our ships. We'd seen Åldran fire in action, but nothing like that. That kind of destruction would bring even the Maker down in godly wrath if the people that set it hadn't died then too. I'm sure the Maker gave them their dues when they stood at the gates of the afterlife."

The truth clawed at Axel's throat, but he wouldn't release it. These people would stick Petra's head on the end of a bloody pike if they knew she was the one who brought that destruction. Godly wrath wouldn't even be warranted.

"You believe it was one of ours that set the fire? I've seen Sidans use Åldran fire as well." Enzo had spread it over the bog outside of Ljust Löfte to defeat the draugr and escape.

Caeso shook his head. "We didn't have access to Åldran fire until a couple years ago. Even if our men had found it in Holmberg, why would they have destroyed the city? How would they have? It had to have been orchestrated beforehand."

Axel straightened. "You think the Åldrans—*my father*—would have ever thought to do something so horrendous? My father loved his people. All of Holmberg was populated with the best men and women Åldras had to offer."

"And that brings us to the crux of the problem, doesn't it? The Åldrans insist they had nothing to do with it, but six Sidan langships never came home after what was supposed to be nothing but an extraction mission. You and Petyr—excuse me, *Petra*—are the only ones to survive that night." The general stood, leaning over his table. "And trust me when I tell you that we were most eager to hear what happened on those shores once you were discovered. We sent spies to gather reports of what happened. When they returned with the tale that two children had been found and blamed us for this war, the entire council had to talk King Leonardo out of sending our entire army to sweep across your kingdom. He lost his childhood best friend the night Holmberg fell. Captain Enzo, the prince's namesake, was a hero to many. The entire kingdom grieved his loss."

An ache bloomed under Axel's ribs, and he swallowed the truth back until it stuck down in that ache. "We've all lost people in this war." Too many. And for what? A misunderstanding? Would Åldras and Sida have avoided conflict completely if Petra's magic hadn't manifested? Probably not. There had been contentions between the two kingdoms for ages before. But could some of these people have been saved?

If Axel looked at the answer too closely, he was likely to break.

"So, what are we going to do?" he asked. "If we want to avoid more bloodshed, we'd best come to some arrangement."

Caeso blew out a breath. "Well, I was hoping you and I could figure out if there was perhaps a trade we could make with Åldras to appease your high king. If we could cool tempers over there, it may give everyone more time to prepare for the battles ahead."

If they could come to some sort of agreement, perhaps the answer to this entire mess would reveal itself to Axel, and he could get his crew out of Bellator before Petra reached the end of her sentence to the queen.

Settling into a chair across the desk from Caeso, Axel picked up a few of the pages the general had set on his desk. They talked over farming endeavors and weather patterns along the northern islands in comparison with those on the southern edge. Åldras had always boasted a thriving wool trade but had difficulty with grains, as the harsh winters could stick around for months. The mountain outside of Harligdam had held onto snow through the last three summers. There were several questions Axel didn't have answers to. He'd always had an interest in trade, but when Caeso brought up things like economics between Åldras and Tatawar, he could only give the most basic information. Doran had always tried to keep Axel apprised of the most pressing things, but anything outside of the war had held little significance.

Axel leaned back. "I don't know that I'm even the best person to ask about all this. If you're amenable to it, I'd like to bring the rest of my crew into the conversation. My skipper keeps up with a lot more than I do. Ulf might be helpful as well, being one of the best weapon traders on the Vit Sea. If they don't have some of these answers, I have a raven keeper on my ship who can send for information discreetly."

Caeso rubbed his chin. "That was going to be my next topic of conversation. We ought to bring your ship into the harbor. I've been getting reports of a ship slipping between my patrols this morning. I've had my captains ignore them up to this point, but it might be best to get them here before they do something foolish trying to get to you."

Axel wouldn't put it past Erik to launch a full-scale invasion if it came to it either, though he probably wouldn't need it. "I'll send word."

"Excellent." The general got to his feet. "Now, I've got to make rounds about the training yard. Come along."

If Firmin were as amiable as Caeso, Axel might have actually enjoyed being under his command. Axel stood from his seat and followed the general out of his office. The guards that had escorted Axel to the command center fell into step behind them. Their gazes on the back of Axel's neck made his spine crawl, but he flashed them a smile as they stepped out of the building.

In the light of day, the military headquarters bustled with activity. Men and women in crisp green uniforms raced back and forth across the footpaths connecting the buildings. Uniformed guards stood in perfect lines, their shields shifting in unison as a captain shouted orders.

Axel trailed Caeso all the way to a round arena dug down into the ground. Rows of benches encircled the ring, staggering up the sides to give any spectators a good view of the sand pit. In the center, two men faced off against each other, each with a practice sword in hand. A sour taste coated Axel's tongue as he watched them, having seen so many similar fighters on the field of battle.

Whispers started up as the audience around the ring became aware of his presence.

"It's Mighty Axel."

"Does he have that sword of his?"

"He doesn't look that tough."

Axel allowed a smirk to spread over his mouth. Even in an enemy city, the whispers were still the same. Every encampment he'd ever walked into had buzzed with the same questions.

"Hey, Mighty Axel!" one of the men shouted, standing from a spot on one of the benches encircling the arena. "You here to give us a show?"

The man's friends pulled him back down to his seat, their gazes flicking everywhere but to Axel. The fight in the arena had slowed, everyone's attention now directed at him.

The smirk on Axel's cheeks stretched to an all-out grin. He turned to the general. Caeso's gaze was already on him, an expectant quirk to his brow. So the man had dragged him out here for this, had he?

Axel folded his arms over his chest and turned back to the man who had addressed him. "Why? You looking for someone to show you how to use that blade strapped to your hip?"

A few chuckles sprinkled the crowd. The man's head ducked in chagrin, but he stood back up. He was courageous, Axel would give him that. The guards surrounding him looked on with a mixture of pity and eagerness.

"What's your name?" Axel asked.

The man straightened his shirt. "Dex."

Axel pointed to three of the man's friends. "You three can join Dex in the ring. We wouldn't want your friend to look too bad, would we?"

Another round of snickers rippled through the crowd, but the four fighters got to their feet.

# CHAPTER 8

## A LESSON

Petra rubbed at the back of her neck as she trailed a guard through the waking halls of the palace. No sleep had come before dawn touched the horizon and the faint light of the coming day had pointed to where Axel had slept. Or pretended to sleep.

Two guards trailed behind her as they made their way to wherever Queen Kelda waited. They'd left the halls of the palace and walked through a gate at the southern edge of the wall. The guards nudged her in the direction of one of the buildings close to the palace.

If only Axel hadn't agreed to stay. It would have been so easy to take down the pair of guards and the unarmed servant.

But Axel had to go and run his fool mouth.

"Here we are." The servant gestured to a doorless archway.

Petra clenched her hands into fists and stepped forward. Without a weapon, she would have to either relieve one of the guards of their sword or find something through the archway to bludgeon any attackers with.

She may have agreed to serve this bloody queen, but she wouldn't go down without a fight if it came to that.

When she cleared the archway, she had to keep her mask of indifference in place.

All along the sides of the room, girls sat on small cushions. Some of the girls were as young as seven or eight, while others were well on their way to adulthood if they hadn't reached it already. There were girls with golden hair like many in Åldras and girls with darker hair like that found in Sida. Small cups and baskets sat on the ground around them. One of the older girls held a stone in her hand, her face scrunched in concentration as she scratched something onto the face of it. A younger girl seated next to the stone carver held a hand out, and a feather hovered over her open palm.

The same scene repeated over and over down the lines. Air, water, stone, plants, every girl held some sort of catalyst before their face, their eyes fixed on the magic in front of them.

The torture chamber Petra had assumed awaited her looked much nicer than anything her imagination could conjure. Rather than racks of manacles and buckets of hot tar or coals, the walls boasted large windows, gauzy curtains hanging down from the ceiling to keep only the most intense light from spearing through the openings. Pools of water sat in every corner. Potted plants leaned toward the sun through the windows. There were shelves of different types of stone along a wall. The room felt almost welcoming and pleasant chatter rippled through the space as the Häxa worked on their magic.

"Glad you were able to join us," a voice sounded from the other end of the room.

Queen Kelda sat in a circle of cushions, several girls and a smattering of women gathered around her. Where she'd worn a light lavender ensemble the night before, she now wore a pastel blue. The cut was much the same, from the veil atop her head to the silk of her skirts. Did she always wear a veil? There wasn't much Petra could gather about her apart from her hands, which sat primly in her lap. They weren't the bronze color of the Sidans. She was clearly from Åldras, but how had she become queen?

A guard stood in an alcove off to the side of the room. Petra's fists clenched tighter when she saw the head of blonde hair. It was the stone carver captain that had caught them outside the city gates. The same one that had chased them through the city and used her magic over stone to waylay their progress toward the palace.

The woman's blue eyes narrowed when they met Petra's.

The queen stood, clapping to command the attention of the girls. "My friends, I would like to introduce you to Petra. She'll be joining us for the next little bit."

Petra winced. Being introduced as herself could cause some potential problems. At least no one here assumed she was also Petyr Mallorysson. To these girls, she likely looked like any other Åldran. If she was to keep her secret, she needed to distance Petyr from Petra. If word reached Åldras about her, it could make this entire mess much worse.

A few of the younger girls whispered to one another, but one of the older ones raised a hand. "Your Majesty, are we to set up the trial tray?"

Petra widened her feet slightly. If she needed to make a run for it, she would have to move quickly. The guards wouldn't be the biggest threat to escape now. She would have to catch this whole room by surprise if she was to make a clean getaway.

The queen shook her head, her light blue veil rippling with the motion. "No, Petra won't be joining us as a student. She's merely here to watch." Queen Kelda held out her hand. "Come. You can stand by Hildi while we continue our lesson."

With careful steps, Petra followed the queen through the room and stopped along the wall next to Hildi, though she stayed out of reach.

Hildi's gaze never wavered from Petra, though her jaw seemed to clench tighter the closer Petra got. The woman wouldn't have any teeth left by the time Petra finished for the day if she didn't let up. A small dagger sat at her hip, but she likely didn't need much more than her magic as a weapon.

"Let's settle in for a review," the queen said, gliding over to stand in the middle of the room. She clasped her hands in front of her; veiled face pointed toward one of the older girls in the row. "Linnea, what is the purpose of a förändra?"

The girl, Linnea, perked up. "A förändra is a magical catalyst, used to activate a Häxa's innate magic—both the control over an element and the added gift that element invokes. The elements are found in the natural world, created by the Maker."

Queen Kelda nodded. "Excellent." She turned to the slightly

younger girl next to Linnea. "And what elements can be used as förändra and for what type of Häxa?"

The girl's cheeks reddened slightly at the attention. "Water for wielders, stone or earth for carvers, plant life for healers, air for whisperers, bone for shifters, blood for walkers, and flame for charmers."

"Good," the queen said.

Petra had collected most of this information over the years, though she hadn't actually known about the spirit walkers and she'd only learned what her own förändra had been through experience. She'd heard the term *fire charmer* in the past. The fact they'd compare such a gift with charm seemed misleading.

Someone raised their hand. "But what about Mighty Axel? Isn't he considered Häxa?"

A few of the girls tittered. Of course Axel even had the females in an enemy kingdom swooning over him. *Ridiculous idiot.*

"It is quite the conundrum, isn't it?" Queen Kelda asked. "But magic is bound by the laws of the universe, which leads us to believe even Mighty Axel is subject to a förändra. Many have speculated over the last several years how he has access to magic, and most believe the answer is found within the prophecy left to him as a babe. Perhaps, we can figure it out."

Something crept up Petra's spine, settling in between her shoulder blades. Axel's prophecy wasn't a secret. All of Åldras knew about it. Asher had never hidden his son's destiny, even when Axel had been young. The fact the other kingdoms paid attention to it only added to the gravity of the foretelling.

The words of the prophecy rolled off the Sidan queen's tongue like she'd tasted them many times before.

> *"Behold the yield of the witch's womb*
> *The she-bear's shield the eagle's doom*
> *Sent to save the land that bore him*
> *No mortal foe dares stand before him*
> *True, born below, yet godly made*
> *Unchallenged in bow, unmatched in blade*
> *Too strong to bend in battle's din*
> *With flame his friend and death his kin*

*In war's dark fray, steadfast, unharmed*
*Until one day by love disarmed*
*When, with a maid his heart is traded*
*By gods betrayed—in war unaided*
*The hero's strength in battle fails him*
*At last, at length, his foe impales him*
*The reaper calls from deathly hollows*
*The hero falls, the she-bear follows."*

As it always did, the prophecy thickened the air, smothering any sound. The words encircled Petra's throat. They'd been echoing in her head since Axel had kissed her in Ljust Löfte. Since she'd kissed him back. Since their entire lives had been flipped on their heads.

Queen Kelda's head swiveled, looking about the room. "Can anyone take a guess as to what the boy's förändra is?"

Petra nearly scoffed. Axel hadn't been a *boy* for a long time. This queen had to be ancient if she thought Axel anything less than a man. Only the Great Mother had ever considered Axel's youth.

One of the girls raised a hand. "His weapons?"

Another raised her hand. "His muscles?"

Another round of giggles rippled through the room.

"It's his heart."

Petra nearly winced at the answer from the guard standing next to her. Hildi's expression remained the same and if every pair of eyes in the room hadn't turned on them, Petra could almost believe the woman hadn't even spoken.

Queen Kelda gave a slow nod. "Correct. From what we can gather, the state of his heart is how his magic is determined. Should he fall in love and the woman he falls in love with return his affection, his magic will change."

How could the queen know that? Petra swallowed back the tumult of questions. Had someone in the past been born with the same gifts as Axel? If he did trade his heart, would it completely dissolve all his magic? The prophecy didn't say how his magic would change, only that it would lead to his defeat and the fall of Åldras.

And Axel would only let Åldras fall over his dead body.

A few of the girls sighed. One piped up and said, "So all we have to do is get him to fall in love with one of us, and he'll be defeated along with his cruel kingdom?"

The vice around Petra's throat tightened. Her fingers reached for the heads of her axes, but the lack of weight at her hips only made her heart pound more. She didn't even boast a bloody knife in her boot to help her if things got out of hand.

The room broke out into squabbling, some of the girls arguing over who should approach Axel and others about the cruelty of it. Queen Kelda and Hildi simply watched on as Axel's death circulated the room like a murder of crows.

With slow steps, the queen glided back toward Petra. "What do you think, Petra? Do you think there's a woman who could steal the heart of Mighty Axel?"

Petra kept her face blank as Queen Kelda studied her—or at least she seemed as if she was looking for Petra to reveal something. The veil was quite concealing.

Even as Petra's pulse galloped against her throat, the lie slid from her tongue. "No. Unfortunately, his heart belongs to his kingdom."

Several of the students groaned in disappointment, whether from their discouragement to woo Axel or defeat him. But the queen didn't turn away. She remained perfectly still except for her head, which tilted slightly to one side.

If she was looking for a break in Petra's façade, she wouldn't find one rocking crack. Petra wouldn't let any of these women know that it was her. That she was the one the prophecy spoke of. And that she would never allow herself to give him her heart. She had lost everyone she'd ever loved, and she'd bloody kill herself before ever allowing Axel to fall. They would get to the end of this war. Stop the Sidans. Stop Firmin and his stupid brother. Then, if she survived it all, she would leave. And Axel would be safe.

A flash of color burst into the room. Lady Idalia skidded to a stop just inside the door, her skirts a flurry of pale green and white. Her long, black hair was pulled back from her face, but a few wayward strands had escaped during what looked like quite the run. Her eyes were wide and her face slightly pale as she met the queen's gaze.

"I'm so sorry I'm late," she nearly whispered, stepping more slowly into the room and fidgeting with her hands. "I didn't realize what time it was."

The queen glided up to her, wrapping an arm around the lady's shoulders. If she noticed the lady's flinch at the touch, she didn't show it. "There's no need to fret, Idalia. You're more than welcome to come and go as you like."

Something in Lady Idalia's posture relaxed. As if she had been waiting for a strike. "Thank you. I'll try not to be late next time."

If Petra hadn't already hated Anders, she would then. How was Axel going to live with himself if they forced the woman to return to Åldras? How would the crew be able to look each other in the eye? Freyja's golden tears, Axel would have never been able to go through with it. It was likely why Firmin had agreed to send him in the first place. The mission was doomed to fail from the start.

A pair of younger girls popped up from their seats and met the lady. "Idalia!" one chimed. "Come sit by me."

"No, me!" another urged. "You have to see what Her Majesty showed me with the water."

Lady Idalia was dragged toward a cushion, but her face was anything but displeased. In fact, she looked excited as she sat between the girls. The paleness of her features disappeared as color returned to her cheeks and a light seemed to spark in her eyes. She looked different in Sida. More relaxed. She complimented one girl's hair and another's dress, which only added to the fuel of the girls' chatter.

The air next to Petra shifted. "Are you shocked, Åldran?" Hildi whispered. "Your lady has become one of us far easier than she ever had in that rock-hole you call a kingdom."

Petra didn't turn back. "It'll just make it that much more miserable for her when she has to go back to her husband."

Hildi hissed, but any biting comment she had to retort with was cut off by Queen Kelda clapping her hands together again.

"The day is getting away from us. Let's begin our lesson."

The girls settled into their cushions as the queen began directing them through a series of practices. There were several whisperers and healers, a handful of carvers, and a pair of wielders. The girls made shapes with their elements, lifted objects, and studied the lore of their magic.

Was this what Häxa had once been? Had the elders gathered the youth around them and showed them how to control their magic? Would Petra have had an opportunity like this if magic hadn't been banned in Åldras? No, it didn't matter. From what she could tell, her magic was still enough of an oddity to separate her from even these girls. She would have simply singed off all their hair or brought a building down on top of them.

Queen Kelda called for the end of class, and Petra blinked, turning to look out the window behind her. The sun was nearly at its zenith, her time with the queen having passed in the blink of an eye. Each row cleared of the young Häxa, but Queen Kelda remained at her post in the middle of the room, a gentle hand on Idalia's shoulder as the lady went on and on about the lessons.

"Do you all find the magic comes from the same place? I know the förändras are all different, but what about the source of magic?"

The queen turned toward Petra and Hildi, who had remained in the exact spot she'd been in all morning. "Hildi, will you and Idalia join Petra and I for a light lunch? I suspect none of you will find yourselves with much time to think about food later on."

Hildi pushed away from the wall. "Is that a prophecy, Your Majesty?"

Queen Kelda didn't answer, instead gesturing for Idalia to follow her. She didn't offer the same to Petra, but it wasn't like there was any other choice except to join them. Perhaps the bloody captain would choke on her lunch.

Idalia and the queen glided through the halls, the lady bubbling over with questions about the palace and Queen Kelda's life. The queen's answers came softly but didn't exceed more than a few words at a time. Not that she needed to speak. It seemed Lady Idalia had enough words for the both of them.

"If I wasn't sure I could make this floor swallow you whole, I'd worry about you watching Idalia like a hawk."

Petra glanced out of the corner of her eye. Hildi continued to face forward, but a small smirk curled at the corner of her lips. Petra flicked her attention back to Lady Idalia. So what if the captain suspected Petra of scheming? If she was worth half the arrogance she exuded, she would be wary. If there was an opening, Petra would take it to get Idalia out, no matter how much it made her want to gut Anders and leave his entrails for his dogs to eat.

A pair of what looked like guards—their clothing didn't match the garb most of the guards Petra had seen—ran out into the hall ahead of them. Hildi's hand strayed to the stone hanging around her neck. The guards disappeared just before a gaggle of servants broke out from a door and poured into the courtyard ahead.

Queen Kelda paused as a guard, in uniform, raced past the servants.

"My queen!"

Hildi leaped forward, putting herself between the oncoming guard and the queen.

The guard skidded to a halt, placing a fist to his heart and bowing. "Excuse me, Captain. I was just on my way to find you. Mighty Axel and Prince Enzo are in the arena."

Hildi frowned, her blue eyes narrowed as she turned back to Petra.

Petra clenched her hands behind her. "What?"

Hildi marched forward and grabbed Petra's arm. "Your man is fighting with Enzo, and you're going to stop it."

Petra refrained from rolling her eyes as Hildi dragged her down the hall. "He's not my man," she mumbled, her quick fingers slipping the small dagger from Hildi's waist into her pocket.

# CHAPTER 9

# SWORDS

Axel stood in the center of the sparring ring, a pile of practice swords at his feet. The rules of the game had been simple. If either combatant lost their weapons, they had to leave the ring. Two dozen men and women had entered the arena one after another with swords in their hands and two dozen had left without them. If these Sidans hadn't fully grasped the power of Axel's gifts, they did now.

The sword Caeso had offered him at the beginning of the bouts remained strapped at his side. All he needed were his hands anyway.

A soldier raised a spear over his head, his face set in grim determination. At least the Sidans were stoic fighters. There had been many an Åldran who hollered and made a big show of their aggression. The Sidans had always been silent killers.

Axel caught the head of the spear before it could poke him in the eye and ripped it from the soldier's hands. In one fluid motion, he snapped the leaf-shaped blade from the shaft.

"If you could refrain from damaging the practice weapons, I would be much obliged," called Caeso. He'd taken up a seat on one of the benches nearly half an hour ago and called for a writing desk not long after that.

Axel didn't have a moment to respond before a woman with two short swords swung for his legs. Even though the blades couldn't pierce his skin, he didn't want his clothes torn to shreds. There was already a tear on the sleeve of his tunic from where someone had caught him with the tip of a spear. He'd have to sew it up later that night, as all his bone needles were on *The Phoenix*.

Sweat coated the back of his neck as Sol's light reached for the highest vantage point to witness these idiots continue to push their luck against Axel's gifts.

Axel grabbed the swords by their blades and yanked. The soldier came with her weapons, stumbling over one of the practice swords on the ground. Axel pulled her close, lifting the blades high enough overhead that the woman could meet his eye.

He smirked. "You forgot to let go."

She headbutted him.

The shock of the hit made him stumble back a step, but as always, no real pain accompanied it.

The soldier, however, fell to her knees. With a groan, she cradled her head in her hands. The large red mark on her forehead would be swollen in minutes.

"Should have known better than that," Caeso called to the woman as she stumbled back to the benches.

Axel dropped the short swords onto the pile. "Anyone else?"

"I'll try my hand at it."

Every head in the arena turned to the back of the benches where Prince Enzo stood, the smugness from last night still residing on his face.

*I haven't met a woman able to resist a Sidan man's charm.*

It had taken all of Axel's will power not to kill the man where he stood in the hallway next to Petra. If she had felt even a modicum of discomfort, Axel would have carved out the prince's liver with a bloody spoon and made him watch as he fried it with onion over a cookfire.

Prince Roman stood next to his brother, dark eyes sharp, calculating, as they flicked about the thick crowd.

Axel spread his arms. "By all means." It would be the best part of his day to send the bloody prince limping out of the arena. The tips of his fingers tingled with the thought of it.

Several of the soldiers lingering around the sparring ring leaped to their feet, gathering the weapons from the horde Axel had gathered.

Enzo pulled the sword from the scabbard at his hip, spinning the blade before handing it off to his brother. He met Axel's gaze. "For a man known for carrying a famous sword, I'm surprised to see you in the arena without a blade in your hand."

Axel shrugged, adjusting the borrowed sword at his hip. "Didn't have much choice considering I don't have my sword at the moment, and your flimsy practice swords wouldn't last more than a couple swings in my hands." He grabbed the collar of his tunic and pulled it over his head. No need to subject the garment to any more abuse. Enzo's abilities with a sword were nothing to scoff at. The few battles they'd fought opposite one another had proven that.

Enzo shucked his own tunic and picked up one of the blades moved to the edge of the ring. The blade wasn't as fine as the one that had sat in his scabbard, but it still boasted a wicked edge. He tossed it to Axel, who caught it by the hilt, and picked up another.

"If I'm going to fight Mighty Axel," he said, "I want to do it right."

Axel twirled the blade in his hand. There was nothing like the shine of a sword and often the bit of showmanship caught the eye of a crowd. "Rules?"

"Same as the others." Enzo stepped into the ring. "First to lose their weapon concedes."

"Stakes?"

A hush settled over the crowd.

Enzo smirked. "Loser buys drinks for everyone at *The Timber Horse* tonight."

Axel matched Enzo's smirk, removing the blade from his waist and tossing it to the side. "I hope the pockets in your trousers are deep. You'll need them to carry all the coin."

Enzo made his move.

Right for Axel's throat.

Axel brought his blade up, deflecting the jab and sending it to the side where it barely slid past his ear.

Murmurs took flight around the arena.

Predictions echoed around the ring.

Coins slipped from one hand to another.

Enzo's sword came swinging toward Axel again.

The prince jabbed as quickly as a snake and as powerful as a bloody dragon. Axel felt the cold of the steel as he dodged it. If his hair couldn't be cut without runed blades, there would be more than a few pieces littering the ground under their feet.

The soldiers cheered as their prince danced around the arena. He was a showman, of that there was no doubt. A people's prince. A master of hearts and minds. The blade in his hand flashed inches from Axel's nose, catching the glint of Sol's blessing. A lesser man would have been skewered ten times over.

A shadow shifted just out of the corner of Axel's eye.

Petra hovered at the edges of the crowd, a small quirk to her brow. *When are you going to put the idiot out of his misery?*

Axel's cheek twitched with a suppressed smile.

He turned back to the prince as the man jabbed at his shoulder. Axel caught the middle of Enzo's blade with his own. As Enzo moved to bring his sword out of the bind, Axel let go of the hilt with his left hand. He pressed his sword overhead, covering his back, and grabbed the hilt of Enzo's sword with his free hand. All it took was a twist of his wrist and the prince dropped the sword. Before Enzo could move an inch farther, Axel brought the blade to Enzo's wrist, allowing the sharpened edge to kiss the skin over his artery.

The crowd went silent.

Enzo's dark gaze held Axel's, the knowledge of his defeat evident but the promise of vengeance flickering beneath.

"I concede," Enzo said.

Axel dropped the grip he had on the prince's sword and took a step back.

The silence broke apart as General Caeso slowly clapped his applause. He pushed himself to his feet. "As I always say, everything in fighting that's not dying is education. What have we learned?"

Enzo's mouth stretched in a wide grin that didn't quite meet his eyes. "Never make a bet you know you aren't going to win."

ᚠᚻᚲᛋᚠᛦᛚ

Axel fiddled with the scrap of parchment in his palm as he strode through the streets of Bellator. Enzo had written down directions to *The Timber Horse* and a time to meet back in the city after dusk, but he would have to wait until after Axel had met with the crew. Would the prince try to kill them if they never showed up? He'd probably wish to. Being beaten in the arena had already wounded the prince's pride. Being stood up would only rub salt in the wound. It might be worth the trouble just to prove to the man that Axel and Petra weren't going to bow to every whim of these bloody royals.

Petra stepped almost silently next to him. Since the argument the night before, there had been nothing to say to her. He couldn't summon the words to ask how her time with Queen Kelda had gone. It couldn't have been too bad. She still had all her fingers, and he hadn't heard of anyone getting murdered. He blew out a breath. They were stuck in this bloody kingdom until they could figure out how to convince Idalia to return or war came to these shores. The latter felt more and more possible with every passing moment.

Big Hal grunted behind them, glancing over his shoulder every few seconds.

Four guards trailed behind them. Wise of the Sidans not to give them too much leash. Perhaps angering the prince only the second day into their stay wasn't the best plan.

Fading sunlight scattered across the road ahead of them. Being farther south, Sida's evenings held on to the heat far more than nights in Åldras did. Axel would take his shirt off again if it wouldn't cause a spectacle. Not that they weren't already turning heads. Faces peered out of windows and gangly children ran from house to house with whispers on their lips. Gazes trailed them down the street, not all of them friendly. Perhaps they ought to have gone around the city to the docks rather than through it.

But Axel had wanted to see it. What these Sidans fought for.

Unlike the dark, speckled stone found in Åldras, the stone making up most of the buildings was pale. Almost white. Some were painted in bright colors, visages of the Maker the Sidans worshipped brought to life in the images. A woman with life in her right hand and death in her left. Dandelions bloomed in between the stones paving the road under their boots. Trees had been planted in neat lines along the street, their long branches holding up clouds of green foliage high above the rows of buildings. Lines of clothing in between some of the buildings, the vibrant fabrics waving in the light breeze coming off the coast.

The street opened up into a large square. A fountain squatted in the middle, clear water bubbling from the top of a pillar and spilling down into three large bowls.

Big Hal gave a low whistle. "Think they've got a water wielder under there pushing that water out?"

Axel chuckled, walking toward the water. It pooled in a basin at the bottom where it looked like people had tossed in coins. Seemed like a waste of perfectly good coin to let it sit around like that.

Petra's fingers tapped at her leg. The faintest imprint of a blade's hilt pressed against the side of her tunic. Someone in the palace was likely missing a dagger. Petra never did feel comfortable without the chill of a blade against her skin. Axel opened his mouth to comment on it, but the words died on his tongue. It wouldn't be worth it if they devolved into an argument. Again.

Instead, he continued toward the city wall. He'd sent Little Hal's raven back with directions for Erik to push *The Phoenix* onto shore a little ways from the harbor. While it would have been easier to leave the ship tied to the docks, he didn't like the idea of leaving it in easy access to the Sidans. Though Caeso had assured him it would be safe, it still likely wasn't wise.

They reached the northern gate, slipping out behind a cart filled to the brim with stacks of fabrics and barrels marked with a Sidan eagle. None of the other guards made a move toward them, but more than a few turned their way as they left the city behind them. The four that had tailed them through the city didn't follow them out, but Axel had no doubt they were being watched.

"Think that'll be an issue?" he asked.

Big Hal shrugged, but Petra narrowed her eyes. *Not yet*, that look said.

Axel could only agree. If they thought the guards not following them out was a sign of trust or even lack in judgment, they were likely wrong. There were likely Häxa watching from the wall, ready to let the sand swallow them or the water to break apart *The Phoenix* if they made one wrong move.

The harbor glittered ahead of them, but they turned west toward the open beach. It didn't take too long until they spotted the ship. *The Phoenix* bobbed her way onto the shore, the small waves cresting underneath her hull sliding her into the sand.

Ulf dropped down from the stem of the ship, his bare feet splashing into the water.

"Thought your luck might have finally run out," he quipped, grabbing the rope hanging over the edge of the ship. He tossed the line to where Axel stood on the shore.

Axel wrapped his hand around the rope and pulled it taut. Another line crashed into the water a few ells away and Big Hal grabbed the end. Between the two of them, they pulled the ship onto the beach. *The Phoenix* groaned as she settled fully onto the shore.

Little Hal leaped down over the edge. "Where's Ludvig?" An empty raven cage swung from his hand. The bird hadn't returned from delivering Axel's missive to Doran then.

"He's all right," Big Hal answered. "Just broke a leg. He's got a nice fluffy bed and a pretty healer to keep him company."

Worry creased the space between Little Hal's brows.

The rope ladder made its way over the side just before Erik's head of unruly red hair popped into view. A pair of crutches and his mismatching peg legs landed in the sand next to the ship. Axel really ought to carve him a matching pair.

"About time you lot showed up," Erik groused.

Axel grinned. "It's been quite the adventure."

Erik pulled himself over the gunwale, settling what was left of his legs onto the rope ladder and quickly climbing to the shallow water beneath. "Your note was vague."

As Petra and Big Hal climbed back into the ship with the others, Axel caught Erik up on the events since they last saw each other. Much had happened in a single day and none of it very good. He recounted them getting arrested by the guards outside the walls, their escape, and being caught by the princes in the palace. When Axel got to the part about Petra's deal, Erik frowned.

"I don't like the sounds of this queen," he said, scratching at his beard. "Why would Pet take the deal?"

"He—*she* hasn't been too forthcoming about her thought process." Not that she had ever been very forthcoming.

Erik huffed. "The two of you need to get over whatever issues you're having. Being divided whilst running around enemy territory will get someone killed."

As if in spite of Erik's words, Petra leaped down from the ship, armed to the teeth. Her axes hung from her waist once again. Daggers stuck out of the edges of her boots and a bandolier of little knives was strapped across her chest.

Erik smacked Axel's knee. "Or someone is going to be doing a whole lot of killing."

# CHAPTER 10

# A CONTEST

*The Sidans boast a rather varied selection of exports. The warmer climates lend to a higher crop yield than what Åldras can supply in a season. Sidan merchants trade exotic fruits and grains for Åldran iron and Tatawarie copper. One of their highest earning exports is their wine. While fresh fruits may spoil on the seas, the fermented drink only grows more valuable as time goes on. Many of the kings around Åldras have acquired a taste for the drink, as well as the people of Tatawar.*

*— FROM THE WRITINGS OF DORAN FINNSSON,*
*THE LAST KING OF GROVÖ*

The sun had fully set by the time Petra had followed Axel back into the city. The weight of her axes hanging from her hips settled the coil of tension that had been growing in her shoulders since they'd arrived on Sida's shores. It would be good to have the crew in the palace with them as they continued to debate how to get out of this bloody kingdom. Erik hadn't been keen on leaving *The Phoenix* behind, but his discomfort had quickly abated at the mention of Caeso's collection of maps. They would divvy out the four rooms between the seven of them, though Axel had been adamant about remaining in the room he shared with Petra. Ulf would likely end up with the last room, being the noisiest snorer of the group. Axel had sent the crew to the palace with a few small trunks and supplies.

If only he'd sent his puke-green cowl with them.

Ahead of her, donned in that ridiculous color, he referenced the small note Enzo had sent after their duel that morning. The duel that kept popping up in her mind every time she looked at him. She hadn't been able to get the image of him shirtless out of her head. The way the sun had made his hair glow. How the muscles of his torso, his arms, had moved so fluidly. The way his eyes had glittered with amusement as he'd toyed with the prince.

It was almost stupid. She'd seen him shirtless a thousand times over the years. Freyja's golden tears, she'd seen him completely nude more than once. But things had changed between them. That bloody kiss in Ljust Löfte had ruined everything. If he hadn't said her name, if she'd walked away from him that day, none of this would have happened. Firmin wouldn't have been able to kill the Great Mother. Petra wouldn't have been captured. They wouldn't be in this rocking kingdom on a fool's errand.

"Are we really not going to talk this entire walk?" Axel asked.

She blinked. He'd never been good with silence.

Petra could almost see the words come and go as he shuffled through what he wanted to say. They hadn't had this big of a fight since they'd been eighteen. Axel had been putting aside money to pay for his own ship once they were old enough to sail on their own. Petra had found it and gambled it away. It had been for a good cause. The other gamblers had been a group of Ekte and thought her an idiot. They'd let slip where a few of their next targets were that night. Axel had been raving mad when she'd returned to their tent. He didn't talk to her for a week, even after she'd gone back to the gambling table the next night and won it all and then some back.

But this time had been longer than a week, and he still wouldn't talk to her. At least, not without it turning into a fight.

What did he expect her to say? She'd laid every sordid detail at his feet. All her sins had been revealed for his perusal. He had every right to be angry, but she didn't understand what he expected from her after that. She'd moved her piece on the hnefatafl board, so to speak, and it was up to him to make the next move.

He let out a long breath and shook his head. "The wine hall should be up ahead."

They turned a corner and found *The Timber Horse* wedged between two other buildings. Instead of the pale stone of its neighbors, the wine hall was constructed of different kinds of wood. It stood three stories tall, the entire face of it pocked with windows of different shapes and sizes. The sweet smell of Sidan wine and warm bread wafted on the salty breeze. Laughter rang out, brightening the entire street in spite of Mani's faint glow. People poured in and out of the open door, several in uniform. It made sense, as the military headquarters sat only a few blocks away.

When Axel crossed the threshold, a cheer went up through the whole building. Petra's hands instantly went to her axes as Axel stiffened. She took a step back, ready to make a run for it if anyone pulled a sword.

"Mighty Axel has finally joined us!"

The holler elicited more cheers.

Petra glanced around Axel's bulk in time to see Prince Enzo jump up on one of the tables, arms wide. The calculating look of the fight earlier in the day had been replaced with the flush of excitement. Was it excitement at the crowd or something else?

"And now, I must fulfill my bargain," the prince exclaimed. "Drinks are on me!"

The entire hall burst into cheers once again, wooden cups beating on the tables scattered around the room and boots stomping on the planks of the floor. Thunder's beard, the whole hall really embraced the *timber* part of its name. Men and women streamed out from behind a counter at the back, trays of bottles and more cups overhead. All wooden. Everything from the tables to the decorations adorning the walls were crafted from wood. The only thing not made from some sort of tree were the glass bowls with a short stub of candle giving light to every table. Each flame sang its whispering siren song. Petra had to force her gaze away.

The prince leaped down from his makeshift stage and sauntered through the crowd toward them. "Come, I've a table for all of us by the window." He gestured toward the corner, where a table had been tucked near a large window looking out onto the street.

A table where a familiar glare of blue eyes met them.

Hildi took up one of the four chairs. She'd shed her green captain's uniform and donned a light blue dress, but that stoic wariness remained. Her blue eyes were as sharp as daggers when she met Petra's gaze over her shoulder.

*Of all the people to have to sit across a table from...*

Had Prince Enzo brought this about to make their meeting more uncomfortable? Was the glaring captain there for backup once the prince sprung his trap? There was no way he simply wanted to sit across a table from Axel, breaking bread and sipping wine as if they were nothing but the best of friends.

Axel slid into the chair across from Hildi, facing the rest of the room. "Good evening," he greeted.

Hildi's eyes narrowed slightly. It seemed that was all they were good for.

"Good evening," she finally bit out.

Prince Enzo slid into the seat next to Hildi's, leaving the chair next to Axel open. The candle on the table flickered as Petra plopped down into the open seat, her hand straying to the dagger hidden under her tunic. Had the captain noticed her missing weapon yet? Did she suspect Petra had taken it and that was why she'd joined Prince Enzo tonight? If the captain wanted it, she'd have to fight Petra for it.

Besides, it would be so much more fun to stab Hildi with her own dagger if it came down to a fight.

Enzo's gaze flicked around the table, calculating. "Well, I suppose a wine hall is as good a place as any to begin our star-crossed friendship."

This had to be a trap. Petra's grip on the dagger tightened.

Without even blinking, Hildi slammed her elbow into the prince's gut.

Petra straightened in her seat next to Axel, meeting his gaze as he glanced over at her, then back to the prince. The captain's reaction was far from deferential.

"Maker take me!" Enzo coughed, pressing a hand to where Hildi had hit him. "Was that really called for?"

Hildi glared at him. "You told me we were meeting friends, Enzo.

If I'd known you were leading us into a viper pit, I would have at least brought another dagger with me."

Petra's fingers twitched.

The temptation was too great.

She whipped the dagger out and tossed it onto the table.

"There you go."

Hildi and Prince Enzo stared down at the blade, both with looks of incredulity.

Quick as Donar's lightning, Hildi lunged across the table.

Axel's arm whipped out in front of Petra as if to keep her in her seat. Not that he needed to. Petra was more than happy to let the captain attack her. Best to get it out of the way now rather than when the rest of the wine hall was expecting it. Any element of surprise they could use to their advantage would be needed if they wanted to make it through this night alive.

Prince Enzo wrapped his arms around Hildi's waist and hauled her back into her seat.

"My love," the prince said, "can we save the bloodshed for after we've all had enough wine to laugh about it afterward? We don't need to give the rest of the hall permission to start another war."

Petra glanced past Prince Enzo's shoulder where more than a few pairs of eyes watched them. He wasn't waiting for the rest of them to attack then. *Thunder's beard.* She glanced back at the prince, who smirked at her. Then what was he doing?

Hildi sat back with gritted teeth and glared out the window. A pity. Fighting the stone carver would have been the highlight of Petra's day.

Axel cleared his throat. "I didn't realize the two of you were attached."

Not missing a beat, Enzo grinned. "I have the marvelous privilege of claiming this glorious woman as my wife."

Petra blinked. Hildi and Enzo were *married*? Was the Crown Prince of Sida allowed to be married to an Åldran Häxa? Hildi had no claim to any title Petra knew of. And if she had, Åldras would have certainly known about it.

"You're a captain and a princess?" Axel asked, practically echoing

Petra's own thoughts. "How does someone who obviously comes from Åldran heritage accomplish something like that?"

Hildi turned back to the conversation, though her expression said she was anything but pleased to be included. "Don't go imagining you could accomplish the same thing. Just because you're used to being the exception to the rule doesn't mean you can waltz around here like you do in Åldras—even though you have magic running through your veins and the rest of us who do get killed for it. This isn't a land of hypocrisy. No one in this kingdom would trust you with a chamber pot, let alone a throne."

"Oh, good," Enzo chimed. "The wine's here."

A tray of cups and a pitcher of dark liquid materialized on the table, the server ghosting away before Petra could even get a good glimpse of the man's face. Enzo set to pouring out four cups and placed one in front of each of them. She watched his hands, but if he'd done anything to the drinks, she hadn't seen it.

Sidan wine wasn't something found commonly in Åldras, though she'd seen it sitting on feasting tables in Firmin's great hall and in the cellars of other kings. She'd never touched the stuff though. The liquid was dark, almost purple. Petra picked up the cup and sniffed the contents. The pungent scent of overripe fruit and some kind of spice tickled her nose. Definitely fermented. Definitely intoxicating. Petra set the cup back down.

Hildi snatched hers from the table, draining the wine quickly.

Enzo watched her with wide eyes. "If I'd known the evening would get this exciting, I would have insisted we bring horses. Or at least changed into something more comfortable." He pinched the leather jerkin he wore over his tunic.

Hildi grabbed the pitcher and poured herself another cupful. "If I'd known you were tricking me into coming, I would have insisted you take a horse with you. Maker knows you would have needed it after Mighty Axel here knocked you unconscious after you inevitably said something foolish."

Enzo waggled his eyebrows at Petra. "She has such a way with words. You can see why we're so in love." He looked down at her untouched cup. "Is the wine not to your liking?"

She gave him a flat look.

The prince turned to Axel, who also hadn't touched his wine. "And what about you?"

Axel shrugged. "I've never been much of a social drinker. Especially when it doesn't do much for me besides leave a bad aftertaste."

Enzo scoffed. "That's a challenge if I've ever heard one. Sidan wine is not that watered-down swill you Åldrans call mead."

There was little doubt the prince had a competitive streak. Petra had witnessed it enough times on the battlefield. Had previously boasted the scars to showcase when she'd gone up against it.

A smirk bloomed across Petra's face, and she leaned forward. "I bet he could drink you under this table." If they got the couple drunk enough, perhaps they wouldn't be too cautious with their words. Petra had learned very little in her meeting with the queen, but perhaps the night wouldn't be a total waste.

Axel kicked the leg of her chair. "Pet. Don't."

Enzo leaned back, his eyes glittering. "What's the matter, Axel? Scared of a little friendly competition?"

"It's not that simple," Axel said. "I don't feel any adverse effects from drink. I'll literally drink everyone in this place under a table no matter how stalwart their stomachs."

Hildi poured herself a third cup. "Can't even drink his nightmares away." She threw back the wine. "Maker above, I'm going to have a headache in the morning."

Enzo pulled the pitcher out of reach. "Come now. What if we make it a game?" He refilled his cup. "One of us can ask a question and if the other refuses to answer, we take a drink."

Leaning back in her chair, Petra glanced between the two Sidans. Hildi looked as if she was ready to throw herself out the window. The glitter of Enzo's eye only brightened as Axel settled farther into his chair.

"Any question?" Axel asked.

"Why not?" Enzo slid Axel's drink closer, then turned to Petra. "Care to play, *Pet*?"

She pushed her cup toward him. "Someone has to help Axel haul you out of here after you drink yourself into a stupor."

Enzo grinned and turned to Axel. "Well?"

He glanced at Petra for only a split second, but the message was clear. *He's being too friendly.*

Petra tilted her head toward the prince. *Use it to our advantage.*

Axel leaned toward Prince Enzo. "I've already warned you this won't end well. If you want to play this game, you're the one who will be sorry by the end of it."

Enzo lifted his cup. "Ask your first question."

"How many men do you have stationed in Grovö?"

Oh, Axel wasn't going to make any of this easy for the prince. It was common knowledge in Åldras that Sida had men tucked away in many of the places they'd taken over before the armistice. Many of the citizens in the southern regions had already fled to the northern isles, but the Sidans had done well blending in with those that had stayed.

"Playing dirty right from the start." Enzo scowled but took his drink. He set the cup back down with a thump. "We know Åldras has a safehouse somewhere in the western part of Sida. Where is it?"

At least the prince would fight back. Petra settled into her chair, folding her arms over her chest. The safehouse had been dug into one of the hills south of Lacus. She'd been to it only once after a battle on one of the isles along Sida's coast. One of Doran's crewmen had been injured badly during the fight and had needed more attention than the ship's surgeon could give him. Firmin likely still had men hidden in those hills.

Axel raised his cup in salute and downed the liquid. Immediately after he swallowed, he stuck out his tongue in disgust. "You really all drink this stuff? It tastes like rotten berries."

"It's grapes, actually. Yes, we all drink it, and that counts as your second question."

Hildi chuckled and Axel scowled.

The two of them continued back and forth that way as the rest of the wine hall grew less rambunctious. The questions ranged from military strategy to fighting styles. Enzo told Axel he bought the Åldran fire they used in the draugr bog off a Tatawarie who had bought it off a smuggler. Axel told Enzo about what happened in Ljust Löfte, which had Hildi calling for more wine. Axel drank far more than Enzo did, but it was Enzo's cheeks that took on a hint of pink with every sip. The only change in Axel was that he finally quit cringing every time he had to drink the wine.

Axel looked to Hildi. "How did the two of you meet?"

"Easy," Enzo said, setting his cup back down. "Hildi was adopted by my father's best friend when she was rescued from Åldras as a child. I met her for the first time when I was eleven and she eight. I was smitten the moment I saw her."

Hildi snorted. "Yes, right before I punched you in the nose for telling me my hair looked like straw."

That had to have been nearly two decades ago based on their age. Had the Sidans really been rescuing Häxa for so long? How had they gotten away with it all these years? Why hadn't anyone in Åldras known?

Petra turned to Hildi. "You escaped Åldras before Firmin was crowned?"

"Ah, ah," Enzo tsked. "If you wanted to play, you should have said so earlier." He gestured to Axel. "Why did you take the princess from Åldras to the Great Mother?"

Axel met Petra's eye. *Should I tell him the truth?*

She shrugged. It didn't truly matter to her. Ella was safe within the forests of Ljust Löfte now. At least as safe as she could be. It wouldn't be surprising to learn the entire Häxa colony relocated after Firmin found the location of their new home and burned down most of it.

Axel fiddled with the cup on the table. "She's a Häxa. We took her to the Great Mother to keep the Ekte from getting their hands on her."

Hildi spat at the Häxa hunters' name. "I hope those demons rot in whatever realm the Maker has set aside for them."

A laugh burst from Enzo's chest. "Oh, that's too good! One of Firmin's own children being gifted. That was divine providence if I've ever seen it." He frowned. "But that also means the rockhead lied about you stealing the girl. I hope you gave him an earful for that."

Axel's face hardened only the smallest bit. He wouldn't reveal what Firmin had done. Wouldn't reveal Petra's role in all of it. Instead, he leaned back. "My turn. Why did your brother take Lady Idalia?"

"I wish I could tell you it was for some kind of scheme." Enzo rolled his eyes, the words falling easier than they did earlier. "Honestly, I really hoped it would be when he first told me he'd stolen her out of Oxe. The idiot wrote to me as I was returning from chasing you around Isberg—which was *not* fun I'll have you know—and told me what he'd planned. He'd already arrived home with her by the time I did, and instead of finding he'd actually done something brilliant for once, he'd fallen in love with the woman and had no intention of returning her to King Anders."

Petra blew out a breath. *What a mess.* If Prince Roman had done it simply to get the Tatawarie freed from their deals with Åldras, it would make it so much easier to fix. But emotions could muck up the simplest things.

"You couldn't talk him out of it?" Axel asked.

Enzo shook his head, not noticing how Axel had skipped his turn in the game. "I tried convincing him, but he was adamant he couldn't send her back even if he wanted to. Kelda was more than supportive of Idalia remaining here, and Roman's always taken her council at face value, being she's the only mother he's ever known."

Petra's head tilted to the side. "Is the queen not his mother?"

"No," Hildi answered this time. "She became queen after Queen Regina, Maker receive her, passed. Enzo was fourteen, old enough to remember his mother well, but Roman was only seven when it happened. The king mourned his queen for a year before he finally took Kelda as his wife."

Pieces fell into place. Why the queen had magic. Why no one had realized a Häxa sat on the throne. She was a second wife. A second queen. While the marriage of a second queen would have been of note, it wouldn't have been as scrutinized as the first. Not with the king's rule cemented and two heirs to take the throne after him. If there had been any news of it, Petra would have been too young to care anyway.

Enzo picked up his cup. "And now I sit here, the only Sidan royal with a Sidan wife."

Hildi squinted at him. "Darling, I'm as much a Sidan as Her Majesty or Idalia."

He straightened. "Oh, right. I guess none of us could do what my grandmother would have liked and married a normal Sidan girl like she nagged us to."

Axel chuckled. "So why does Queen Kelda wear the veil?"

Enzo shrugged. "She always has. She keeps the kingdom safe by concealing her identity. As one of the strongest seers we've come across, she would be quite the help to any kingdom who could get her to work with them—willingly or unwillingly."

Petra tapped her fingers against her leg. It was wise. The queen could go out among the people, and no one would think anything of it. If she needed more security, she could dress anyone else up to act as decoys and no one would be the wiser. But why would a seer need such protections if she could potentially see them coming?

"Doesn't it cause complications?" Axel asked, his brows drawing together. "How do you know you can trust a person who hides all the time?"

Enzo laughed. "I think you've asked plenty of questions and haven't had nearly enough drink." He poured the wine into Axel's cup. Well, mostly into the cup. His hand swayed back and forth, splashing wine onto the table when he missed.

Axel grabbed the pitcher, pulling it from his grasp. "Why did you want to play this game, Enzo?"

The prince's friendly expression slipped. His dark eyes met Axel's. "You can't be completely perfect, Mighty Axel. There has to be something I can beat you at."

And there it was. Enzo was looking for Axel's weakness.

Axel set the pitcher down. "Perhaps we should find the two of you some horses."

"Don't think this is the end of our game." Enzo sank back in his chair with a sigh, his face growing somber. "I don't think it will end until one of us winds up in a grave."

# CHAPTER 11

# APOLOGIES

Axel leaned against the wall of Caeso's office as the general sat across from Erik, maps spread over the desk. Ulf stood across the room, watching out the window at what had to be the courtyard below. They'd left the others back at the palace, though Little Hal was hopefully running amok in the city, gathering information. The lad could be as sneaky as Petra when he wanted to.

After meeting with the prince and princess at the wine hall ten days ago, they'd gone back to the uneasy silence between them. It didn't help that she left before the sun was up every morning and avoided him the rest of the time. Not that he hadn't been in the same space as her, but she'd done her best not to be alone with him. Hel's halls, she'd been doing that since they'd left Harligdam nearly three weeks ago. Since she told him what happened in Holmberg.

He needed to get her alone. They needed to resolve this.

Caeso leaned forward, his finger stabbing into the spot where Doran's Storm whirled on the page. "I've lost more ships in this blasted storm than I have to any Åldran armada."

Erik scratched his beard. "Aye, only the best sailors make it through and never unscathed. We nearly lost our bloody mast when we went through."

"*Sidan's Shield* took quite a few hits on the rocks near the coast. It was a miracle from the Maker the ship didn't get crushed."

When Prince Enzo's ship had finally caught up to *The Phoenix* in the draugr bog, there hadn't been any holes in the hull, at least none Axel had seen. The damage must have been somewhat easy to fix. Bloody prince could pilot a ship as good as Erik.

Erik and Caeso spoke over every spot of water from the Stiga Sea to the dark waters of the Vit Sea north of Harligdam. They swapped stories of sailing through the deathly Död Isles and the whales off the coasts of Isberg. Even as Axel watched for any malicious intent behind Caeso's questions, he couldn't help smiling at the two old sailors swapping tales of the mercurial waters connecting the kingdoms. When Caeso asked about *The Phoenix's* construction, Erik lit up.

"I didn't have much to do with the design of the ship," Erik said, "besides the modifications made for me to be able to come on as skipper, but I couldn't complain any when Axel showed me the designs. He'd been sketching the schematics for years and had met with the dwarves in the mountains to put together the design just before he approached me about joining the crew."

Caeso looked to Axel. "I didn't realize you knew how to design ships."

Axel smirked. "What can I say? I'm a man of many talents." Or hobbies, as Petra would say. He couldn't stick to one hobby once he mastered it. There were a few things he would return to—wood carving, nålbinding, music—but once he understood the principles of a skill and could perform at a moderate level, he moved onto the next obsession. At least, when he wasn't attempting to stop a war from reigniting or keep his head on his shoulders.

A knock sounded on the door and a younger man stuck his head into the room. "There's a boy, General, asking to speak with Mighty Axel."

Caeso waved a hand. "Send him in."

Little Hal popped into the room a moment later, his cheeks flushed and hair windblown. A small piece of parchment stuck between his fingers. "Axel! I've got a missive."

Axel took the paper and unrolled it.

His stomach sank as he read the three words on the slip of parchment.

*He's gathering forces.*

Axel had no doubts about who *he* was. Hel's halls, if Firmin was gathering men, he obviously never intended to wait for Axel to return with Idalia to launch an attack on Bellator.

And if they weren't careful, Sida wouldn't hesitate to wipe them from their shores.

Axel glanced out the window. It wasn't quite midday yet. The crew would need to gather. They had to figure out what to do next. He needed Petra to help him draft another note to Doran. To come up with a plan.

Caeso cleared his throat. "Good news, I hope?"

Axel tucked the note into his vest. "Of course."

ᚠᚢᚲᛟᚠᚤᛚ

"How long do you think we have?" Erik asked, sitting next to Axel on the floor of Ludvig's room. It had become somewhat of a headquarters for them since Ludvig hadn't been able to move the first two days. Now, he sat in a chair, his leg weak, but healed. The healer told him he should be back to normal activity by tomorrow, thank the Allfather.

Axel fiddled with a string sticking out of the woven rug beneath him. "If he's only gathering at this point, we still have time. Doran would have given a date if Firmin had planned an attack."

If Axel knew Firmin at all, the High King was probably just riling up the other kings. Anders likely ran around Åldras spouting on about the injustice of having his wife taken from him. They would use Idalia's abduction as fuel for the fire. It would put Firmin in the position to rally the kings to his side for when he was ready to attack Bellator.

But it also meant they were running out of time.

Ludvig tugged at a knot in his hair. "If His Majesty never intended to let us succeed, what was the point of sending us out here?"

"I imagine most of it was that he was put on the spot," Erik said. "He had to maintain peace with all the kings present. Having Idalia returned would still work in his favor, considering the ties with

115

Tatawar, but I don't imagine bringing the lady back would have been enough to satisfy his pride."

Little Hal shook his head. "I don't want to take the lady. She shouldn't go back to Anders no matter what happens."

Axel blinked down at the lad. "What do you know about it?"

"Probably more than you lot," Little Hal said. "I've been listening in the palace. Idalia arrived in Bellator with bruises, and they definitely weren't from Prince Roman. She still has nightmares too if the guards are to be believed."

*Hel's bloody halls.* Axel would kill Anders. He should have torn his bloody head from his fat body the day he'd made a spectacle of himself in Harligdam's great hall.

"We already knew it wasn't a good situation," Erik said, his voice low. "Did you expect any different?"

That was the question, wasn't it? Axel wished he could say he did hope Anders was a better husband than he seemed, but it was like wishing for tulips to grow in the middle of winter.

Axel glanced up to meet Petra's gaze. She had perched herself on one of the two windowsills, the sunlight streaming through haloing her hair and turning it gold. She didn't move, her body still as the stone statues decorating the palace grounds outside as her mind put everything together.

"What do you think?" he asked her.

Everyone turned to face her, their brows knit in consternation.

She shrugged. "I think no matter what we do, Firmin is going to make a move for Bellator."

Ulf hummed his agreement. "Aye, but what does that mean for us? If we don't bring Lady Idalia back, we face Firmin as the enemy. If we do, we have to deal with Sida."

"Are we going to ignore orders, then?" Big Hal asked. "Turn our back on our kingdom for one woman?"

Petra glared at the back of his head.

"I think, at this point," Axel cut in, "our kingdom is being put in jeopardy. This has become so much bigger than one woman. Even if we could take Lady Idalia back, if Firmin plans to attack, there's nothing we could do to stop him. Not in time, anyway. It might be better for us if we *don't* take her back."

"Either way," Ludvig said, "we're going to watch our kinsmen die when they set foot on this shore."

"You think one measly city guarded by a bunch of women could withstand the force of Åldras?" Big Hal argued.

Axel straightened, but it was Erik that smacked Big Hal. "The stupidest things come out of your mouth, boy."

Big Hal glared at Erik, but his gaze flicked over to Petra. It had been an intentional jab then. Axel's hands clenched into fists. If that idiot kept prodding her, he was going to get a knife in his back.

"Haven't you visited General Caeso's office with Axel yet?" Ulf asked. "If you have, you'd have seen most of the army headquarters. Have you noticed their training?"

"What does their training have to do with anything?" Big Hal asked.

Ulf raised one bushy eyebrow. "Training has to do with everything. What I saw today wasn't the training you'd see in Åldras. There were sparring matches, of course, but most of the soldiers were practicing subduing tactics."

"So?" Big Hal asked.

"*So*," Ulf answered, "that means the Sidans aren't preparing for a defense. They aren't even training for a battle. They're training to capture people."

Ludvig's face scrunched in confusion. "What are they planning to do? Capture all of us on the battlefield? How would that help them defend their home?"

"They aren't worried about defending their home," Petra cut in. "It means they're fully expecting to win whatever fight is coming and readying themselves to subdue skirmishes. They have full confidence in their victory over Åldras."

The room went completely silent, horror and indignation sharp in the air.

"Why?" Little Hal asked. "Why do they want to take Åldras so badly?"

Again, Little Hal asked the questions on everyone's mind. What little time Axel had spent in King Leonardo's presence only proved the man was different than Firmin. He sought council from others and looked for opportunities for peace. So what was driving the king to take Åldras?

Axel got to his feet.

"We need to keep our ears to the ground. If we can figure out what Sida is planning, maybe we can find a way to stop Firmin from rallying the kings. I know Doran is doing everything in his power to keep the peace with the council, but if we don't figure out how to stop Firmin from coming, we aren't going to be able to help those we swore to protect. We were sent here to keep the armistice in place, and that's what we're going to do."

Ideas bounced back and forth across the room, each of the men suggesting this scheme and that solution. Everything from going back to Åldras, to assassinating King Leonardo, to burning down the entire city with Åldran fire was presented and discarded. Everything they came up with ended in death. How could they keep the peace? This war wasn't worth all this.

Petra still sat at the window, her blue-green eyes tracking the lines of conversation. Axel slipped from the middle of the group and joined her at the window.

"Can I have a minute?"

Her gaze flicked up to his face, the blue-green turning dark with wariness, but she gave a short nod and strode to the door.

"Be right back," he told the rest of the room and followed her out.

She didn't stop at the door to their shared room but turned and made her way down the hall. He kept pace with her, not breaking the silence. Not yet. A set of guards peeled away from the wall behind them and followed. They trailed through the halls until they found an opening into one of the palace gardens. The area boasted a square fountain, mosaics creating a picture of the sea in the tiles around the pool. Spearhead-shaped trees lined the perimeter of the space and fragrant blooms bunched together in flower beds. The guards stationed themselves at the doorway and Petra stopped on the other side of the fountain, sitting on the edge of the pool. The sound of the water would at least help mask any words they spoke from the guard's ears.

Axel sat next to her. "This mission is going to get everyone killed."

"Aye," she agreed.

"I don't know how we're going to stop Firmin from bringing ruin to our home."

"Aye."

"I need you."

She stiffened, her short hair falling to cover her expression.

"Pet, I *need* you. This contention between us is only going to get our crew killed. I need my master schemer. My second in command." He took a deep breath. "I need my best friend."

Petra sat completely still, her hair concealing her face. He didn't dare brush it away. Didn't dare touch her. It would break him if he did. Because he also needed her in a thousand other ways. He needed her to look at him with that spark of mirth and that slight curl of a smirk. He needed her to tell him the truth, to let him kiss her again. Gods, how he wanted to kiss her again.

She finally shifted, just enough that he could glimpse the corner of her eye. "What if I can't give you what you need?"

*You're all I want.* He kept his face neutral, blank. He wouldn't pressure her. He'd told her all he'd felt in that kiss in Ljust Löfte. He would wait it out.

"Then I guess I'll have to rely on Big Hal and that thick skull of his." He gave a dramatic sigh. "Though, if I let him come up with all the plans, he'd probably get the lot of us killed before we even get to supper tonight."

Petra shook her head, a smile touching the corner of her mouth. "Things aren't that dire. Not yet."

Axel slid from the pool's edge and crouched in front of her. "Tell me what to do, Petra. Tell me how to get all of us out of here alive. Tell me how to bridge this divide between us. I'm so tired of being angry. Of trying to do all of this on my own."

She looked at the ground between them. "What about what I did?"

The fire. The lies. If Axel told her he was over them, she'd see right through the falsehood. The hole he'd carried in his heart for the last nine years had been scraped open once more and left his chest aching. She could probably see it every time she looked at him. He saw it in her too, the wound that had never healed. And now that he knew why, he understood her bitterness. Her scars.

"I wish you would've told me," he whispered. "I wish I'd have known."

She met his gaze. "You would have hated me. Would have blamed me for the death of our families. For this war. What would have kept you from throwing me to Firmin and his wolves?"

"I wish I could say that I would have been a good friend. That we would have figured out something together that kept you and Åldras safe, but I just don't know. I don't know how I would have reacted. But I know that how I've reacted now isn't right either."

He rubbed at his face. "I don't blame you for what happened in Holmberg. How can I? We were children, ones with the wool of childhood bliss and our parents' protection over our eyes. No one is prepared for tragedy when it strikes. You were scared and believed you were alone. You kept your secrets. But you're not alone. While I'm still hurt you didn't tell me, I'm glad I know now. I'm glad all these questions I've brushed aside all these years are answered. That now we can move forward. We can work together to fix this. We can stop Firmin from waging this war and stop the Sidans from destroying everything we love."

"And what about us, Axel?" she asked, a thin line of tears gathering for just a moment before she blinked them away. "You say you want me to be your friend, but what happened in Ljust Löfte isn't something between friends. That friendship changed the moment we...you know. We're never going to go back to what we had before, no matter how much you want us to."

His stomach did a little flip, and he couldn't help glancing down at her lips. While her words should have hurt him, they didn't. If anything, they only confirmed what he himself felt in his soul. That kiss had shattered their friendship, and he didn't want to go back. If anything, he wanted to pursue those feelings with as much ferocity as he fought with on a battlefield. But pushing her into a corner and making her tell him how she felt would only hurt both of them. He was still hurt and she was definitely still scared. Even if he could convince her to give them a chance, they would still have to face the chasm between them, and he wanted to bridge that before he really allowed the feelings he'd harbored for so long to come fully into the light.

Before he exchanged his heart with hers.

Because if he'd learned anything from that kiss, it was that she felt for him too. That she wanted him as much as he wanted her.

He forced his heart to slow its flutter, his stomach to stop flipping, and meet her eyes with a flirtatious smirk.

"You're right. Things have changed. But I think we can both agree to set aside this raging inferno building between us for the sake of our kingdom, don't you?"

She scoffed and shoved him back. "Your sense of humor needs a major readjustment. I'm being serious, Axel."

*So am I.* He tucked those words far down where they wouldn't surface. "All right, I'll be serious. Will you accept my apology?"

Her brows drew together. "What do you need to apologize for?"

"For all of this. For being snippy and yelling at you for the last three weeks every time you attempted to speak to me. For being a brute and brooding for so long. For not trusting you and for getting us into this mess."

She shook her head. "None of this is your fault."

"That isn't true, but even if it is, I've been nothing but unhelpful while trying to deal with it. I'm sorry, Pet." He felt a prickle at the backs of his eyes, and he blinked back the sensation. "I'm sorry you've had to carry this for so long, and that when you finally trusted me with it, I responded with anger when I should have been mourning with you this whole time."

Petra let out a sigh. "I shouldn't have kept the truth from you. I should have trusted you."

The fountain splashed into the pool behind her as the words settled along the edges of that hole in his chest. There was still healing to do, but they could work this out. They'd faced monsters before and come out on top every time.

He settled his hands on her knees. "You good?"

She took a deep breath and ran a hand through her hair. "Aye. But our little make up isn't going to fix everything else."

Axel chuckled. "If only. Unfortunately, we still have a war on the horizon."

Petra's mouth flattened. "I think we've been going about this the wrong way."

"This apology? Should I have brought some of that disgusting wine to drink to our inevitable demise?"

She rolled her eyes and pushed to her feet. "No, idiot. I think we really do need to allow Lady Idalia to stay. You and I both know taking her back would destroy the crew. We are meant to be heroes and reuniting her with Anders would bring everything we've accomplished since we set sail on *The Phoenix* into question."

"I agree. But that still doesn't solve the Firmin problem."

"What we need to do is figure out how to force Firmin to call off the battle. There has to be something we can do."

Axel stood as well. "You know what would really help?"

She turned back to him.

"If you weren't bound to the bloody queen."

Petra rolled her eyes. "Well, you and I both know I'm not going to get out of that any time before Firmin shows up."

The deal had been for her to play companion to the queen until either Firmin arrived in Sida or they reached the next spring. Firmin would certainly push to get to Sida before the sea storms hit at the end of fall.

"But we do know me and the crew being amiable could help with that. What if you were able to lessen your sentence as well? What if you could convince her that it's in Sida's best interest to let you go back to Åldras?"

"How do you propose I do that?"

"By getting her to trust you."

"I literally tried to skewer her with a sword."

"You're being obtuse."

Petra's eyes flashed. "I'm not like you, Axel. I can't try to stab people one moment, then charm them into playing a drinking game with me in the next."

"Don't sell yourself short." He set a hand on her shoulder.

"You're a hero in Åldras. There are plenty of people who have endeared themselves to you because you've helped them."

She glanced down at where he touched her. "There's no one in this entire bloody palace that I've ever helped."

Axel tapped a finger against her knee. "Oh, but isn't there?"

# CHAPTER 12

## A TRAP

*I do not know what to make of the events of the last several days. The Council of Kings has vacillated between righteous indignation and fierce worry over the state of our kingdom. High King Firmin sat among us this afternoon and about halfway through the meeting, he received a missive. After reading it, he began laughing as if he'd gone completely mad. He'd called an end to the meeting, barely able to stand from his chair. I worry for the state of our High King. I worry for the state of us all. If Axel and Petyr don't soon return with Lady Idalia, we may all find ourselves laughing as the Sidans slit our throats.*

— *FROM THE WRITINGS OF DORAN FINNSSON, THE LAST KING OF GROVÖ*

The gods hated Petra. There was no other explanation for her life. She had stolen the gift of fire from them and now they were out to get her.

Queen Kelda had sent a guard that morning, letting Petra know she was to report for her morning slave duty at the palace gates. Though which bloody gate, Petra actually didn't know. There was a wall around the palace, a wall around the buildings surrounding the palace, and another around the whole rocking city. Praise the Allfather, the guard stayed with her the entire time, directing her out through the north gate and onto the road leading down toward the outer city wall. The guard's boots clopped on the stone road as she nodded to her comrades on the palace wall.

The queen stood between a pair of wagons, the edge of her veil catching the slight breeze. Even her neck was wrapped in the blue fabric of her dress. Petra would think the confining outfit would be sweltering under the Sidan sun, but it probably offered a measure of protection. Petra could feel the bridge of her nose already burning even through the thin morning fog. Her skin still hadn't tanned back to what it had been before her healing in Ljust Löfte. The plant healers had done some work on her when they healed her from the draugr bite.

Next to Queen Kelda, Hildi spoke to a group of half a dozen guards, her hand resting on the hilt of her short sword. Her expression was set in that stern way of hers, the face of the guard captain. It was still odd Prince Enzo let his wife continue to act as a captain. The kings in Åldras practically hid their wives behind closed doors, only bringing them out when they needed something to show off. There were a few exceptions to that—King Gudrun's wife could be an absolute dragon when she needed to be—but most of the ladies stayed out of their husband's way, content to be shiny trinkets on a shelf.

Idalia—as she'd insisted Petra start calling her—stood a little ways from the small group, her dark eyes wide as she looked out over the city ahead of her. From their place at the gate, one could see all the way to the glittering waters along the coast. Petra couldn't see her face, but she could see the ease in her shoulders. In Åldras, the woman had been all poised perfection. Here, she was a new creature entirely.

How on Midgard was Petra supposed to get the lady to trust her enough to help win over the queen and free herself from this bloody bargain? Axel's plan was absolutely stupid. She was the least trustworthy person on the planet. Freyja's golden tears, she didn't even trust herself. There was no way the plan she and Axel had come up with would work.

"Ah, good morning, Petra," Queen Kelda greeted, gliding up from behind. "I hope you're up for a bit of exercise today."

It wasn't like Petra had much of a choice but to follow after the queen, even if she wasn't up for the exercise. She shrugged.

Queen Kelda swept over to Hildi, setting a hand on her shoulder. "Petra is here, so we can go whenever you're ready."

Hildi glanced at her, brows lowered. "Do you truly think bringing her and Idalia is wise?"

Petra met her gaze, folding her arms over her chest. She certainly didn't want to run around with the surly princess. Though they'd been around each other for the last ten days, not much had changed. At least the scenery would be a pleasant diversion.

"Petra is supposed to attend me, and Idalia hasn't had the opportunity to see anything outside the city walls," the queen said. "Besides, I'm sure they'll surprise you."

Hildi nodded and barked orders to the guards huddled around her. They immediately loaded into the wagons, the guards taking the front and rear of each. The queen and Hildi went to the first wagon, leaving Idalia and Petra to follow in the second.

"I can't believe Hildi is letting us accompany her today!" Idalia practically squealed in delight. Her eyes widened and her cheeks flushed. She ducked her head a bit, as if waiting for someone to reprimand her. Her voice was much quieter when she said, "I've wanted to go with her on one of these since I found out she does this."

Petra glanced over at her. "Does what?"

"Hildi is part of an elite team that helps take care of magical beings," she said softly. "Apparently, when a monster problem pops up, she's the one sent out to take care of it."

The princess wasn't just a captain, but a monster hunter as well? Thunder's beard, if Petra didn't hate her, she'd probably like her.

"What are we going after?" Petra asked. If she'd known they were hunting a creature, she would have brought more than just her axes and the one dagger strapped to her back under her tunic.

Idalia's eyes brightened. "A vätte, apparently."

Petra blew out a breath. A vätte shouldn't be too much for their small group. The creatures could be malicious but weren't more than a nuisance. They regularly stayed close to livestock, only wreaking havoc when they were upset about something. If they got angry enough, they would start killing animals. It was smart to be wary of the little beasts, but they were easy enough to trap and dispose of if one knew how to.

Idalia's attention trailed off, taking in the scenery of the city as they rode down the street connecting the palace wall to the inner-city wall. Honestly, there were a lot of walls, but at least they were built out of stone and made the Sidans seem like they actually cared about the security of their citizens. *Firmin should take notes if he ever lays eyes on this place.*

They crossed through the second gate and onto the third. Petra searched for conversation topics. Anything to speak to the princess about. But this was Axel's area of expertise, not hers. He was the charmer, the socialite. Stabbing herself in the leg felt less painful than trying to come up with small talk.

She cleared her throat. "Have you ever seen a vätte?"

Idalia turned back to her, dark brows drawn together. "Not that I can remember. We don't have them in Tatawar, and I never saw any in Åldras. I didn't have much opportunity to see anything when I lived there."

Petra picked at her bottom lip. It wasn't surprising to hear Anders had shut her away for the most part. The man was a rock-head of the highest degree.

"What about you?" Idalia asked. "Have you seen one?"

Petra nodded. "A few."

Idalia grabbed her arm. "What did it look like? I've read a few books in the palace library, but there weren't many descriptions."

Petra did her best not to startle at the lady's lack of personal space. "They're small, only reaching up to my knee. The females are smaller than the males, and often with spindly limbs where the males can be a bit stockier."

"And they have hats," Idalia added.

"Aye. Most of the time they're made of fur, though I've seen one made from some kind of leather." They had a fox-fur hat on *The Phoenix* collected from a vätte they'd come across along the coast of Hjärta a couple of years ago. The little beast had killed an entire flock of sheep because the shepherd had planted a new kind of bean to feed the flocks and the vätte hadn't liked it.

Idalia sighed. "I envy you and Hildi immensely. The two of you have gone on such marvelous adventures."

Petra nearly snorted. "It's not as exciting as you think it is."

The battles and monsters were always romanticized in the songs, painted in a way to make the hero seem like some kind of mighty warrior and the beasts these dark creatures easily fought off. Unless they were children's songs. Those were sung with a wary tone and a warning in their words. Petra had nightmares about marbendill for two weeks before her brother Gram had finally told her they were basically just sea lions. While his reassurances hadn't been completely true—the creatures could kill you in your sleep if you didn't light a fire on the beach at night—it had helped her sleep after that. If only he could wipe away the things that kept her from sleep now.

The conversation fell off once again. Perhaps this idea of befriending the woman was a lost cause. Or, at least, Petra was. Axel would really have to spook the queen into letting Petra go back across the Vit Sea or charm the queen into being his friend himself. Though, that could exacerbate the problem rather than solve it.

The wagons trundled out into the open plains outside the city. In the daylight, Petra could see for miles even through the thin fog that clung to the hills. Short trees and shrubs covered the dusty ground. The grass was a mixture of sage green and yellow. Being this close to water, Petra thought the vegetation would be thicker, but it seemed the farther they got from the sea, the livelier it became. A mountain range pierced the sky far away, their tall faces nearly purple at that distance. Petra knew from maps of the kingdoms the mountain range stretched for hundreds of miles, splitting the continent in two.

That morning's thin fog finally cleared as they crossed the river east of the city and rode into a small village tucked near its banks. It was little more than half a dozen houses and what looked like some trade stalls gathered around a square. A wide well squatted in the middle of the square, surrounded by villagers. A round man stepped away from the crowd, his nose a giant beak taking up half his face. Honestly, it would be less of a shock to see wings sprout from the man's back than it would be to find a vätte running around the village.

"Your Majesty," the round man bowed to Queen Kelda. "We weren't expecting such exalted company to attend to us."

The queen gave a small nod of her head, barely a tilt of her chin. "It is an honor to join Princess Hildigunn to offer our help. Tell us, what has happened?"

A tale bloomed from the man's lips, and Petra slid closer to catch it. A vätte had been spotted several weeks ago around a new herd of goats the village had invested in to bring more industry to their area. Nothing had happened at the beginning, but a week ago, they'd found a dead goat lying at the back door of one of the houses. Another followed a couple days later. Then another. They suspected someone was attempting to sabotage their new business, but a group of children had spotted the vätte when it had left the most recent goat.

"While we've set our best men to tracking the beast down," the man said, "we have had no success. With Midsummer so soon, we didn't want to risk the creature ruining preparations for our festival."

Queen Kelda set a hand to her chest. "Then it's good you've reached out to us."

Petra glanced around the village. Something had to have set the beast off. They didn't often attack without provocation, but it could be something as simple as the creature not liking someone's flowers they planted in their garden.

When Idalia had made her way to a group of children—where she had already instigated some kind of game with them—Petra stepped away from the group. While the rest of the party comforted the traumatized village, Petra could actually look around for the little nuisance.

It wasn't difficult to slip between the wagons and glide toward the closest building. Nothing seemed out of place. Even the barrels on the side of the house hadn't been moved in weeks based on the way the dirt hugged the bottom. A clothesline had been stretched between two posts at the back of the house, but no clothing hung from the rope.

The faint call of animals sounded from somewhere past the buildings. Petra followed the sound until she found the small herd. There were goats in Åldras, but these goats had shorter hair and their horns angled straight back from their head rather than curving around their ears. A few of them turned to her, chewing cud as they stared with their square-pupiled eyes. One of them stepped away from the middle of the herd, opening up space between a few goats.

The vätte stood in the midst of them.

Vätte didn't often come out in broad daylight, preferring to dwell in their dens in the ground during the warmest hours of the day. Most sightings of them happened in the early morning hours, just before dawn. This vätte had been waiting for someone to spot him.

It was a male, his hat made of what looked like skunk fur. His eyes were black from corner to corner, his cheeks a ruddy red. He stared at her, his hands still at his sides as the goats mingled around him. A slow grin stretched across his face, showing rows of blunt, crooked teeth. The little beasts were herbivores like the livestock they liked to hover around, but those teeth could break bones.

"There!"

Petra spun around. Hildi stood at the corner of the house, sword pointed toward the vätte.

The little beast gave a howl and bolted. A few of the goats startled as he zipped away, racing for a line of scraggly trees.

Hildi and a pair of guards ran after the creature.

The vätte looked back at them, glee obvious in his face.

Setting her hands atop her axes, Petra watched the Sidans crash through the brush. Vätte were conniving little monsters. The bloody idiots were going to get themselves killed.

Idalia rushed around the corner, a quiver of arrows peeking up from behind her shoulder and a bow in her hand. "What's happened?" Her eyes widened when she spotted the creature taking Hildi on a merry chase. "Is that the vätte?"

"Yes," Petra answered, "and he's going to lead Hildi into a trap."

She'd seen it before. When the vättes were especially displeased, they would turn their anger onto humans instead of the livestock.

Idalia gasped. "We have to help them." Before Petra could grab her, the lady took off toward Hildi and the guards.

*Freyja's golden tears.* Now Idalia would get herself killed.

But was that such a bad thing?

It would certainly save Petra the effort of having to befriend her. If she died, perhaps the Sidans would be blamed and the Tatawarie wouldn't think about siding with them. Though, more likely than not, Firmin would figure out a way to blame Axel for Idalia's death, and they'd be mired in another mess.

With a growl, Petra drew one of her axes and raced toward where Idalia was attempting to catch up with Hildi. The lady's dress kept snagging on the brush and allowed Petra to reach her. Honestly, the woman was a fool to be running out here in a skirt. She'd get herself killed before she ever hoped to help Hildi.

Petra caught up to her and grabbed her arm, pulling her to a stop. "What are you doing?"

"I'm trying to help." Idalia ripped her arm free and cupped her hands around her mouth. "Hildi! It's a trap!"

Hildi didn't seem to hear though. She continued to stalk forward after the creature, barking orders to the two guards trying to box in the vätte.

Idalia pushed forward, and Petra trailed after her.

"How are you going to help—"

The sound of rocks crashing cut through the air.

Petra turned just in time to watch Hildi, and the two guards fall through the ground.

"Hildi!" Idalia screeched, gathering her skirts and racing toward the hole.

"Idalia! Stop!" Petra hollered. She sprinted after the lady, gaining on her quickly.

Idalia was two feet from the hole when the ground beneath her fell out from under her feet.

Petra grabbed her arm and yanked her backward.

She took the fall instead.

Idalia screamed as Petra hit the side of the hole and rolled the rest of the way down. She hit the bottom, her still healing shoulder screaming at the abuse.

"Hel's bloody halls," she hissed.

"Don't move!" Hildi yelled.

Petra froze, but when she glanced up at Hildi, who had gotten to her feet, the princess wasn't looking in her direction. Petra followed her gaze up to see Idalia crouched down on a ledge halfway down the hole. *Rocks.* While Petra had taken the worst of the fall, the lady was still in danger.

One of the guards moaned, holding his arm hanging at an awkward angle. His comrade stood next to him, a sword in her hand.

Hildi clambered over a few of the rocks toward where Idalia crouched several ells above them. With a stone tucked into her tunic, she built up the ledge holding Idalia up.

Pushing herself to her feet, Petra took in the vätte's trap. It looked as if the bottom of the hole had been carved ages ago. Mud sucked at her boots. There was water somewhere close, which wasn't a surprise considering the river on the other side of town. Vätte tunnels pocked the sides of the hole. The fall had been a little more than ten ells, and the bottom was probably twenty or thirty ells wide. The little pest had been hard at work making this trap, which meant he'd been upset for quite some time and it likely wasn't with the humans. To Petra's right, a wider tunnel led into the earth. There may have been dwarves in the area previously. That wouldn't be surprising.

Hildi held up her hands. "Without shifting your weight too much, can you reach up and grab the edge of the hole?"

Idalia shook her head emphatically. "I can't!"

"Idalia?" a voice called from above them. The edge of the hole slowly turned white with frost and Queen Kelda's veiled face came into view. "Maker above, is anyone injured?"

Idalia let out a little sob and Hildi took up a status report to the queen as the wielders' magic bled into the dirt, hardening it so it would be more stable for Idalia to stand on. Stone and ice mingled carefully under Idalia's feet. Once she was settled, hopefully both wielders could get them out of this hole.

The sound of crumbling stone echoed from behind her. She whipped her head in the direction of the large hole in the side of the wall. The light from above only pierced the dark a few feet into the tunnel. The shift in the dirt could have been the earth settling under Hildi's magic, but something made the hairs on the back of Petra's neck stand on end.

Without looking away, she carefully stepped toward the guards. "Ready your swords."

The guard still standing shifted closer. "I don't see—"

A draugr leaped out from the darkness.

The beast's sole arm clawed the air as it snapped its broken teeth. Idalia screamed.

*"Ready your bloody swords!"* Petra bellowed. The monster lunged at her, and she met it near the mouth of the tunnel. Her axes took off the draugr's head, and the decaying body fell to the ground in a heap.

Two more stumbled out of the tunnel, teeth clicking.

A shudder ran down Petra's spine as she took down the largest of the pair. *It just had to be rocking draugr.* She turned to attack the second, but Hildi's sword had already lopped it's head off.

Hildi whirled toward the other guards. "Alexander, get to the wall and stay out of reach as much as you can. Liv, you take the right. Petra, the left. Idalia, you stay right where you are and don't let any of the beasts try to climb the wall. Your Majesty—"

"I'm already working on it," Queen Kelda answered. The hole grew a degree colder as more frost stretched down the walls.

*The princess definitely knows how to boss everyone around.* Petra bit back the words as she took her position to the left of Hildi. The captain held her sword in one hand and the stone hanging around her neck in the other. The ground under Petra's shoes shifted as Hildi's magic slithered about.

"You don't want to use that fancy magic of yours to get us out of here?" Petra asked.

Hildi's eyes narrowed. "And let the monsters out right after us to terrorize the village?"

She was right, unfortunately. If they left the draugr in the hole, they would only tear themselves apart to get up to the surface and terrorize the town. And the vätte would likely help, seeing as how it had led their merry little band right to the beasts in the first place.

"Then collapse the tunnel," Petra suggested.

"If we weren't so close to the water, perhaps I could do something, but if I shift the ground too much without the proper time to stabilize it, I could shift the way the river runs down here, and it could potentially collapse the village into the river. Best to take out the monsters, don't you think?"

Freyja's golden tears, what was the point of having magic if they couldn't use it?

Idalia hovered above them, the ledge almost completely frozen over from Queen Kelda's magic. The lady had her bow nocked and the arrow poised at the hole. Not that an arrow would take out a draugr, but it would slow it down.

It didn't take long for the other draugr to follow the scent of living flesh through the tunnel. They came in a flood, a dozen of them scrabbling through with feral eyes and gnashing teeth. Petra's axes became a blur of steel in front of her, taking limbs and heads with abandon.

Stones flew around the space, Hildi wielding magic in one hand and a sword in the other. Liv, the uninjured guard, was apparently an air whisperer and shoved the draugr away from her injured comrade. Alexander held his sword poised, waiting for one of the beasts to break through.

Petra's ax cut through a draugr's neck, even slicing through the ragged sheet of dark hair hanging from its head. Black water sprayed across her face, likely a mixture of old blood and whatever water kept them alive in whatever underground water source they'd found to sleep in.

A hand grabbed the back of her shirt, and she spun, severing the bloated limb from the monster.

The draugr didn't even wince as its arm fell to the floor between them. It reached for her with its other hand and before it could touch her, the tip of an arrow shot through its eye socket. The creature stumbled slightly, and Petra took the opportunity to decapitate it.

A scream echoed around the hole, making Petra's ears ring. She took down another monster just in time to see Liv get dragged down by three draugr. Her screams cut off when one of the beasts tore her throat out with its teeth.

*Rocks.* Petra spun and sliced through the neck of another draugr.

Hildi roared, sending a wave of stones over them, using the earth to swallow the mob of draugr whole, Liv included.

With their right side open, the draugr made for Alexander.

A wall of dirt shot up between the monsters and the guard. It didn't stop the creatures from attempting to dig through the stone to get to him.

Another wave of the creatures surged through the tunnel. Petra couldn't even tell when the horde ended.

Her heart seized for a single moment before she sliced through the neck of the closest beast.

They were all going to die down here.

Gritting her teeth, she raced for the wall under Idalia, putting the dirt to her back so she could face the beasts head on. The frost had made its way all the way to the base of the hole, hardening the mud under her boots.

A draugr dragged itself toward her, the bottom half of its body completely missing. She kicked it back as another draugr lunged for her.

*"Any time now, Your Majesty!"* Hildi bellowed, her sword flying as she backed up to the wall of stone surrounding Alexander.

Hildi couldn't see the draugr climbing on top of it. She was too focused on the pair in front of her.

Petra chopped the head off another beast, then finished off the legless one, pushing past them to the back of the tunnel.

The draugr scrambled to its feet atop the shell.

Idalia saw it and shot an arrow right through the beast's eye.

The draugr stumbled off the top of the shell, falling right onto Hildi's head.

"Hildi!" Idalia screamed.

Petra reached the pair Hildi had been battling, kicking the smaller of the two away and taking out the second.

Hildi was on her back, the draugr on top of her, the arrow sticking out of its rheumy eye. She held the creature back with only her hands.

The draugr's head turned, crooked jaw widening as it lunged for her arm.

Petra's ax slid straight through its neck.

Ichor sprayed across Hildi's front as the decapitated head fell next to her.

Hopefully, the princess had the wherewithal to get off her arse and fight. Petra dodged a swipe from another draugr and pulled the dagger from the sheath at her back. She cut the creature's hand off with the sharp dagger and finished it off with the ax.

When she stepped back away from the wall, she nearly slipped. Water pooled along the bottom of the hole, slicking the icy layer underfoot.

"To me!" Hildi hollered, taking out the closest draugr.

Petra cut down another and dove toward Hildi. Arrows flew past her head, sinking into more than one eye socket as she went. Thunder's beard, Idalia really knew her way around a bow.

Petra reached Hildi and the princess snatched the neck of her tunic, pulling her through the wall of dirt surrounding the guard. Hildi sealed the wall behind them, slicing through one of the draugr's arms, which fell limp to the ground at their feet.

"Down!" Hildi barked.

Petra followed the command, but Alexander was a beat late and hit his head as Hildi brought the capsule of earth down. The space went completely dark as Hildi packed more dirt on top of them, leaving only enough space for them to kneel together.

The ground under Petra's hands quaked and a roar pierced through the stone shell.

Water seeped through the dirt, soaking into the knees of Petra's trousers.

Hildi growled in Petra's ear, the sound one of spite and determination.

A drop of water splashed on Petra's cheek.

Wōden's one good eye, she was holding up water. And likely not just around them. If the queen had brought the river this way, that meant Hildi was likely also holding up the tunnel so the village didn't collapse above it.

*Bloody magic.*

The roar of the water faded along with the quake of the dirt beneath Petra's feet.

Cold seeped in between the stones. She felt it at her back, though the center of their shell was warm with the heat of their bodies.

Hildi let out a breath and the shield of stone around them crumbled.

Petra shot to her feet, her ax still in hand. Ice glittered along the sides of the hole, casting sparks of light where the sun glanced off the crystalized water. The draugr had been swept away and a wall of ice blocked the tunnel's entrance.

Hildi's braid had come almost entirely undone and her face was streaked with mud. She glanced at Petra. "Sometimes, when dealing with magic, you have to be patient. You have to think of the ramifications of what will happen. You have to work alongside your sisters."

She bared her teeth and stretched her hand toward the tunnel.

The entire thing collapsed. Petra shielded her face as mud and rock sprayed out, but none of it touched her. Hildi's other hand was clenched in a fist in front of her and the rocks and mud ricocheted off an invisible wall in front of them.

When the dust finally settled, Petra looked to the tunnel. The earth didn't collapse above them. There were no screams of terror as the village above them fell.

Hildi had waited for the queen to fortify the ground to minimize the damage that could have been created by her collapsing the tunnel on her own. She'd put herself in danger, when she could have saved herself, to make sure everyone was safe.

*Rocks.* The princess was actually worth her crown.

Petra looked up to the ledge. Idalia shook with cold, but she had kept her place on the icy ledge.

A shadow fell over the lady and Queen Kelda's veiled head came into view.

"Everyone still alive?"

Hildi sank to her knees, and Idalia burst into tears.

---

# CHAPTER 13

# FAMILIES

Axel rested his head against the wall, the back of his tunic sticking to his skin. Honestly, someone could bake honey cakes out in Sol's glaring light if they wanted. The only reprieve was the faint breeze whistling through the airy space. The construction of the palace made more sense now. If they'd built a great hall like the ones in Åldras, everyone would roast themselves the moment they stepped inside.

After his morning with General Caeso, Axel had waited for Petra in their rooms back at the palace, but she didn't return once her allotted time with the queen had ended. After nearly an hour of waiting, he went searching for her. It didn't take long to discover Queen Kelda had gone to visit one of the villages outside the city walls.

So, after an afternoon of thrashing Enzo in the sparring ring again, Axel had parked himself on a bench near the northern entrance to the palace to await their return. He'd give them until dusk, but the moment the sun fell below the horizon, he would go after her. To Hel's halls with the bloody queen. If Petra had been harmed, he would make Queen Kelda pay for it.

He could see the gate of the palace from where he sat. Little Hal discovered Petra had gone to a village to the east of the city, so if they were going to return before sundown, it would be through this entrance. He'd sat for over an hour, long enough to take in the space. Pillars held up the roof over his head, protecting the entrance to the palace from any harsh weather. Runes had been carved in the ceiling above his head. He likely wouldn't have noticed if he hadn't been staring at it for so long. Now that he thought about it, there were runes throughout most of the palace. What they did, he had no idea, but there had to be a reason the stone carvers created them. Based on how open the palace was, there were likely plenty of defensive runes.

"Awaiting our lady heroes?"

Enzo strode into the courtyard, a smirk on his smug face. He took a seat on another bench along the same wall as Axel's. His hair was wet, likely from bathing after their grueling spar in the arena. Enzo had been sure to challenge Axel every day since their first match. While the prince would have beat him a handful of times, Axel's magic made the fight completely unfair. But Enzo persisted. As if he simply couldn't abandon this crusade to find Axel's weakness. To win.

"Aye," Axel answered. Apparently, Enzo's wife had also gone with the queen. Were Sidans so used to their women going out on their own, leaving the protection of the walls to take care of monsters in the outlying villages? It was so alien from what Axel had grown up seeing, though that certainly hadn't kept him from taking Petra with him on the ship. He'd always thought it was foolish to keep the womenfolk out of the fight. Mila had drilled into him that women were just as strong as men—both in word and deed. While he'd never seen Petra's mother pick up a sword, she was as fierce as any man he'd fought beside on the battlefield. Petra was like her in that way.

Enzo hummed, rolling his left shoulder. He'd wrenched it when he'd challenged Axel to a weightlifting contest at the end of their spar. "I'm sure they'll be back. Hildi doesn't like to miss bedtime."

"What?" Axel tilted his head. Bedtime? The sun was barely going down.

A squeal cut through the space. A little girl dressed in a bright green dress toddled into the courtyard. She couldn't have been more than one or two years, her light hair only a sprig of fuzz tied in a small bow on the top of her head.

"Papa!"

Enzo grinned, hopping up from his seat on the bench. "Hello, princess." He scooped her up and nuzzled the babe's cheek. The lass squealed, her tiny legs kicking as Enzo kissed her over and over.

Something in Axel's chest squeezed. Hard. It was easy to paint the Crown Prince as a villain when all Axel had seen from the man was the way he slaughtered Åldrans. When Axel could pretend all the man wanted was to make his life miserable. It was easy to forget he was a man, with his own dreams. With a family.

Hel's halls, Enzo had a *family*.

With a grin as wide as the Vit Sea, Enzo led the child over to where Axel sat.

"Aggie," he said, speaking to the lass, "do you want to show Axel here what you and Nana have been practicing? Show him how to fight."

The toddler squirmed out of Enzo's arms as he leaned down so she could stand in front of Axel. She pulled up her skirt until she showed her belly and stomped on the top of Axel's foot.

A laugh burst from him. When she looked up at him expectantly, a fierce line between her brows she'd very much inherited from her captain of a mother, he met Enzo's gaze.

"Play along," Enzo whispered.

With a chuckle bubbling up in his chest, Axel grabbed the top of his boot and gave a howl of pain.

"You've wounded me!" he cried, clutching his foot. He carefully slid to the side, lying on the bench as if in great pain. "Oh, great princess, you have felled me."

The little child walked carefully up and grabbed his cheeks in her tiny hands. Without provocation, she pressed her thin lips to his forehead.

"All better," she said, the words barely discernable in her tiny voice.

"I am?" Axel gave her a little grin and sagged down in dramatic relief. "You're my hero."

The child giggled at his antics, large brown eyes sparkling.

Enzo scooped her up once more. "My kind little Aggie. You saved him, though you did defeat him first like Nana taught you."

Aggie wrapped her arms around Enzo's neck, hugging him

tightly. She pulled back and pointed at the strip of fabric tied on the top of her head. "Bow."

Enzo followed her gaze to the tiny scrap of cloth holding up her one stalk of blonde hair. "Yes. Did Nana tie you a bow?"

The child shook her head. "Mama."

Axel watched the two of them as they continued to exchange words—Enzo asking questions about her day and Aggie giving answers in a language all her own.

Something in Axel's chest ached at the softness in Enzo's face and the adorable babble of the child in his arms. He hadn't heard Enzo was a father. Wōden's one good eye, he hadn't heard *anything* about the Sidan royal family apart from the king and his two sons. From what Firmin had always boasted, they had spies all over the place. Where were they when this all came to be? Was Åldras so out of touch with this kingdom they didn't even know the state of the royal family? Or did no one truly pay attention to the enemy they were fighting?

What did that say about Åldras?

"Oh, look," Enzo said, turning Aggie to see down into the city. "There's Mama."

Axel pushed to his feet as two wagons lumbered in through the front gate. The first wagon held Lady Idalia and Queen Kelda, but the second carried both Petra and Hildi, covered head to toe in dust.

Axel swept past Enzo and Aggie, jogging down the front steps and down the brick road leading to the gate. The guards piled out first, their faces a mixture of haggard relief and solemn exhaustion. Only one other guard was as covered in dirt as Petra and Hildi were, and his arm had been strapped to his chest with a length of cloth. Axel came around the back of the second wagon right as Petra hopped down.

Her face was creased with exhaustion like all the others, but a spark lit her eyes in a way he hadn't seen for weeks. She looked at him, and a small smile touched the corner of her lips.

His traitorous heart skipped.

He folded his arms over his chest, praying it concealed the sensation at least a little from Petra's sight, though he doubted it. "You're later than usual."

Her head tilted slightly, eyes narrowed as if searching his expression for something. After their conversation a few nights ago, things had been...easier. Not back to normal. Not at all. But it was better. The anger between them had fizzled out, though it made other things between them more fraught.

Like the fact that he would like nothing more than to kiss her right there and then.

She cleared her throat. "Things didn't go according to plan."

Hildi clambered down after Petra, her own eyes shining as she looked past him. "There's my sweet girl."

"Mama!" Aggie called from behind him.

Petra's eyes widened—as Axel was sure his had when he first saw the lass—as Hildi joined Enzo and Aggie.

The child pointed at Hildi's face. "Mama bath."

Enzo burst out laughing and Hildi smiled.

The three of them together, with the golden light of the setting sun, did something to Axel's insides. Like he was seeing a dream he had forgotten he'd had. They were beautiful, and Axel had to rub the heel of his hand against his chest to ease a little of the ache that settled there.

Would he ever have what they did?

Petra bumped him with her shoulder. Her dirt-caked brow rose in question, but he shook his head. He couldn't even put a name to what he was feeling himself. There was no way he could express it to her.

"What happened to you?" he asked, gesturing to the chunks of dirt plastered to her clothing.

"Vätte trap. Dropped us in a draugr hole."

"Are you hurt?" Memories of her bleeding out after the draugr bite flashed through his mind. He reached out to grab her shoulder, but stopped, the air between them still stiff. There weren't any visible injuries, but all the dirt made it hard to see anything.

She shook her head. "Just tired and in need of a bath."

Hildi stepped toward them. "I'll have my own servants bring up hot water. I owe you that much."

Petra's shoulders rose a fraction as all eyes turned in her direction.

"What happened?" Enzo asked.

Hildi gestured to Petra. "She saved me. Alexander had injured himself in the fall and Liv had fallen to the draugr. I'd put Alexander in an earth shell, but one of the draugr used it to get behind me. It landed on top of me and if Petra hadn't reached me, I would have been draugr food."

"She kept all of us from becoming draugr food!" Lady Idalia cut in, materializing between Petra and Hildi, her expression more open than Axel had ever seen it. "She was the one to notice the monsters in the first place. If she hadn't called for the guards to arm themselves, the draugr would have caught us completely by surprise."

Axel bumped Petra with his elbow. "And here I thought you only saved your heroics for when I'm around." Not that he really thought so. Petra was a hero in her own right and had done plenty of good for Åldras without Axel about.

Petra silently protested, sending a blunted glare up at him.

The captain gently flicked the bit of fuzz on Aggie's head. "I owe you far more than a hot bath, that's for certain."

Petra tucked herself slightly behind Axel, shrinking back further. "Don't reward me for saving my own skin. I wasn't going to beat them on my own."

Enzo snorted, shifting Aggie in his arms. "Modest, are we? And here I figured being Åldras's demon would have instilled some arrogance in you."

A grin pulled at Axel's mouth. "Challenge her to a game of hnefatafl, and you'll see plenty of arrogance."

"A woman after my own heart," Enzo replied, pressing his empty hand to his chest.

Lady Idalia bounced on her toes. "We'll have to put together a tournament. Maybe you can finally beat Kelda. She holds the winning hnefatafl title in the palace apparently."

Axel turned, finding the veiled queen already halfway up the steps to the palace. A gaggle of servants skipped down toward her, several stopping near the queen while others scurried down the steps past her. In the latter group, Roman took the steps two at a time until he reached Lady Idalia.

"I just heard what happened." He cradled the lady's face in his hands. "Are you all right?"

Lady Idalia blinked up at him several times as if she were dispelling tears. "Yes, I'm fine."

Had Anders ever held the lady so tenderly? No wonder she left him for the prince. At least Roman acted like he cared about her wellbeing.

Hel's halls, Axel really was starting to respect these bloody princes.

The servants trailing behind Roman finally caught up to them, one stopping at Axel's side.

"Mighty Axel, the council has gathered in the hall to speak with you."

Petra blew out a breath. "I guess we'll have to put that bath on hold."

Roman grimaced. "Just be careful. Mother doesn't like dirt on the carpets."

The entire group turned toward the palace, trailing behind Axel as he followed the servant to the council hall. This procession contrasted sharply with the last time he'd walked into the hall. Instead of in shackles, he walked beside the princes. It had been less than two weeks, and already he found himself on even ground with them.

How could it all have changed so quickly? Was it really that the Sidans were easy to get along with and it was Firmin that had been making things difficult this entire time? Firmin being difficult wasn't necessarily a novel idea, but would the High King really be so bad as to allow this war to continue on for so long all for his pride? King Leonardo was obviously a good man. One who cared about his kingdom and taught his sons to live with honor.

At the doors to the hall, Enzo passed Aggie off to an older woman, setting a kiss to the child's fuzzy head. Hildi did the same, and the little girl was swept away. The moment she disappeared, the Crown Prince and his captain reappeared. It was like a mask fell into place. Their faces turned stoic and their backs straight as they swept past their entire group, entering the council hall ahead of them with their chins held high.

What if Åldras was led by such people?

Would it really be so bad if Sida did win this war?

What would happen to Åldras if they did?

The council hall was much the same as it had been the last time. The councilors green robes fluttered in the breeze coming from the large windows, and fires crackled in their bowls. The only difference was this time, King Leonardo stood among them, nodding along with something Caeso was telling him. The king's dark gaze alighted on Axel, and he pulled back from the general.

"Mighty Axel," the king greeted, his deep voice echoing off the walls, "I hear you have news from Åldras."

Axel had to take in a breath. While he'd told Caeso that morning word had arrived from Harligdam the day before, he'd kept exactly what that information was to himself. Giving away any intelligence that could be used to harm Åldras went against everything Axel had been taught.

Roman and Lady Idalia found seats on one of the benches, and Enzo and Hildi took their places at the foot of the dais below the throne.

Axel gave a slow nod. "Aye, Your Majesty. I was informed High King Firmin is gathering men."

Caeso's head whipped in Axel's direction, his brows lifted high. He obviously hadn't been expecting Axel to be so forthcoming.

One of the councilors stood up. "Why would he be gathering forces when we haven't even sent a reply in regard to Lady Idalia's departure from the kingdom?"

King Leonardo glanced at Hildi, then Petra, likely noting the state of their clothing. "You think a man whose pride has been dragged through the mud is going to simply roll over once he gets his toy back? No, I have no doubt he was planning to retaliate regardless of whether Lady Idalia returned or not. It was what made the decision not to send her back easy for me to make."

Axel blinked. The king had come to that conclusion so quickly? Even Axel had hoped Firmin would allow the armistice to run its course before he attacked. Had he been plotting an early attack this entire time? No, he couldn't have. The kings would never have agreed to it.

"So, what are we to do?" another councilman asked—his name started with *a*, but Axel couldn't remember it. "Should we let him come baying like hounds at our city gates? Or do we finally crush the fat little grub?" His eyes widened and he looked over to Axel and Petra.

If Axel actually cared about Firmin, he might have found the description offensive. As it was, he just shrugged at the councilor as if he couldn't find fault with his words.

King Leonardo climbed the few steps up the dais and took his place in his throne. "I would like to hear what the Crown Prince has to say."

Enzo's eyes flicked over to Axel. "Should we discuss possible scenarios with Åldrans present?"

The king met Axel's gaze again. "What do you think, Mighty Axel? Would it be in our best interest to allow you to stay and contribute your own expertise to the conversation? Or will you take the plans we discuss here and share them with your comrades across the sea?"

Petra shifted next to Axel, her sleeve nearly brushing against his arm. She placed a lazy hand atop the head of her ax hanging at her waist.

But Axel didn't think the king meant his comment as a threat. More like a test.

If he and Petra stayed, they would basically announce to the entire council they were on the side of the Sidans. That they had abandoned their kingdom. It was a tempting prospect. After seeing the might of Sida's military firsthand, it was obvious Åldras had no real chance against the Sidans. Not in a head-to-head battle. Not only did Sida have the numbers, they also had unity. They loved their king and countrymen. While Åldrans were loyal to a fault, there was dissension. The Häxa hunts had turned families against each other. The war had only increased desperation. Åldras was weakening, and if they weren't careful, Sida would sweep through and take the entire kingdom with a wave of King Leonardo's hand.

A small voice, one that was getting louder the longer he stood in that room, whispered into his heart.

*Would that be such a bad thing?*

The answer was still too far out of reach. If Axel and Petra didn't stay to plan with the Sidans, they would show these people they could be trusted, but their allegiance was to their kingdom and they were still enemies.

But that didn't feel completely true.

And what if these people weren't his enemy anymore? Firmin would still arrive on these shores. He would bring war right to this city's doorstep. There was no way Firmin would leave the bloody Ekte and their protective runes behind in Åldras. They would bring down as many Häxa as they could while they were here. And Firmin wouldn't have forgotten his anger with Axel.

Axel looked to Petra out of the corner of his eye. *What do we do?*

Her blue-green gaze flicked up to him. *I'll follow your lead.*

He took a deep breath and met King Leonardo's gaze. There was a small crinkle on either side of the king's eyes. As if he already knew the answer.

Axel turned and walked out of the room, Petra following in his shadow.

The people of Åldras still needed him. They still needed Mighty Axel to try to save them.

## CHAPTER 14

## A SURPRISE

Every day of the next week followed the same routine. Petra would wake up and step carefully through the room, doing her best not to wake Axel from the second bed he'd dragged into their room the second night they'd slept there. She would still fail, and his green eyes would track her through the room as she readied for her time with Queen Kelda. Ignoring that look, she would slip out into the hall with a whisper of a farewell on her tongue.

The one thing that did change was how she saw the women she worked with. She would make her way through the palace with two guards trailing behind her, almost looking forward to the lessons the Häxa took part in. They would escort her out of the palace to the Häxa study hall and leave her in Hildi's care. The two of them would stand at the back of the room as Queen Kelda led the Häxa girls in their lessons. The tension between Petra and Hildi had nearly dissipated after their fight with the draugr. Petra had even stopped looking for ways to best the captain. After the queen finished, they would gather with Idalia for a quick luncheon and Petra would leave.

But exactly one week after the fight with the draugr passed and none of that happened when she woke.

She crept from her bed, but Axel's green eyes didn't greet her. His bed was empty except for her small clay tablet on the pillow.

*Meet me back here when you're finished with the queen.*

Petra tossed the tablet back on the bed and stuck her feet into her boots. Maybe Axel found something that would help them figure out how to get them out of these bargains. Little Hal had been trying to collect information on the queen, but even the citizens of Bellator seemed to view this Häxa queen with the quiet reverence everyone else did.

Slipping out into the hallway, Petra listened for the telltale signs of life, but only Big Hal's snores from the room next to hers cut through the air. The guards that met her every morning outside her room didn't greet Petra in the hallway. She carefully crept down the hall, finding the corridor completely empty. It hadn't been unguarded since they'd arrived, though the guards had definitely grown more lax in their post. Little Hal and Ludvig had snuck past them only two nights prior. Ludvig had some sweetheart in town whose heart he was going to break when they finally returned to Åldras.

Petra settled her hands on the tops of her axes and treaded carefully through the empty halls of the palace. The sound of bustling servants rang out of sight, but she didn't cross anyone's path. If she didn't meet with Queen Kelda, would she think Petra hadn't met her end of the deal? Axel would be absolutely livid if she ruined this and got herself trapped here for longer. While Ludvig and Big Hal had made a full recovery, it would be a bloody nightmare trying to get all of them out of the city and to *The Phoenix*. Not to mention getting the bloody ship out onto the water.

When she arrived at the Häxa training room, she didn't even have to walk through the open entrance to know it was empty. The regular shift of stones and trickle of water didn't fill the space. Even the breeze didn't rustle the leaves of the plants near the open windows.

Petra bit the inside of her cheek and turned to walk away.

Hildi leaned against one of the trees.

Petra nearly jumped. "Thunder's beard."

A smile stretched across Hildi's face, revealing a dimple in her left cheek. "Queen Kelda is busy with preparations for tonight's festival. She told me to take over your morning activities while she's busy."

Petra narrowed her eyes. The captain looked almost pleased at the prospect. That couldn't be good.

Hildi pushed away from the wall. "Come along. Idalia's waiting for us."

*Great.* Petra stretched out her fingers, leaving them hanging down by her axes. If Hildi tried anything, they would be in easy reach but letting the princess know Petra was slightly worried wouldn't do.

She followed Hildi back the way she'd come but instead of turning left toward the rooms the crew were staying in, Hildi kept going straight. They walked out of the palace and down toward the north gate.

If the princess was taking her out of the palace to rid the Sidans of her, she would be in for a surprise. There was no way Petra would go down without a fight.

But the princess continued walking. Before they made it to the next gate, Hildi turned left, heading toward one of the larger buildings. There were several surrounding the inner wall near the palace. Little Hal had done some reconnaissance over the last couple of weeks and had reported on the surrounding areas with their possible escape routes. This building was the royal library, the one building taller than the wall. Ludvig had made the suggestion of using the vantage point from the roof in case they needed it. Seeing how close it was to the wall, the crew might even be able to use it as a possible escape route if they could get a rope across the space between the building and the city wall.

Hildi pushed through the large wooden door, not even glancing back to see if Petra was following her.

She did.

Petra stepped into the space and the scent of paper nearly punched her in the nose. There were three stories worth of shelves, scrolls and leather tomes crammed into every available space. She did her best to tread across the polished floor with care, the glistening marble almost reflective with its sheen. If Doran ever stepped foot in this place, she and Axel would have a bloody difficult time getting him out.

There was nothing like this in Åldras. The closest thing Petra's kingdom had to a library was whatever stash of scrolls Doran had collected over the years. Most of Åldras didn't know how to read anyhow—though Mama had insisted Petra and Axel learn from a very young age. Sharing knowledge was important and the written word was one of the easiest ways to do that. This library was a wealth of knowledge.

Hildi walked toward the back of the building, stepping up onto a set of twisting stairs. Petra's skin felt rough against the smooth handrail as she climbed up behind Hildi.

They reached the top of the library. The tomes on these shelves seemed a little more disheveled, scraps of paper sticking out of some of the scrolls and frayed ribbons hanging limply from their places at the edges of books.

Hildi reached up above their heads and pulled on a brass ring bolted into the ceiling. A section of the ceiling detached, swinging down to reveal a set of steps.

"After you," Hildi said, gesturing to the steps.

Petra climbed up, ready to slip her axes from their loops if she needed to. If there was an ambush, she would need to figure out how to get back down from the roof. With Hildi behind her, the only way left was forward.

When she could finally peer up over the lip of the opening, she paused.

The flat roof of the library had been transformed into a garden of sorts. Potted trees stuck up out of stone boxes filled with soil. Flowers poured out of hanging baskets, trailing down to the stones making up the roof. Sol's light just peeked up over the city, casting brilliant colors across the sky and turning the entire space gold.

The scent of something sweet drew Petra's attention to one corner, where a small sitting area had been put together under a canvas canopy. Idalia flitted about a table laden with fruits, pastries, and bowls Petra couldn't quite make out the contents of. The queen didn't seem to be there, and no guards patrolled the perimeter of the roof.

"Are we just going to stand here on these steps and gawk?" Hildi asked from behind her.

Heat attempted to scorch Petra's cheeks, but she pushed herself forward. Idalia looked up from her ministrations, a grin on her face.

"Happy birthday!" Idalia spread her arms wide. "I hope you came hungry. I didn't totally know what to put together, so I helped the cooks at the palace kind of give us a sample of everything."

Petra glanced back over her shoulder at Hildi. "If I'd realized it was your birthday, I would have insisted Queen Kelda charge someone else with babysitting duty." Besides, wouldn't a princess have such a day off? Even the princesses in Åldras were toted around Harligdam, flowers thrown at them and gifts left on the stone steps of the great hall every year. But perhaps Sidan birthdays were a quieter affair.

Hildi poked Petra's shoulder. "It's *your* birthday, idiot."

Petra stood frozen as Hildi swept past her. Was it really her birthday? She counted the days since they'd received Doran's letter. *That was the first day of Sólmánuður because it had taken five days for it to come across the kingdom.* She counted the days since then.

*Nine. Midsummer.*

It was her birthday.

Not every one of her birthdays fell on Midsummer, but some of them did. With all the preparations for the festival going on around the palace, she hadn't even thought about it.

No wonder Axel hadn't been in his bed that morning. He was likely plotting something. The idiot always remembered her birthday and attempted to make something grand out of it. There had been some years when he hadn't made a bloody mess of it—like the year he'd crafted everyone on *The Phoenix* a fishing rod and they'd had a competition to see who could catch the most. Little Hal hadn't had to fish for an entire week. But that had only happened the year after he'd taken her to a Tatawar festival. He'd sworn he hadn't known the kingdom had a penchant for fire dancers.

"Come over here," Idalia pressed. "I'm not the only one going back to the palace with a stomachache today, that's for certain. Gods above, I'm probably going to be sick tomorrow after this and the festival tonight."

Petra quirked her brow, but Hildi laughed.

"I'm hoping the both of you will have to roll me off this roof," Hildi joked. "I haven't seen a spread like this since Maker's Day."

Idalia waved a silver plate at Petra. "Come on. You know you want some."

Petra ducked under the edge of the canopy and took the plate. "How did you know it was my birthday?"

Hildi stuffed a spiced bun into her mouth. "Kelda," she said around the food.

Petra's brows pinched together. The queen was a water wielder, sure, but she'd cared enough about Petra's birthday that she'd had Idalia and Hildi put something together? Why?

Idalia grabbed one of the bowls filled with different types of nuts. "Everyone should be able to celebrate their birthday. Besides, we owe you for what you did in that draugr-infested hole." She shuddered, dropping a round red fruit into a bowl of spiced porridge.

Petra picked up a purple fruit shaped like a drop of water and an apple to be safe. The warmer seasons were always good for fresh fruit. Her eyes caught on a bowl of raspberries. A pang shot through her chest. Memories of her and her brothers with stained fingers as they picked from the berry patches all around Holmberg flashed one after another. Gram would have loved trying all the different fruits on this table. She plucked a few berries from the bowl and popped one in her mouth, savoring the tiny bit of tartness around the sweet.

"Grab that water skin, Petra, and we'll sit over here," Idalia said, balancing a precariously piled plate in each hand.

Petra grabbed the waterskin and followed behind them with her own plate. It wasn't heaping as theirs were, but there was a good array of foods. Fruits, buns, puddings, and even a little pie that looked like it was filled with some kind of cream.

A fur rug and several cushions had been placed under one of the trees. Idalia nearly lost her plates as she plopped down onto a large blue cushion. Hildi chuckled as she took a more sedate seat on a tan cushion. Petra found one leaned right up against the box for the tree where she would be able to see most of the rooftop.

"Oh, I'm glad you grabbed one of the tarts." Idalia picked up a similar tiny pie to the one Petra had on her plate. She bit into it with a moan.

Hildi pointed out the tear-dropped fruit. "When I came to Sida,

I hated figs. They might look tasty, but I still have to roast and drench them in honey to enjoy the flavor."

Petra picked up her bun. Perhaps it was better to start with something that looked familiar. She bit into the bun and flavor exploded on her tongue. The inside was stuffed with some sort of fruit, the spices blending in with the sweetness and creating a warmth in Petra's mouth.

Idalia giggled. "The stuffed buns are *amazing*. I made the same face when I had my first one."

"The food is certainly nothing to scoff at." Hildi bit off a hunk of her apple.

They fell into silence as food took up their attention. Petra took bites of everything. She nearly spit out the tart Idalia had mentioned, the flavor making Petra's lips practically pucker. The fig was much better, though the outside flesh was a bit chewy. Every type of bun was as glorious as the next. After living off brown bread for so long, it was like eating clouds from Valhalla itself.

Idalia groaned, leaning back in her large cushion with the last half of her second plate balanced on her stomach. "How old are you now, Petra?"

Petra swallowed the last raspberry she'd had on her plate. "Twenty-two."

"Really?" Idalia perked up. "I turn twenty-four in the winter."

Petra had guessed the lady to be much younger. Perhaps it was the youthfulness about her, but even when she'd been in Åldras, Petra had guessed her to be twenty at the most.

"Aw, lambs," Hildi said. "You haven't hit the stage where your joints start to creak and the wounds you sustain in training linger a little longer than they used to."

"You can't be that much older than us, Hildi," Idalia said.

"I turned twenty-eight just before spring."

Idalia tossed one of the nuts at Hildi, hitting her right in the forehead.

"Ow!" Hildi rubbed at the spot.

Petra set her plate on the top of the tree box, clearing her throat. "You have very good aim. I noticed it when you shot those draugr down." The compliment was genuine, even if Petra had said it to endear herself to the lady.

A flush stole over Idalia's cheeks. "I've used a bow since I was very young. My auntie insisted I have some way to defend myself, though my *father* hadn't appreciated it once he found out." She spat the word "father" as if it were a curse rather than an endearment.

"Good for you," Hildi said. "You ought to have shot the brute before he sold you to Anders."

Shadows bloomed in Idalia's gaze. "I wish I had. Maybe none of us would be in this situation, though I would have simply been replacing one tyrant with another. My brother is cut in my father's perfect image, though perhaps even crueler. I would have been glad to leave Aiktisah if I hadn't been trading one tormentor for another."

Petra's knuckles cracked she was clenching them so hard. "If you'd have asked us, Axel and I would have helped you disappear." She'd practically offered as much when they'd met. When Anders had abused her in front of an entire hall full of people. Idalia had been so quiet, but Petra had seen the fire in her. The creature waiting for the doors of her cage to crack just enough for her to escape.

Idalia sighed. "I thought about it. After Eva and I reached out to your crew to help Ella escape the Ekte, I considered asking you to take me. I even came up with a plan to fake a Häxa gift just to make it look like I needed you to smuggle me to Ljust Löfte."

"Wait." Hildi pointed a finger at Petra. "*You* were the ones smuggling Häxa out of Åldras?"

"Aye," Petra answered. "Though, from what Axel tells me, not at the same scale you lot have been."

Hildi leaned back on her hands. "Maker above, I should have known. It makes sense Mighty Axel would want to save the women like him. I just couldn't see how such an Åldran patriot would go against his beloved High King."

Petra snorted. "There is little love lost between Firmin and Axel. If Firmin could have, he would have killed Axel years ago and Axel would like nothing more than to tear the man's head from his shoulders."

"Then why fight for him?" Idalia asked. "If he hates High King Firmin so much, wouldn't he want to work against him?"

Petra picked at the skin of her lip. Idalia's question was valid, and Petra couldn't say she knew the answer anymore. Before, Axel had fought for Firmin because he'd believed they were avenging their families by fighting against the Sidans. But now that he knew the truth, what did he think? There had been hesitancy in his eyes when he'd been in the council room last week. A battle had raged there before he'd walked out.

A battle had raged in her own soul when he'd asked her what she wanted to do.

If she was being honest with herself, she wasn't quite sure anymore.

"It's probably because he blames us for Holmberg," Hildi said, "even though he wasn't the only one to lose family on that Maker-forsaken isle."

Petra blinked. The bite of Hildi's words told a story all their own.

"Who did you lose?" Petra asked.

Hildi met her gaze, and Petra saw a reflection of her own wounded soul.

"I lost my father that night."

Idalia reached over and touched the princess's arm. "I'm so sorry. I didn't even know. You talk of him as if he were still around."

Hildi nodded. "He wasn't even supposed to be there, but he'd arrived back from another mission early. Somehow, he ended up taking point to retrieve the Häxa."

Petra's entire body felt like a hive of wasps had crawled under her skin. "Your father went to save the Häxa?" Axel had told her about Caeso's list, that the mission to Holmberg had been to save Häxa in their town. But he hadn't said it was Hildi's father.

The story unfolded before Petra's eyes as Hildi spoke.

Her father had gone to Holmberg as captain of an elite group of fighters tasked with retrieving Häxa and smuggling them out of cities around Åldras. Sometimes, he would be covert, slipping in and out of towns like a wraith. Other times, he would set up a distraction to help draw attention away from what they were doing to keep the Ekte off their tails. Holmberg had been one of those. With Axel's powers being what they were, apparently the Ekte had kept special watch on the isle. The fight on the beach had to be believable. The

Sidans sent several ships to come close to the beach, while Hildi's father had taken a team into the town. Petra could see him. The hulking man with the hawkish nose and the dark eyes. *Demon eyes*, she'd once thought. He'd been confused when Mama had thrown her stones at him. He'd been there to save them. He'd been there to help them get out of Åldras.

And Petra had killed him for it.

The spiced buns in her stomach roiled.

Idalia shook her head. "I'm so sorry. That's a horrible way to lose your family." She looked to Petra. "Both of you lost those you love on that isle."

Petra could only nod. She didn't trust herself to speak. If she confessed to what actually happened that night, there was no way she would ever earn either woman's trust. No way they would ever forgive her for what she'd done.

"When I get to the gates of Valhalla or Heaven or wherever death takes me," Hildi said, "I fully plan on finding out who on that isle started that fire, and I plan on making them regret they ever existed."

# CHAPTER 15

## FESTIVALS

*Midsummer swept through Harligdam like a limping dog this year.
While the city was decorated in bright colors, the faces of the people
still held onto that deep-rooted exhaustion. The citizens did their best
to put on their smiles as the High King rode through the city on his
largest stallion, but once he disappeared, so did the smiles.*

— *FROM THE WRITINGS OF DORAN FINNSSON,*
*THE LAST KING OF GROVÖ*

The clip of his boots echoed down the hall, but Axel couldn't care less. It had taken him all day to gather the package tucked under his arm. Everything had to be just right. Petra was picky about certain things. Like the texture of her trousers. She hated when hair stuck to them and some of the wools weren't the right kind of itchy. She also hated cheap leather. If she found an item she liked, she would use it until it was practically falling apart.

When he'd gone with Little Hal on a tour of the city the week before, he'd seen the cloth merchant. The woman had practically taken the shirt off his back with what she charged for the gray wool, but he'd gotten the fabric and a full spool of dark thread. He'd had to sneak away to *The Phoenix* to put it all together, but Petra still had no idea what he'd been working on. She'd discovered the last four years' worth of gifts. It was hard to put together a surprise when you

159

didn't leave each other's sides for more than a day or two at a time. But this year would be different.

"Ho, Axel!" Enzo raised a hand in greeting as he came up the hall.

Axel gritted his teeth but slowed. When they were within a few feet of each other, Enzo stopped.

"I hope you and your crew aren't busy tonight. The festival has already begun in the city."

Axel held up the parcel, which had taken him at least an hour to retrieve from the bustling city. "I noticed."

Enzo grimaced. "I hope the insanity didn't put you off. It would be wonderful to have you join us."

"We plan to take in the sights, but we don't wish to cause any trouble. We'll keep our heads low."

"Right." Enzo snorted. "Because Mighty Axel is capable of being discrete."

Axel gave him a smug grin and continued past him. Just because he was well-known didn't mean he didn't know how to keep attention away from himself. He wouldn't have been nearly as successful smuggling Häxa out of Åldras if he didn't.

He chuckled as he rounded the corner toward their set of rooms, finding Petra, Hildi, and Idalia standing in the hall. Hildi said something and Idalia threw her head back and laughed. Petra's eyes glittered with humor as she met Axel's gaze.

It had been quite some time since he and Petra had been so often separated—the last being when the two of them had saved a Häxa family outside of Poppel. They'd had to split up for two weeks to leave false trails for the Ekte while the family escaped to Ljust Löfte.

Since the bargain had been struck with the queen, Axel continued to meet with Caeso every day, and Prince Enzo often asked Axel for time after noon had come and gone. Petra had spent more and more time with Hildi and Idalia. Axel had to admit he was a little jealous of their mornings together, but he couldn't begrudge Petra that time. While she was still closed off, something in her had brightened the day they'd gone after that vätte and had sparked every time she was with either Hildi or Idalia. He recalled words Mila had shared with him when he'd sat with her in one of the weaving huts in Holmberg.

"Women need each other," she'd said. "Like wolves, we gather together to support one another and protect each other. It's not good for any woman to be alone and often another woman is what one needs to heal and find strength."

He'd done his best to make sure Petra hadn't been alone, but even he could see he hadn't been enough. It stung, but it also showed him how much more Petra had been hiding behind her mask.

When this was all over, perhaps they would go to Ljust Löfte and she would have everything she needed. Though, watching the three of them stand there together, it seemed like she might need what was here in Sida.

"Good afternoon, ladies," Axel said, adding a little swagger to his step as he joined them.

"Axel," Idalia greeted, bobbing her head. "We were just returning Petra to you after our blissful morning."

Axel quirked a brow, looking at Petra.

Something in her eyes darkened and she shook her head. *I'll tell you later.*

Hildi groaned, setting a hand to her stomach. "I don't even know if I'll have room for the feasting tonight."

"At least you didn't actually make us roll you off the roof," Petra mumbled.

Idalia snickered. "Though it was a close thing."

Hildi rolled her eyes and turned to Axel. "Are you and your crew going to be joining in the festivities, Mighty Axel?"

He gave a small nod. "We hope to. Though, I do worry about how we'll be received." He'd gone into the city enough to feel the animosity toward anything Åldran, except the Häxa. If anything, the gifted women were revered.

The princess gave a flippant wave of her hand. "Your crew will be fine. Besides, everyone will be so far into their bottles of wine by sunset they won't even be able to see straight."

Axel should have guessed there would be more wine. He shifted the package under his arm. "I'll let the crew know they are free to join."

He wouldn't force anyone to go. Erik would likely stay in the palace to avoid the crowds as he was wont to do. Big Hal would figure out how to get into a party regardless of whether he was invited or not. It would probably do all of them good to get out and mingle with the Sidans. It would help for more of the crew to see that this war was folly. That they needed to stop Firmin from storming these shores.

Hildi nudged Petra with her elbow. "Make sure to keep this big oaf out of the wrestling matches. We don't need to start a riot."

A grin stretched across Petra's face. "I make no promises."

Idalia dragged Hildi away, both of them practically skipping down the hall.

Axel watched Petra as her gaze followed them. Her brows lowered slightly.

"I really wish I didn't have magic," she said. The comment cast a shadow over the light the women had left in their wake.

Axel carefully grabbed her elbow and drew her toward their room. "What's brought that on?"

She sighed, opening the door to their room and slipping in ahead of him. "Hildi. Her father was killed in Holmberg. He was the one that came to my house."

The parcel in Axel's hands crinkled as his hold on it tightened. "He was there to get you and Mila out."

"And I killed him." She sat on the edge of her bed as if she couldn't bear the weight of it anymore. "Is this all I'm ever going to be?"

Axel set the package down beside her and crouched in front of her knees. "What do you mean?"

Her gaze met his. There were no tears in her eyes, only a weariness belonging to a woman far older than her twenty-one—no, *twenty-two*—years.

"I mean am I cursed to burn everything and everyone good in my life? Am I only ever to be a revenant of secrets and death? A shadow? A demon? To taste hope and life only to have it snatched away every time? I can't even attempt to make acquaintances or, Allfather forbid, actual friends without ruining their lives. I mean, just look at us, Axel! What's the point of trying to make the world better if this bloody magic running through my veins is going to ruin it all?"

Axel set his hand on her knee. "You haven't ruined anything, Petra."

And he meant it. The hurt that had pierced him had lessened to a dull ache, one that bled for the young girl who never thought she had another choice. He wasn't perfect, and he well knew he had been a hothead as a youth. If she had told him back then, he had no idea how he truly would have reacted. He might have thrown their friendship to the wind and allowed Doran to haul her off to who knew where. Her secrets had kept her safe, but now?

"Are you going to tell her?" he asked.

Petra shook her head. Emphatically. "I can't. Whatever truce has built up between us will snap. The civility between the Sidans and the crew would evaporate. She'd have my head—or at least try to take it."

He didn't blame Petra for feeling as she did. How could he? It wasn't like he'd told the rest of the crew what had happened on Holmberg. He had kept her secret because he knew there would be no peace once the crew knew. Even the secret of her gender hadn't remained hidden more than a few weeks after they found out, not that they could be totally blamed for the bloody seer queen knowing the truth.

But these secrets wouldn't last. They couldn't. Not forever.

"Perhaps," he edged, "tonight could be a way for us to show these Sidans we're not all bad. You've obviously already formed an attachment to Hildi and Idalia. Maybe we ought to take the crew about today and prove to these people we're the same as them."

She reached up to pick at her lip, but he grabbed her hand. Her eyes narrowed in a half-hearted glare, but she refrained from tearing at her face.

"I think you'll have to worry more about Big Hal acting like a bloody idiot than garnering goodwill with these people," she said. "It's almost like they *want* us to be their friends."

Did the Sidans actually want that? There were always people attempting to get on Axel's good side, trying to weasel their way into his circles in the hopes they could use him. He was a weapon. He knew it. But, while the Sidans would definitely use him against Firmin in the coming skirmish, he couldn't imagine them forcing him to. Couldn't imagine King Leonardo or Caeso or even Enzo forcing him to throw his honor to the wind as Firmin had over the years.

It made something in Axel's stomach knot uncomfortably.

He nudged the package next to Petra with his elbow. "I got you something."

She half-heartedly glared at him. "I knew you were up to no good when I woke and you'd already disappeared."

He grinned. He'd met with Caeso earlier than usual so he would have time to collect the gift before Petra finished her morning. He'd hardly been able to sleep the night before, imagining what today would hold.

With nimble fingers, she unraveled the twine keeping the bundle together. The fabric opened to reveal the silver fur lining inside. The fur he'd had in the ship's hold already. If he remembered right, it was from one of the wolves that had targeted a village outside of Hjärta a year or so ago.

"A new cloak?" She shook it out, settling it over her shoulders. The gray fabric draped over her arms down to her calves.

"There's hidden pockets in the sides and bottom," Axel said. He grabbed the hem of the cloak and showed her where she could tuck things away.

She met his gaze. "It's wonderful. You even got it in gray instead of puke green."

"You're just jealous of my glorious cowl." He stood and went to his trunk to retrieve the garment. He glanced back to see her admiring the cloak and he couldn't fight back the grin that took over his face. It was precisely the reaction he'd hoped for.

"At least I'll be able to see you through a crowd," Petra said, running her hand over the soft fur of the inner lining. "No one but you would ever wear something so atrocious."

The lid of his trunk shut with a click as he slipped the cowl over his head. "Maybe I'll make it a fashion in Sida before we leave."

ᚠᚼᚢᚲᛟᚠᛦᛚ

AXEL WATCHED Petra as she studied the wares of the blacksmith in front of her. The burly man hadn't even looked their way, attending to other customers and avoiding them completely, but Petra likely didn't mind. She would have already chosen a blade if one had caught her eye.

Ulf picked up a set of kitchen knives, turning them this way and that. "Not half bad."

"I like the look of this." Big Hal studied a helmet, the steel shining in the flickering torchlight brightening the street. The helm covered from the base of the skull all the way to the forehead. There were slits for the eyes and a faceplate that covered the bottom half of the wearer's face. White horsehair added some flare to the top. Even Axel could admit the helmet was striking.

The blacksmith's face turned toward them slightly at Big Hal's enthusiasm, but he still said nothing.

Big Hal set the helmet atop his head. "Maybe Pet should get a helmet," he said, his voice muffled by the faceplate. "No one will realize she's a girl if her face is covered up all the time."

Petra glared at him, her fingers wrapping around the hilt of a large butcher knife on the table.

The two of them were going to kill each other one of these days.

Before Axel had to intervene, Little Hal popped up next to Petra.

"Do you think there's a spice trader close by?" Little Hal asked. "I'd love to get my hands on some cinnamon. I convinced one of the cooks in the palace kitchens to teach me how to make those spiced buns."

Ludvig was turned completely away from them, standing on tiptoe every few seconds to scan the crowd, as if looking for someone. "Pet, as a woman yourself, do you think this tunic is better for catching a lady's eye? Or should I go back to the palace and put on my brown?"

Petra rolled her eyes, releasing her hold on the huge knife, and Axel chuckled.

As Axel had thought, Erik had remained at the palace for the evening, though Little Hal would be going to join him so he could watch for their ship's raven. Not that the bird would have returned that quickly. It had only been a week since they'd sent the missive, and they couldn't expect it back with Doran's reply before next week. The wait might drive Axel to madness.

They finally left the blacksmith behind, trailing through the crowd as they moved from stall to stall. The Sidans had brought out their best for the festival. Traders from Tatawar had brought bright silks and colorful spices. There were traveling merchants with Åldran wools and dwarven steel—though the prices were steep, as such products were likely hard to get their hands on with the trade ban between the kingdoms. It didn't stop smuggling or trades through Tatawar though. Carts overflowing with baked goods, cups of wine, and every color of fruit Axel had ever seen stood on every street corner. His ears nearly rang with all the sound, but he would subject himself to it if it meant his crew would keep smiling.

What would it take for Åldras to enjoy this kind of happiness? Festivals in Åldras were always a time to celebrate, but Axel had never attended a festival like this. The air practically buzzed with excitement. With joy. There was nothing like this back home.

But if Sida won this war, could there be? Eventually?

Axel stopped in the middle of the street, his chest aching. Was he really even considering such a thing?

A gentle hand pressed into his shoulder. Petra met his gaze; her eyes filled with the very same ache he felt.

*The same questions plague me too.*

He took a deep breath and had to push the questions aside. They would wait for him until tomorrow. Tonight, he was supposed to forget these people were meant to be his enemy.

The six of them spread out through the stalls, each one caught up by the wares. It didn't take long until he'd lost sight of most of them. Even Little Hal had dashed off somewhere—hopefully he remembered to return to Erik before it got too late. The rest of the crew knew to keep a low profile, especially in enemy territory. They wouldn't go off on their own, staying in pairs.

"You have to try one of these," Petra said, materializing at his side with a warm bun in her hand. She couldn't have made it through one of the lines streaming out from the closest baked goods cart without him noticing. Hopefully, she'd left a coin or two behind.

When he bit into the bun, flavor exploded across his tongue.

"Whoa," he said, stuffing the rest of the bun in his mouth. "We're definitely going to need more of those."

She pulled another from her pocket, and he snatched it from her hand.

When they reached the next street, the crowd opened up into a familiar square. A fountain stood tall in the center, many of the partygoers tossing coins into the pool as they passed.

"If it isn't the infamous crew of *The Phoenix*!" a voice called.

*So much for keeping a low profile.*

Axel turned and found Enzo striding toward him, Hildi on his arm. The princess had completely transformed. Instead of her captain's uniform, she wore a dress of the deepest blue. There was still that sharpness about her, but the outfit transformed her from an intimidating warrior to a regal commander.

Idalia materialized right next to her, similarly dressed but in a bright yellow, hauling Roman behind her. "We're all here!" she hollered over the crowd. She pulled away from Roman and attached herself to Petra's arm. "Have you seen the Häxa display yet?"

Petra shook her head. At the flash of interest that brightened her eyes, Axel took a step closer. If she wanted to see the Häxa, he would take her. Tonight, he would give her anything she wanted. She deserved this kind of revelry. If it were up to him, every single one of her birthdays would have her feeling like the entire world was celebrating her.

"You can't miss the demonstrations," Enzo agreed. "Kelda helps the girls come up with their tricks, and they usually put on quite a show. Come along."

The merry group followed behind the prince. Axel held back so he and Petra could be at the rear. There was still so much to see, and he really didn't want to miss any of it. That, and it was easier to pretend they were alone when no one was watching from behind them.

"Is there anything in particular you're hoping to do tonight?" Axel asked, his voice low.

Petra shrugged. "Not really."

As they turned down another street, Roman and Idalia worked the crowd, Roman flashing charming smiles and Idalia greeting every person who met her eye. She complimented almost every stall they passed and accepted many a small flower from children who gifted them to her. If Anders wasn't such an idiot, he might have realized how easily the woman could get people to like her. Her charm was a force to be reckoned with.

Enzo and Hildi were their own sort of charming. As the next ruling couple, they greeted the people with grace and kindness. Undisguised respect beamed from the faces of the citizens that greeted them.

Like they had earned the regard of their people, not demanded it.

Axel had to pull his eyes away, lest someone see a similar feeling in his own expression.

Petra walked beside him, her gaze flicking across the crowd. The vigilance was still present, but there was also interest in her eyes as she took everything in one moment at a time.

"I heard there's dancing in one of the squares," Axel said, leaning down next to her ear. "Maybe after the Häxa demonstration, we could go."

She looked up at him, a strange squint to her eye. As if she were hiding something. "You want to dance?"

"It could be fun to watch. Besides, I think it would behoove us to mingle as much as we can. The Sidans might not look at us with such daggers in their eyes if we can show them we're just here to have a good time."

Enzo and Hildi slowed their steps, coming to either side of them.

"What are you two whispering about back here?" Enzo asked from Axel's left, a mischievous glint to his eye.

"Probably how to slaughter us in our sleep," Hildi answered from Petra's right.

Axel coughed, but Petra smiled.

"You've found us out," she said.

It was Enzo's turn to cough.

Hildi threaded her arm through Petra's. "Now, don't hold back. I expect the worst. Poisoned daggers, hot iron pokers, the works." She pulled Petra after Roman and Idalia.

Axel remained only a step behind, Enzo keeping pace beside him as the women spoke back and forth.

"If I didn't know any better," Enzo piped up, "I would say the two of them were friends."

*Friends.*

It was exactly what Petra had been working toward. Exactly what he was afraid of.

The street wound north, down away from the castle. The buildings grew smaller the farther they went, closer together. Children lifted wooden swords and wreaths of flowers over their heads. Couples walked arm in arm, leaning close together as they pointed out different wares.

Wind brushed past Axel's ear, ruffling his hair and bringing along the sweet melody of voices and trill of flutes. The breeze carried away the song before Axel could even grasp it. The farther down the road they walked, the more the wind carried the tune until Axel heard the familiar lyrics. He'd heard it played back in Åldras. His voice joined the throng of singers as the crowd around him took up the song.

*"Sisters, it's time again.*
*Look and you'll find*
*The solstice has past,*
*Nature's forces aligned,*
*The power of your mirth*
*Has been there all along.*
*Now let it find worth.*
*Give it life with a song."*

The street finally led them into an open square. Streams of water shot through the air, catching the light of the lanterns scattered throughout the space. A large platform had been erected around this square's fountain, holding young women above the crowd. The whole structure was a latticework of stones, woven together with flowers that bloomed in different colors. A current of air carried petals across the square, raining them slowly on the crowd.

*"It came from within*
*But now flies about.*
*As quiet as a whisper,*

*Then loud as a shout.*
*You can't flee its pull.*
*The music will find you.*
*It's left, then it's right.*
*Now it's right behind you.*
*Is it gone? Have you lost it?*
*Not so. It has found you.*
*It's above. It's below.*
*Now it's all around you.*
*Let it into your feet.*
*Just give it a chance*
*And walk on the wind*
*In a wind-walker's dance.*

Petra picked a white petal out of her hair even as her eyes remained transfixed on the stage where several of the girls sang and played instruments. Around the base of the platform, dancers had cleared the space and were spinning in a circle, their feet pounding the same beat as the drums on the stage.

*"First, it's so quiet*
*It's almost unheard.*
*Soon, it's so loud*
*Some may find it absurd.*
*Then it takes wing,*
*Over hill over dale.*
*But soon it returns,*
*Like a thunderous gale."*

"Come on!" Roman hollered, capturing Idalia's hand and dragging her through the crowd. Idalia threw her head back with a laugh but let him carry her forward until they were fully immersed in the dance.

Enzo bowed to his wife. "Your Highness, will you join this fool in a dance?"

Hildi smacked his arm, but they joined the throng as well.

A tingling feeling started up in Axel's limbs, his foot tapping out the beat as the dancers continued to spin to the rhythm of the chorus. He nearly jumped when a hand touched his arm.

Petra tilted her head toward the dancers. "If you want to dance, you should. There are plenty of girls to choose from."

If it was the feel of her skin on his, the beat of the dance, or the slow ache in his heart, he didn't know, but the cautions he regularly had to repeat in his head when he looked at Petra in the way a man looks at a woman fled him.

> *"Sisters, take hands.*
> *The song's power is ours.*
> *The tune greens the Earth*
> *And gives bloom to the flowers.*
> *Hold tight to it, sisters,*
> *For soon it is gone*
> *And cannot return*
> *Till next night yields to dawn."*

Axel placed his hand over hers and leaned in close. "I would dance, but the only woman I would ever want to dance with is standing right here."

# CHAPTER 16

# A FRIEND

If Petra could even come up with any words to respond to Axel, she was saved from having to utter them as the crowd burst into applause. She quickly snatched her hand away from his grasp.

Wōden's one good eye, all she'd been thinking about was how he'd looked at her the same way in the forest outside Ljust Löfte. When he'd said her name. When he'd claimed her lips with his own. When he'd broken through walls Petra had built for so long. Her pulse galloped at her throat, the fires around the square seeming to flare at the corners of her eyes. With one look and a few words, they were back in that forest.

What was he thinking? He knew what she was. Wasn't there still a part of him that was angry with her? That would still look at her and see his father's murderer? Yes, they'd come to some sort of accord, but his words threatened the tentative bridge they were trying to rebuild between them. The words shook her at the least and would break her if he kept it up.

She couldn't let herself fall for him. Couldn't give him her heart.

It would kill him.

"That was marvelous!" Idalia cheered, appearing with Roman in tow. "I've seen some of the girls practicing during their studies, but I never would have guessed the actual event would turn into something this grand."

"It certainly lends to a good time," Roman agreed. He frowned up at Axel. "You two ought to have joined us."

Idalia bounced on the tips of her toes. "That can't possibly be the last dance of the evening. I certainly hope all of us go to bed with sore feet in the morning."

Petra didn't know if she wanted to throttle Idalia or kiss her. The conflicting temptations churned with the words Axel had whispered in her ear.

Freyja's golden tears, she needed another sweet bun. Or something stronger.

Hildi slid up next to them. Her dark blue dress shimmered in the torchlight like the ocean on a starlit sea and made her skin glow like moonlight. It was similar in style to the one Petra had worn in Ljust Löfte, except the sleeves stopped at her elbows. Her appearance was in sharp contrast to Idalia's bright dress and dark skin. Even the cuts of their dresses were different, Idalia's all soft curves and layers with the yellow overdress over a creamy underdress while Hildi's was all sharp angles and simplicity. Hildi's was also far more daring with its neckline and light beading on her bodice where Idalia's was almost sweet but with far more embellishment on the overdress. Night and day. Sol and Máni. Two opposites, yet complementary to one another.

And in very sharp contrast to the rough clothing Petra had put on. She looked down at her brown trousers and gray tunic. It had been far too hot to wear the cloak Axel had gifted her, but she almost wished she'd put it on.

Hildi met Petra's gaze when it finally lifted. A smile stretched across the captain's face. It was as sharp as the sword she usually carried at her side. The threat of it certainly seemed just as deadly.

"Roman," she said, "I think you ought to take your brother and Axel over to the wrestling matches. Us girls need to freshen up."

Enzo slipped through the crowd and joined his wife. "Did I hear someone say wrestling?"

Axel shifted beside Petra. "I don't think—"

"Good idea," Petra cut him off. She didn't look up at him. She had to wrangle her thoughts back under control. Between the siren song of the torches around them and Axel's warmth next to her,

Petra couldn't think. Couldn't stop herself from doing something foolish. Putting some distance between them would give her a moment to gather herself.

"That sounds *divine*," Idalia agreed. "I've needed to use a chamber pot for a good half hour."

The princes chuckled and Hildi shook her head in exasperation.

Petra finally turned to Axel. "We'll meet you at the matches."

There was definitely an argument forming on his tongue, but he seemed to swallow it back and gave a nod. "Just don't get into any trouble."

She plastered a wicked grin on her face. "I'm definitely not going to make that promise."

Idalia and Hildi both took one of her arms.

"Off we go!" cheered Idalia.

They dragged her out of the square and back up the large hill toward the palace. People approached both Hildi and Idalia, hawking their wares and giving the women free samples of their inventory. Idalia received nearly twice as much as Hildi did, the people of Bellator enamored with the lady and her romantic story. Several citizens welcomed her warmly to Bellator and Idalia walked about with a bright flush to her cheeks. They passed at least two public bath houses before Petra finally pulled them to a slower pace.

"Where are we actually going?"

Hildi gave her that dangerous smile again. "What? You can't wait and find out?"

There was a challenge there. Petra pursed her lips as her stomach twisted slightly. "I don't do surprises."

"Well, I like surprises," Idalia said, pulling Petra up the road again.

"That's because you seem to always be in the know about them," Petra retorted.

Idalia flicked her dark hair back over her shoulder. "Precisely."

They dragged her down the street until they reached a stall. A woman stood behind the display table covered in strips of fabrics and beads, stitching what looked like the branches of Yggdrasil onto a stretch of brown fabric. Behind her, several garments hung on frames. Vibrantly colored tunics and cloaks shimmered with embellishment in the torchlight. Dresses in multiple sizes and styles draped down to the ground, beads sparkling in different patterns down the skirts and across the bodices. One ensemble was a forest green over-dress, nearly the color of Axel's eyes when he looked at her a certain way, over a blue underdress with a wide neck and silver knots beading along the edges of the collar and elbow-length sleeves.

"If it isn't my favorite customers," the woman said, getting to her feet and greeting Hildi and Idalia.

Hildi grinned. "Juno, I need another one of your wraps for my friend here."

Juno looked to Petra. Mainly, at her chest. "Doesn't seem like she needs much of my help."

Idalia tugged Petra closer. "I believe she's already wearing something similar, but we know it can't be half as comfortable as what you make."

An amused, if not slightly flattered, expression flashed across Juno's face. "Come with me, girl. You'll want to step into the changing room."

Hildi and Idalia pushed her around the table to the back of the stall where curtains had been stretched between two buildings. Juno reached into a trunk, rifling through straps of cloth until she drew out what she'd been looking for. She held out two different items, one just a thick band of cloth that laced up somehow and the other with two thin strips of fabric hanging off it with even more laces.

"Go in there and try them on," Juno said.

Petra took them. What on earth was she supposed to do with them? They were too short to be any sort of scarf. Too big to be a sort of head wrap.

Hildi cleared her throat. "They're for your breasts, idiot."

"Oh. *Oh*." Petra slipped back behind the curtain and yanked her vest and tunic off. Now that Hildi had said it, she could see it. She carefully unwound her chest wrapping, doing her best not to let it touch the dusty ground. She tried not to get it dirty as much as she could. It was hard enough finding the right kind of material to bind her breasts properly and not chafe her skin. She tried on the strapless wrap first. Wouldn't the bloody thing simply slip off when she was doing anything? But once she had it tied with the laces in the front, she found it didn't even budge from her chest, the way it was sewn hugging her skin. Thunder's beard, it felt like her skin was breathing for the first time. The binding still hid the curves of her chest but didn't make her skin itch. It also took way less fabric and adjusted with the laces.

The other one had a very different effect.

With the way the straps pulled up her chest and the thicker fabric formed over her chest, there was no way anyone would ever be fooled into thinking she was anything but a woman.

Heat suffused her cheeks, and she quickly changed back into the other piece.

She put the rest of her clothing back on and slipped back out onto the street.

Idalia and Hildi met her with knowing smiles.

"How do you feel?" Hildi asked.

"Like I can actually breathe."

Idalia giggled. "Isn't it fantastic? Hildi brought me the second day I was here, as I hadn't arrived with any clothing. I nearly bought everything in Juno's shop that very day."

The seamstress grinned. "You can come by my shop any time you like, my lady."

The three of them laughed as Petra reached for her money pouch. The blue dress caught her eye again, but she had no need for one. Especially after what happened the last time she wore a bloody dress.

Hildi grabbed her hand. "This one is on me." She turned to Juno. "We'll buy three more of each wrap and that dress she's been eyeballing since we arrived."

Petra shook her head. "I can pay my own way, and I won't get the dress."

Idalia flounced forward. "Hildi can pay for her wrappings, but I'm buying the dress. Consider it a birthday present. You can send a bill up to the palace."

"I really don't—"

"Done," Juno said, reaching back to pull the dress from where it hung.

Petra turned to Idalia. "Why are you both so insistent on this?"

"Listen, Petra." Hildi put a hand on Petra's shoulder. "I know you're used to doing things on your own and isolating from others to protect yourself. You know better than everyone else when someone acts nice they're actually looking to exploit you. If anyone understands that it's Idalia and me."

Idalia snorted. "We understand more than most people on this planet."

Juno placed Petra's new clothing on the table and took Hildi and Idalia's coin.

"I'll be totally frank," Hildi continued as Juno counted out the change, "and say that even we're trying to get something from you. We can't say that we don't hope that getting into your good graces will mean you can influence the Åldrans in our favor. We'd be hypocrites to say we don't hope to get you to like us so we can use you to help us get what we want. But, more than that, we want to be your friend. Even if you weren't Åldras's demon and you didn't have Mighty Axel wrapped around your little finger, you're a remarkable woman, and we want to spend time with you and do silly girl things and ogle the men we get to call ours just because we like doing it together."

"Absolutely!" Idalia took both their hands. "I think the Maker or gods or whatever brought us together. Three women from vastly different worlds who can change each other's lives for the better. We can help one another. Like going to the Häxa lessons. I might not be able to use magic at all, but I've learned so much about how their magic works just by sitting and talking with them."

Petra's fingers tightened around theirs. This was exactly what she and Axel had hoped would happen, but now that it was here, she faltered. She didn't deserve this. She'd killed Hildi's father and had planned on sending Idalia back to her rotten husband. There was no way she could truly tell them everything she'd done to hurt them.

But they weren't asking her to share the past. They were asking her to help them carve the future. A future where none of them would have to hide. Where they could be themselves. Where they wouldn't have to be alone. Maybe Petra could stay in Sida. Could figure out her magic and keep it controlled. Eventually, she could leave Åldras behind her.

And, perhaps, Axel would consider staying too. How could he not after seeing what life was like here? If anything, being here had only proven how backwards Firmin ruled over Åldras. What if they stayed and let themselves carve out a future free of Firmin and his ilk? Free of the Ekte. They could be with the Häxa. Could help them in ways they'd never been able to in Åldras.

They wouldn't have to hide anymore.

She met Hildi's gaze, then Idalia's. Her stomach turned in knots even as her ribs loosened around her lungs.

"I'll think about it."

Idalia let go of her hand and threw her arms around her. "I just knew it. Even that night when you took me out of Firmin's great hall, I knew you and I were going to be great friends." She pulled away. "Of course, I didn't know you were a woman at the time. Really, I have no idea how you do it. There was no doubt in my mind that you were anything else but Lord Petyr."

Petra shrugged. "People see what they want to see, especially when they have no reason to suspect anything else."

"Well, I want to see some more of those spiced buns," Hildi said, grabbing the package holding Petra's new clothing, "and then some shirtless men try to throw each other around a sparring ring while I drape myself on the arm of my deliciously attractive husband. Though, by the time we get to the ring, he'll likely be included in the lineup of fighters, and I'll have to be satisfied with watching him compete."

It didn't take them long to rejoin the throng of festival goers. It was so much bigger than any festival Petra had attended in Åldras, likely because Sida was far more traversable than the isles of her homeland. If one didn't have a boat to get around with in Åldras, there was no chance of getting out of a town. Here, people could walk with their own two feet and get to any one of the villages.

Most of the crowds were making their way toward the military headquarters on the east side of the city, where the competitions were taking place. The sounds grew more and more boisterous the closer they got. When they finally reached the road leading to the headquarters, the crowd was so thick Hildi had to take lead and use her captain voice to get people to move out of the way. By the time they reached the edges of the fighting rings, they had a retinue of guards escorting them through. If Caeso wasn't careful, Hildi would take his job out from under him, though Petra suspected Sida wouldn't be too upset over it with how many of them followed Hildi's progress through the crowd with stars in their eyes.

The thickest throng of people stood on the far side of the street. A boisterous roar thundered as their hands flew into the air with their cheers. While Petra was taller than most, she still couldn't see what the commotion was about.

Hildi turned back to Petra with a curved brow. "How much do you want to bet our boys are right in the middle of that?"

Petra shook her head. "I know better than to make a losing bet."

Idalia laughed and practically skipped alongside them as they finally breached the crowd and pressed up against the fighting ring.

Axel and Enzo stood in the center.

Both shirtless.

Petra's gaze focused on the muscles of Axel's back. They rippled every time he shifted. The gold of his skin and hair only deepened with the light of the singing torches surrounding them. Petra's gaze trailed from his shoulders to his lower back, her mouth going dry for some reason. Why his shirtless torso had been affecting her lately, she refused to even think about. He towered over the crowd around him, a god among men.

As if he felt her gaze, Axel pivoted in her direction. His smirk turned absolutely smug when his green eyes met hers. Wōden's one good eye, he was such a showoff.

The words he'd said only an hour ago echoed in her head.

*The only woman I would ever want to dance with is standing right here.*

Why did he have to say things like that when she was trying so hard to keep the walls up between them? He already knew all her secrets. Knew the worst parts of her. Why would he want to be with her at all? All of this would be so much easier if he hated her. It would be so much simpler. She could help him fix their kingdom, then she could disappear and let him live the rest of his life in peace. Let the past be the past.

Hildi chuckled, leaning against the wooden railing put up around the ring. "My night just got ten times better."

Enzo was certainly a specimen to behold. His sweat-soaked skin glimmered in the torchlight. There were faint scars all across his torso, the story of his years of fighting battles told in the pale lines written on his flesh. At least two of the scars had been gifts from Petra herself, if she remembered right. Hopefully, he didn't hold too deep of a grudge. Dark hair coated most of his chest. His feet were bare, toes digging into the sand that made up the ring. His dark eyes glittered as he charged Axel.

Petra sucked in a sharp breath, but Axel went limp, allowing Enzo to take him to the ground. She blew out the breath. When they were younger, Kol had been angry with Axel and had tried to tackle him. He'd broken his collarbone and dislocated his shoulder. Axel could hold himself as stiff as a stone wall with his strength, but he'd always been so aware of his own body.

The sand sprayed as the two men grappled, Enzo trying to lock Axel into a hold. Axel's laugh shook the ground under Petra's boots.

His green eyes met hers across the space. His grin turned slightly dangerous. *Enjoying the show?*

Heat raced up her chest into her cheeks. She narrowed her eyes. *Show off.*

He got an arm free from Enzo's grip and used it to push himself up. Without even a moment's hesitation, he stood, dislodging Enzo and sending him back into the sand.

Groans echoed through the crowd as the judges called the end to the round and Enzo pushed himself to his feet. Axel grabbed his shirt where it hung on the railing and shrugged it on.

Hildi's displeasure joined the crowd's. "It shouldn't be legal to be that strong and handsome."

"It's to make up for all the stupid ideas he comes up with," Petra responded.

A smug grin stretched across Axel's face as he strode to where they stood. The mischief in his eyes told her he'd definitely heard what she said.

Enzo joined them, and Roman materialized at Idalia's elbow.

"Well?" Idalia asked. "What's next?"

# Chapter 17

## Ravens

*The kings have all been summoned by Firmin, though Haukr and Leif are taking far longer than the rest of them. While they were just here for Axel's trial, there isn't much room to ignore the summons of the High King. Especially not one who seems to be losing his temper at every inconvenience, more so now than I've ever seen. I suppose we'll all need to make sure our ships are ready to follow Firmin's whims to and fro. Though, when haven't we done so?*

— *From the writings of Doran Finnsson, the last King of Grovö*

The entire crew sat on the deck of *The Phoenix*, watching the sunset at the end of their fourth week in Sida. Erik had decided they all needed a break from palace life and put them to work on the ship. Axel leaned against the gunwale, a carving knife in hand and a pile of wood shavings at his feet. The little wooden horse finally began to take shape.

*Hopefully, Princess Aggie likes horses.* He'd attempted a bird earlier, but he kept breaking the wings off on accident. The driftwood in Sida seemed to be more brittle than that found on Åldran shores. He'd have to make the horse's legs a bit thicker so they wouldn't snap in the little girl's hands.

"We can't possibly abandon our mission," Big Hal said, aggressively polishing the handle of his battle hammer. "Even if we wanted to let the Sidans get away with everything, Firmin would see our heads roll."

The image of Olav's head landing at his feet flashed through Axel's mind.

He glanced over at Little Hal, the boy's face having gone slightly pale.

"Watch it, Big Hal," Petra snapped, her own gaze flicking to Little Hal.

Big Hal tossed down his rag. "Don't growl at me, Pet. This is more your fault than anyone else's. If you hadn't dressed up like a stupid girl and gotten kidnapped in Ljust Löfte, we wouldn't be in this situation. We'd be happily sailing around Åldras taking care of our people rather than bowing and scraping at the bloody Sidans. But no! You had to put on a skirt and ruin everything. We're all going to die because of you."

Petra's face slipped into a blank mask, but Axel could see the fury in the white knuckles of her fingers as she detangled a net beside Erik. Big Hal was going to pay for that comment.

"Enough," Axel said. "Sniping at each other isn't going to get us anywhere. We have a meeting with the Sidan council again tomorrow night, and I'd like to go to them with some sort of idea about how to stop war from breaking out."

Because that was what needed to happen. Axel couldn't possibly let Firmin win this war. Not after what he'd seen. If Åldras was to have any chance of a future, they needed the Sidans on their side. They needed to stop Firmin's reign of terror and find harmony in the isles once again.

Ludvig's head of unruly hair popped up from the hold in the middle of the ship. "If there was a way to find common ground between the two kingdoms, we might be able to start up a conversation that could mutually benefit both sides."

"What do you think everyone's been trying to do during this entire armistice, idiot?" Big Hal rolled his eyes.

Axel stood. "Enough, Big Hal. If all you're going to do is gripe, you can go for a swim. Ten laps the length of the ship for your words and twenty for being a bloody moron."

Big Hal ground his teeth together but stood and kicked off his boots. With curses dripping from his lips, he leaped over the side of the ship and stomped toward the water.

"He's not completely wrong," Ulf said. "There isn't much we can do to stop a battle from happening. This war has become too bloody and gone on too long for anyone to simply let it go. One of the kingdoms is going to come out the victor in this, and I'd like for it to be the right one if we can make that happen."

"But which one is right?" Ludvig folded his arms over the edge of the hold and set his chin atop them. "Do we let High King Firmin and King Anders continue persecuting Häxa in Åldras, keep letting them rule over everyone with an iron fist and no end in sight? Or do we sit back while we watch our brothers be slaughtered on the fields of battle without our help?"

"I think the question we should be asking ourselves," Erik said, "is what is best for Åldras? Will Firmin's rule and the rule of his kin bring about the peace we are striving for, or will Leonardo and his sons be the ones to usher in a better Åldras for the future?"

Axel rubbed a hand down his face. Everything Father had taught him about loyalty to one's country screamed at him to say they couldn't give up fighting for Åldras because it was their homeland. They had sworn to serve her king and protect her people. But what he knew to be right seemed to push against the traditions he'd grown up with.

No matter what, he didn't know how Åldras could find peace with Firmin on the throne.

What did the High King believe he could do? Even if he hadn't been to Bellator and seen how equipped the Sidans were for an attack, he surely had spies in the city to feed him that information. So, he had to have something in his pocket. He had the Ekte, sure, which would even the playing field against the Häxa, but there were still numbers to consider.

Unless Firmin didn't think they were going to win. Unless he believed they had one last ditch effort to turn the tides of the war and he'd been waiting for something to rally the kings together, to help him. Was that why he'd attempted to frame Axel? Why he'd gathered the kings to charge Axel with kidnapping Princess Ella and taking her to the Great Mother? Was he trying to sow helplessness in the other kings by framing Axel to call into question their loyalty to Åldras's hero? Trick them into believing only in what Firmin could offer them instead of what was right for their kingdom?

Axel sat on his trunk. If Firmin had gotten away with his deceit, it could potentially have united the kings to him. There were quite a number of the kings who shared Axel's feelings about the war—both in regard to the Häxa and the Sidans. There were several who had voiced their desire to resolve the conflict after the armistice had been signed. They were likely the only reason Firmin had entertained the idea of a treaty and allowed the princes to negotiate. But if those kings had become suspicious of Axel as the High King had hoped they would be, there would have been a waver in their resolution. Likely, Axel's betrayal would have been only the beginning of his machinations.

Queen Eva had saved not only Axel the night she'd confessed to sending him with Princess Ella, but likely the kings up to this point as well. Firmin still would have rallied the kings to gather their men, but no one would have been given the time granted to them by the mission to retrieve Idalia.

But why? Why now?

Little Hal sat at the edge of the hold next to him. "I like Bellator. I don't want Firmin to come and attack the city. There are good people here."

Axel could do nothing but agree. "Aye, but what about the good people in Åldras? Do you think we ought to abandon them?"

The lad's face turned solemn. "But if Sida is able to finish this war, won't that mean the people in Åldras will be safe too?"

When the question was said out loud, the answer felt obvious. Åldras could have what Sida did. The Häxa could be with their families. Firmin would no longer abuse the loyalty of the citizens.

Sida winning this war seemed more and more like an inevitability.

And Axel didn't think it would be such a bad thing.

A flutter of feathers sounded overhead.

Black wings descended on Little Hal's head. The lad hardly flinched as the large raven planted its feet on his shoulders.

The raven hopped down, showing the band of metal cuffed to its ankle.

Little Hal pulled a nut from a pouch at his waist but paused when he looked at the bird. "Oh, hello Munnin."

It was Doran's raven, not theirs. Axel straightened. Little Hal had helped raise both ravens, naming them Huggin and Munnin after the famous pair of ravens who attended to Wōden and whispered the events of Yggdrasil in his ears. Little Hal had given one to Doran a little over a year ago, after training him as a messenger. Doran had three ravens he used regularly, but Munnin was his swiftest.

Little Hal held the nut out to the raven and slipped a scrap of parchment from the metal ring on the bird's ankle. He didn't even break the wax coating, protecting it from the weather.

Axel cracked it open.

*F and A will attack at the start of Heyannir.*

*Plague in Hjärta and Generös*

*I am coming.*

"Rocks," Axel breathed. He ran a hand through his hair.

Petra appeared in front of him and snatched the note from his hand. Her eyes darted over Doran's words. "So that's why he's rallied the kings."

Axel nodded, words escaping him.

Firmin wouldn't want to wait if there was a plague.

He would attack Sida now, before he lost more men.

Before the plague had a chance to take his army.

If the sickness had already spread from Hjärta to Generös, it was on two of the biggest isles in Åldras. There were hamlets and settlements scattered throughout those isles, many likely not even on maps simply because of how remote they were. If it already moved across water, it had likely made its way to other isles as well. The last plague to sweep over Åldras had been half a century ago, but it had taken the lives of many and crippled the kingdom. It had been what started the animosity for the Häxa. Many had blamed them for the illness, mostly because the Häxa had been the only ones able to heal the people. But once suspicion bloomed, it was as difficult to kill as a plague.

"Allfather save us," Erik said, reading the note for himself. "This is no longer about pride."

"No," Petra said, coming up beside Axel. "Now, it's about survival."

ᚠᚼᚲᛟᚠᛦᚱ

"THE HIGH KING and his brother will arrive in three weeks' time," Axel announced. He held his hands stiffly behind his back as the councilors in their benches jumped to their feet.

Outrage swept through the council hall. Idalia's face had gone ghostly white and Roman reached for her hand; his own expression twisted in rage. Enzo and Hildi stood with grim faces next to Caeso, their voices quiet as they spoke back and forth with each other.

The only people not boiling over with shock were the king and queen.

While Axel couldn't see the queen's expression, he watched the king sitting back in his throne. King Leonardo's dark eyes were trained on Axel, not a spark of surprise crossing his face. No, he actually looked a bit sad. As if he'd known all along this would be the result of this war. That peace had never truly been an option, yet he'd hoped.

Axel knew exactly what that felt like.

The king pushed himself from his throne. The room quieted as he slowly stepped down from the dais and stopped in front of Idalia. He crouched down in front of her, eyes crinkled at the edges as he gave her a soft smile.

"I'm sorry, Idalia, that so much of this has been on your shoulders, but we need you to be ready to face what comes next. When your husband arrives on that beach, will you fight at our side?"

Two tears tracked down each side of her face as she blinked. "Your Majesty?"

King Leonardo set a large hand on her shoulder. "I need you to be sure when your husband provokes you that you will be strong. Your husband isn't a man who takes loss with honor. He will attack you personally. He'll say things to make you question your choices and attempt to cast doubt on your character as well as ours. It won't be easy, but you must not forget that what he says and the things he does are not your fault. You are a princess of Tatawar. You are a beloved lady of Sida. There are many people who love you and are willing to fight for you. You must not allow him to make you forget."

Idalia shuddered and Axel could hear her pounding heart from all the way across the room. "I won't. I care about your people too. I'm willing to fight for them."

The king gave her shoulder a soft squeeze and got to his feet. "We are to prepare for a siege. We have three weeks to gather those from the outlying villages, but we aren't to incite panic. We must have order. We'll use this time to bring our people together not only in body, but in heart and mind as well. We'll meet again three days from now to discuss possible strategies to accomplish this. This meeting is adjourned."

Axel turned away, Petra at his side.

"Mighty Axel, a word?"

The king's voice was quiet, not his usual boom. No one else in the hall even glanced at him. Had they even heard the summons?

Axel twisted back around and found the king standing next to his throne, a female guard at his side.

An air whisperer.

Axel turned to Petra, but the air stirred around by his ear.

"Tell your demon to go."

Axel stilled. The king was up to something. Axel nearly told him to go stuff his commands up his arse, but he grabbed Petra's elbow.

"Will you go check with Little Hal at the ship? I told the lad to keep his eyes out for Huggin."

Petra glanced over her shoulder at the king, her gaze sharp with obvious knowing. She met his eye, lowering her chin in an almost imperceptible nod.

*I'll stay close.*

She strode out of the room, making a show of clearly leaving.

Once she disappeared along with the rest of the council, the doors shut, leaving him with the king and queen in the empty space.

Axel could almost hear Petra's steps as she skulked back around. Where she would find a place to perch, Axel had no idea.

"Is something the matter?" Axel asked.

The king raised a finger, and the air whisperer spread her fingers.

The air moved around them, creating a bubble of silence.

*Hel's halls.* Even if Petra could find somewhere to eavesdrop, she wouldn't hear a bloody thing.

King Leonardo lowered his hand. "We know what is happening in Åldras."

Axel's gut twisted into knots, but he kept his hands loose at his sides. "I would hope so. I've been keeping my end of the bargain and apprising you of any developments."

"You and I both know that's not what I was referring to. We know about the plague." He gestured to Queen Kelda. "We've known about it since you arrived. The illness is not one I would wish on even your people, Mighty Axel. It will be for those afflicted as if they are drowning inside their own bodies. It's an awful sickness that will take many if your kingdom does not put a stop to it before it's too late."

Axel took a step toward them. "Is that why you've been so at ease with all of this? Why you've been preparing your men for a conquest rather than a battle? I've seen the drills Caeso has been running in the barracks. You're not thinking of peace any longer."

"All I've ever thought about is peace." King Leonardo leaned back in his throne. "Peace is the reason we haven't conquered your kingdom in the twenty years I've sat on this throne. In the forty years my own father sat here as well. Sida isn't a nation built on bloodshed. We preach in our temples and our houses of worship that we are to be makers like our Maker before us. We are not to be makers of destruction or war but of peace and life. It's why we were the first to offer aid to the Häxa when they needed refuge. Why we don't allow Tatawarie slaves within our borders. But that does not mean we won't fight for what we believe is our right to protect."

The king stood, taking measured steps until he stood before Axel, standing eye to eye.

"I am through with this war, Mighty Axel. We will finish it."

The resolve the king spoke with reverberated in Axel's bones.

He'd known it would come to this. Hadn't he been asking for it? Wasn't this what he wanted?

Axel didn't break his gaze from the king's somber face. "Why are you telling me this?"

"Because you're going to have to decide which side of this war you're on. You're going to have to choose who you're willing to watch die and who you are willing to let live."

# CHAPTER 18

## A CATALYST

When Petra arrived for her morning duties with Queen Kelda, only the queen and Hildi occupied the training room. After their demonstration at midsummer, the Häxa had been given the week off. Apparently, they only attended classes once a week until the two months leading up to the midsummer festival, where they would gather with the queen to practice for the demonstration. The other times, they would be taught by their mothers or others at home and would meet at the end of the week to practice together.

Hildi had opened up about much of what it had been like to grow up in Sida after she'd fled from Åldras. Without her mother to teach her, Hildi had been instructed by some of the elder Häxa in the city. Queen Kelda had also taken her under her wing when she had been a councilor to the king. Before she became queen.

Petra took a seat in one of the cushions next to them, folding her legs underneath her. The cushion across from her sat empty. Idalia usually joined them, but after the council meeting the night before, it wasn't surprising she had holed up somewhere. Petra hadn't spotted Roman skulking around either.

Two stones hovered above Hildi's open palms. One shifted into the form of a bear and the other an eagle. They rippled, not holding their shape for longer than a second at a time.

"Don't let your emotions get away from you," Kelda said, her voice soft.

The stones shifted again, turning from animals into buildings. A miniature of the library took form as well as another Petra didn't recognize. It looked like some sort of house, with a large tree that had grown to stretch over a portion of the roof.

"Petra," the queen addressed her, "do you know that a förändra isn't the only thing that influences a Häxa's magic?"

Petra brought her knees up and rested her elbows atop them. She'd picked up little pieces of knowledge about Häxa magic as she'd listened in on the lessons, but this was potentially new information. She shook her head.

Queen Kelda dipped her fingers into a bowl at her side. The water inside slid up over her skin. "From what we've learned in ancient texts, magic itself is influenced by two things: the Maker and the user. As Häxa have come and gone, we've seen a correlation between a gift and the emotional maturity of a woman. Two sisters could be born of the same mother, the same father, with the same gift, and grow into two completely different levels of power. What makes them different is how the Häxa uses their emotions and mental fortitude."

The stones above Hildi's palms shifted again. A heart and a head —one that looked very much like Petra's own—took form.

The water covering Queen Kelda's hand broke away and formed seven different shapes, each representing the seven known Häxa förändras. Petra didn't allow her gaze to linger on the small curl of flame closest to her.

"For me," the queen said, "I have to keep my mind in a place roiling in emotion. Water is fluid and cares not what shape it's poured into, only that it's water and that it can be held together. If I don't allow myself to get swept away by my emotions, the water will not yield itself to me. However, I cannot lose my focus, which takes effort. I must allow the emotions to crash over me but recede like the tide."

The water förändras began to spin lazily in the air between them.

"Hildi's is somewhat similar."

A snort shot from Hildi's nose. "Except completely different.

Mine comes from a sense of having a solid foundation. Like stone, I have to stick to my purposes. Stone is immovable and my will must be stronger than it if I am to wield it. If I want to carve runes, I have to know exactly what I want the rune to do, or the magic won't imbue itself into what I'm carving. When I want to form the stone, I have to know exactly what shape it needs to be. I center myself in one emotion, in one purpose."

Petra leaned forward, watching the stones above Hildi's hands. Mama had been a stone carver. At least, that was what Petra suspected. The stones Mama had tossed at the feet of the Sidans in their house had been runed. The way Hildi spoke about it, Petra could easily see why the gods had gifted Mama with that particular gift and how it had affected the way she thought. Mama had been stubborn nearly to a fault. When she was angry, she stayed angry until she decided it was time to be something else. When she knew something was unjust, she stood her ground against it. She had been the foundation of their family, the one all five of Petra's brothers, her father, and even Petra herself had relied on.

"Do you find that each kind of Häxa uses their gifts in the same way?" Petra asked. "Do stone carvers all rely on their emotions like you?"

Hildi caught the two stones in her hand, both perfectly round spheres. "I think a lot work similarly. I've also always believed we're given gifts that our hearts will find strength in. Even before I knew what gifts I would have, I always stood on principles. For me, things are very black and white. I don't do well when I don't have a clear path before me, so I do my best to figure out what is the right thing to do and follow course. Many of my stone carving sisters are the same way, though some have a different way of thinking of it."

Petra turned to the queen.

"It's the same with water wielders," she said.

The two women went back and forth, describing the different gifts and their emotional catalysts. Plant healers had to have full empathy for the person they were healing, which was why they often would stay out of a fight. They could feel no discord with the person they were healing, or the magic would only make the person's condition worse. Air whisperers had to have quiet minds in order to allow their magic to flow through them. Animal shifters had to allow their instincts to take over both their heads and their hearts. From what records said, spirit walkers had to rely solely on their intellects, detaching them from any sort of mortal emotion and allowing themselves to separate from the emotions of a body.

Hildi frowned, looking down at the symbols of the Häxa still floating in the air. "I haven't heard about fire charmers though."

Petra's ribs tightened. "I thought there weren't any fire charmers left."

"There's not." Hildi shrugged. "There aren't any more spirit walkers either, but we have some record of them passed down through the Great Mothers. I wonder if the current Great Mother knows anything about the charmers."

If she had, she hadn't shared it with Petra when they'd been in Ljust Löfte. Hopefully, the elders had some record. Perhaps if Petra survived the coming battles, she could return to the colony and seek out answers.

At least, if she made it out of the queen's bargain alive. While she'd become friends with both Hildi and Idalia—well, as close as she could be friends with them—the queen remained somewhat aloof. As if they had all the time in the world.

She shifted on the cushion. "Is there really so little known about them?"

Hildi shrugged. "They're mentioned in several of the older documents. Apparently, they were often put into positions of great importance to the Great Mothers of the past. They were Häxa warriors, which was probably one of the reasons they were taken out by the Ekte first. It's said they were nearly undefeatable in a battle."

Petra licked her lips. Häxa warriors? Undefeatable?

"That was mostly due to their secondary gift," Queen Kelda said. The water she wielded joined together until it created one large flame over her hand. "So long as they had access to their förändra, they could self-heal."

Petra's stomach sank.

Hel's bloody halls, of course. Flashes of the healer's house back in Ljust Löfte flew through her mind. The scorch marks around her fireplace. Petra's complete lack of any scar on her body. Even when

Holmberg fell, she'd climbed out of the ruins of her house without a scratch on her.

She'd healed herself.

And the Great Mother had known it too. That was why she'd told Petra she could stay in Ljust Löfte. Why the old bat had said she belonged there. She'd known all along.

And she'd died for it.

Petra held her face completely neutral, even as her entire body felt like it had been taken over by bees. "If they could self-heal, how did the Ekte defeat them?"

"They took them out like the Häxa did in the days of the old law." She slid her thumb across her neck. "Decapitation was how Häxa were executed. A fire charmer couldn't heal if she was already dead."

"Let's move onto runes, shall we?" Queen Kelda said, pouring the water back into the bowl at her side as Hildi set aside the stones. As if the two of them hadn't just dropped earth-shattering revelations in Petra's lap.

Petra picked up one of the perfectly round spheres, her hands shaking.

ᚠᚺᚲᛟᚠᚤᛚ

AFTER THEIR LESSONS with the queen, Hildi had insisted Petra meet her at the palace gates after supper that evening. Idalia was still nowhere to be seen.

"My fingers are going to ache for days after that lesson." Hildi groaned as she trundled beside Petra down the road. The captain had carved nearly two dozen stones that morning, so her complaints were somewhat warranted.

Petra was pretty sure her entire body had gone into shock that afternoon. It had been a bloody miracle she'd made it through the rest of the lesson that morning without losing it.

She still might lose it.

Petra had gone to the lady's rooms after luncheon, only to find the way blocked by several guards. At least she was safe. Petra imagined Idalia would rather jump from the top of city wall than let Anders get his hands on her again.

The street opened up into the fountain square ahead of them and Hildi turned east, taking Petra's arm in her own.

Petra glanced behind them, noting the pair of guards trailing behind them. The guards had grown more alert since Axel's announcement to the council.

They turned down a familiar street, the sound of music and creaking wood harmonizing with the ring of laughter and hiss of whispers. *The Timber Horse* looked even more lopsided than it had the last time Petra had been there, but it might have simply been the feel of the place. They passed by several soldiers who gave Petra uninviting glares, but Hildi walked on as if ambling down the road with one's supposed enemy were an everyday occurrence.

Axel and Enzo sat across from one another at the table they'd occupied the last time they'd been here. Their hands were locked together across the table in an arm wrestle. Enzo's face contorted with strain as Axel sat still, an amused curl at the corner of his mouth.

Petra stared at him, a small voice in her head telling her to look away, but she couldn't.

She'd kissed that mouth.

She wanted to kiss that mouth again.

Her spine stiffened. That line of thought was not at all welcome. But something had happened at midsummer. Something in her had shifted and it couldn't be good.

Why was absolutely everything in her life turning upside down right now?

"Arm wrestling?" Hildi asked, letting go of Petra's arm and sliding into the seat beside her husband. "Why would you think this would be the thing you could beat him at? He's stronger than an ox."

"He has a weakness," Enzo hissed between his teeth. "I just have to figure out what it is."

"Well, it wasn't swordplay, wrestling, or drinking." Hildi counted off her fingers. "Nor was it climbing, ax throwing, or swimming."

Petra met Axel's gaze with a quirked brow. *You both have had time for all that?*

"There's only so much Caeso could talk about in front of me." He grinned up at her, completely nonplussed as Enzo pressed almost all his body weight into his hand. "Enzo decided he would help wile away the hours we were waiting for you to get away from the queen."

Enzo huffed a breath. "It's a wonder that woman hasn't run both of you off yet."

Hildi smacked his arm. "Just because you don't particularly like your stepmother doesn't mean everyone else shares your dislike."

Finally, Enzo dropped back in his chair and Axel released his hand. He wiped a hand down his reddened face. "If everyone else knew her like I did, they wouldn't like her very much either. I think there's a reason the Maker gave her gifts with water. She's nothing but icy veneer."

Hildi rolled her eyes. "Don't listen to him. Queen Kelda has been a wonderful queen."

"I never said she wasn't a good queen. I just said I never quite liked her." He turned to Petra. "Now, my good friend Petra..."

Petra gave him a flat look.

"Please," Enzo begged, "*please* tell me how I can defeat this big oaf in physical prowess. I beg of you. There must be something this prime specimen of mortal flesh isn't good at."

She shrugged. "He's usually good at everything he tries."

Like kissing.

*Oh, Hel's bloody halls.*

Enzo groaned, his head thumping on the table.

"We didn't come here to engage in friendly competition, my love," Hildi said, patting the top of Enzo's head of dark hair.

Petra glared at the married couple in front of her. This had to be their fault. If they weren't such an affectionate pair, Petra wouldn't be thinking about kissing Axel. About how soft his own hair had been under her hands. How he'd held her against him, as if neither of them could get close enough to each other.

"Why are we here?" Axel asked, green gaze flicking between the couple. The question brought Petra back to the present, thank the Allfather.

Enzo sat up abruptly. "We're here because we need to figure out what on our Maker's blessed earth we're going to do about your foolish High King showing up on our shores in a few weeks."

Petra's fists clenched under the table. Even she couldn't figure out what to do about it. Part of her wanted to wash her hands of the whole thing and run for the hills. There was probably a nice mountaintop south of Bellator she could hide out in. The mountains along the border were said to be nearly impassable. Neither Firmin nor Queen Kelda would be able to find her there. Or she could escape to Tatawar and hope she wasn't snatched up by slave traders. Another part wanted to simply intercept Firmin before he arrived and slit his throat in his sleep. There was an innate pleasure in the idea of watching the brute choke on his own blood after all the misery he'd caused.

But the biggest wish? She really just wanted to go back to how things were. Before she met these people. Before Idalia and Roman. Before she'd been taken by Firmin and locked in a cage. Before she'd kissed Axel.

It wasn't possible though. Not when Axel kept glancing at her out of the corner of his eye with that glimmer she'd never noticed before. Not when Enzo and Hildi were humorously bickering with one another in front of her. These people saw her. The mask was crumbling.

What would they all find underneath?

Axel glanced toward her, his brow set low. *What should we do?*

As if she knew the answer.

"What are you all doing?" a sharp voice snapped.

Petra looked over Hildi's shoulder and found Roman storming toward them. Idalia trailed behind him, her cheeks ashy.

"Brother," Enzo greeted.

Roman sneered. "Seriously, Enzo? We have enemies arriving on our doorstep any day now and you're out here sipping wine like there isn't a care in the world?"

Enzo leaned forward. "Seeing as you are also here, likely looking for a night among friends where you can enjoy what time we have together, I'm going to pretend you didn't just attempt to impugn my honor."

Petra stood from her seat, stepping past Roman to where Idalia stood. "You good?"

She let out a deep sigh. "I will be after a few cups of wine."

With little more than a sniff, Idalia grabbed a chair from the closest table and sat next to Hildi, though there was barely enough room to fit her around the small table. "I assume we're attempting to convince Axel and Petra here that their king is an absolute lout, and it's finally time to admit they like us more than him."

Petra's gaze flicked between all four of their expectant faces before finally turning to land on Axel.

There was a crease between his brows and a sliver of sorrow in his eyes. *Are we really going to admit it?*

She glanced back at the others. Their friends. Because they had become friends. Even though Petra had been the one trying to worm her way into their good graces, they'd been silently sneaking behind her defenses and finding a place in her heart.

And she knew the same had happened with Axel. Even if he didn't say as much out loud, she'd watched him struggle with it these last few weeks. He was a man of deep loyalty, and his entire soul had ached with the thought of letting go of the promises he'd made, even in his own ignorance. This decision was not one either of them could approach lightly. It would put everything they'd worked for at risk. It could put the crew in danger. Could harm all the people they cared about in Åldras.

But she already knew what her answer would be, and she couldn't make the choice for Axel. Not for this.

She turned back to him. *I'll follow your lead.*

He blew out a breath, a sad smile curling the corner of his lip. *You're no help.* His gaze shifted back to the Sidans. "Has this been your goal the entire time? You've been plying us with kind words and wine to attempt to sway our allegiances?"

Idalia sat up straight. "Of course not!"

"Yes."

Petra turned to Hildi. Her blue eyes met Petra's before turning to Axel. "After Petra made her bargain with Kelda, Enzo and I decided to approach things differently. We realized we wouldn't make things better by antagonizing the two of you. With the realization that Petra is who she is, it made sense that you, Axel, would feel threatened by us. We needed to mitigate damage, so we devised to in the manner things should have always been approached between our two kingdoms."

Axel sat back in his chair. "And how is that?"

"With diplomacy," Enzo answered. "I have often wondered what would've happened if my father hadn't retaliated that night in Holmberg the way he did. What would have happened if our kingdoms had actually sat across a table from one another, sharing a pitcher of wine instead of crossing swords."

"What we didn't expect," Hildi continued, "was that the two of you would actually be bloody likeable."

Petra's lips twitched. The Sidans had certainly surprised them as well.

Enzo chuckled. "So now, here we are. The six of us unlikely friends. But war is coming, and this friendship could change the course of both our kingdoms. And so, we must ask you whose side you are going to take when your High King arrives on these shores."

Petra swallowed, looking up at Axel.

His eyes were already waiting for hers, as if she were his north star and he was begging her for direction. As if she were the one who would guide him toward the right course.

But he already knew the answer she would give, just as she knew what he would choose.

He shifted so their knees touched under the table, as if the small connection could give him what strength he needed to give his answer.

"We are going to take Åldras's side."

Idalia sucked in a breath and Roman's mouth opened with what was likely to be a slew of curses, but Enzo raised his hand. "Let the man speak."

Axel took Petra's hand. "I have given my life to bring peace to Åldras, to work toward a future for my kinsmen I can be proud of. After having spent time in your kingdom, after seeing how your king seeks the wisdom of his council, and how your people treat the Häxa, I believe the best way to help Åldras is to rid them of Firmin and allow Sida to claim the victory of this war."

Hildi's eyes slid to Petra. "And what about you?"

Petra's head tilted to the side. "Haven't you heard? I'm Mighty Axel's shadow. Where he goes, I'm not far behind."

Enzo shot to his feet, a hand raised as he looked across the room to the counter. "Wine! We need your best wine right here!"

Idalia stared up at the Crown Prince and broke into giggles. Roman looked to her, his own eyes wide with shock until he too broke into laughter. Soon enough, the entire table was bent over laughing.

Petra met Axel's gaze, her smile stretched wide and her belly aching.

His own smile was absolutely radiant.

When the wine finally arrived, Enzo cleared his throat. "So, who's ready to end a war?"

For the rest of the evening, they went back and forth, calling for writing implements as the candles burned low around them. Roman was as sharp a mind as Petra, scenarios falling from his lips as fast as she could discard them. Enzo was ingenious with methods of mental manipulation, tugging at the strings of Firmin and Anders's motivations. Hildi's intimate knowledge of the city was imperative as well as her network of city leadership—both official and apparently unofficial. Axel poked holes in defenses and pointed out weak parts in their plans. Even Idalia contributed, giving numbers of men from Anders's city and spilling secrets Petra and Axel couldn't share themselves. Though, that didn't make them stop her.

It wasn't long until their pitchers were empty of wine and the sky lightened with the coming dawn.

Petra stared down at the scattered papers across the table.

She prayed to whatever gods were listening that all of this would work out. That these friends she'd made would help change their kingdoms for the better. That they would make the right choices.

And she prayed none of the people seated beside her would die.

# CHAPTER 19

# REGRETS

Axel tugged on one of the loose pages of parchment as Enzo and Roman laid out their late-night plans to the general. The piece of charcoal in his hand split in two.

*Rocks.*

He set it on the desk and swallowed.

Caeso glanced down at the pages, his brows rising higher and higher with every word the princes spoke.

"*The Phoenix*'s crew will no doubt have more for us to work with," Enzo said. "We plan on meeting with all of them this evening."

After their confessions at the wine hall two nights ago, Axel and Petra had returned to the palace and gathered the crew together to discuss the future and their allegiances. They wouldn't make promises for all of them without speaking to them. He'd expected them to be angry, for them to call dishonor on Axel's head.

But none of them had.

Sida had been working her magic on all of them.

Ulf and Big Hal were the two with the most to say about it, but most of their concerns were with the reactions of those they'd left behind in Åldras. Ulf had family that had tilled the grounds outside of Grovö for generations. Big Hal had a father in Gudvangen who would hate his son siding with their enemy, no matter that they still fought for the future of their kingdom.

But Erik's words had answered for all of them.

"We have been working against Firmin since *The Phoenix* first touched the waters of the Vit Sea. As long as she spreads her wings over the water, her crew will continue to work toward the betterment of Åldras and her people—High Kings be rocked."

And now, Axel sat across from the leaders of Sida's army, expected to bare Åldras's throat to them.

Thunder's beard, was he really doing this? Was he really sitting here while the very men who had once been his enemies were discussing ways to defeat his countrymen? His kin? When they'd sat in the wine hall, he'd felt the strings that tied him to those at the table. How all of them wished for peace, to get through this with the least amount of bloodshed. But was any of this the right answer?

Would all this work only end in more bloodshed? Firmin was coming. There was no stopping that. The Sidans would win. It was inevitable. He knew this. Standing in the command center of Bellator, he knew there was no way for Åldras to come out of this war as the victor. Not if King Leonardo was prepared to finally end things. Not if the plague would kill their people and the ones left were coming to Sida to die on these shores. What if his plans didn't work? Firmin could simply ignore the evidence right in front of his face. He was certainly going to rage once he found out Axel had betrayed him. What if the kings didn't listen? Even he had been blinded by his loyalty to his kingdom. What if they didn't care that their people would die if they didn't listen?

*I need some air.*

"What?" Enzo asked. "Axel? You need some air?"

Axel finally looked up at him. "I'm just going to go for a walk." Without even looking to the general for permission, he bolted for the door.

"What just happened?" Roman's voice chased him down the hall.

Axel's pace increased with the beat of his heart.

What was he doing?

He was at a full sprint by the time he made it out into the courtyard. A trio of guards nearly plowed into him. He jumped over their heads. Shouts of alarm sprang up, but he was out of the barracks before anyone could follow him. There were too many people talking. Too much happening.

Before he even knew where he was going, he burst out of the city gates and onto the beach. *The Phoenix* sat in the sand, her beak open in an anguished cry Axel felt building in his own chest.

"Axel?" Erik asked, his graying head of hair popping up from the side of the gunwale. "What's wrong?"

Axel didn't even have words to put to the tightness in his chest or the hollowness in his stomach. He climbed onto the ship, going to his trunk. With shaking fingers, he unbuckled his sword and yanked his tunic over his head. He nearly toppled over getting his boots off, but they landed on the deck with a thump. Without so much as a nod in Erik's direction, he jumped back over the side of the ship. The sand sprayed out as he landed on the beach. His strength was out of control.

He ran for the crashing waves behind the ship. The surf slammed into his legs as he ran, but it barely phased him. When the water reached his waist, he dove underneath. The warm sea did little to calm his heart. If anything, it only enhanced the pounding of his pulse. He pushed through the water until he made it past the lines of rock, over the schools of silver fish, until he couldn't even see the bottom beneath him. His chest contested the lack of air, but like always, it didn't so much as spasm.

The quiet of the sea brought his pulse to a normal rhythm. The darkness of the water pushed away the glaring realities of the city behind him.

He couldn't take it. He couldn't watch all of them die. He didn't have it in him.

The buoyancy of his body pulled him to the surface of the water. He floated on his back, letting the sun kiss his skin as he closed his eyes. This far from the shore, the waves were calm, rocking him like a babe. If he knew he wouldn't just sink back under the water and come up spluttering, he'd let himself be lulled to sleep and allow Njord to take him wherever the currents willed. Perhaps he would find his way back to Ljust Löfte. Or to the red rocks of Tatawar. Or even to the world beyond the three kingdoms. Maybe the gods would simply strike him down right there and be done with this entire thing.

Sol's light slowly made its way across the sky, reaching its zenith and descending toward the edge of the sea. Axel looked to the south. The faintest line of coast painted the horizon. He'd gone out farther than he'd thought.

A scratchy *caw* rang across the air.

Axel shaded his eyes and found a raven soaring over his head.

It had to be either Huggin or Munnin. When Axel squinted, he saw the cuff of metal on his left ankle.

*Huggin.*

The bird had already made it back from Doran?

*Rocks.* He had to be close then. Likely past Holmberg already.

Axel dove back down under the water, turning back toward Sida. His arms cut through the waves, not even weary from being in the sea almost the entire afternoon. The current must have been strong, because the city came into view far quicker than he'd have liked.

When he could touch the sand under his feet, he found Petra standing at the stern of the ship. The wind tugged at her short hair and the gold light of the setting sun kissed her cheeks. Her neck.

The ache in Axel's chest nearly drove him back into the sea. But she was a lighthouse and he a lost ship. He could do nothing except turn toward her.

As he pulled himself out of the water, she leaped down to the beach. There was a weariness in her blue-green eyes. One Axel felt in his very soul.

She took a seat on the sand, kicking off her boots then her socks and setting them out of the sea's reach. Her toes dug into the sand, and she folded her arms around her knees.

Axel laid out next to her, not even caring that he'd have to take another swim to get all the sand out of his hair. The wind cooled the water across Axel's torso, making his skin prickle with gooseflesh, but the sand was warm under his back.

Petra's face angled toward the water, her expression flickering with one emotion after another. It wasn't often she allowed her mask to fall, but it happened in moments like this. When no one else was around. When her mind mulled over a problem. It wasn't so much that her entire demeanor changed, but there were small twitches in her brows, a light curl of her lips. Her eyes said the most, that blue-green hazel shifting colors with each thought and feeling.

Wōden's eye, he wanted to kiss her.

He wanted her to kiss him back.

He wanted her to want him like he wanted her.

*Until one day by love disarmed...*

He would give anything for that to happen. He'd give up all his magic if that was what it took for her to give him her heart. His very life if she asked it of him.

She finally turned to look at him, her eyes the same shades of the sea, as if staring at it so long had soaked the color into her irises. "Why do you keep looking at me like that?"

"Like what?" He was sure his thoughts were plain on his face. There was no way they weren't. They suffused his entire body. He felt them all the way from his toes to his scalp.

She shook her head, looking away. "It doesn't matter. Why'd you run off?"

Axel blew out a breath. "Who told you I ran?"

"Erik. Said you leaped out into the water like Fenrir was snapping at your heels."

"Of course he did." Erik could be such a busybody sometimes. Axel couldn't get away with anything under the man's all-seeing gaze.

Shaking the sand from his hair, Axel sat up. "I couldn't sit in that room and listen as the princes and Caeso talked about how they were going to take down our kinsmen. How they were going to defeat Firmin. If anyone on this bloody planet wants the High King kicked off his bloody throne, it's me. But I couldn't watch as they laid out plans to go up against our people. Our kingdom. We've fought for Áldras our entire lives. While I know this is the right course, I just hate the idea of harm coming to the people we've sworn to protect."

Petra turned her gaze back to the water, shadows lining her face. "I'm sorry."

"None of it is your fault."

She barked a laugh, eyes filling with tears. "Isn't it? Isn't all of this my fault? Aren't I the one who started all of this? If I hadn't killed Hildi's father, if I hadn't burned down our isle, if I'd known about the magic—"

Axel took her chin in his hand, forcing her to face him. "None of that was your fault, Petra."

Tears slipped out between her lashes. She scrunched her eyes closed. "I don't know how you can say that."

He wiped the tears from her cheeks. "Because it's true. You can't keep blaming yourself for this. For something that was so completely out of your control. It's over. It already happened. Now, we have to fix it. We have to figure out how to stop people from dying. How to help Sida bring peace to our kingdom."

Petra blew out a shaky breath, placing her hands at his wrists but not pulling away. It was as if his touch centered her. How badly he wished it really did. If he could be any kind of comfort to her, he would be.

She opened her eyes again, capturing all his attention. If she didn't look at him with so many questions, he would have captured her lips with his. He had to use every ounce of self-control not to glance down at the soft curve of her mouth.

"I—I've been learning a lot about magic lately." She swallowed. "About the förändra and how it all works. About how emotion plays a big role in it."

Axel nodded. "Aye. Even my magic is tied to my emotions."

Her eyes flicked down. Had she just looked at his lips? After he'd been so careful not to look at hers. After he'd held himself back from crushing her to him. He licked them and her eyes shot down once again. Her chest rose and fell, and slowly, those blue-green eyes of hers trailed back up to meet his gaze.

"Why do you keep looking at me like that?" she whispered.

Slowly, he brought her face close to his. He gave her plenty of time to pull away even as his entire body told him to claim what he'd always wanted. To crash against her. To show her just how much he'd thought about kissing her. Touching her.

He brushed the very tip of his nose against hers, but she didn't pull away. In fact, her fingers clamped down on his wrists, keeping his hands cradled under her jaw.

"Petra..." His voice rumbled from under his ribs, almost a plea.

She closed her eyes, her soft breath touching his lips only a hairs-breadth from hers.

"Axel!"

Petra sprang away from him, nearly falling onto her back. She scrambled back, her cheeks pink and eyes wide.

To Hel's bloody halls with whoever had just ruined this. He shot to his feet, only to find Little Hal come around the side of the ship, Huggin on his shoulder.

"There you are," Little Hal said. He frowned at Petra. "Pet? You good?"

Petra leaped to her feet. "Fine. I'm fine. I'll go." She practically sprinted away, not even glancing once at Axel and leaving an owlishly blinking Little Hal behind her.

"I don't think I'll ever understand girls," Little Hal said.

Axel burst out laughing. He slapped the lad on the back, making the raven on his shoulder squawk in displeasure. "Aye," Axel said between chuckles, "you and me both."

Little Hal gave a confused look and shook his head. "Uh, Doran reached out." He held out a hand, an open missive taking up a good portion of his palm.

Axel unrolled it.

*Midnight.* A short list of directions for Erik had been scribbled just below.

Axel handed the missive back to Little Hal. "Gather the crew. We're expecting a reunion tonight."

ᚠᚺᚲᛟᚨᛁᛚ

AXEL PUSHED against the hull of the ship. Had she always been this light? She slid through sand like warm butter over bread until the waves picked her up.

Big Hal looked over at Axel, a furrow in his brow. "That was easy."

Axel shrugged and grabbed the edge of the gunwale. It was slightly easier to push the ship through the soft sands of Sida's beaches than the cragged pebbles of Åldran shores. He pulled himself up over the edge, the bottom half of his trousers dripping onto the deck.

The rest of the crew took up their oars, taking orders from Erik who counted out the beat as he watched the sea behind them. Slowly, they turned the ship around and pulled away from the coast. With a few tugs of rope, the sail unfurled above their heads, pulling them away from Sida.

Axel helped tie down the oars and took up post at the stem of the ship. It was a perfectly clear night, the evening fog having already been swept away, leaving the sea open for miles ahead of them. The stars glimmered above their heads, ever watching.

A glitter of orange peeked out to the northwest of them. Axel pointed it out and *The Phoenix* shifted under his feet, heading in that direction.

He felt her approach before he saw her. Petra materialized beside him; her eyes trained on the sea ahead.

"How bad do you think it is that Doran decided to come ahead of Firmin?" she asked.

Axel followed her gaze out onto the water. "I don't know."

They watched the orange glow turn from one spot of color to two to four. A striped sail rippled in the breeze above a familiar ship, a skeid that could hold nearly two hundred men comfortably on its deck. The head of a dragon breathed fire down toward the sea, its snarling visage staring down in rage. Axel hadn't seen *Sorrow* in years. He'd grown into a man on that ship. It was easily three times the size of *The Phoenix*, built to carry men from one battle to the next. Her hull gleamed in the light of the lanterns hanging from the gunwale. Dozens of heads bobbed as they scrambled back and forth across the deck, taking orders from the skipper. Old Harald's commands rang out over the water. The man had a voice like thunder that had reprimanded Axel more than a few times over the years. The skipper was also the reason Axel and Petra had ever made it off Holmberg.

*Sorrow*'s sail gathered up on the mast at the same time *The Phoenix*'s did. The two boats slowly glided the rest of the way toward each other. The crew on *Sorrow* brought long boards to the gunwale and laid them over the edge until they met the side of *The Phoenix*. Axel grabbed one of the boards, tying it into place and locking the ships together. He was sure there were hooked platforms on Doran's ship as well. He must not be too upset with them, or he would have considered using them and leaving marks in *The Phoenix*'s deck.

As if summoned by the thought of his anger, Doran jumped up on the board, walking across as if it were solid ground. His beard glistened with spray from the sea, longer than Axel ever remembered it being. There were more gray hairs running through it as well. He stopped when he reached the end, his brows drawn together over his flashing eyes.

Axel had been the recipient of that particular look many times in the past, and he'd seen others tremble beneath it.

Doran stared down at him. "What in Hel's bloody rock-covered halls have you been doing, Axel?"

Axel had never seen Doran so angry, not in all the years that he'd been chasing him and Petra around like naughty toddlers.

"What do you mean what have I been doing?" Axel asked. "I've been trying to accomplish this bloody fool's mission you and Queen Eva sent us on."

Doran gritted his teeth. "Oh really? Because from what I've been hearing, the bloody lot of you have been dancing around Bellator like a merry band of children, breaking bread with our enemies, and having a jolly good time while our people have been waiting for you to return with Lady Idalia to restore pride to our kingdom. Instead, we've had to receive reports about how Mighty Axel plays games with Enzo the Scourge and Åldras's demon follows after a queen like a puppy on a leash. You have made us all look like *fools*."

Axel sucked in a breath. The rest of the crew did too.

"You're lucky I don't dump every single one of you in the sea with stones tied to your ankles. You've done nothing but disgrace our kingdom's name. You should be kissing my rocking boots for all the trouble I've gone through to keep Firmin from taking his entire bloody armada and coming himself. For weeks, I've reassured every single king in Åldras that their most revered hero is doing it all for a reason. But even I couldn't ignore the reports of *The Phoenix*'s crew carousing with Sidans, seen courting Häxa women and lounging around with the very royals they should have slaughtered in their beds."

"*Enough*," Axel growled. "How dare you board my ship and threaten my crew. How dare you throw shame in our faces. You know *nothing* of what has been happening here."

Doran snorted. "I know *plenty*. And so does all of bloody Åldras. But I'm here to fix it all before Firmin and Anders get here and get the men of Åldras killed while the rest of the kingdom is left to die by a bloody plague."

He grabbed both the collar of Axel's shirt and the back of Petra's and yanked them toward the back of the ship where Erik was keeping the tiller straight.

"You two need to tell me *exactly* what is going on," Doran hissed between gritted teeth, "before the bloody spies on my ship report that the three of us are cavorting against Firmin."

Axel's entire chest loosened. Of course Doran was still on their side. Of course he was angry, but it wasn't solely at them.

Doran shook both of them. "Don't you dare ruin my ruse. You have two minutes to explain yourselves, and you better look like the two most repentant rockheads on Midgard to fool everyone." He shoved them, and Axel fell to his knees beside Petra.

"Erik!" Doran snapped, his voice carrying over the water. "I expect to see every single page of your bloody log."

Erik glanced sideways at Axel, who gave him a nod. The skipper reached for the leather tube holding his papers.

The entire crews of both ships watched them with equal curiosity and anger. Ulf had a firm hand on Big Hal's shoulder, and Little Hal's face was as hard as Axel had ever seen it. They would jump to his aid the moment Doran made any wrong move.

"We can't take Idalia back to Anders," Axel whispered. "Not only is she under the protection of the Sidan King, but the entire bloody city is half in love with her. If we return her to Anders, it will cause more problems for everyone."

"Of course not, you idiot!" Doran boomed. He grabbed Axel's collar and lowered his voice. "I already bloody knew that. What I don't know is what you lot are planning to do about it."

Petra slid between them, pretending to push them apart as she kept her voice low. "The Sidans know about the plague. They're planning to take Åldras peacefully if possible and we've agreed to help them."

He stared at her, the first flashes of shock marring his face. He'd believed the rumors to be unfounded. That Axel wouldn't have actually sided with the enemy. He buried the expression, frowning deeper.

"They're attempting to come up with a strategy that'll endanger less lives," Petra continued, "but they aren't going to roll over and let Firmin walk all over them. If it comes to it, they plan on fighting here on their home turf and exhausting Firmin's resources until he turns tail and runs. Then, they will chase him back to Harligdam, claiming Åldras as they go. They plan on bringing every healer in Sida with them and saving the people, turning their opinions away from the Ekte propaganda."

"They'll be saviors after Firmin's apathy." Doran grabbed Petra's tunic, pulling her up so his face was close to hers. Axel had to clench his fists together to keep from jumping to her aid. "You better pull out a bloody dagger so they don't get suspicious."

Petra pulled a blade, making sure the crewmen could see it glitter in the lantern light as she set it against Doran's throat.

Axel got to his feet and pulled them apart. Even if they were playing a part, he couldn't stop himself. "Pet! Fighting him will only make it worse!" He glanced over Doran's shoulder. "We don't know what to do. We don't want to see our people's blood shed on these shores, but we also don't want to help Firmin destroy a kingdom who only wants peace."

Doran frowned. "If they wanted peace so badly, why take Lady Idalia?"

"They're in love," Axel replied. "Roman and Idalia. He saved her from Anders. From the reactions of Enzo and the king, it wasn't something anyone was happy about. They knew it would break the armistice and Firmin would happily use it as an excuse to attack."

Doran pretended to angrily pace back and forth in front of them. "He was right. Firmin started gathering men the day after you left, though I didn't catch on until King Gudrun told me he'd been ordered to call in his ships. That was when I sent you the first missive."

"So how do we stop this?" Axel said. "How do we stop Firmin from bringing the kings here and keep Åldrans from dying?"

Doran sighed and ran a hand through his hair, the angry façade melting away to one of genuine worry.

"We can't," Petra said. "It's already too late."

ᚠᚻᚳᛟᚠᛁᛚ

THE SIDAN'S were ready for them when they arrived back at the city. Little Hal had sent Enzo word before they'd met with Doran, so no one would think they were abandoning the bargains they'd struck. The promises they'd made.

Axel stood at the stem of *The Phoenix* as *Sorrow* followed behind them. All along the shore, torches burned, and the green of the Sidan guards bled onto the sand. Enzo's proud shoulders stood at the front of the crowd, Hildi beside him with her arms crossed over her chest. Idalia and Roman were nowhere in sight, but that wasn't surprising. Behind them, three large tents had been put up in the sand, the green flag of Sida's proud eagle flapping in the wind from their peaks.

The crowd moved back as the two ships slid onto the shore. Axel was the first to jump from *The Phoenix* and pull her onto the sand. He'd almost done it all on his own before Big Hal joined him for the last couple of feet. *Sorrow* took a team of ten men to pull her onto the shore. The hiss of whispers crackled between the torches held up by the Sidans.

Doran jumped over the side of one of the *Sorrow*'s dinghies, his boots splashing into the shallow water. The skeid was too large to beach as far up as *The Phoenix* and they had to use smaller boats to carry them onto the shore. His broadsword peeked out from under the dark cloak hanging off one shoulder. With the scowl on his face, he looked like a vexed king ready to lay down the law to his subjects. His acting skills had always been unmatched. He'd always said even one's reactions were a strategic choice. Axel had learned a lot from him over the years about what it took to be a man people respected.

"King Doran," Enzo called, striding toward them. "We hope you have come to our shores with thoughts of peace."

There was a threat in those words. Hildi positioned herself

behind Enzo, her right hand out of view. Just in case. The woman would bury Doran in the bloody sand if he so much as flinched.

Doran gave a small bow, barely bending at the waist. "Prince Enzo, I've come with a message from my High King. Do I have your word that my ship and crew will meet no ill will while we address one another?"

Enzo looked up at the tall stem of *Sorrow*. "So long as your crew means no ill will toward my people, they are welcome on these shores."

Doran turned and gave a nod. The dinghies bobbing near the ship sliced forward through the surf.

"Come," Enzo said. "I'm sure my father will wish to greet you." He gestured for Doran to follow him.

"Petyr, Axel, with me," Doran barked before turning to the others. "Get the tents up and some fires going. We won't be long."

Axel followed behind him, setting a hand on the hilt of his sword. Petra kept on Axel's heels, shadowing him.

When they passed Hildi, the captain took up position behind them. She leaned closer to Petra than she did to Axel, but he still heard when she mumbled under her breath.

"I assume this conversation isn't actually going to be that short."

"You'd be right," Petra muttered back.

Four guards stood at the entrance to the tent. The two in the middle grabbed the tent flaps and pulled them aside. Enzo slipped through first, followed by Doran and the rest of them.

The inside was a clash of opulence and utility. A long table stretched against one wall, covered in maps and stacks of reports. Along the other wall, a row of chairs settled atop an emerald rug. There were no lumps of sand beneath it and when Petra stepped onto the edge, she found whatever was beneath didn't yield under her weight. The Häxa had probably created a flat surface on the beach.

King Leonardo sat on a throne. Roman sat in a chair on the king's left, leaving one open on either side. Enzo proceeded to the chair to the right hand of the king and Hildi slipped past Petra and took the empty one next to it.

"King Doran," King Leonardo greeted, "it's my pleasure to welcome you to Sida."

Doran gave another bow, this one slightly deeper than the one he'd given Enzo. It was certainly a sign of respect Axel hadn't expected from him, and based on the way the king's eyes lit with intrigue, neither had he.

"King Leonardo," Doran said, "thank you for meeting with me."

The king raised a ring-studded hand and a horde of servants swarmed forward. Chairs were procured for Axel, Petra, and Doran. Three round tables were brought together to form one long table and food was brought out.

They'd passed some kind of test.

Doran let out a breath. "You honor us with your hospitality. I didn't know if my presence tonight would be received well."

King Leonardo took a plate offered by a servant, already filled with food. "You have always been one of the few Åldran kings with a calm head on your shoulders. When I heard it was *Sorrow* making her way toward our shores, I knew tonight would at least begin with civil conversation."

Doran bowed his head. "You flatter me, Your Majesty."

King Leonardo waved away the compliment. "We aren't here for flattery or felicitations. You have come with a message."

With a sigh, Doran reached into the inside of his vest.

Several of the guards stepped forward, their hands on their swords, but Enzo held up a hand, stilling them.

Doran pulled out a thick roll of parchment. "My High King has come up with a list of demands to be met for reparations in regard to the breaking of the armistice between our kingdoms. This writ has been signed by all twelve of the current members of the king's council, including myself, and if all items of the list are met, this war is over and a truce will be signed between both kingdoms. I have been assigned by the council to present this list verbally to the king and his sons."

King Leonardo gestured to him. "Then proceed."

"Firmin Witchkiller, Son of Vilgot the Steadfast, High King of Åldras, and the Council of Kings have written on this the twenty-ninth day of Skerpla a treatise to the King of Sida. With the abduction of the property of King Anders, Son of Vilgot the Steadfast, the armistice created on the seventh day of Haustmánuður is now void. As Sida acts as the dishonorable party, Åldras has put forth a list of demands Sida must meet to instate peace between both Åldras and Sida. The list is as follows. First, Sida will yield all lands conquered within the borders of Åldras as well as the surrounding isles. They will retreat into their own borders, disbanding all forts, safe houses, and command centers on Åldran soil..."

Axel sagged back in his chair. His stomach sank lower and lower as the list went on. The Sidans were prohibited from making any new treaties with Tatawar until ten years had passed after the treaty was signed. They were to pay a king's ransom for the damages done to ships and for the last eight years' worth of taxes they would have been forced to pay to the crown as Åldran citizens for living on the land. They were also to send back any and all Åldran refugees who had run to Sida—including the Häxa.

"That bloody fiend," Enzo cursed, taking his wife's hand in his. Hildi's face was set in a flat expression, but anger simmered in her eyes as she listened to the demands.

Doran continued to read, making all sorts of ridiculous demands of the Sidans. The last of the demands was that Idalia be returned to Anders.

"If King Anders's property has been defiled in any way," Doran recited, his voice taking on an edge, "the hands that touched Idalia of Oxe will be severed from the perpetrator and delivered to King Anders as recompense for actions against him and his property."

"This is more than an insult!" Roman roared, shooting up from his seat. "This is evil in the vilest form! I won't have it!"

"Sit *down*, Roman," King Leonardo thundered.

Roman practically threw himself back into his chair, his hands gripping the armrests with white knuckles. He was ready for a fight. Axel's own grip on his chair tightened. Wōden's one good eye, the prince would have to get in line behind Axel if he wanted a chance at Anders. The demands were absolutely ludicrous, and everyone in that tent knew it.

The king kept his gaze on Doran. "If we don't agree to the terms of the truce?"

Doran pulled out another sheet of parchment and presented it to King Leonardo. "Then the war will remain, but the High King has included a reinstitution of the armistice to finish out the rest of the ten months of peace and resume war once that time has passed."

King Leonardo gave a nod and took the page.

Doran pulled a smaller paper from the stack he held. "If Sida does not agree to the truce, the High King of Åldras will allow one form of reparation to be made in regard to the dishonorable conduct by Prince Roman and the abduction of Lady Idalia. King Anders will challenge Prince Roman to a duel."

Roman nearly jumped to his feet again, but with one glare from his father, remained seated.

It was madness. The king would be an absolute fool to take it. Anders was a seasoned warrior. He might have been a buffoon, but Axel had seen him kill men three times the size of Roman. And he did it with sadistic glee. He wouldn't just injure Roman, he would slaughter him.

The king took a deep breath, straightening in his chair.

"No. My son will not accept Anders's challenge."

Axel let out a sigh of relief.

"Father, I can do it!" Roman demanded. He knelt at the king's feet. "Please, I can fight him. I'll reclaim the honor of our kingdom and win Idalia's hand. Let me prove to that tyrant that Sida is the far greater kingdom. Let me face him."

King Leonardo's face turned hard, and he ignored his son's plea. "What does Firmin have to say now?"

Doran set aside all the papers except the smallest one.

"If Sida rejects all proposed reparations, Åldras will have no choice but to carve out their dues from the very shores of Sida's borders and from the cities under their feet. We will take back what is ours, including the Häxa who have violated our kingdom's laws and Lady Idalia who abandoned her oaths. We have offered mercy, and if the Sidans desire none, they will have their wish."

Doran set the paper down and met the king's eye.

"May the gods have mercy on their souls."

# Chapter 20

## A Choice

*I am going to have to step in with whatever is happening between Axel and Pet. The two of them have grown much fonder of each other in the few weeks since I saw them in Harligdam. If Firmin finds out about who Pet truly is, he will kill her quicker than Axel would be able to spear him through with his own lysande blade. I pray the both of them will keep their heads.*

*— FROM THE WRITINGS OF DORAN FINNSSON, THE LAST KING OF GROVÖ*

The ceiling of their shared bedroom brightened as Petra stared up at the dark wood paneling. Even as Sol prepared to make his debut, Petra couldn't make herself get up from her bed.

So much had happened over the last day.

Axel had said he wanted to help her fix the past.

She'd nearly let herself kiss him again.

Doran had arrived.

Firmin had made his demands.

Everything was about to change and there was nothing she could do about it. Firmin and Anders would arrive on these shores. It would be her kingdom's last stand. The final fight. They would either come out victorious or Sida would wipe them from the face of the earth.

And she couldn't decide which would be better.

"I can hear that brain of yours whirring from all the way over here."

A breath escaped her. "I'm so confused."

Axel chuckled. "Me too."

She threw her hands up. "That's helpful."

The bed he laid on creaked as he shifted. "What happens when Firmin arrives? How do we convince him to leave? Do we run away from it all and pray the gods don't strike us down? Or do we lay ourselves between the two sides and let them hack at us with their swords?"

"Definitely not that last one," Petra muttered.

Another sad chuckle. "No matter what we do, I feel like the people we care about are going to get hurt."

Those were the exact words to her feelings. For all her adult life, she'd fought mercilessly for her kingdom, not caring who fell under her blade because she couldn't care. She'd made her proverbial bed of filth, and now she had to lie in it. And she did. Happily. Because she knew that Axel would remain by her side if she did.

But now? The filth had been let out into the sun, and she didn't know what to do with it. Axel forgave her, but no one else knew she was the cause of this war. This war that had brought her to people who understood her, who accepted her even with her secrets. She'd learned under the hand of an enemy queen, befriended a rival, and found her heart turned for a traitorous lady. Even the bloody princes had broken down a bit of her resolve.

"I like them too," Axel whispered.

She sat up and turned to meet Axel's gaze across the room. "I don't know how we're going to get through this without losing any of them," she whispered.

"Nor do I," he said.

Blowing out a breath, she grabbed her clay tablet off the floor next to the bed. "We need to come up with how we're going to deal with Firmin when he arrives."

Axel rolled over, settling his hands behind his head. "I say we ignore him and stay here. He can throw his barbs at the city, and we can sit here sipping at that nasty wine Enzo keeps insisting is good."

"You know that's not going to work. You would hate sitting back and watching people fight our battles." She picked at her bottom lip. "We need to figure out how to get the lesser kings to question Firmin's command."

"Like that's going to happen." Axel scoffed. "Doran's been trying to do that for ages."

If only Doran had been successful. It was true that he'd swayed some of the other kings in the past. Especially the reasonable ones like Gudrun and Agnar. He wouldn't have trouble helping them see reason. But if they were to turn the tides of this war back on Firmin, they would need more than a couple of the kings to back them. Freyja's golden tears, they'd need more than half, which would be impossible without killing some of them. Most were blindly loyal to their High King, and it would take something miraculous to persuade them from Firmin's side.

"What about the plague?"

Petra glanced at Axel. "What about it?"

"What if we use it to our advantage like King Leonardo is going to? Do you think the kings would waver in their loyalty if we told them Sida had the cure? We don't have to tell them it's the Häxa, but we could tell them there's a way to heal their people if they help us stop Firmin."

The idea wasn't half bad. She jotted it down onto the tablet. "How would we get word to them without Firmin knowing what we were doing? If he figured it out, he would convince them the Sidans were trying to gain access to the people to make them sicker."

Axel's lips puckered in thought. "It's likely too late to get missives to any of them. They're coming to Bellator. If we can convince Doran, he might be able to gather those we know will wish for a cure first. If we get enough of them to agree to abandon Firmin's vendetta, they could convince others to join us. We could stop the fight and take Firmin out at the knees before any blood was shed on the shore."

"Leif and Haukr would likely cut their own arms off for a cure," Petra mused, "if what the king told you about it is true."

She jotted down the names of the kings. They went down the list, marking which of the kings would likely be receptive to such a scheme and which wouldn't. There were at least five who would likely sell their souls to the Sidans to end this war, but it wasn't enough and they couldn't be sure a cure to the plague would be enough incentive to bring those kings to betray their loyalties.

"And what if that doesn't work?" There were so many ways approaching the kings could go awry. It would be so easy for one of them to expose Axel and allow Firmin to retaliate. Though, that particular risk hung over their necks like a giant ax, ready to take their heads.

Axel chuckled. "We pray."

She glared at him. "That's not good enough." They would need a backup plan in case one of the kings turned on them, which was more than likely. Most of those brutes would throw their own people to wolves if it meant they kept their thrones.

Petra's hand stilled over the tablet. "What if we decide to play the Sidan's game? If we can't get the kings to go against Firmin, we go to Åldras herself. We slip past the Vit Sea while Firmin and Anders hit their heads against Bellator's wall and rally the people ourselves. With all the kings trapped here by Firmin's demands, we could take Åldras right out from under their noses."

"And if we took a few of the healers here back with us," Axel added, "we could heal the plague as we went. It would turn the people not only against Firmin, but against the Ekte as well. It would take longer than convincing the kings, but it could work." He turned to her; a smile stretched across his face. "You're brilliant."

The faint light cast dramatic shadows over the sharp planes of his face. If she was any good with a piece of charcoal, she could have closed her eyes and drawn that face from memory. She would try to capture this moment, before they finally fell from the cliff. Before the world crashed down on top of them.

Axel sat up. He pushed the blanket off his legs and padded over to her, crouching in front of her knees. "Why do you look at me like that?"

Petra nearly shuddered at the words she'd spoken to him repeated back to her.

His hand came up and brushed a stray hair from her temple. The light touch of his fingertip against her skin made her heart skip in her chest. That fingertip traced her hairline. Her jaw. Her cheek.

"You can't do that," she protested, but even her voice sounded as weak as her resolve.

"Tell me why," he whispered. He trailed a finger over her eyebrow. Her nose. The curve of her bottom lip. "Tell me why and I'll stop."

She closed her eyes. *Because I don't deserve it. If I let myself have it, I'll ruin it.*

His hand slowly trailed down her neck. "Petra, look at me."

She opened her eyes.

"My feelings aren't going to change." His gaze followed the slow trail of his fingers as they brushed against her shoulder. Her arm. "I've felt this way from the moment I even understood what it was. I've lived with it for years, and it has only ever grown. I kept the feelings at bay because I knew you didn't feel the same way. I knew you didn't look at me the way I looked at you because I know every one of your expressions. I can see the thoughts in your head as if I thought them myself. You never once considered the possibility of us."

She should stop him. Should pull away. She should tell him she still felt that way. That she couldn't give him what he wanted. That there was no way she would put him in danger.

But she was selfish. She was terrible. A shadow. A demon. She was weak. She was a bloody coward.

She didn't want him to stop touching her.

His hand trailed back up her arm and his gaze finally met hers.

"But that changed the day I kissed you in Ljust Löfte. I know it did, because I saw those same feelings I've been harboring for our entire lives mirrored in your eyes. That was the day I fully lost my heart to you. I left it back in that forest, and you took it."

Petra couldn't think. Couldn't breathe. Only the pounding of her heart told her she was alive.

His fingers finally stopped under her chin. With the slightest pressure, he lifted her face until only a knife's edge of space remained between them.

Petra's eyes fluttered close.

His lips brushed hers. It wasn't a kiss, but the faintest touch. His lips moved from her mouth to her cheek to her ear.

"You took my heart Petra, and I'm not going to stop until I take yours."

Then, his fingers were gone from under her chin, his lips from her ear.

"I'll go tell the others about the plan," he stated.

She blinked her eyes open, but only the brightening ceiling overhead greeted her.

All she saw of him was the gold of his hair as he shut the door to their room behind him.

She fell back to her bed and buried her face in her pillow.

*Coward.*

But whether she was thinking at Axel or herself, she couldn't tell.

He wasn't playing fair. Not at all.

Shaking her head, she quickly readied for her morning with the queen. The dress she'd bought at midsummer sat on the top of her trunk. She ran her fingers over the soft fabric before she shut the lid. There wasn't anywhere for her to even wear such a thing. She stuck her axes through their loops at her waist and stepped out into the hall.

Big Hal slouched against the wall across from her, his brows furrowed.

"Going off to play with your little girl friends?"

She shut the door behind her. "What's your problem?"

"My problem?" He scoffed. "My problem is that you're prancing around this bloody palace like you own the place while the rest of us are trying to figure out how to stop a war. You go gossip with a bunch of women, then come back and distract Axel from what's really important. I've seen the way the two of you have been acting. If I didn't know any better, I'd think all this talk of a better future for Åldras is actually you just trying to keep Axel to yourself when he belongs to all of us. Ever since you revealed what you are, you've been ruining everything."

Petra turned away from him. "Go jump off a wall."

He grabbed her arm. "Don't walk away from—"

She spun, her fist flying for his face. Her knuckles smashed into his cheek.

He released her, cursing.

Her hands strayed to her axes. But she couldn't kill the bloody rockhead. She yanked the axes from their loops and dropped them to the ground.

Big Hal had recovered enough to get his feet under him. He raised his fists up. "Don't think just because you're a girl, I'll go easy on you."

She charged him and he swung at her, holding back even though he said he wouldn't.

*Idiot.*

She moved quicker than he did and avoided the blow. His momentum carried him forward and Petra spun to land a hit to his lower back. Big Hal growled through clenched teeth and spun back toward her.

He was a brute, and if she let him land a blow, she would lose what little advantage she had over him.

Luckily, she knew how he fought, and he hadn't landed a blow on her in years.

The door behind him opened, Ludvig peeking out into the hallway. Erik and Little Hal's door opened only a second later.

"What are you two rockheads doing?" Erik asked.

Big Hal ignored them, charging Petra and attempting to tackle her. She let him wrap his arms around her, but she kept her feet and slammed into the wall behind her. She grabbed his head and bashed her knee into his face.

He reared back with a roar. His fist came flying at her head.

She dodged his swing, sliding past his guard and kneeing him in the groin.

He gasped, staggering back.

She met him step for step. "Must be terrible being a man." With him curled over, she punched him in the face again.

He fell to his knees.

Her fingers grabbed the wavy blond hair atop his head and yanked his face up to look at her.

"You shouldn't have held your punches back."

She smashed her fist into his jaw.

His eyes rolled back in his head, and he slumped to the ground.

Erik's shuffling gait came up behind her. "We all saw that coming."

ᚠᚼ<ᛟᚠᛁᛚ

PETRA STARED across the small table as Queen Kelda poured water into cups. Her knuckles ached from her fight with Big Hal, but she ignored it as she watched Idalia.

The woman's face was pale, dark circles marring the skin under her eyes. Her hollow gaze stared at the still full plate in front of her.

Hildi reached for her arm, grasping it tightly. "You're going to be fine, Idalia. Nothing is going to happen to you or Roman or any of us. The Åldrans are just blustering about, trying to make us uneasy. We're the ones they should be afraid of."

Idalia's head bobbed up and down in a nod, but even Petra could tell Hildi's words didn't penetrate whatever shell Idalia had built around herself.

Petra's fingers tapped her leg under the table. She couldn't keep still. Since Axel had touched her, it was like her entire body was filled with crickets. Every flash of gold turned her head. Every laugh perked her ears.

Hel's halls, she was so rocked.

Queen Kelda set the pitcher of water down on the table. "Perhaps we ought to take a walk." She stood from her seat.

The rest of them stood with her, though the queen had to thread her arm with Idalia's to get her to move.

"What are we going to do?" Hildi asked, falling back with Petra. "She looks as bad as a draugr."

Petra watched the back of Idalia's head. It had only been a day since Doran's arrival, but Idalia had aged years. She knew as well as Petra did that everything would change when Firmin and his brother arrived on these shores.

"We should take her to *The Timber Horse*," Hildi whispered. "Get her out of the palace. Maybe peruse the library. What do you think?"

"We should get her out of this bloody city," Petra muttered.

Hildi frowned. "What would that do?"

"She needs a change of pace." Petra's fingers tapped against the head of her ax. "How would you feel if every word you heard walking around this place was about the coming skirmish? She needs to feel safe and not trapped in these bloody walls like a fox cornered in her own den."

They turned a corner, an archway to one of the many gardens ahead. A pair of braziers stood to either side of the archway, still lit even though the sun had risen two hours earlier. Petra's magic responded to them, and she had to breathe through her nose as they got closer. The temptation to reach into the flames ached fiercely within her. Would it be so awful if she only brushed her fingers over the flames? She shook her head. It would be awful. Freyja's golden tears, this magic would be the death of her.

A servant holding a tall stack of linens came through the archway at the same time as Idalia and the queen. The servant slammed into Idalia, sending her to the floor, and careened backward, the tower of linens tumbling from her hands. She fell into the brazier behind her, making it wobble.

"Look out!" Hildi shouted.

Petra raced forward just as the brazier fell.

Hildi lifted her hand and caught the bowl of flame, but the oil within crested the edge of the bowl, pouring down onto the ground at the servant's feet.

Idalia cried out as some of it caught on the hem of her dress.

Petra slid to the ground in front of Idalia, grabbing her skirts.

The fire sang as it touched her skin.

The ache in her knuckles disappeared along with the small twinge she felt in her shoulder.

Quickly, she bundled Idalia's skirts, smothering the flames.

The song went silent.

Petra let out a breath, bringing her head to the cold stone floor. The warmth suffusing her aching limbs dissipated, though the throb in her fingers and the ache in her shoulder had disappeared.

"Everyone good?" Hildi asked. The sound of grinding stone and twisting metal accompanied her words.

A hand settled on Petra's shoulder. The one that had ached up until now.

"Petra?" Idalia asked. "Did you get burned? I swore I saw your hands go right into the flames."

Petra sat up straight. "No, I'm fine. See?" She held up her hands.

Her only slightly bruised hands.

Idalia let out a breath and dove forward, wrapping her arms tightly around Petra's neck. "Oh, I was so frightened. I thought for sure it would burn me and then there you were, grabbing the dress and smothering the flames. You saved me."

The words carved themselves into Petra's chest.

Wōden's one good eye, she'd just touched fire.

No one had died.

No one had seen.

In fact, nothing had even really happened besides her aches easing. She could still feel the slight crook to her nose and her hands hadn't healed entirely. Perhaps it would all be fine.

After a few more seconds, Petra finally pulled away. Tears pooled at the corners of Idalia's eyes.

"It's good to have such amazing friends."

Hildi crouched down next to Petra. "Us women have to stick together. We've all had some rocking hard times befall us, but we were meant to find each other, to save each other."

Idalia chuckled. "Well, Petra was meant to save us. The only thing we've really saved her from is sore breasts."

The three of them burst out laughing and Hildi actually fell to the floor.

"I can assume the three of you are just fine then," Queen Kelda said, standing under the archway.

Petra looked up at her, having completely forgotten she was there. Swallowing back her dying laughter, she stood. "Are you unharmed, Your Majesty?"

The queen raised a placating hand. "I'm completely well. It's fortunate no one was seriously injured."

The servant still lay on the ground, but now she was bowed low at the queen's feet.

"Please, Your Majesty, forgive me. It's my fault. I should have looked where I was going. I should have—"

"Peace," Queen Kelda said. She helped the woman rise. "You have done your duty to the utmost perfection."

The servant nearly sagged in shock. "Truly, Your Majesty, I didn't mean to run into her ladyship. I should have held onto the linens better and not let them fall to the ground. It won't happen again, I swear it."

The queen set a gentle hand on the servant's shoulder. "I believe you. Now, go fetch someone to help clean this up and to put out these braziers."

The servant bowed low and scurried away, only stopping to bow at Petra and the others as she left. Her face was as white as the sheets she'd been carrying.

"Poor girl looked such a fright," Idalia said. "I hope she wasn't injured."

The queen swept toward them. "Hildi, will you take Idalia to the fountain? I'm sure she'll want to clean off any remaining residue from the oil."

Hildi gave a sharp nod and led Idalia out through the archway.

Petra stayed where she was. She knew a distraction when she saw one.

The queen's head tilted to the side, as if listening to the patter of Idalia's slippers and the thump of Hildi's boots grow fainter. Queen Kelda leaned forward until the edge of her veil brushed against Petra's ear. "When you're finally ready to control that fiery gift running through your veins, I'll be waiting."

# Chapter 21

## Engagements

*Sidan marriage customs are very different than those in Åldras. In Åldras, there are marriage contracts to be signed, ancestral swords and gold rings are traded, and a cord tied around both the bride and the groom. The couple has to wait until an available Frigg's Day, when the families can gather and be married by the king of the isle they wished to wed on. In Sida, they gather with a priest of their temple and the couple exchanges vows. No pomp. No celebration. There are a few witnesses, but it can be as big or small as they want.*

*— FROM THE WRITINGS OF DORAN FINNSSON, THE LAST KING OF GROVÖ*

"We'll have to increase the patrols on the northern wall," Enzo said, rubbing at his chin as he stared down at the map spread across Caeso's desk.

Axel grabbed a paperweight off the corner of the map. The orb was made of glass or possibly crystal, though there was a liquid inside that swirled up bits of glittering sand. He tossed it up. The thing nearly brushed the ceiling.

He caught it, glancing over at Caeso, but the general was staring down at the map beside Enzo.

"What about carvers on the towers?" the general asked. "I imagine Firmin will have Ekte on the front lines. If we can keep the

Häxa up above the fight, they still might be able to use their magic on this side of the trench. The Ekte might not be able to be hit by manipulated earth, but they can't walk on open air."

"Yes, but it'll take a substantial number of carvers to pull off something like that." Enzo rubbed at the stubble shading his chin. "And it'll be difficult to differentiate the Ekte from the regular men at such a distance. If King Doran is to be believed, their numbers are far greater than they have been before."

Doran had been in Sida for a week already and in that time had offered priceless advice to the Sidans. All of it had come through Axel, seeing as Doran was doing his best to keep an eye on the spies Firmin had sent on his ship. If Axel and Petra were going to get away with tricking Firmin into believing they were still on his side, they needed it to seem as if nothing had changed. As if Doran had reprimanded them thoroughly and Axel and Petra were more than repentant. They had even moved most of their things from the palace, returning to their ship with the rest of the crew. The walk into the city every morning was a hassle, but Axel didn't mind it too much, considering he was able to spend those quiet minutes with Petra.

Axel tossed the paperweight up with less force than he had the last time. It didn't get close to the ceiling.

"We should meet with Hildi to see how many carvers we could get on the towers," Enzo said.

What would Firmin do when Axel finally revealed his intentions to help the Sidans? Doran had said not to say anything yet, to wait for the High King to show his own hand before divulging anything. The fact that Doran was on their side still made Axel's chest feel like a hafgufa had been sitting on it and had finally decided to go somewhere else. While Axel still would have kept his promises to the Sidans, having Doran's approval still made it feel like it all hadn't been a mistake. That maybe this wild idea was worth something.

Roman burst into Caeso's office, his eyes bright and face almost frantic.

Axel threw the orb up and it smashed into the ceiling. Shards of wet glass rained down on top of him.

*Freyja's golden tears.*

"What did you do that for?" Caeso asked, coming around the

desk to look up at the ceiling. He narrowed his eyes at Axel. "Perhaps we'll refrain from throwing things in the office from now on."

Axel winced. "Aye."

Enzo walked to Roman. "What is it? Has something happened?"

"No, no. Nothing's happened yet. But by the Maker, something is definitely going to happen. This very night, if I have my way!" He slapped a hand on Enzo's shoulder. "I've talked to Father, and he's finally agreed to allow Idalia and I to marry."

Axel's stomach twisted and Enzo glanced at him quickly before turning back to Roman. "You can't just marry her, Roman. She's another man's wife."

Roman frowned. "Father has gone to the temple to procure papers of divorce. As she was not married of her own free will and as her husband broke the oaths of marriage, Father believes it's finally time to help her break the last ties she has to that man."

Axel shook his head. "But Åldras will not recognize it." Divorce in Åldras was no small thing. It was an honor to be married under Åldran law. A divorce had to be agreed to by the heads of both families and the king of the couple's isle. One signature on a piece of paper would not hold up in the eyes of the Åldrans.

Roman squared his shoulders. "It doesn't matter what your people think. Only what Idalia thinks. I've given her my heart, my body, everything that I have. In my eyes, I'm as much hers as any husband ever should be. Even if a marriage on these shores won't matter to the people of the husband who didn't even truly care about her, it'll matter to me, and more importantly, to her. I'll give this to her before she has to face what's to come, even if that happiness lasts only days. She deserves to know that she's loved. That I won't abandon her. I'll make oaths to her, and I'll keep them until my dying day, no matter if the paper on which they are written is void or not."

Axel put up his hands. "I meant no offense to you or her. I just pray you both know what you're walking into. If word of this gets back to Anders, it will not end well. There will be no hope of reconciliation between the two of you if this happens."

Roman lifted his chin. "Then so be it."

Axel took a deep breath but gave a nod. Idalia did deserve this.

None of them were ever going to let Anders take her back and they knew full well Firmin would do everything in his power to attack Sida now. If they could have this moment of happiness, Axel would not keep them from it.

"You are a fool, brother," Enzo said. "A lucky, lovesick fool, but still a fool."

Roman's scowl melted into a smile. "I came to seek your help. I haven't asked her yet. She doesn't know about any of it. I want it to be a surprise. She deserves to feel cherished. To find some happiness."

Enzo grimaced. "Well, don't look at me. You know my proposal to Hildi literally consisted of me saying 'You know I'm planning on marrying you right?' and her responding with 'I've been thinking the exact same thing.' I'm hopeless."

Axel could just see Enzo and Hildi sitting across from one another at *The Timber Horse* sipping wine and casually talking about getting married as if it were a given. He chuckled.

Both princes turned to him.

A grin stretched across Roman's face. "I have the perfect idea."

ᚠᚾᚲᛟᚠᛁᛚ

"THIS IS A TERRIBLE IDEA," Petra hissed as she clung to Axel's shoulders.

He reached above his head and pulled them higher up the wall. "You have to admit it's rather romantic. Besides, Enzo told the guards what we're doing, so we don't need to worry about getting shot or anything."

"I'm not saying putting ourselves in danger is stupid. I'm saying this sneaking into Idalia's rooms is stupid. She's going to kick him right between the legs."

Axel chuckled. "In that case, you and I will get to enjoy ourselves at his expense."

She huffed. "Did the three of you even stop for a second to think about what pretending to kidnap her will do?"

Axel paused. How would Idalia respond? They had certainly not been quiet about their plans to take her back to Anders when they arrived in Bellator over a month ago. Would she think they'd cast aside their promises and take her anyway now that Firmin was coming?

"I hadn't thought about that," he admitted.

She smacked him in the head, obviously not caring that he was the only thing keeping her from plummeting to her death three stories below them. "No, none of you were thinking."

"We may need to come up with a new strategy."

"Freyja's golden tears, you think?"

Axel gritted his teeth. "Well, what would you want if you were in her shoes?"

Petra's hold around his shoulders tightened. "I don't know. I hadn't thought about it much."

Axel's hand slipped and Petra nearly cut off his air supply.

"Rocks, Axel! If we fall, you're hitting the ground first!"

Axel's ears rang. *Hadn't?* She *hadn't* thought about it? Did that mean she was thinking about it now? He'd certainly thought about it. He'd almost done it once. The desire had nearly taken over his entire mind. When he'd been working on getting the dwarves to build *The Phoenix*, when he and Petra had left Doran's crew the summer they'd turned nineteen. He'd approached the dwarves with plans to build the ship in the shape of a dragon, just like Doran's skeid. When they'd asked him why, he'd said it didn't really matter to him what it looked like. They'd told him he wanted the ship to mean something. That the vessels became part of one's soul when they tied it to something. That if he cared about it, the ship would care about him. He'd thought hard on it. It had been when he'd seen Petra sitting in the shipyard he'd realized what he'd wanted.

A home. For the both of them.

The desire to marry her had crashed into him harder than the waves in Donar's Storm. He'd thought about it for three days. Obsessed over it. He'd had to avoid Petra the entire time in case it slipped out.

Then, she'd had another nightmare. One that had plagued her since Holmberg.

And he realized he couldn't do it.

That he had to wait.

So instead, he'd built *her* a home. Anything she wanted on the ship, he made sure it was there. She'd picked the kind of wood it was made from. The color of the sail. The shape of the hull. When the dwarves had asked again what creature he wanted, the answer came to him.

A phoenix.

A creature of fire.

One that rose from the ashes of its old life as something new.

He'd built Petra a home. One that he had slowly found his own home in. But it was because she was there. She was his home.

"Why did you stop?" Petra asked.

Axel shook himself, the memories clinging to his mind like webs. "Just trying to figure out what we're going to do about Idalia."

Petra puffed out a breath. "No matter what, we're going to have to get off this wall. So, up or down?"

Axel kept climbing. Roman would be waiting for them in the center of the palace, the courtyard all decorated and a holy man from their temple waiting for them. The prince was certainly sure of himself, believing Idalia would marry him on the spot like that.

Axel pulled them the last few feet onto the roof of the palace.

Petra stumbled from his back, shaking out her limbs. "I hope we never have to do that again."

They walked around the roof of the palace, the moonlight glowing on the white stone of the city below them. The sea stretched out from the coast, catching the light from the city. As if the whole world shone with anticipation of the night ahead.

Axel stopped on the edge of the west wall of the palace. A balcony sat twenty ells below, a faint light slipping between the curtains blocking the view into the room attached.

"Do you think she's still awake?" Axel asked.

Petra crouched next to the edge. "Let's hope so. We don't want to wake her and scare her to death."

Axel nodded and scooped Petra up from her crouch.

She squeaked. "What in the Allfather's name—"

He couldn't help himself. He pressed a soft kiss to the top of her head and before she could respond, leaped from the top of the roof.

She clung to his neck, her eyes trained on the quickly approaching balcony below them.

Axel landed on the balcony, allowing his knees to take the brunt of the fall.

"You're absolutely insane," Petra hissed, pushing herself away from him.

He smirked as she rubbed at the spot where his lips had pressed into her hair.

She crept toward the curtain, carefully parting it just enough for a beam of gold light to brush her cheek. She quickly dropped the curtain and slipped back toward him.

"She's still awake," she whispered. "And she's in a bloody nightgown. Honestly, Roman expected her to show up to her wedding in a nightgown?"

Axel snickered at the image of the lady walking down the aisle towards a wide-eyed Roman, and Petra smacked him in the chest.

"Here's what I'm going to do," Petra said. "I'll go in there and tell her Hildi and the boys have planned a late-night excursion and to wear something fun. After she's dressed, we can pretend to be sneaking past the guards and when we get to the courtyard, she can still be surprised."

Axel nodded. "A much better idea than what Roman had planned."

She slipped away from him, thrusting the curtain open to make her entrance obvious.

"Petra!" Idalia squealed. "What are you doing in here?"

ᚠᚺᚲᛟᚨᚠᛁᚾ

AXEL STOOD next to Doran and Petra in the farthest corner from the ceremony. The Sidans had swarmed the courtyard in all their pomp, even though it was practically the middle of the bloody night. Sniffles sprinkled the crowd as the couple echoed the priest's words.

"This is the end of it then," Doran said, his voice so low only Axel could hear.

Idalia stood across from Roman—not in her nightgown—both their eyes overflowing with tears as the priest spoke the vows. They were similar to the ones spoken in Åldras. The two of them promised to care for each other. To cherish one another. To build a life together.

Until the Maker called them home.

*How long would that be?*

Petra's arm shifted beside him.

Her pinky carefully brushed his.

While she didn't have tears in her eyes, they were shining, a green so bright it nearly scattered the shadows that had lived in her eyes for so long.

The couple finished their vows. Roman pressed his lips to Idalia's. She wrapped her arms around his neck.

The entire courtyard burst into cheers. Flower petals rained down from the ceiling, carried over the crowd by a magical breeze. The royal family crowded around the new couple, all with smiles and welcoming hugs.

They were the picture of bliss.

Yet, once the sun came up, nothing would change.

War would still come for them. Perhaps not that very day, but it would come.

And all they could do was pray they would see the future they were fighting for.

Axel wrapped his pinky around Petra's.

## CHAPTER 22

---

# A HOUSE

The wagon hit a bump and sent Petra sliding into Hildi next to her. Idalia had insisted the three of them ride together in this carriage and the men in the other. She'd wanted to discuss some things with Hildi—which Petra had not appreciated being privy to, being the only unmarried woman in the wagon—and sequestered them together.

Hildi covered a wide yawn with the back of her hand. "If I'd known how many hands I'd have to shake and how many smiles I'd have to return, I would have stayed happily back in the nursery with Aggie last night."

"But I'm so glad you were there," Idalia said. She reached for Petra's hand. "That you're both here with me now."

Petra smiled, though it felt a bit more forced than she would like.

In another fit of stupid surprises, Roman had announced they would be doing a short wedding trip outside the city. When Petra had gone to meet with Queen Kelda that morning, the queen had insisted she and Axel, along with Hildi and Enzo, accompany the couple to one of the safehouses right outside Bellator. That she would count it toward Petra's penance.

Why everyone thought it a good idea to send the two royal couples out of the city while they awaited the arrival of their enemies any day now was beyond her.

But Idalia had looked so hopeful.

Petra had bit back her words.

Like a bloody coward.

This woman had made her soft.

"Oh, Hildi," Idalia sighed, looking over their shoulders at the road ahead, "you told me it was beautiful, but I really didn't picture this."

A house sat atop the largest hill. The building was two stories tall, the roof a rusty red color and the walls the same white stone making up so much of the city on the road behind them. A tree practically butted up against the side of the house, its canopy stretching up over the top as if adding another roof to shelter the house.

"Welcome to my childhood home, ladies." Hildi brushed back a lock of her blonde hair that had slipped from its braid. "Well, at least the home I finished my childhood in."

The wagons trundled up a well-worn road and stopped at an iron gate. Two guards pulled open the gate to allow them entrance. An entryway greeted them, a single woman standing on the doorstep. She was older, her back stooped and curly white hair framing her face. She didn't have the look of the Sidans, but she wore one of the simple dresses most of the servants in the palace donned.

Hildi jumped down from the wagon, her arms wide. "Gullveig, you are looking as beautiful as always."

The woman, Gullveig, batted Hildi's arms away. "And you are as impetuous as always. You don't hug a housekeeper, child."

Hildi still wrapped her arms around the older woman. "How is the house?"

"Quiet and empty," Gullveig huffed. "At least, it was until your men showed up and sniffed about an hour ago. I nearly had to hit one over the head with a broom for peeking into your wardrobe. No one has any sense of propriety anymore."

Enzo had hopped out of his own wagon and joined Hildi in greeting the housekeeper. "Perhaps it would be best if I took a look in the wardrobe. You know, for safety's sake."

Gullveig scowled. "I'll have none of that indecent talk here, Prince. And the tree has done more than enough in keeping the house secure, I assure you."

Petra couldn't help glancing up at the tree. It was large, but it made the house more scalable than add any sort of actual protection. It wouldn't be hard to hide away half a dozen men in the branches. There was even a branch that led right under one of the windows. Someone could scale the tree and climb through in less than a minute.

The branch moved.

Not in a breeze, but it actually twisted about, shifting from below the window to curl up over it.

Petra turned back to the housekeeper.

The older woman's gray eyes were already watching her, fingers curled around a twig sticking from a pocket in her dress.

"No point standing around," Roman said, pulling Idalia toward the house. "We have to return to the palace tomorrow. Might as well get right into enjoying our time here."

He practically rushed through the door and disappeared with a giggling Idalia in tow.

Gullveig frowned. "I suspect we won't be seeing those two anytime soon."

ᚠᚾ<ᛟᚠᛦᛚ

AFTER HILDI SHOWED Petra to her room—a separate one from Axel, thank the Allfather, as she wasn't sure she would have been able to sleep at all with him so close to her—they cleaned up from the wagon ride and met in the kitchen. There wasn't a separate room set aside for a dining room, just one large space at the back of the house that allowed a view of the sea. Planter boxes overflowing with flowers and vegetables spread out over the back patio.

Gullveig was definitely Häxa. There were crocus blooming next to red campion and the small trees in their boxes sagged with fruit. It was a garden of the gods, one not found anywhere on Midgard. Unless one was gifted by the gods, of course.

The long dining table stretched from the open patio to the entrance. A robust kitchen stood off to the side, a sleeping fireplace tucked between two ovens. Herbs of all kinds hung along lines of string, and clay jars sat in neat rows along the closest wall.

Hildi and Enzo had already taken a seat at the far end of the table, a bowl of fruit and a platter of flat bread sitting between them. Axel leaned back in one of the wooden chairs, pushing it to balance on its two back legs. He bit into an apple as he watched Petra walk into the room. He'd been doing that lately, turning to her anytime they were in the same space. He'd always been aware of the area around him, but lately it was as if he were purposefully drawing attention to the fact he knew she was there. Like he wanted her to know he was thinking about her.

Something in Petra's gut did a flip and she didn't know whether to eat something to crush it before it took life or throw up.

Axel's eyes darkened.

"Please, just ignore us while the two of you make sultry eyes at each other." Enzo sagged back in his chair. "Maybe all of us ought to ignore one another for the duration of our stay."

Hildi tore one of the flat breads in half. "You know I wouldn't mind. We haven't had this much time to ourselves since Aggie was born."

Enzo shot her a wicked grin.

Warmth prickled against Petra's cheeks. She ducked her head and slid into the seat next to Axel, who finally stopped looking at her.

"I was sad to hear the little princess wasn't coming with us," Axel said. "I've been working on something for her."

So, the little set of wooden horses was for the tiny girl. He'd always had a soft spot for children and they for him. Axel had never met a babe that didn't like him.

A soft smile touched Hildi's lips as she swallowed a bite of flat bread. "That's kind of you. Honestly, that girl is spoiled. Everyone she meets falls in love with her."

Enzo grabbed the other half of Hildi's flatbread and tore into it. "That's because she takes after her mother."

Petra grabbed one of the flatbreads before her stomach could decide it wanted to throw up.

They sat around that table for hours, discussing their families and things they did when war wasn't looming on the horizon. Enzo continuously challenged Axel to competitions—who could eat the most berries, chug water the fastest, hold their breath the longest—

and continuously lost. Hildi and Petra watched them with exasperated amusement, using the time to talk about Hildi's childhood home.

The building had been in her father's family for only a couple generations. When she'd been brought to Sida after the Ekte had executed her family for their magic, she had been sequestered in the house under the supervision of her newly adoptive father for some of the time and the house's staff for the rest of it.

She'd been eight.

"It took five different people to watch me back then," Hildi said. "I'd only recently discovered my förändra and nearly knocked the house down on more than one occasion."

Eventually, her father had brought her to the palace where she met the royal family and developed a friendship with the two princes. The king and his captain had been the best of friends—Enzo having been named after Captain Enzo—and their children had grown up practically as another family. They got into all sorts of mischief, both in the palace and here in Hildi's childhood home. Hildi painted a colorful picture of all of them as youth, one both Axel and Enzo laughed about as the stories progressed.

"The first time the captain caught us kissing," Enzo said, "he nearly stuck my hide to the tree out there. I was twenty-one and Hildi seventeen. He told me if I wanted to kiss her, I had to wait until she'd made it through guard training, and he could be sure she knew how to kill me and get away with it if I ever broke her heart."

Axel burst out laughing.

Petra's fingers knotted together under the table. Captain Enzo had been a father. A brother. A friend. She hadn't often thought about the men who barged into her home the night of the fire. All they'd been were dark eyes and angry faces in her memory. But they'd been people who were trying to make the world a better place.

And she'd killed them.

She was really going to throw up.

"I'll be right back," she said, shooting to her feet. Axel called after her, but she had already slipped out through the patio and into the gardens.

Steps led down the grassy hill until her boots sank into the white sands of the beach. Night would be upon them soon, but Sol's light still hovered in the sky, banishing any shadows Petra could have used to hide in. That was all she wanted to do. Hide. But this bloody house and its bloody occupants kept finding ways to dig their claws into her soul and rip it out of the shadows, throwing her lies into the light for all to see.

She made it to the edge of the water and kicked off her boots. She tore her tunic over her head, her skin prickling as the breeze struck what wasn't covered by the chest wrap she'd received at midsummer. A cold swim in the ocean would clear her head. Would help her gather her wits. Would quiet this burning in her blood.

The water lapped at her legs as she ran into the waves. She dove in as soon as she got deep enough to fully immerse herself. A few more quick strokes and she was past where the waves crested on the beach. She stopped just far enough where she could touch the sand with her toes between the waves. The sea was wide ahead of her, framed by the shores of the inlet. Gulls bobbed in the waves a few ells away from her, their white plumes like clouds hovering in a sky of water.

Freyja's golden tears, she was so ready to get off this bloody continent. To escape this war and the memories it plagued her with.

"Pet!"

She closed her eyes. She couldn't look at him. Not now. Not when there were holes in her mask and wounds in her chest.

"Go back up to the house, Axel," she called back when she was sure her voice wouldn't wobble. When she wouldn't choke on the lump she felt forming in her throat.

But he didn't go back to the house.

He came up out of the water just behind her.

"What happened?" He didn't touch her, but she felt him in the sea behind her, felt how the water moved around the both of them. "You ran out of there like you'd seen a draugr."

Petra shook her head but didn't turn. "I'm fine. Just needed to get out for a minute. I wasn't feeling well."

"Aye, I could tell."

He still didn't move.

"What?" she snapped, finally spinning around. The rest of her words died on her tongue.

He stood not even half an ell away. The water only reached up past his chest—his very bare chest. He was looking at her again. Like *that*. With that burning desire in his eyes. That simmering intensity that made her brain go too fast and too slow at the same time. Like if either one of them moved, they would both go up in flames.

"You can't look at me like that," she said, the words sounding weak even to her own ears, as if every time she said them, she believed them a little less.

He didn't move. Didn't reach for her. He barely seemed to breathe.

"Tell me why, Petra."

She swallowed, her mouth almost completely dry. "Because you should hate me."

His shoulders seemed to fall. "Why do you think I should hate you?"

"Why wouldn't you?" The words fell from her lips. "I killed everyone you loved. I killed Hildi's father. I started this war. And I've never even apologized. Why wouldn't you hate someone who does that? How could you possibly forgive me enough to look at me like you want me? How do I not absolutely disgust you?"

The sea lapped at her back, but she wouldn't let it push her toward him. He would realize what she said was true. That there was too much between them. That he did hate her.

"Oh, Petra." He reached for her, one hand coming up out of the water to cradle her cheek. To hold her still as he studied her face. His green eyes took in every inch, likely seeing into her very soul. He trailed a thumb over her cheek so softly it made the backs of her eyes prickle. He took a deep breath, his lips twisting in a sad smile.

"You never needed my forgiveness."

Petra nearly drank sea water as she lost her footing. "What?"

He grabbed her, pulling her toward him so that he held her above the water. "Petra, there wasn't even a moment where I blamed you for what happened. I never once thought you capable of hurting our family with any kind of malicious intent. What happened on

Holmberg was an *accident*. You were never to blame for the deaths that happened that day. No one is."

She set her hands on his shoulders to steady herself. "But you were so angry."

"Oh, I was *furious*," he admitted, "but not because of what happened with your magic. I was furious because you felt like you had to hide the truth from me. You didn't tell me, and even now I'm still trying to figure out how to reconcile what I thought the truth was to what it truly is. I have my own sins I have to come to terms with—ignorant as they were. But I understand why you did it. I understand why you made that choice and I want you to know that you don't need to be afraid. Not with me. Not anymore."

He pulled her closer until they were flush against one another, his skin practically scorching hers in the cold water. They were so close Petra could see the flecks of gold in his green eyes.

"Don't hide from me," he whispered. "Don't let this be the thing that keeps us apart. If I have to keep pretending my heart still beats in my chest instead of in your hands, it might kill me."

Petra's ribcage squeezed against her rapidly beating heart. "But what if this is what kills you? We can't forget about your prophecy. If we let this continue, it could be the death of you. What if I destroy you just like everything else?"

His gaze never left her face, the resolve in his eyes unwavering. He didn't loosen his hold on her. If anything, it felt like he pulled her closer. As if he believed he would end if he let her go.

"Then at least," he whispered, "I'll have finally lived first."

# CHAPTER 23

# TRUTHS

Axel finally broke.

He couldn't wait any longer. Not with the feel of her hands pressed against his chest. Not when her eyes were the blue of the sea, deep, open.

He wasn't strong enough.

She was worth the long road ahead. She was worth dying for.

His mouth crashed into hers.

Her lips were as firm as her bloody resolve, then she was pressing herself against him, those firm lips softening around his.

Gods, she tasted sweeter than anything he'd ever experienced.

He groaned, moving from her lips to her jaw to her neck. Even though he was the one holding her above the waves, he was drowning. Wave after wave of the kiss beat against the walls they had put up against one another until they finally crumbled.

Salt and smoke coated his lips as he pulled her mouth back to his. His fingers dug into the skin of her back as he pulled her toward him. She was so bloody small when he held her. Yet she fought him for every touch of his lips. She threaded her fingers through his hair and tilted his head back to deepen the kiss. Her legs wrapped around his waist, locking them together as she took her fill of him.

She could have all of it.

All of him.

There was nothing he wouldn't give her in this moment.

Nothing he would hide from her.

His soul was bare before her and if he died in that very moment, he would have simply gone from one heaven to the next.

He'd wanted this for so long it felt like it wasn't real. Like it couldn't be possible. After what happened in Ljust Löfte, he wasn't sure he'd ever get the opportunity to kiss her again. Didn't know if she would ever actually let him. But he'd seen the desire in her eyes. Caught the glances she thought she was being discrete about. The almost kiss a few days before.

There was no chance on all of Yggdrasil's branches he wouldn't kiss her after that.

She shivered and he felt the cold in her fingertips as they scraped his scalp.

He moved his hands to her thighs, spinning around in the water and walking toward the shore.

She pulled away from him for only long enough to ask, "What are you doing?"

The sound of her voice, breathless and rough, made gooseflesh break out across his back.

Her mouth was on his again, demanding, feasting.

*Thunder's beard...*

It took him a few seconds to gather his wits enough to pull back. "You're shivering."

She pressed her lips to his neck. "I'm not the only one."

He nearly crashed to his knees as they broke away from the surf. He didn't even pull his feet all the way out of the sea before he sat, still holding her against him. She left a trail of kisses against his neck. He caught her lips with his, the heat of their kiss smoldering down to a warmth he felt through every limb.

Petra finally pulled away, but only far enough to press her forehead to his. Axel's chest rose and fell at the same quickened pace as hers, their bodies in near perfect sync. Like they always had been. Like they were always meant to be.

The sound of the waves finally registered, and Axel opened his eyes. Petra's eyes were closed, her brows soft and the lines of her face relaxed in a way he'd never seen. It made his chest ache and his soul rejoice all at once.

He couldn't so much as blink, wanting to take in every piece of it, praying this moment could last for an eternity.

But Petra let out a small sigh, her brows drawing together.

"You said you were going to take my heart," she whispered, "like I took yours in the forest outside Ljust Löfte."

Axel kissed the corner of her mouth. "I did, and I still plan to."

She chuffed a laugh, a small, vulnerable yet joyful thing. She opened her eyes, the blue as bright as he'd ever seen it.

"I'm afraid you just might have."

A grin pulled at Axel's mouth.

He captured her lips once more.

ᚠᚺᚲᛟᚠᛖᛚ

EVEN AFTER THEY'D returned to the house, Axel couldn't stop grinning. His cheeks were starting to ache with the strain, but he couldn't bring himself to care.

Petra loved him. It was still new, still only a fragile flame between them, but there was no denying it anymore. There was no hiding it. No smothering it. He felt it under his ribs, in his blood. She loved him and it felt like he could take on the bloody world.

He'd changed into dry clothes, not wanting to sit around in soggy clothing as they ate a late dinner with the others. Candles had been lit throughout the house, giving it a warm glow. When he finally reached the dining room, he found the other couples seated at the end of the long dining table, a spread of cold meats and fruits in front of them.

"The mighty Åldran returns," Enzo said. "I hope you and Petra enjoyed the beach." A gleam settled in Enzo's eye as Axel pulled back one of the wooden chairs and sat. The bloody prince probably knew *exactly* what had happened on the beach. If he hadn't before, he could probably guess by the stupid grin Axel still couldn't keep off his face.

"It's definitely a nice beach," he replied, grabbing a small red fruit out of a bowl. Wōden's eye, it was the best beach he'd ever been to. No other beach would ever compare.

Enzo snickered, and Hildi rolled her eyes.

The air in the room shifted, the shadows growing starker, more defined, as the candles seemed to burn a little brighter.

How had he never noticed that before? He'd always thought the shadows changed when Petra walked into a room, but it had never been the shadows. It had always been the flames.

She stepped through the door and Axel nearly swallowed the red fruit in his mouth whole.

She was in a dress.

It was stunning, a green overdress over a blue underdress. Silver beading decorated the collar and the ends of the elbow length sleeves. Her hair held more curl than wave from the swim, soft tendrils framing her face. She glanced at him. The green of her dress brought out the emerald in her own eyes.

Axel stood from his chair, sending it toppling to the floor. Thunder's beard, he really needed to keep his head. He picked it back up, setting it next to the table. What was he supposed to do with his hands? With everything? Should he go to her? Should he pull out a chair for her? Should he throw her over his shoulder and run back down to the beach to resume that life-altering kiss?

That. He definitely wanted to do that.

"I knew that dress was too perfect to pass up," Hildi said. She kicked out the chair across from her, the one to Axel's right. "Have a seat. Axel was just telling us all about the beach."

Petra's eyes narrowed at him, but a very becoming shade of pink spread across her cheeks.

If she kept looking so bloody divine, he might not even steal her away to the beach. He'd kiss her right there, to the rocks what Enzo and Hildi would think.

Petra sat, nearly throwing herself in the chair as if to spite the knowing looks Enzo and Hildi sent their way. She grabbed a slice of meat and folded it into a piece of flatbread before stuffing it into her mouth.

Oh, she was flustered. It made Axel's stomach flip. He couldn't stop himself from sliding his knee over until it touched hers.

Her movements slowed at the contact. She didn't flinch. She didn't glance at him. But he could practically feel her attention on him, on that point of contact.

"So," Enzo drawled, "while the two of you were taking in the sights, Hildi and I were discussing travel back tomorrow. We're hoping to get moving before sunup so we can get back to the palace before noon."

Their little outing had been a bit of an ask from Roman. They'd all known it could be a risk to leave the palace walls with Firmin on the way, but Roman had somehow convinced the queen to let them come out and she in turn had convinced everyone else. There seemed to be little she wouldn't indulge in for the prince's sake.

"I think that's wise," Axel said. "It might also be a good idea to take watch shifts tonight." The grounds were guarded, but there really could never be enough people on patrol.

Enzo smirked, glancing between him and Petra. "You and I could take the first shift and allow the ladies to take the second." He turned to Hildi. "If that's agreeable with you, of course."

"That should be fine," Hildi agreed. "Idalia deserves to feel whatever peace she can find here. If we can give her even a small measure of safety so she can enjoy her time with Roman, I'll make it happen."

"Then it's settled," Enzo said, speaking around a mouthful of apple. "Axel and I will take first watch, and we'll wake you two for the second."

"What's this about taking watch shifts?"

Roman and Idalia stood at the door to the kitchen, his arm around her back. The two of them looked the picture of marital bliss. Idalia was the most changed, her expression void of any of the shadows that had dwelled there in the few months Axel had known her. Even the weight of Anders's imminent arrival seemed to have fallen from her shoulders.

She'd healed. She'd shed the weight of this war, of her past, and found something to hope for.

Axel glanced over at Petra, her focus on the bowl of fruit in front of her as she picked out the best raspberries.

She stilled when she caught him looking at her and tilted her head. *What?*

He smiled. *I really want to kiss you again.*

The blush bloomed across her cheeks once again, and she set the raspberries on her plate.

"We were just assigning some watches for the night," Enzo said. "None of us want to sit under this roof for longer than we have to."

Roman pulled a chair out for Idalia and sat next to her. "I'll take a shift."

Hildi shook her head. "No need. It's only a night. The rest of us will happily take turns not being under the same roof as a pair of newlyweds."

Enzo snickered again.

Idalia ducked her head, reaching forward to snatch a piece of bread from one of the platters.

"However," Hildi said, "since we are all here, we should discuss what we're going to do when the Åldrans do arrive."

Enzo theatrically groaned. "Leave it to my lovely captain to bring the business into our pleasure."

Idalia rolled her shoulders back, lifting her chin. "I think we should talk about it. I don't know what all of you expect to happen and I'd much rather go into this with my eyes open."

Roman wrapped an arm around her shoulders.

It was commendable, especially for someone who would come face to face with her tormentor. Nothing about this would be easy for Idalia. Not until Sida took care of Firmin and Anders.

"Petra and I have discussed what comes next." Axel leaned forward and settled his arms on the table. "Firmin and Anders will be here within two weeks. They won't come with anything less than five thousand men. They'll likely arrive with fanfare as well. It'll be a show for them. They'll want to be putting on their best for the kings and will be looking for any cracks in Bellator's walls—physical or otherwise. But that means Firmin will be bringing all the kings with him."

"We believe some of the kings won't wish to be part of the battles to come," Petra continued. "We plan on convincing them to abandon the fight and return to Åldras to help their people."

"And how would you convince them to do that?" Enzo asked, skepticism deep in the furrows between his brows.

Axel swallowed. If they were truly going to take the Sidan's side in this war, they needed to be open about their hopes. Their plans.

Petra moved closer to him, offering him strength.

"I don't know how many of you already know, but there's a plague sweeping through Åldras. It's why Firmin is making this push. Åldras is already crumbling."

Roman and Idalia both went wide-eyed, but Enzo and Hildi held Axel's gaze. There was no surprise. No shock. They'd already known. Yet, they hadn't shown their hand. Hadn't used it to convince Axel or Petra either way. They'd held back, when they could have used it against them.

Perhaps Axel could trust them more than he'd thought.

Hildi ran a hand over the top of the table. "You're hoping to convince the kings to turn traitor in exchange for a cure—a *Häxa* cure."

"Yes," Axel answered. "In exchange, the kings would be indebted to Sida, thus allowing Sida to take control with minimum bloodshed."

"And it would leave Firmin and Anders defenseless," Petra said. "They would have no grounds to stand on and Sida could choose what to do with them and any other kings that don't join our side."

"Convincing the other kings is great and all, but what about Idalia?" Roman asked. "I refuse to subject her to being in the same city as that man. Maker above, I tried to get her off the same *continent.*"

*And look where that got you.* Axel would have kicked the prince if he didn't agree with him.

"If there still ends up being a siege," Enzo said, "the palace may be the safest place for her. We have precautions for royalty during an attack."

"But that's right where Anders will expect her," Roman argued. "He'll likely have plans to take her from the palace."

Axel shook his head. "Anders doesn't think in terms of subterfuge. He'll come for you openly."

"You've wounded his pride," Petra said. "He'll want an audience for the moment he faces you, which would work to our advantage.

While he's posturing, we can be working against him behind his back."

Petra was right. While Anders was a boor, he was a showman as much as his brother. He'd already made a spectacle of himself when he'd barged into the meeting of kings in Harligdam and demanded Firmin go after Idalia. It was beyond a husband losing his wife to another man. It was a king losing his pride to a second prince who wouldn't even inherit a throne. And Firmin would come with all the pomp he could, putting on a good face for the three kingdoms as he waited for the death toll to rack up from a plague back home.

"Then what are we supposed to do while you're convincing the kings?" Hildi asked. "I'd much rather not subject Idalia to the torment of that man if we can help it, but I also want us all to come out on top of this fight."

Petra folded her arms on the table. "We strategize."

"Aye," Axel agreed. "From the way Caeso has been talking, it won't take much to keep the Åldrans away from the walls. It'll be the Ekte and any kind of subterfuge Firmin enacts that we will have to watch for. You'll need to be prepared to have dishonor thrown in your face. He won't hold back."

Firmin wouldn't make this easy on any of them.

"But this is talk for another night," Hildi said, smiling at Idalia. "We're supposed to be celebrating."

"I hope we haven't put all of you out," Idalia said. "I know we took a risk coming here today. When Kelda brought up the house likely being the safest spot, I jumped on it immediately. I didn't want today to be another day waiting for Firmin and Anders to come. I wanted it to feel special."

Hildi reached across Roman to take Idalia's hand. "There's nowhere we'd rather be."

"Speak for yourself, wife," Enzo drawled. "I'd much rather be sitting back at the palace, twiddling my thumbs." He winked at Idalia, biting off a chunk of his apple.

Roman rolled his eyes. "All that to say, we're grateful you're here." He met Axel's gaze. "Even you. Who would have thought I would trust an Åldran with something as precious as a day like this?"

Axel smirked. "Oh, you trust me? See, I thought all of this was a trap to lure us into a false sense of security so you could dump our bodies somewhere." He turned to Petra. "We're going to have to tell Big Hal to scrap those eulogies we told him to write. Probably for the best, anyway. The idiot would definitely botch them."

Petra kicked him under the table.

"Not to make the moment any mushier," Enzo said, "but I can't help agreeing with Roman. I never thought I'd be sitting across a table from Mighty Axel Ashersson and Petyr Mallorysson without a blade in my hand or poison in my cup. The Maker really does have a sense of humor."

The conversation moved from there, flowing from different beliefs to favorite foods to childhood antics. Petra even shared a story of the time she and Axel had pranked her older brothers, Brand and Corey, by swapping all their things in Petra's house and calling them the other twin's name. Petra's other brothers had even joined in and made the twins question their very existence for a solid three days.

Had Axel felt anything like that since their families had passed? That sense of family? Of community? Their families had never been perfect. Father and Mallory had been in plenty of arguments and Petra's brothers had all been hotheads—well, besides Gram who never had anything bad to say about anyone and often was the one to broker peace between everyone. There had been fist fights and rows. Pranks and teasing. It had always been loud, but it had been home. There had never been lies tucked into corners. They'd never had to watch their words or bite their tongues. Mila had loved every single one of them as they were. Mallory had tanned their hides for their errors and taught them honor and respect. Father had protected them and taught them how to work together. To find a family in spirit as well as blood.

Yet, as Axel sat at that table, surrounded by liars, enemies, and sinners, he felt connected to all of them. His heart was reflected in the small glimmer of Petra's eyes. His hope in the glow of Idalia's cheeks. His mirth in the curl of Enzo's smirk. His honor in the set of Hildi's shoulders. His stubbornness in the line of Roman's brow.

There was something beautiful growing at this table and Axel wanted it with every fiber of his being.

He wanted this war to end. He didn't want to fight anymore. He wanted to sit around a table like this every day, with these people who understood him, who accepted Petra.

A flash of light caught Axel's eye. Without thought, he snatched a wooden bowl, scattering tiny red fruits across the table, and raised the bowl in front of Enzo's head.

An arrow sank into the wood, flames licking at the edges.

Hildi leaped to her feet. "We're under attack!"

# CHAPTER 24

# AN ATTACK

*The Sidans have always fought with a calculated ferocity not found in many attacking forces. They are a unit, working together seamlessly as they face their foes on the field of battle. They will sweep across a stretch of land, trampling their enemies underfoot. However, those units can be broken and that is when blood is spilled. Åldrans have always been particularly adept at breaking things.*

*— FROM THE WRITINGS OF DORAN FINNSSON, THE LAST KING OF GROVÖ*

The room went from warm to hostile in a blink.

Petra grabbed one of the knives off the table and spun in the direction the arrow had come from. Wood shot out from the sides of the patio, branches creating a barrier and blocking access into the house.

Gullveig walked through a doorway, her knobby hands thrust out toward the open patio. The branches obeyed every twitch of her fingers as she shielded them from the intruders.

"To the front!" Gullveig barked. "I'll barricade the house."

Enzo drew a sword from where it had been hidden under the table. Hildi's magic tore out a section of the kitchen wall, revealing a weapons cache. She tossed Roman a short sword and shield.

Roman handed Idalia the shield. "Keep this over your head and I'll cover you."

Hildi shoved him to the side, taking the shield away and handing Idalia a bow and a small quiver of arrows. "Anyone tries to kill any of us, kill them right back."

Idalia nodded, throwing the quiver over her shoulder and stringing the bow.

Roman stared at her, eyes wide. Apparently, he hadn't been aware his new wife could hold her own in a fight.

A smirk tugged at Petra's mouth as she followed Axel out of the kitchen.

Their rooms were only a few doors down. She bolted into hers, grabbing her belt and wrapping it around her dress. Of course, the one night she decided to be bold, she regretted it. She was never going to wear a dress again. Things always lit on fire when she did.

"They're coming around the west side!" Enzo shouted, his voice muffled by the sound of groaning wood.

The window of Petra's room went completely dark. Leaves broke off from a branch as it scraped against the edge of her open window.

"Petra!" Axel hollered, bursting through her door. "That old bat is using the tree to swallow the house."

Petra pulled her vest of knives on and followed him down the stairs. Smoke billowed down the hall. One of the rooms was alight.

The flames danced in front of Petra's eyes.

"Come on," Axel urged, pulling her through the front door and out into the courtyard.

She turned back to the house.

The tree really was eating it.

The northwest corner, the one farthest from the tree, was in flames.

The others had already run out of the house and were now facing off against the intruders. Idalia stood back by the foot of the tree, her arrows finding their marks as Enzo, Hildi, and Roman stood beside the guards, shields locked together as they pushed toward the intruders.

Petra nearly stumbled when she recognized them as Åldrans.

There were two dozen of them, likely a whole snekkja's deck

worth, up against the dozen guards Hildi had called to travel to the house. Petra didn't recognize any of them, which could signify any number of things, but it likely meant these were a set of scouts whose steersman was an opportunist. Or they'd received word about Roman and Idalia's little trip and one of Firmin's cronies in Bellator had sent a group to take them out. Had they known Axel and Petra had joined them?

"Traitors!" one of them boomed, pointing at Axel and Petra. He pulled a knife from his belt and threw it straight at Petra.

She stepped to the side to avoid it, but Axel's hand shot out, catching the blade in his fingers.

A growl rumbled in his throat, and he turned on the man who had thrown the blade.

The man's face paled, and he spun to run.

He didn't make it far before his own blade sank into the back of his neck.

Petra couldn't even move. She stared up at Axel.

He'd killed an Åldran.

The other men had seen it too. Their shocked expressions hardened, betrayal rippling across their faces.

Mighty Axel, the hero of Åldras, had just killed one of his own.

Axel turned to Petra, his face set in stone. "Kill them all."

They leaped into the fray. Petra threw one of her smaller knives, taking out a tall man who had raised a bow at Idalia. An ox of a man charged Petra, hammer swinging toward her head.

She ducked, using the ax in her hand to take him out at the knees. He crumpled and she buried the blade of her ax in his throat.

If any one of these men made it back to their commander, they would find themselves in far more trouble with Firmin than they already were. Getting rid of the witnesses would have to do.

Axel had already taken out four men, his sword severing limbs in one sweeping blow. Several of the men turned to charge him and he cut down every single one.

She'd never seen him do that. Yes, he was strong, but not like this. His lysande blade sang his fury as it flashed in the light from the flames behind them. Petra didn't even have time to attack anyone before he had already cut them down.

A shout from the row of shield's pulled Petra's attention away from the fight.

"Hildi!" Enzo bellowed. His face was turned back toward the house.

Petra spun, finding Hildi racing back inside.

*Bloody woman.* Petra raced after her. She'd get herself killed in there.

Hildi's boots disappeared up the stairs, and Petra chased after her.

"Stop!" she hollered, but Hildi ignored her.

The farther up the stairs she climbed, the hotter it was. The louder the flames sang.

Petra reached the top and all the air left her lungs.

Fire danced at the end of the hall, beckoning to her.

"Gullveig!" Hildi's voice called out, breaking Petra's trance. "Gullveig!"

Hildi ran out of one room and into another, closer to the fire.

A cough sounded behind Petra.

She spun to find the old woman at the bottom of the stairs, her face creased with ash.

"What on bloody Midgard are you doing up there?" she called. "Those rooms are going to crumble any second!"

Petra spun. She charged into the room she'd seen Hildi disappear into.

Hildi stood inside the door, eyes wide as she watched the flames eat away at what looked like a study.

Petra grabbed the collar of her shirt, yanking her backward right as part of the roof collapsed.

"Come on!" Petra yelled.

Hildi didn't argue, and the two of them raced for the stairs.

The door to their left burst open, flames roaring out into the hallway.

Petra wrapped herself around Hildi and dove for the floor, keeping herself between Hildi and the fire.

The flames found her.

They cooed as they wrapped around her ankles, wove their tendrils through her hair.

She gasped, rolling off Hildi so the flames wouldn't touch her.

"Petra!" Hildi reached for her, but Petra pulled away.

Flames danced at the edges of her fingers, and she tried to quiet the fire. Tried to make the burning in her blood go away even as her heart roared in her ears. It had moved from her ankles and shoulders, but it only grew bigger as she stared at her palms.

"Petra..." Hildi stared down at Petra's hands. Her eyes, widened with shock, narrowed. The light from the flames created haloes of fury in her eyes as understanding dawned. "All this time, it was you?"

A crash sounded, and the house groaned again.

Hildi grabbed her arm, not touching the flames along Petra's hands. She pushed her toward the stairs. "Get to the bottom."

Petra felt tears building as they raced to the ground floor of the house. She fell to her knees at the bottom, the fire growing up her arms. The heat made her entire body shake. Flames sang to her, begging to be released. They dripped onto the hard stone floor.

*Falling into the fire in her house.*

She couldn't go outside like this.

*Mama's sad eyes.*

Her breaths came in rapid bursts.

*The wall of fire shooting out from her.*

She needed to get the flames to stop.

The stone at her feet shot up and encased both of her arms all the way to her shoulders.

The heat left her instantly.

"Gods," she gasped.

Hildi skidded to her knees in front of her, pulling the stone away. The captain's eyes were hard as the stone she wielded as she grabbed Petra's arm.

Because Hildi knew now.

She knew who had killed her father.

They burst out of the front door and nearly hit a solid wall. It wasn't until arms came around her and Hildi's grip on her upper arm fell away that she realized it was Axel.

"Pet?" He pulled back to peer down into her face. "You good?"

She looked up at him and the tears she'd been holding back finally fell.

*No. I'm not good.*

The sound of a blade being drawn from a scabbard sounded from behind him.

Axel whirled, keeping her tucked behind his back, but she saw Hildi standing with a sword in her hand, facing them.

"Did you plan for us to be attacked tonight?" Hildi asked, her voice cold.

Petra pushed away from Axel. "We had nothing to do with this."

Enzo rushed forward, standing just behind Hildi. "They fought with us. Axel took out half the men with his own two hands. Why would they have planned this?"

Hildi raised her sword. "Because they're *liars*."

"Hildi!" Idalia scolded, coming between them. "Petra is our friend. She's done nothing but help us since she got here. Axel too."

"*Ask her*," Hildi barked. "Ask her what happened the night my father died. Ask her what really happened on Holmberg all those years ago."

Axel's face turned to Petra, his eyes wide. *How does she know?*

Petra swallowed back the lump forming in her throat. "I can explain."

"Explain?" Hildi asked through clenched teeth. Tears tracked down the sides of her face. "You've had eight rocking years to *explain*, Petra. Yet you and lover boy here have kept *all of us* in the dark this entire time."

Petra's lungs practically seized, but she stood her ground. If Hildi wanted a fight, Petra would give her one. She'd take the punishment brewing in the princess's eyes.

Enzo's eyes flicked between them. "I'm not following. Explain what?"

"Explain that it was *her*," Hildi seethed. "That she killed my father. That she's the reason we're all in this mess to begin with. That she has led all of us to believe a lie and let hundreds—no, *thousands*—of people die for it."

Petra's chest grew too tight. Too heavy. "I couldn't tell anyone. I didn't know why your father was there. I didn't know anything until that night."

"Know *what*?" Roman asked, taking his place next to Idalia.

"She's a bloody Häxa," Hildi spat. "A fire charmer. The first one in centuries. I bet that's exactly why Kelda has been so insistent she stay close. She's found the only girl in the entire world that can control fire."

They all turned to her, their eyes wide and faces pale.

Hel's halls, how had everything fallen apart so quickly?

Axel tucked her behind him once more. "If you blame Petra for the things that happened on Holmberg, you're no better than the Ekte that have gone after our kind for decades."

Hildi's nostrils flared. "Don't preach to me about the wrongs of our people. You have no idea the things that have happened to Häxakind. The things I've seen. I've lost more than you could ever understand to this bloody war—no, I'm not talking about the little skirmishes we've been fighting for the last eight years. I'm talking about the one that's slowly been building for the last century. The one that sparked the moment the Åldran kings decided they didn't like sharing their power with the Häxa. When they decided to blame all their problems on the only women with the power to fix things."

"Then you should understand Petra's position," Axel said. "What happened was an accident. No one told her what she was. If anyone would have discovered the gift she had, she would have been hunted to the edges of Midgard."

"You're just as complicit as she is," Enzo cut in, standing at his wife's side. "Neither of you ever thought to change the story. You didn't have to blame our people for what happened on Holmberg. This whole war started because we were all blaming each other when no one understood what happened. You could have come up with any story. You're both liars."

Axel's spine stiffened.

"I didn't tell him," Petra said. She wouldn't let Axel take the blame that was squarely at her feet. Wouldn't let him villainize himself for her. "I made him believe the lie as well. He didn't know until recently."

Idalia gasped.

Petra stepped around Axel, setting her shoulders. "I knew if I told him, he would hate me, and I needed him. I was young. I was an idiot. By the time I was old enough to realize I might have made a mistake, it was far too late. My family was dead. My people were dead and dying. I'd killed countless Sidans both that night and many nights on a battlefield after. There was no going back, so I pretended it never happened. I let everyone believe the lie because how much worse would it have been for you all to know the truth? I realized I saved myself. As a child, that was all I knew how to do, and I don't regret it. I would have died for the lies that had been told to me."

"Oh, poor little Petra," Hildi mocked.

"I wasn't like you, Hildi!" Petra snapped. "I didn't know anything about magic. My parents didn't *die* on a pyre so I could learn about my gifts."

Hildi roared, diving toward her.

Axel reached an arm out to guard Petra.

Enzo grabbed Hildi around the waist. "There's no time for this. We need to get back to the palace. Then you can kill each other."

"You can't expect us to take them back with us," Roman said.

Enzo shook his head. "Splitting up right now won't help us. We'll all get back to the palace and sort through this when we don't need to worry about Åldrans jumping out of the shadows."

Petra clenched her hands at her sides, shoving Axel's arm out of her way. Instead of moving, his arm remained a firm barrier between her and Hildi.

"Enzo's right," Axel said. "While we may have taken care of everyone that came to the house, they couldn't have been the only group of Åldrans."

Hildi glared at Petra. "Fine. Get in the bloody wagons."

They all raced over to where the wagons sat outside the gates, the guards swarming them like green locusts. Axel clambered into one of the wagons, gently dragging Petra behind him. The others took the second wagon.

Idalia climbed in next to Hildi, tears in her eyes. Both of them stared at Petra as if they didn't know her.

As if they finally realized she was the monster she'd always known herself to be.

# CHAPTER 25

# SCARS

Axel had killed an Åldran. He'd killed more than one. Their blood stained his hands. It had been inevitable. Since the moment he decided to support the Sidans in this war, he knew he would have to face his kinsmen across battlelines.

He just hadn't expected it to be so soon.

The night devolved too quickly for Axel to wrap his head around. Was this how it would always be? Slivers of absolute joy only to be trampled by destruction?

The wagon hit a rut in the road, throwing Petra into him. Her face was a blank mask, which he knew only hid the roiling emotions within her. He'd seen the hurt when she'd stumbled out of the burning house. The shock. Whatever happened in that house had shaken her. Hildi's vitriol had only exacerbated it further. Petra had donned her demon mask once more.

Axel scanned every inch of her. The hem of her under dress had burned, the edges blackened. Soot streaked her cheeks, but he could see how pale her skin was. The shadows skittering across her eyes. The fire had affected her far more than she pretended it did.

He slowly reached over and set his hand atop hers where she dug her fingernails into the bench. Her fingers tightened their hold for only a second before they loosened. She glanced up at him, a small crack in her mask showing in the slight squint of her eyes.

"We should probably move our things back to *The Phoenix*," she said.

He nodded. It would probably be best to give Hildi and the others time to think things over. Besides, if the Åldrans were already arriving on Sidan shores, the crew's days in the palace were running out. If they wanted a chance to sue for peace when Firmin arrived, they needed to act as if nothing had changed.

The driver at the front of the wagon shouted, yanking on the reins of the horses.

The wagon thrashed back and forth across the road as it tried to slow. Guards yelped as they were thrown around the back of the wagon. Axel caught one by the leg before she could go tumbling over the side.

The wagon skidded to a stop, and Axel got to his feet, looking past the guards to the road ahead. A pile of trees had been laid across the road.

He unsheathed his sword and jumped out of the wagon just as the second wagon slowed behind them.

"What is it?" Enzo called.

Axel held up his hand, silencing him.

Their position was not favorable, which was exactly why they'd been stopped there. Hills butted up against the road on either side, blocking any view of the surrounding area. The trees blocked any way forward, and it would take several minutes to clear.

Which meant the attack would come from their rear.

Petra was already striding past the wagons, her axes dangling from her hands.

Always a step ahead of him.

A shadow slipped from the hill to their right and Petra's ax went flying.

It sank into a man's skull.

Before he could even sink to the ground, men swept out from the shadows, some even having buried themselves under cloth on the sides of the hills.

"Circle up!" Enzo hollered from somewhere at the front of their caravan, but Axel couldn't turn away from Petra. Not when she was in the middle of it all.

She'd retrieved her second ax already and immersed herself in the dance of the fight. Everyone called her a demon. It was times like these when he saw what they did.

Her expression went completely blank, every inch of her attuned to the fight. She cut men down with an almost clinical precision. She didn't get flashy with her swings, simply watched, waited. She didn't play with her opponents. Not when she already knew she would win. You could see it in the tilt of her head. In the surety of her movements.

A man barreled toward Axel, a long spear in his hands. Axel caught the spear with his sword, tucking it between the metal of the spearhead and the wood of the shaft. With a twist of his wrist, he popped the weapon from the man's grasp.

He recognized him.

*King Bjorn.*

He was ruler over Koli, one of the isles farthest east from Harligdam. They'd fought beside one another on more than one battlefield. Broke bread around dozens of fires over the years. He was a fine warrior, though he made questionable choices in his friends. He and Anders were usually found on the same side of things. He'd probably been one of the first to offer his men up to come to Sida. It was more than likely it had been his men who had attacked the house and drove them this way.

"Rocking traitor!" the lesser king snapped.

"Bjorn," Axel growled. "What are you doing?"

Bjorn drew a large knife from his belt. "I'm following orders, Axel. As you should be."

Axel held up his sword between them. "Call off your men. No one needs die tonight."

"I may not be able to kill you," Bjorn spat, "but I will hold you back while the rest of my men take out the Sidans."

The king swung his knife.

Axel didn't flinch. Didn't raise his sword to deflect the attack. If this foolish king thought his paltry knife was going to—

Something happened to Axel's arm. The sensation was odd. Like his skin was screaming.

Something was very wrong.

He looked down at his forearm, finding a line of red.

Red? That couldn't be right. Why was there blood on his arm?

A searing sting bloomed from the spot and Axel nearly dropped his sword. He reached for the spot, gently prodding at it. His fingers came away wet.

Blood.

He was bleeding.

Why was he bleeding?

Bjorn stared at the blood, his own eyes wide. "Gods save us."

The searing sensation disappeared, and Axel's mind cleared.

He could bleed.

His gaze met Bjorn's astonished one.

And this king knew it.

Axel raised his sword.

Bjorn didn't so much as gasp as Axel's blade plunged into his chest.

He met the king's eyes, watching as the light went out and the gods collected his soul. Axel prayed the man found peace in Valhalla, that the death at his hands would be honored. Because he didn't want to kill this man. He was a father. A brother. A king. A friend.

But he'd seen Axel bleed.

Axel pulled his sword from Bjorn's chest and let him fall to the ground.

No one could know. His invulnerability was protection for not only him, but the people he loved. No one could find out.

He spun back to the fight, finding Petra surrounded by dead bodies on all sides. A brute stood over her, a two-headed ax swinging toward her head.

She was a blur of shadow as she bent backward, the blade only an inch from her nose. Before the man could finish his swing, Petra had already straightened and sliced into his side. The man stumbled, and she used his momentum to carry him forward past her and she buried the other axe in his spine. He fell and she finished him off with a dagger to the base of his skull.

When Axel turned to the Sidans, he found Enzo standing atop the wagon, his eyes taking in Axel.

There was a question there. A small frown between his brows.

The rest of the Åldrans fell to the Sidans. Only one remained, his face bloodied as he was brought to kneel before Enzo.

Enzo looked down on him with cold eyes. "Give me one reason why I should allow you to live."

The man stared up at the prince with defiance. "Kill me. It doesn't matter. My High King is coming, and there's nothing you can do to stop his wrath from taking out every rocking Sidan in this kingdom." He spat, the spittle landing on Enzo's tunic.

Enzo didn't so much as blink, even as the spit dripped down his front.

The man laughed, a crazed sound, looking at Idalia. "Hope you enjoyed your little Sidan prince, Lady Idalia. Anders is going to enjoy cutting him up piece by piece, starting with his—"

Petra materialized behind him.

The dagger in her hand stuck from the man's throat.

She yanked it out, and in one fluid movement, stabbed him in the heart.

"Petra!" Hildi barked, pushing through the guards. "You killed our only source of information."

Petra's head tilted to the side, her demon mask still in place. She didn't reply, only stared.

Axel saw the moment the effect hit Enzo and Hildi. Enzo's nostrils flared, but he'd seen Petra fight on a battlefield more than once. He knew what Åldras's demon was like.

Hildi flinched.

Axel strode to where Petra stood and set a hand on her shoulder. She didn't actually move, but he felt the tension dissipate. Felt the fight leave her.

"We need to clear the trees," Axel said, sliding his hand down Petra's shoulder to rest at her lower back.

Enzo gave a sharp nod and called for the guards to start moving the trees.

Axel led Petra to the front wagon. "You good?"

She gave a sharp nod. "Someone got a nice hit into my side, but nothing that won't heal."

He dropped his hand and pointed at the trees. "I'll be right back."

Once she was inside the wagon, he jogged toward where the guards gathered.

Enzo caught up to him. "Axel, you've got blood on your arm."

Axel's heart nearly stopped dead in his chest. He looked down, but only the smear of his dried blood marred his skin. The wound was gone as if it had never existed. As if it had all been a trick of the eye.

"Oh," he breathed. "Must have gotten some on me during the fight." He wiped at it with his fingers, revealing the skin underneath.

Enzo blew out a breath. "I could have sworn..." He shook his head. "Never mind. I'm glad you and Petra were able to help us. I can't imagine what you both must be feeling, but I'm grateful to you."

Axel nodded absently, slowing as Enzo began giving orders for the men to move the trees and check the surrounding area to make sure none of Bjorn's men had escaped.

Axel's thumb rubbed against his arm where the blood had been.

Where a white scar marred his skin.

ᚠᚾᚲᛟᚠᚤᚷ

WHEN THEY CAME into view of the city gates, a group of green-clad guards poured out from the city to meet them. Caeso rode at the front of the group, meeting Enzo's carriage at the head of the caravan.

"What happened?" Caeso asked, taking in their haggard group. Sol's light had just come up less than an hour before, but they hadn't been supposed to arrive back at the palace until that afternoon.

"Åldrans attacked the house," Enzo said. "From what I would guess, someone got word we'd left the palace and decided to try their luck."

Axel's knuckles cracked as he clenched them between his knees. It was dishonorable, what Bjorn had done. There was little honor in attacking someone off a battlefield. Especially by burning down a house. What if Aggie had been there? What about Gullveig? Petra said the old woman had gotten out, but Axel hadn't seen hide nor hair of the old housekeeper.

The guards circled the wagons, but Axel stood. "I think it best if Pet and I part ways with you here." They needed to tell everyone what happened. Needed to be prepared for questions that would arise should anyone find out what happened to Bjorn and his crew.

Would someone discover them and give them proper funeral rights? Generally, after a battle, the crew would take their fallen and build funeral barges to usher the bodies out to sea. There would be a requiem, and a flaming arrow would light the barge. Would anyone honor those fallen? If it wouldn't look so condemning, Axel would even do it himself.

Caeso's dark brows drew together. "You need to be debriefed and the lot of you need checked over by a healer."

"I don't think it wise for us to return to the city. Not after tonight. We'll return to *The Phoenix* with our men."

"Will you abandon your pact with us? To the queen? Will you return to the city tomorrow as promised?"

Axel grabbed Petra's hand and pulled her from the wagon, careful of the side she'd injured. "We slew our people in the name of friendship with Sida. I think we've paid our end of the bargain tenfold, don't you?"

Caeso gave a slow shake of his head. "I won't make either of you stay in the palace, but it is for the queen to decide." He looked to Petra.

Axel huffed out a breath. "Then we'll go to our ship first to speak with our crew to let them know what's happened. We will resume our agreed to service tomorrow morning."

The crew needed to prepare for the backlash that would come from this. While Axel had made sure none of the Åldrans had escaped, the rest of Bjorn's crew was still out there somewhere. Their king had died last night, and they would blame the Sidans for his death.

Caeso gave a sharp nod and turned his horse around. The wagons trundled forward after him and a squad of men broke off in the other direction, likely to scout out any other ships and see to the bodies they'd left behind.

Axel swallowed and met Petra's eye.

Her brows furrowed. *Time's up.*

He turned away from the city gates. Petra was right. Their time in the city was up. The fantasy they'd lived for the past few weeks was about to be ripped apart, and there was nothing either of them could do about it.

"Come on," he said. "We need to gather the crew."

## CHAPTER 26

---

# A FIGHT

Petra leaned her head against the cool stone at her back, staring up at the vaulted ceiling of the classroom. Sol had yet to light the room, but she'd needed to get away from the ship. The crew had been very disgruntled the night before, the obvious change to their circumstances chafing. Thank the Allfather Little Hal and Ludvig had supplied the ship over the last few weeks. Sleeping in a palace had made them all soft. She'd been glad to leave all of them to their grumblings this morning.

Petra needed to convince Queen Kelda to dissolve their deal so she could return to *The Phoenix* and ready for Firmin to arrive. It certainly wouldn't do to have him show up and see all of them getting chummy with each other. It had been wisdom on Axel's part to kill the Åldrans that had attacked them the night before last. If word got back to Firmin they were protecting the Sidans, it would be more than just their heads that rolled.

Footsteps echoed from outside the room, the quiet shush of slippered feet. Petra pushed herself up and stood.

Hildi stormed in ahead of Idalia, her face twisted in a scowl. "I didn't know if you'd actually show up."

Petra shrugged. "Not like I had much of a choice."

The two of them stopped across the room, an invisible line drawn across the stone floor.

Idalia stepped forward slightly. "If you want out of the agreement with the queen, we could talk to her." She looked back at Hildi again for a moment, as if unsure she would stay put. "I don't think Kelda would make you stay if it would cause problems in the palace."

"As if the queen would let the only fire charmer in existence walk out of this deal." Hildi scoffed. "There's no way Kelda will let little miss firecracker over here skip off into the sunset."

Petra clenched her hands at her sides. Even if Hildi was right, the agreement was nearly finished. Firmin would arrive on these shores in days, and Kelda wouldn't be able to keep Petra here even if she wanted to.

And if Hildi and Idalia didn't want her here, she would leave.

Frowning, Idalia turned back to Hildi. "She saved your life last night."

"And that's supposed to erase everything she's done?" Hildi's expression turned thunderous. "She's killed *hundreds* of people, Idalia. She lied about what happened on Holmberg. This whole bloody war is all *her* fault. Saving my life one time doesn't fix all the wrongs that came before. It doesn't change the fact that she's been lying to everyone this entire time and never had any inclination to bring the truth to light."

The words dug their claws into Petra's chest, finding purchase in her heart where they had beat out the truth to her for the last nine years.

*Liar.*

*Imposter.*

*Killer.*

She was everything Hildi said. She always had been.

Petra folded her arms over her chest. "Yes, I was the one who burned down Holmberg. I was the one who lied and blamed Sida for this war. All of this is my fault. What are you going to do about it?"

The floor under Petra's feet disappeared.

Petra tried to fall to the side, away from the hole. Her stomach hit the edge, and she scrambled to pull herself out of the hole. She'd made it almost all the way out, but the stone swallowed her foot.

She reached forward to unlace her boot, but a stone flew at her head.

"Hildi!" Idalia grabbed Hildi's arm. "Stop it!"

The distraction gave Petra just enough time to reach for the dagger she'd sheathed under her tunic. With her foot caught at such an awkward angle, it was difficult to aim correctly, but she threw the dagger at Hildi's leg.

Hildi dodged it, throwing Idalia to the side.

The stone under Petra's foot released and she nearly faceplanted. She rolled into the stumble, popping back up onto her feet.

Hildi screeched, her hands clenched into fists at her sides. Practice stones from all over the room flew out of their places, revolving around her.

"Give me *one* good reason I shouldn't kill you where you stand."

Petra widened her stance.

A stream of water shot through the entryway. The liquid surrounded Hildi's arms, yanking them to her sides and freezing solid. Hildi staggered to her knees; her jaw gritted together as the weight of the ice pulled her down.

"Cease this nonsense at once," Queen Kelda demanded, sweeping into the room. Small bubbles of water collected the stones and placed them back into their baskets. The ice cracked around Hildi, shattering to the floor.

The queen's veiled face turned from Hildi to Petra. "Are we to be barbarians in these halls? Slaughtering our friends in our home?"

Hildi shook her head, still on her hands and knees. "No, Your Majesty."

The queen settled her hands behind her back, as militant as General Caeso. "I haven't trained any of you to be brash. If you're going to kill someone, at least have the decency to do it correctly."

"Yes, Your Majesty."

"Get up."

Hildi shoved herself to her feet, her eyes still staring down at the floor.

"Now, the three of you need to figure out how to work together again. Petra, you need to determine how to use your gifts without turning into a mess of memories and regret." She turned as Petra's jaw clicked shut. How the bloody queen imagined the three of them would ever get along again only the gods knew.

"You've really been trying to get her to use her magic this entire time?" Hildi seethed. "You've let a murderer walk around our palace? Near our children?"

"Petra has helped kill more people with her axes than her magic," Queen Kelda said, "yet you didn't complain one bit until you knew about her gifts. Besides, what happened on Holmberg was a result of her awakening, not some young girl's foolishness. You brought down half a mountain and nearly killed your village when you discovered your förändra. Don't let your hunger for vengeance blind you to truth, Hildigunn. If you let it rule you, it will make you sloppy."

Hildi's attention whipped back to Petra. "You truly didn't know you had magic until that night?"

Petra glanced at the queen but gave a single shake of her head. How did the queen know all of this? How long had she been watching all of them? She was powerful, but there had to be limits to that power. Right? If she'd truly understood what was going to happen, she would have been able to stop this war from coming.

Idalia's hand pressed to her mouth, her eyes glittering with tears. "It was all just a mistake?"

Petra shrugged. She didn't even have words to respond. What else did they want from her? The bloody queen was laying it all at their feet. Freyja's golden tears, when would everyone finally be able to move past this? It was so much easier to bury it, to not talk about it. Now, too many people knew and all they wanted to do was *talk*.

"Honestly, it's a miracle you didn't discover it sooner, Petra," Queen Kelda continued. "Though, being that your förändra would be fire, it makes sense that by the age your magic would have been ready for you to take hold, you were old enough to learn that fire burns."

"Is that why you dressed up as a man?" Hildi asked. "So you could stay in Åldras, and no one would guess?"

Petra shook her head. "It was for Axel."

"Ah, yes," the queen said. "The mighty hero. *The she-bear's shield, the eagle's doom.*"

"It kept the two of you together," Hildi concluded, eyes wide. "If you admitted to being a girl, they would have shipped you off to whatever family or house would have taken you in. They would have separated you."

"Do you see what happens when we get the whole picture, Hildigunn?" Queen Kelda asked. "Not everything is so black and white. We must understand our enemies to know if they are truly the ones we ought to be fighting in the first place."

Hildi met Petra's eye. There was still a glimmer of steel there. While she had more of the picture, she was not even close to appeased. "Yes, Your Majesty," she responded dutifully.

With careful steps, Idalia stepped forward and took one of Petra's hands. She didn't speak, but she squeezed Petra's fingers in apology. In camaraderie. She wouldn't hold this against her. Wouldn't let this come between them.

The queen clasped her hands in front of her. "Now that we have that all out of the way, we need to discuss what comes next."

They gathered at the head of the room where cushions were circled around a low table. Idalia smiled at Petra as she sat across from her, and something in Petra's chest settled back into place. These women had become important to her. Their opinions of her meant things. It was foolish, but she couldn't help it. She'd let Hildi tear into her if it made it easier for them to mend the rift. Let Idalia cry at her until the tears dried up and she could smile again. Petra would give anything for these women.

And it scared her.

"Now, let's discuss the coming days," the queen said. "Idalia, your former husband will arrive on these shores in six days."

Idalia's face turned ashen.

"We aren't going to let him get within sight of you." Hildi reached over and took her hand. "I swear it."

Idalia nodded, closing her eyes and taking a shuddering breath. "Six days."

The queen turned to Petra, the outline of her profile visible through the veil by the light coming in from the window behind her.

"Which means we only have six days until our bargain is finished."

Petra turned toward her, though she couldn't truly meet her gaze through the veil. Did she hide because she was trying to protect herself from those who would use her against those she loved, or was there more to it? Was she more like Petra? Hiding behind a mask so others would only see what she wanted them to see? To distract them from the truth of what she was? As Petra studied her, she saw so many things that felt familiar. Felt like maybe her and the queen were more alike than any of them realized.

She turned to Idalia, then Hildi. All of them had faced terrors worthy of nightmares.

"Then teach me." Petra straightened her shoulders. "Teach me how to use this magic so I can help all of us make it out of this fight."

The queen leaned back, obviously pleased. "We will. But there are things you need to understand before we get to practicing."

Water dribbled up from the small pool under the window, spreading over the top of the polished table in front of them. The tree of Yggdrasil grew from the ice. Queen Kelda's voice lowered as the story spread before her.

"The Häxa have long believed the gods created man and set them on the earth to toil and labor to earn their place among the gods. We were taught in Åldras that as mortals worshipped the gods that gave them life, the gods bestowed blessings upon them. In Sida, we have accounts of a Maker of the world, passed down from generation to generation. Of a being of light and life that walked the earth long before us, that created the ground beneath our feet and fills the world with magic."

"Which is true?" Idalia asked.

Hildi's expression turned contemplative. "I think all religion is founded in truth. It has to be. We all feel that little bit of light and connection when we find those little slivers of truth. It's how that truth is interpreted by men, by imperfect and unintentionally igno- rant people, that creates the division. Perhaps, the Åldrans found an account of some sort of deity in the past that led someone to believe there were more than one and that line of belief grew. Or, someone literally met more than one god, and it expanded their knowledge even though others didn't adopt the belief. All I can say is that I think all of us have been given truth and all of us get to choose how, where, and what we worship."

Worship wasn't something Petra had ever thought about too

hard. Mama and Da had been fearless in their beliefs, teaching Petra and her brothers about the gods who held stewardship over the world they lived in. Axel was far more prayerful than she, but she'd never truly considered the differences between what Åldras believed and what Sida did.

"For today," the queen said, "we will focus on the Åldran side of things, considering most of the Häxa lore we have is written in that context."

Her story unfolded further, the tree transforming to a group of women.

"A blessing was given to a group of Åldran women who had proved their mettle in the eyes of the Allfather, who could give power over the very world He created. To each of these women was given the power to control the elements of the world. It has been lost to time exactly how many of those elements were given, but we have records of seven."

Seven women remained on the table, their icy hands holding aloft the förändra of each Häxa. The fire charmer of the group looked suspiciously like Petra. The stone carver like Hildi. None of the other women looked familiar. The air whisperer stood taller than everyone around her. The water wielder had a riot of curls trail down her back. The shifter almost looked like an older Viveca, the granddaughter of the Great Mother. The women stepped closer to one another, tightening the ring.

"Kings bowed to these women," Queen Kelda said, "and nations flourished and fell under their care."

The isles of Åldras bloomed in the ice.

"We're unsure where the term Häxa first originated, but they were revered, given positions of power and influence in their communities. They flourished within the isles of Åldras, the magic blooming under their feet as they thrived. For generations, the magic strengthened. The other kingdoms looked to Åldras for wisdom, sought alliances with them, hoping their magic would spread to their own kingdoms. While there were a few instances when a Häxa was born outside the isles, it was a rare occurrence. Åldras was a seat of power—not only in magic, but in every aspect. The Häxa ruled beside the kings and the kingdom only prospered."

Fissures formed in the ice.

"But it wasn't enough. With power comes greed. The kings of Åldras grew jealous of the Häxa and their magics. They wanted all the power for themselves. They began to spread their ideals across the kingdom."

Åldras fell away, reforming into women being dragged out of their homes, decapitated in front of their children, stuck to burning pyres.

Idalia gasped. Even Petra's heart ached at the sight, though it was a familiar one.

"Did you know the Ekte learned their marks from the Häxa?" Queen Kelda asked, forming a man with marks all over his body. "Stone carvers have a knowledge of the language of magic, given to them through their gifts. No one knows exactly how it happened, but the Ekte gained similar knowledge, except they realized if they carved certain marks into their skin, it would work to give them powers against magic. Every Ekte is marked from head to toe in all the markings of their order, so the knowledge cannot be taken from their minds."

The man melted, as did the grotesque scene. It was replaced by a map of the three kingdoms.

"So, the Häxa became powerless. It started out with restrictions. They could only practice in certain ways, under certain conditions. Then, it was only certain women that could practice, those given leave to under the king's thumb. The Häxa revolted, but the revolution lasted a week, divided as they were between the past and what some believed the future would be. After that, magic was banned from Åldras. Anyone found practicing was brought to a swift end."

The ice wavered slightly, as if the emotions were almost too much for the queen, but it formed into the seven elements once again.

"And now, we live in a world where we're killed for the gifts we are born with. For the power of the gods running through our veins."

"But how do we stop it?" Idalia asked. "How do we save the Häxa now?"

The ice smoothed over the surface of the table, then slowly melted as it streamed back to the basin it had originally come from.

"We start here," the queen said, "like our mothers did before us. We start by understanding the past, so we can create a new future."

# ᚠᚺᚲᛟᚠᛁᛚ

THE STARS GLITTERED OVERHEAD as *The Phoenix*'s crew gathered around one of the dozen fires on the beach. *Sorrow*'s crew had set up camp a little ways from them, tents reflecting the glow of their cookfires. The flames danced in front of Petra's eyes as the history of the Häxa replayed over in her mind. She'd come to terms long ago with the fact she hadn't been taught the ways of the Häxa by Mama. The situation had been impossible, and Mama had likely prayed Petra had been born without any magic and when no förändra attached itself to her, there had been nothing to worry about.

But now? Now Petra had this magic running in her veins, and she couldn't even use it. Couldn't wield it like Hildi or Queen Kelda could. She never would have been able to outlast Hildi if the queen hadn't interrupted their fight that morning. She would have been dead in minutes. But if she could wield her own gift?

"Your brain is very loud tonight."

Petra nearly jumped up from where she sat as Axel held out a plate in front of her. She grabbed it, nearly sending the food tumbling to the sand before she caught it.

"Today was an interesting day," she said.

He settled onto the beach next to her, their shoulders brushing.

Since she'd returned to the ship that afternoon, he'd seemed to find ways to keep touching her. His mind had been distracted since coming back from Hildi's house, from facing King Bjorn, and the physical contact appeared almost subconscious. A brush of his hand against hers. His arm around her shoulders. Sitting close enough for their knees to touch.

It was heavenly torture.

What she wouldn't give to be back on that beach near Hildi's house, where no one was watching. Where she could capture his soft lips with hers.

Warmth spread across her cheeks, and she had to choke down the bite of fish she'd taken.

"How many men do you think will arrive with High King Firmin?" Big Hal asked from across the fire. He still sported a nasty bruise on his jaw from their fight in the hall four days ago.

Axel shifted beside her, taking a bite of flatbread before answering. "I imagine he'll have gathered his most ardent followers first. King Bjorn, King Viggo, and King Amund would be the first to offer up their men."

Petra glanced at Axel from the corner of her eye. They hadn't told the crew about King Bjorn, Doran's men bringing far too many listening ears along with them. It wouldn't be long until word reached everyone that he'd fallen while trying to attack the Sidans.

If Firmin was wise, he would have taken a route through the southern isles and gathered men as he went as well. The stretch between Generös to Mötesplats was riddled with cities and towns, a lot of Åldras's population finding homes along the shores there. Those kings would be the hardest to win over though, being close to the plague and having taken the brunt of the war over the last several years.

"And what are we to do about the Sidans?" Ludvig asked, glancing over at the other cook fires ringed with *Sorrow*'s crew. "While I understand King Anders's anger, this kingdom shouldn't be punished for their prince's folly."

Petra took a bite of the goulash Little Hal had thrown together that evening. Ludvig had certainly taken the Sidan's side with enthusiasm, especially since he'd been distracted by whatever girl he'd fallen for inside Bellator's walls. The way he phrased his sentence made him seem like he was still thinking of Åldras, but everyone around their small fire knew exactly what he meant.

Were they going to turn their backs on their friends when Firmin arrived on these shores?

Ulf grunted. "Aye, but that is the way of kings and princes, is it not? They make mistakes and their kingdoms have to pay for them.

The people fight for the honor of the kingdom cast into the mud by their leaders."

No, they weren't going to turn their backs on the Sidans.

"But this fight isn't about kings and princes. It's about a girl. Why do girls always ruin everything?"

All heads turned toward Big Hal.

He stared back at Petra.

So, it hadn't been enough that she'd handed him his arse back in the palace. She set her bowl down by her feet. He still wanted to throw his anger about and expected everyone to be on his side.

"Be very careful with what you say next, Big Hal," Axel growled.

Petra elbowed him. She didn't need him to defend her.

Brows furrowed, Big Hal glanced about the fire. "The lot of you can't pretend we aren't in this *situation* because a girl made things difficult."

They definitely weren't talking about Idalia anymore.

Out of everyone, Big Hal still had the hardest time accepting Petra. And the idiot didn't even know the half of it.

"I think we're in this *situation*," Ludvig parroted, "because of how the women back in Åldras are treated. Lady Idalia would have never felt like she had to run if Anders had respected her the way she deserved. And Pet"—he cleared his throat—"Pet wouldn't have this bargain with the queen keeping us trapped here."

Big Hal rolled his eyes. "Just because you've found yourself a skirt to chase doesn't mean the rest of us don't see the truth for what it is. We want Åldras to make it out of this? Maybe we need to stop letting stupid girls get in our way."

Petra was on her feet and around the fire before Big Hal could start up another tirade. She tackled him into the sand.

"Pet!" Axel called from somewhere behind her, but she didn't look back.

She straddled either side of Big Hal's stomach and punched him square in the left eye.

Big Hal roared, bucking her off before she could move up onto his chest.

She rolled to the side, sand spraying as she came to her feet.

He was already there, a roaring punch coming for her midsection.

It wasn't difficult to dodge to the side, but he came with a hook that she took straight to the nose.

A crunch reverberated through her skull and stars blossomed at the edges of her vision. *Hel's halls.* Blood trickled from her nose.

"Didn't hold back this time," Big Hal snapped.

"I'll kill him!" Axel roared.

Petra kicked one of Big Hal's legs out from under him and looked back to where Ulf and Ludvig held Axel's shoulders and Little Hal stood in front of him. While they wouldn't actually be able to hold him back, at least they were distracting him. She needed to finish this before he got involved.

Big Hal tossed sand at Petra's face.

*Bloody idiot.* Petra staggered back, blinking the grit out of her eyes. "What is your bloody *problem*?"

"None of this would have happened if you'd just been a *man*!" Big Hal raged. "Ever since you were bit by that rocking draugr, everything has fallen apart. All of us are going to *die* because of *you*."

He tackled her and she couldn't stop it. Not when his words had punched through her.

They fell back into the sand. All air sputtered out of Petra's lungs as she fell onto her back. Her breath didn't return as Big Hal's weight settled across her chest. Hel's halls, the brute weighed as much as a horse. Shifting her hips out from under his legs, she kneed him in the side. His arms around her loosened and she wriggled out from under his weight.

Cheers sounded from a way off. *Rocks.* Doran's crew caught onto what was happening. No Åldran could resist the call of a fight.

Petra needed to finish this.

She shoved herself to her feet at the same time Big Hal did.

"You're going to get us caught," she hissed. She brought her hands up. "If *Sorrow*'s crew gets wind of this, we're done for."

He shook his head, fists at the ready. "You can't blame this on me. Everything was perfect. Our crew was helping Åldras. Doing good and saving people. You're the one who forced us into this mess. Axel wouldn't have to keep sacrificing everything for you. If you would have just been a good little girl and done as you're told, none of this would be happening."

Petra snapped.

She swept under Big Hal's guard. Her fist slammed into his stomach once. Twice. Three times.

He reached for her, but his hands found no purchase as she came around behind him. She wrapped her arms around his neck and squeezed.

He flopped onto his back, crushing her against the ground, but she didn't let go.

The sound of boots rushing through sand met her ear.

Axel bellowed, but she couldn't hear what he said over the pound of her own heart in her ears.

"Listen to me, you rocking maggot," she hissed in Big Hal's ear. "Everything I have ever done and will ever do is to protect Axel. If you think for one second I'm going to let you get away with harming him, I won't challenge you to a duel. I won't fight you for all the world to see. I'll come in the darkest part of the night, and I'll be the mare that sits on your chest to plague your dreams. You'll wake long enough to feel the edge of my blade across your neck and meet my eye as your life seeps out onto your pillow. It'll be a dishonorable death, and the Valkyries will scream their rage as they drag you down to Hel's rocking halls."

Big Hal jabbed his elbow into her side. It would leave a mark, but the burning in her blood masked the pain. Her hold on his neck tightened.

"Mark my words," she growled, "if you do anything—*anything* —to jeopardize Axel's safety because you think me being a female is really what's putting you all at risk, this girl will take care of you herself."

Ludvig and Ulf reached them first. They grabbed hold of Petra's arms and pried them from around Big Hal's neck. The big oaf sucked in a breath as he rolled to the side. With help from Ludvig, he got to his knees, the skin of his face fading from purple to red as air returned to his lungs. He shoved Ludvig back and stomped away from the camp.

Brows low, Ulf pulled Petra to her feet. Several of Doran's

crewmen stood behind them, a few groaning that the fight wouldn't continue. Others taking in the aftermath with glee.

Petra glanced past them.

Axel stood at the back, Doran's white knuckled grip on his shoulder. There was no misinterpreting the unbridled fury etched into Axel's face as he glared at Big Hal's retreating form.

"Show's over," Ulf said. "We ought to return to our meals before they grow cold."

The men glanced from Big Hal to Petra to Axel, the bloodlust thick in the air.

Petra wiped the blood from her nose with the sleeve of her tunic and walked past them all back to the fire. Her bowl still sat where she'd left it and she shoved a large bite of goulash into her mouth.

She'd deal with Big Hal later.

# CHAPTER 27

## SWORDS

Axel stared down at the white line on his forearm, the clang of swords in the sparring rings around him echoing in his ears. It was so strange, how such a small mark on his skin could change so much.

He had half a dozen of them now, little marks on his fingers. He'd been too curious the day they'd arrived back in Bellator. He'd taken the bone needle in his trunk and stabbed himself in the finger. The pain had been instant, the sharp twinge completely foreign. Sure, he'd experienced pressure that had caused him pain, but nothing like this. One small droplet of blood had welled up on the tip of his finger before his skin had closed up. The magic still healed him incredibly fast, but what did it mean?

Until he fully understood what was happening, he wouldn't tell Petra. Wōden's eye, he was a coward, but he couldn't tell her. Not now. Not when her eyes glittered when they met his across the cook-fire at night when she didn't shy away from his touch. When the want he felt buried into his bones reflected in her eyes. When everything he'd wanted was finally his.

Petra had said she loved him. Said she'd given him her heart. But he hadn't fallen dead like he'd worried he would when he was a lad. If anything, he felt amazing. He felt *strong*. Just last night, he'd taken Petra in his arms and run down the beach out of sight of the rest of the crew. She'd weighed nothing as he'd carried her. She wasn't a small woman—*thank the Allfather for that*—and should have started to grow heavy in his arms. But she hadn't. He could have run from Bellator to Castellum, holding her against him the entire way, and his arms wouldn't have grown fatigued at all.

"Axel."

His head shot up, finding Enzo staring down at him.

"What?"

The prince rolled his eyes. "Maker take me. Have you not heard anything I said?"

Axel straightened in his seat. Several of the guards standing about the sparring ring looked their way, mirth twinkling in their eyes. Doran stood next to General Caeso a few steps away, his own brow raised. Wōden's one good eye, he really hadn't been listening.

"Sorry, I was thinking about something."

"Yes, I'm pretty sure that something has a pretty face and can kill a man in two seconds flat," Enzo mumbled. He shook his head. "You're up for a bout."

Axel pushed himself to his feet as a murmur started up at the other end of the ring. He'd scaled back on the bouts. Enzo still pushed him into every competition he could think of—yesterday, the prince had challenged him to a game of hnefatafl and after years playing against Petra, Axel had still taken the victory—but he needed to be careful. It wouldn't do to have one of the Sidans see he could bleed, especially not when so many of them still believed Axel to be their enemy.

"Your Majesty," voices echoed.

King Leonardo swept into the arena in all his kingly glory. No crown sat on his brow, and he wore a similar uniform to that of the guards. His boots were worn and the leather of his sword's handle soft from use. Roman stood at his side, a scowl on his face.

"Mighty Axel, a word?" King Leonardo's voice brokered no argument.

Axel strode across the ring, Enzo at his heels. He gave a short bow when he approached.

King Leonardo smacked Roman on the back, nearly sending him sprawling into the sand. "I woke up this morning with the craving for a good sparring session with my sons. As we have uneven numbers, I was hoping you would join us."

Axel blinked. He'd fought plenty with Enzo in the ring, but he'd never seen the king or Roman attend matches before.

Enzo bounced on his toes. "Who would you like to go up against first, Father?"

King Leonardo's eyes glimmered, the same look Axel had seen in his eldest son's eyes on more than one occasion. "Looking for a good bout, Son? I wouldn't mind reminding you who taught you how to pick up a sword."

Enzo bared his teeth in a grin.

Axel turned to Roman. "Shall we leave these two to their posturing?"

Roman gave a short nod, though his expression wasn't one of the cool confidence he usually exuded. There was a flicker of consternation that Axel couldn't quite place.

Did he not want to spar?

Axel plucked one of the practice hammers from the weapons rack. He'd broken too many swords over the last few days and Caeso had banned him from them. Something about not having unlimited funds for supplying the headquarters. Axel had made it a point not to remind the general about the catapult the soldiers had dragged out of the city walls to "test" a few days ago.

Roman selected a short sword and picked up a shield, testing the weight of both as he stepped into the ring. Axel stopped on the other end to allow the prince a few practice swings. He held the sword as naturally as his brother, though the gleam of excitement for a fight was definitely absent. He almost looked bored.

The fight might be over before it even got the chance to get started.

"On your mark, Your Highness," Axel said.

Roman settled into his stance, his brown eyes narrowed in concentration.

He gave a sharp nod.

Axel crossed the ring.

Roman's sword came up, making a jab for Axel's jugular.

Axel knocked it away with his hammer and rammed into Roman.

The prince flew back into the sand, landing on his rump.

"Maker above, you're worse than an ox!" Roman said, shaking himself and getting to his feet.

Axel twirled the hammer in his hand. "Is that a yield?"

Roman shook his head, rolling his shoulders. "Not quite yet, but I can see now why my brother has had the palace healer on standby every afternoon."

Axel laughed, stepping back to allow Roman the space to get his feet fully under him. He didn't want to make him look too bad.

Yet.

Roman charged him, making careful movements, testing Axel's boundaries. There weren't many. At least, there hadn't been. Now that he could be somewhat injured, Axel retreated a bit more readily. He didn't need anyone figuring out he could be injured and word getting back to Petra. She would kill him once he told her.

If he told her.

No, that wasn't right. He needed to tell her. Needed her to know how things had changed. It wasn't smart to keep vital information from a strategist, especially with the coming battles ahead. But telling her would put her walls back up, and he was very much enjoying those walls being down.

The prince made a jab at Axel's side, which he sidestepped.

"Are we courting or sparring?" Axel asked, knocking the top of his hammer against Roman's sword.

Roman gritted his teeth, that Sidan savage in him sparking in the furrow of his brow. He thrust the sword at Axel's shoulder and used the shield to deflect Axel's answering blow.

"Come on, Roman!" Enzo shouted from where he was going toe-to-toe against King Leonardo. The two of them moved with a practiced speed, knowing the move of the other before it was made. Their matching grins were more suited to a party than a sparring match.

Roman's face turned hard.

This time, the swing actually held some weight as he went for Axel's arm.

Axel pulled back slightly, allowing Roman to push him into a retreat but dodging every blow. The prince wasn't as ferocious as Enzo. What little stamina he'd mustered up at the beginning of the fight was already lagging.

Axel dodged another swing, finally smacking his hammer against the prince's shield. Roman grimaced at the reverberations likely shaking the bones of his arm.

"When you told your father you wanted to fight Anders," Axel said, "was this the kind of fight you had in mind?"

Roman swiped at him but chased the movement with a smack of his shield against Axel's side. *Finally.*

"This isn't a real fight," Roman stated.

Axel dropped his hammer and grabbed the top of Roman's shield with his hands. As he lifted it over his head, Roman came with it.

The prince was smart enough to take a jab at Axel, but when the sword came close, Axel turned, allowing the jab to slide past him. The blade skimmed his shoulder. But the momentum carried Roman's hand forward and Axel used his free hand to twist the prince's wrist and take his sword from him. He dropped the shield and spun the sword back to face Roman.

"Is it a real fight now?"

Roman's eyes went wide, and he brought the shield up to protect him as Axel swung the sword at his head. Axel allowed the movement to carry through, slamming the sword into the shield and cracking it.

"Axel!" Caeso barked. "Quit breaking my stuff!"

Axel released the sword and crouched, sweeping the prince's leg out from under him.

Roman squawked as he tumbled to the ground.

Axel grabbed the edge of the shield and ripped it from Roman's arm.

The prince fell to the ground, weaponless.

Axel tossed the sword and shield off to the side. "Yield, Prince."

Roman roared, shoving himself to his feet and barreling at Axel. *About bloody time.*

Roman's fists swung wildly, his frustration making him strong but sloppy. Axel took a couple blows to the side and one to the gut—

Hel's halls, those hurt worse than they had previously—before he tackled the prince to the ground. With quick movements, he encircled Roman's neck with his arm.

The frantic beat of the prince's heart pulsed at his throat.

"Listen, Roman, because I'm only going to say this once."

The guards began to cast their eyes about. Enzo and Leonardo stood off to the side, their matching gazes wary.

Axel leaned forward so only Roman could hear him. "If you go into a fight against Anders with even twice the amount of care you did with me just now, he will kill you and he will make it look easy."

Roman's elbow jabbed into Axel's side, but Axel didn't release him.

"Fight like you have something to live for, Roman," Axel said, "or your new wife will end up a widow far sooner than either of you will like."

"Axel!" Doran barked, shoving through the growing crowd. "Let the man go."

Axel released Roman from the hold and the prince gasped for air, rolling onto his side.

Enzo swaggered up, pulling Roman to his feet and slapping him on the back. "At least I'm not the only one to get thrashed by Axel."

Roman shoved his brother away, not saying a word as he stormed from the sparring ring.

"Oh, brother." Enzo rolled his eyes. "He certainly inherited all the good humor in the family."

Axel watched the retreating prince's stiff shoulders. "I hope that was Roman at his worst."

"He certainly wasn't in fine form. He's a wicked shot with a bow, but his swordplay is something that has always needed improvement —both in attitude and in technique. He's always been a tad bitter about it." Enzo brushed dust from his trousers. "But enough about him. I want to talk about you."

"Me?"

Enzo grabbed Axel's arm, making the skin there twinge. He dragged him toward the offices.

Axel's lungs constricted.

*No.*

He ripped his arm from Enzo's grip. He tugged at the sleeve of his tunic. Roman's sword had sliced through the fabric, and a small line of blood had soaked into the brown linen.

"Keep your arm covered, you idiot," Enzo hissed.

Axel tucked himself closer to Enzo, using the man's shoulder to block anyone else's sight. He followed the prince to one of the buildings, one he hadn't visited before. Men and women in green uniforms crossed their path, bowing at Enzo who greeted them with a friendly smile and a nod, even as his feet raced down the hallway. He stopped at a nondescript door in the middle and yanked Axel into the room.

A small office, barely large enough for a desk and a chair, greeted him.

"Hildi's office," Enzo supplied, locking the door behind them. "Now, what on the Maker's bloody earth happened to your arm?"

Axel yanked his tunic over his head and twisted his arm so he could get a better view.

Flakes of blood stuck to his skin, but the cut had already healed.

He blew out a breath. "It's nothing."

"Nothing?" Enzo nearly screeched. "Mighty Axel just experienced a sword wound."

Axel shrugged back into his tunic, ripping the sleeves off at the shoulders. "You're mistaken."

Enzo shook a finger at him. "Now, I would have believed you if this wasn't the *second* time I've seen a blade cut into your skin. Yes, I saw what that Åldran did on the road. Don't try to lie to me."

Axel blew out a breath. "Don't think this means I'm weaker now."

"Oh, I wouldn't dare," Enzo said. "I just saw you lift my brother and shake him like one of Aggie's cloth dolls."

The words felt genuine, but Axel saw the calculation in Enzo's gaze. The way his eyes kept flicking to Axel's arm as if waiting for him to bleed again.

"Why do you think it's happened?"

The reasons caught in Axel's chest. Would Enzo use this against him? Would knowing Axel could be harmed break the fragile bridge they'd been building together? Enzo's crusade to find Axel's weaknesses hadn't lessened. While it had taken on a good-natured air to it after Axel and Petra had begun working with them to stop Firmin, Enzo still had to choose Sida over everything else.

And maybe that loyalty was enough. For all of them. If there was anyone Axel wanted to trust in this whole bloody kingdom, it was Enzo.

Axel's mouth twitched. "Petra."

Understanding dawned in Enzo's expression. "So, your little prophecy isn't just a bunch of Häxa fluff after all."

Axel folded his ripped sleeves and stuck them in his belt. He rubbed once more at the already healed skin of his shoulder.

"No, it isn't."

# CHAPTER 28

## A GIFT

*The way Häxa freely use their magic in Sida is almost terrifying. Even before I was born, the High Kings had outlawed the use of magic in Åldras. Some of the older kings have told stories from their childhood of watching women water fields with a flick of their hands. I always knew it was real but seeing it before me is something entirely different. Even the Häxa of Ljust Löfte were often quieter in their use of magic in the brief time I was among them. But the Sidans have no qualms with magic breaking down the walls of their city when someone can step up to fix it a moment later.*

*— FROM THE WRITINGS OF DORAN FINNSSON, THE LAST KING OF GROVÖ*

"Focus, Petra," Queen Kelda's voice echoed around the room. But all Petra could do was focus.

The small flames danced in front of her.

The bowl of fire sat on the table like the most tantalizing song and the most torturous poison. It called to the magic running through her veins, practically begging her to touch it. To wield it.

"You're letting the element control you," the queen said. "You need to master your own emotions and use that as your foundation to center the magic."

Petra breathed in deeply through her nose, filling her lungs until her ribcage protested.

"When you discovered your förändra, what happened?" Hildi asked.

That made Petra lift her gaze from the fire.

Hildi leaned against the wall next to the window, her blue eyes sharp.

Petra bit the inside of her cheek. How much could she divulge? Should she tell them about the Sidans breaking into their home? About Mama's stones?

"My mother and I were the only two in the house and the Sidans broke in, saying they were going to take us."

"Wait." Hildi pushed away from the wall. "Didn't your mother know they were coming?"

Petra shook her head.

The captain's brows drew together. "But that was part of the protocol. We didn't take any Häxa that didn't wish to be taken. There was always an understanding between the Häxa and the extraction teams." She looked to Queen Kelda. "Why would my father have gone in without them knowing?"

The queen spread her hands. "That, I cannot say."

Hildi turned back to Petra. "So they attacked?"

"No, they were just talking. But I'd left my knife across the room. When I went to retrieve it, I tripped and fell into the cookfire in the center of our home. The magic took over after that."

The queen folded her arms, tapping her fingers against her sleeve. "Often in the beginning, the magic will root itself to the memory of the first time it is used. It's why it's so important for the younger Häxa to practice with their gifts from the very beginning, to separate the magic from that event. However, in your case, the magic has likely buried itself into that moment so only when you can replicate those feelings will you have the power over the magic."

"Though," Idalia piped up, sitting behind Petra, "I don't think throwing her in a fire is the best idea."

Petra gave her a grateful smile over her shoulder.

Idalia flashed her a grin of support.

"No, you're right, Idalia," Hildi said. "Until we can be sure of

Petra's control, we don't wish to go throwing her into danger. Water wielders have still drowned themselves and stone carvers have buried themselves alive out of foolishness. As there isn't much knowledge about fire charmers, we'll move forward with care."

The queen sat across the table from Petra. "Do you think you can reach into the fire and keep the flames from touching the edge of your sleeve?"

Petra clenched her hands in her lap. "I don't know. I don't seem to have any control over it when it touches me."

"Enhancing that control will help you overcome doubts about your gift." Queen Kelda summoned water from one of the pools. "Just as I can keep the water from soaking into my clothing, you too should be able to keep the flames from scorching your clothes."

The queen gestured toward the fire. "Let's give it a try. Go ahead and touch the flames."

Petra glanced at Hildi. "Are you sure it's wise?"

Hildi snorted. "Don't worry. We'll put you out before you set the palace ablaze."

"You'll be fine," the queen assured her.

Petra rubbed her fingers against the rough fabric of her trousers, attempting to wipe off the sweat. Her entire arm trembled as she reached forward.

The fire nearly leapt toward her as she drew close. Holding her breath, she touched it. Magic sang in her blood as the flames rippled across her skin. The heat licked at her fingers, spreading up her arm and into her chest.

"Keep it centered," the queen said.

Petra's lashes fluttered as she tried to refocus. Something in her nose popped and she could breathe a little easier.

"Did her nose just heal?" Hildi asked.

Queen Kelda held up a hand. "It's the secondary gift. It's healing her body."

Petra jumped to her feet. Big Hal had left bruises under her eyes after their fight four days ago. Thunder's beard, Firmin might recognize her as the girl he'd captured. What would Axel say?

The flames grew.

"Get it off," she said.

The fire spread up her wrists, singeing the edge of her sleeve.

"Get it off!"

Water sprayed over her palms, making the flames sputter until they finally died.

The queen stood, coming around the table. She took Petra's chin in her hand. "Remarkable," she said, turning Petra's face to either side.

Petra ripped her face free from the queen's grip and raced over to one of the pools. There was just enough light in the room to give off a reflection.

Mama stared back at her.

"Hel's halls," she hissed. She smacked the water, distorting the image.

"What's the matter?" Idalia asked. "Isn't it marvelous that your magic healed you?"

"Not when others have seen my face this way and believed me to be someone else." If Firmin arrived and saw her looking like the Häxa woman he had taken to Harligdam only weeks ago, he would put the pieces together. While a few of the Sidans—like the royal family and the council—now knew her identity in correlation with Petyr, most of Sida and Åldras were still blissfully unaware.

Petra turned to Hildi. "I'm going to need you to break my nose."

"Wait, what?" Idalia squawked.

Hildi didn't hesitate. She smashed her fist into Petra's face.

Black creeped into the edges of Petra's vision and she fell to her knees. "Rocks, Hildi, I didn't mean *now*." Blood dribbled onto the floor, and she pinched her nose to keep it from spilling everywhere as she strode toward one of the windows.

"You weren't very specific with your request," Hildi answered, a bit of vindication coloring her voice.

Queen Kelda swept up beside Petra and laid a hand on her shoulder. "I guess you'll have more reason to hold off the fire from healing you if you don't want to have to keep breaking your nose." She turned back into the room. "Let's try it again."

ᚠᚾᚢᚲᛟᚨᛁᛚ

Hildi broke her nose three more times.

Even thinking about it made Petra's eyes water.

She'd had her nose smashed into her face plenty over the years but knowing it was coming was far worse than taking a hit in the middle of a fight. Praise the Allfather it didn't hurt too badly to heal with her magic. Adjusting the bloody thing herself had almost made her throw up.

Squinting through the afternoon light, she traversed the streets of Bellator leading out to the harbor. It was easier to reach *The Phoenix* by going through the west gate, slipping through the grand houses around the palace walls and taking the main road toward the northwest shore where Erik had beached the ship. However, Little Hal had requested she get a bushel of figs—which he'd taken a particular liking to—and some of the spices only found in the market square north of the palace.

A shadow swept across the alleyway next to her.

It was a bloody huge shadow, or she would have missed it entirely.

She increased her pace, not quite jogging, but almost, as she swept toward the market.

A hand shot out and grabbed her arm.

She grinned as Axel yanked her past lines of clothing, wrapping her in his arms when they were out of view of the street.

His lips pressed into her hair. "I missed you," he grumbled.

"Did you?" she prodded his side, making him jump. He still hated being tickled.

He grabbed her hand, bringing it to his lips. When he met her eyes, he stiffened.

"What happened to your face?"

She shrugged.

"Petra," he rumbled, making her skin prickle. He reached for her, setting his hand against the side of her neck and running a thumb across her jaw.

"I had it coming," she said breathlessly. Thunder's beard, why did even the barest touch make her sound like some lovesick fool? She was supposed to remember his prophecy. Remember why they couldn't be together.

Gently, Axel pressed his lips to her cheek, avoiding her nose. His mouth trailed down to her jaw, then her neck.

A small moan slipped from her.

Perhaps she was a lovesick fool. Perhaps, just this once, she could let herself forget.

His hands came around her, and he lifted her in his arms, pushing them back as he continued to press his lips to her throat. Her hands grabbed fistfuls of his shirt, which he'd seemed to have lost the sleeves of. He curled around her, blocking her view of everything but him.

Not that she could pay attention to anything else. As his lips continued to explore the sensitive points of her neck, his hands roved over her back, pulling her closer to him.

A small scream shattered the moment.

Axel straightened, his head whipping to the mouth of the alley.

An older woman stood with a basket on her hip, wide eyes slowly narrowing into a scowl. She shook a finger at him. "Go find somewhere else to ravish each other. Maker above."

Axel flashed the woman a devilish smile and grabbed Petra's hand. "Wonderful advice. I'll do just that."

The woman clutched at the neckline of her dress, muttering remarks about indecency and the folly of youth.

Petra's heart burst out of her chest when Axel grinned back at her. He nearly ran into a cart crossing an intersection and she had to pull him back before he plowed into a pair of laundresses.

She followed him down another street and into a small garden that sat behind a group of houses. In the middle of the day, no one but the bees seemed to be about.

Axel pulled her down to sit on the edge of one of the boxes holding the trees.

"You're going to get us into trouble," she said.

He tucked an arm around her, pulling her flush against him so he could lay his cheek atop her head. Under the sun, it would have been uncomfortable being so close, but under the shade of the tree with a slip of a breeze weaving between the buildings, it was soothing.

"Are you going to tell me what actually happened to your nose?" he asked.

She sighed. "I didn't want Firmin to recognize me when he arrives. I asked Hildi to break it."

He straightened, turning to look at her. "You did what?" He cradled her face. "That idiot doesn't deserve something like this." His thumbs gently brushed the tender skin of her cheeks.

"If he figures out what we did, what I am, we would have more than just this war to worry about." Firmin would have all their heads.

"If you think I care about what that man does or doesn't think, you're wrong."

She rolled her eyes. "Don't be an idiot. You have to care about what he thinks because he's the one holding the ends of our leashes, no matter how much you want to ignore it."

"Then we'll leave."

She stared up at him. "What?"

He got to his feet. "Aye, we'll just go back to Åldras. We'll make Plan B our new Plan A. Or we'll run away. We'll leave this war behind us. We'll find a place in Isberg or past the mountains to the south of Bellator. Something. We'll leave all of this behind us and leave everyone to fend for themselves."

She really couldn't tell if he was being serious or not. She stood, stepping into the path of his pacing. "You and I both know we can't." The regret would eat him alive. He would never be truly happy. Eventually, it would drive him to insanity.

He stopped and pulled her to him. Like he couldn't stand being far from her. Not that she minded one bit.

"I would." He pressed his forehead to hers. "If you said the word, I would take us out of this city this instant. We would walk away."

She shook her head. "I'm not going to make you do that. I'll let Hildi break my nose a hundred times before making you give up this fight. We've said from the start that we would see this war to its end."

"And here I thought I was the virtuous idiot."

She shoved him, though he hardly moved. "You are. I'm just trying to make sure you aren't being an idiot about this. You don't need to save me, Axel. You can't be my shield all the time."

He studied her face, his eyes flicking from her nose to her eyes to her mouth. His brows set in a firm line, his expression growing serious.

"I love you, Petra."

She blinked, a laugh bubbling up. He couldn't just say stuff like that to her. Why did he have to keep surprising her? Though she shouldn't have been surprised. He'd always been better at talking about how he felt. Better at expressing the desires of his heart.

He stepped toward her. "I would give anything for that love. My heart. My body. My soul. They're all yours. I would sacrifice every other dream I have if the dream of getting to call you mine, of knowing you were happy with me and wanted me, were a reality."

"Axel…"

"You want to know something funny?" He took one of her hands, playing with her fingers. "Remember that day that King Leonardo asked me to stay behind? When he'd revealed he knew about the plague? He told me to choose a side of this war. A few months ago, the answer would have been instant. But I realized that the side doesn't matter now. Both Åldras and Sida have their faults and their virtues. What matters to me now is that we're together, as we were always meant to be."

His prophecy echoed in her head, making her ears ring. "But what about your magic? What about what it says if you fall in love with someone?"

"I don't care about my magic or some stupid prophecy."

She pulled her hand away. "Don't say that. Your magic is part of you."

"But it doesn't define me, just as your magic doesn't define you. It isn't who we are. What we choose, how we react to things and what we do with the gifts we've been given? That's who we are. And I'm just a man deciding to choose a life filled with love and light. I choose to love you, Petra."

Tears gathered at the corners of her eyes. "You say the stupidest things."

"And you say far more than you think you do." He wiped the tears away. "Just let me love you."

What little resolve she'd thought she had finally crumbled under those simple words.

"All right, as long as you let me love you back."

# CHAPTER 29

# DECISIONS

Axel leaned against the hull of *The Phoenix*, the warmth from the sand under his legs keeping the chill from the sea breeze at bay. A few of the cookfires flickered along the beach, but many of them had already smoldered, the crewmen from both ships not minding the summer chill off the sea in their bedrolls.

Doran walked about his camp, leaning down next to some of the men on watch, likely gathering reports from the day and checking in with each of them. He'd always been an attentive steersman. After making his rounds, he wove his way through the sleeping mounds of soldiers on the beach until he reached Axel. He plopped down onto the sand next to him.

"I had an interesting meeting with King Leonardo this morning."

Axel smirked. "I knew the two of you would be bosom friends in no time." The two men were similar in their way of thinking. Neither of them truly wanted this fight and both were politicians to a fault.

Doran had been meeting with the king and his councilors nearly every day since Roman and Idalia's marriage. All under the guise of attempting to get Sida to capitulate to Firmin's demands of course. He still hadn't been able to root out the spy on his ship. He and King

Leonardo discussed possible negotiations for when Firmin and Anders arrived, though it was difficult to know how the kings would respond once they got here. Would they be weary from their travels and think better of their threats once they saw the might of Bellator at their feet? Or would the long trek only stir up their anger toward the Sidans and bring about unnecessary battles?

"Based on what his scouts reported back, we only have two days until Firmin arrives on these shores."

Axel sat up. "Two days?" He counted the days in his head. Petra said Queen Kelda had said so, but the days had slipped past him.

"Aye," Doran said, leaning back against the ship as Axel had a moment before. "But it wasn't that particular subject that intrigued me. He told me about possible plans to convince the Council of Kings to switch loyalties."

Of course the old king had told Doran about their strategy. "Sounds like a wise plan."

"Do you actually think that will work?"

The question caught Axel off guard. "I—I don't know."

Doran's brow furrowed. "I need you to be very honest with your next answer, Axel. I know King Bjorn arrived on these shores recently. One of my men saw his ships, yet none of his crew was to be seen. I recall a certain day you and Petra went off with the princes and their wives. Did you happen to cross Bjorn's path?"

Axel swallowed. "Yes."

Doran nodded. "Did you kill him?"

"Yes."

Closing his eyes, Doran blew out a breath.

"Are you going to tell Firmin?" If anyone found out he'd been the one to slay the king, his entire crew would find themselves floating at the bottom of the Vit Sea with stones wrapped around their ankles.

"I'm not going to tell *anyone*," Doran hissed. "You're bloody lucky I'm one of the few that knew where you'd gone and that Bjorn had come to Sida earlier than expected. Hel's halls, Axel, you killed a king."

"I had to," Axel said. "They would have killed the Sidan princes."

"They *should have* killed the Sidan princes," Doran said. "I hate to say it, but that was their bloody job. If Firmin even gets a hint that you had any part in Bjorn's death, any hopes you have of convincing the kings will go to the bloody fishes."

"They would have killed Pet," Axel hissed. "She didn't look like Petyr. They were either going to suspect her as one of the Häxa refugees, or they would have figured out who she was and gone to tell Firmin. Either way, them seeing her put her in danger and I wasn't going to have that no matter what."

Doran blinked up at him. "You're in love with her."

Axel gave a sharp nod. "I have been since I knew what love was."

"And what about her?"

Axel smirked. "I wouldn't dare speak of her feelings without her present, but I definitely haven't been led to believe she doesn't reciprocate."

In fact, he'd been playing the kiss in that alleyway over and over in his head all day. He'd wanted to touch her all week, yet every time he'd gone to her, someone had been around. When he'd heard Little Hal ask for supplies the night before, he'd taken advantage of the situation and didn't regret it one bit.

Doran groaned, digging the heels of his hands into his eyes. "Hel's bloody halls. If the two of you aren't careful, this will get her killed." He rubbed at his face. "Perhaps I should have her come stay on *Sorrow* while Firmin is here."

"It's fine, *grandfather*." Axel rolled his eyes.

"It is certainly *not* fine. My crew has already been eyeing *The Phoenix* with suspicion. You can't get distracted now, when we're about to embark on the most crucial part of this war."

"You think I don't know that?" Axel snapped.

"I think you want to forget it." Doran sat up. "Our people are *dying*, Axel, whether by Sidan blade or this rocking plague, they are dying. It's our job to protect them, and if we allow ourselves to get distracted, we won't protect them from anything—Firmin included."

"What do you want me to say, Doran? Do you want me to take back the feelings I shared with Pet? Do you want me to tell the Sidans to all go jump from their white-stoned palace?"

"I want you to live through this bloody war, Axel. The work

you've done with the Sidans could change the course of our kingdom's future, but none of it will mean anything if we aren't here to make sure it happens." Doran's head fell back. "I want all of us to make it through this bloody war."

The fight drained from Axel's chest. "I know you do. That's all you've ever wanted. You've trained Pet and I nearly our whole lives to live through battle after battle. You've kept our kingdom together even when it was splitting apart at the seams."

Doran stared up at the stars above them. "Then why do I have this feeling it still won't be enough?"

ᚠᚢᚾᚲᛟᚠᛉᛚ

AXEL STRODE into the council hall at Doran's side. Petra stood just behind them, her bruised face adding a sense of danger to their entourage. How she managed to make a broken nose look menacing, he didn't understand.

The councilors sat with their stoic faces and pristine green robes. Idalia wasn't present, but Hildi stood between both princes and the king towered over the back of the throne. The meeting also held a sense of irregularity with the sun streaming in through the east-facing windows. Axel had only seen this room in the moonlight.

King Leonardo left his sons to sit on his throne. "High King Firmin is to arrive on the morrow, and we have rebuffed the challenges he sent with King Doran."

Roman scowled but said nothing.

"We have gathered today," the king continued, "to lay out what our relationship with the Åldrans will look like going forward."

"War," Caeso said brusquely. "There's no other way forward. We must meet them on the field of battle."

Several of the council members nodded their agreement, though others shook their heads as if the very idea were a fool's dream.

King Leonardo chuckled. "I would first like to address the present Åldrans and their indenture to yourself and the queen." He steepled his fingers at his chest. "As king and senior ruler over Sida, I've decided to dissolve the pact made between Queen Kelda and

Petra Mallorysdottir along with the deal between General Caeso and Axel Ashersson. Effective immediately."

General Caeso gave a pleased huff. "Good. I was running out of practice swords."

A few of the councilors chuckled, likely having been privy to Caeso's regular rants about Axel's destructive nature. Not that he'd broken that many swords. Axel numbered the blades in his head, losing count after a dozen.

Perhaps the general's grumblings weren't unfounded.

The king turned to Doran. "I assume you've received word from your High King regarding our reply to his challenge."

Doran nodded. He hadn't said anything about hearing from Firmin before they left the ships that morning. Axel frowned. When had that happened?

"My High King has stated that if the Sidans wish to rebuff Åldras's act of goodwill, it will be death on all their heads."

King Leonardo nodded as if he expected nothing less and the conversation was merely a formality.

"We will meet them on the shore," Enzo said, stepping toward his father. "Once the enemy comes against us, we will take them where they stand. We have the men. We can end this war before it takes any more Sidan fathers or mothers. We'll bathe the sands in their blood."

Several of the council members cheered, in obvious support of their Crown Prince.

Enzo knew about Axel and Petra's plans to try to bring the kings to Sida's side, but Sida would still need to defend the city if their goals didn't come to fruition. If the kings wouldn't abandon the ridiculous crusade, Bellator would need to hold back Firmin so Axel and Petra could return to Åldras to rally the people against the High King and whoever continued to support him. It would take time, and people would still die. But if Axel and Petra could work quickly enough, they could leave Firmin to fight the Sidans and take the ones truly loyal to Åldras back to help their people usher Åldras into a new future.

Axel's grip on the hilt of his sword tightened. There was little doubt the Sidans could rally their forces and wipe out the ones loyal to Firmin. It was only a matter of *when*. Firmin wouldn't go down without a fight, and he'd take as many bloody Sidans as he could with him. The battle would not be as easy as Enzo presented it.

"What other options are before us?" the king asked.

"We could just as easily barricade the city," one councilor said. She stood from her place on her bench. "Bellator could outlast the Åldrans in a siege even with half our resources."

"The outlying towns are already within the city walls," another councilor added. "It would be as simple as closing the gates."

"Or," Roman cut in, "we could take Anders up on his challenge and I can accept his duel. That will give us more time to gather our people and take the Åldrans to battle once the armistice expires."

Axel's own desire to smack the prince upside the head flashed in his older brother's face. The duel was simply a way to goad the Sidans, a flash of petty pride in a pan, and everyone in this room knew it.

"That is not an option," the king said. "Anything else?"

The room stood silent. Everyone could likely hear the pounding of Axel's pulse under his skin. Their plan to convince the kings was risky, but what if the other kings could see what he had? What if they could come to understand what Sida could do for their kingdom?

Axel stepped forward. "Perhaps, having all the monarchs in one place could be a boon."

All faces turned to him.

Petra kicked his foot with the toe of her boot, but he stepped forward. This was very not according to the plans they'd set, but he had to ask it.

"Continue, Mighty Axel," King Leonardo ordered.

Axel swallowed. "What if this war could be settled by airing our grievances? What if all of this has been a big misunderstanding and it's only that we're blaming one another for our problems rather than talking it out and working together to solve them?"

One of the councilors chuffed. "Like we haven't attempted that for eight years?"

"But have we had an opportunity like this to even try?" Axel met the gaze of every council member. "When was the last time we had all our kingdoms' leaders in one place? I believe there are very few of my countrymen who truly want this war to continue, and those that think they do wouldn't be hard to dissuade. This war is in no one's best interest."

"Except we must think of the Häxa," one of the councilors said. "One of the reasons we haven't simply taken out Åldras in all the years we've been fighting them is because we know doing so would have ramifications for the gifted women. We knew if we failed, the Häxa would be the ones to suffer for it."

"But what if we could change the people's minds?" Axel met the king's eye. He knew the plague could change things. For everyone. "What if there was a way to prove to Åldras that the Häxa were needed?"

The king turned to look behind his throne. "My queen? What say you?"

Axel held his breath. It could be enough. If Queen Kelda could be convinced to let the Häxa go and save Åldras, it would do so much good in helping others see what Axel did.

Queen Kelda folded her hands in front of her. "A fight is inevitable, and this war will not end without bloodshed."

Axel's breath left him.

King Leonardo drummed his fingers on the arm of his throne. "I believe that to be true, despite my own hopes aligning with Mighty Axel's. If there's room for open communication, I would take it up with praise to the Maker, but we have no reason to believe such a thing is possible. Not after High King Firmin laid out his desires as plainly as he did. There's too much wounded pride, too much anger, for there to be gentle peace. However, I believe we owe it to our people to give them their best chance. So, we'll begin preparing to hold the city and wait the Åldrans out."

"Father," Enzo said, "I know we can stop them. I know we can take down Firmin and his ilk if you allow us to."

"But at what cost?" King Leonardo said. "Will you measure a man's life to be worth less than a few weeks of patience? Will you be able to live with the possibility that our enemies break through our forces and take our city upon the bones of our citizens? Until we know what the Åldrans have brought to our gates, we'll remain behind them. Our city is strong, our walls tall. We'll make a stand, but we will not shed needless blood to do it."

King Leonardo met Axel's gaze, the hard truth plain on his face.

He knew about the plague.

And he was betting on the gods to do the heavy lifting for him.

# CHAPTER 30

## AN ARRIVAL

*When High King Firmin was coronated at the age of twenty-three, many of the kings didn't know how the boy would fill his father's shoes. While magic had been outlawed by the time he took the throne, High King Vilgot was a man of action, honorable and steadfast. There was little the man couldn't achieve with the right crew and the right plan. The kings had worried over Vilgot's son, Firmin having a cruel streak and a propensity for violence inherited from his grandfather. While I have little memory of life under Vilgot's reign, I wonder if he watches from the gates of Valhalla with pride in his eyes, or if he has had to turn away from it all.*

*— FROM THE WRITINGS OF DORAN FINNSSON,*
*THE LAST KING OF GROVÖ*

Sleep didn't come to Petra as easily as it should have. She stared at the stars above, allowing the crackle of the cookfires around her to sing freely. Midnight had come and gone, but her mind didn't quiet. The conversation in the council hall echoed in her thoughts.

*This war will not end without bloodshed.*

It was as inevitable as the tides. Eight years of death and heartache turned kings into tyrants and men into soldiers. There was no way Firmin would have ever let the Sidans out of this battle without skinning them alive. He still would do his best to do it on the field of battle. He was a warrior king. A man who thrived on the pain of others. On brutal domination. It was why he tortured Axel the way he did. Why it was never enough for him to just leave them all alone.

Petra wasn't looking forward to the backlash of their failure to capture Idalia. Not that she wouldn't take the consequences so long as Idalia was free to choose her own path.

*Freyja's golden tears, I'm worse than Axel.*

The bedroll between her and the fire shifted.

Axel's hand reached out across the space between them, barely brushing her shoulder.

"What are you thinking?" His voice wasn't even groggy with sleep, plagued with the same restlessness that stirred in Petra's limbs.

"I'm thinking that it was a bad idea to come to Sida."

He chuckled. "Aye, I'm feeling much the same."

She turned to face him. "I don't think I'm ready to go back to war."

He turned fully onto his side so he could mirror her. "I'm certainly not ready. I keep praying Firmin doesn't show up tomorrow or that the gods simply descend from their branches of the world tree and strike us all down and start over fresh."

"I'd much rather the former than the latter."

Axel's lips curled up the smallest bit, making Petra's stomach flutter slightly.

A bedroll landed between them, spraying sand into their faces.

Petra spat the grit from her mouth and glared up at Doran, who stood at the foot of her bedroll.

"Don't mind me," he said, crouching down to lay out his roll. "It's just been so long since the three of us have had the opportunity to enjoy a beach camp. When was the last time? Three years ago?"

"Last night," Axel bit out. "Don't you have a nice, cozy tent set up somewhere?"

Doran ignored the question and settled into his roll. He'd been far more attentive in the last few days than he ever had when they'd been his wards on *Sorrow*. He'd let them run almost wild as children, but now he popped up anytime Axel was near Petra. Perhaps the coming battle was getting to him more than he showed on the outside.

"So, what are we going to do when Firmin shows up?" he asked.

"Tell him to crawl back into the bloody hole he came from," Axel muttered.

Petra shook her head. "We'll need a case for why we haven't been able to take Idalia. He won't be satisfied no matter what we tell him, but we can try to mitigate as much damage as possible."

"What's the worst he could do?" Axel asked.

"Kill the crew," Petra answered, "and chain you to the mast of *The Sceptre* to live out the rest of your miserable days on the sea without food, water, or sanity."

Doran nodded. "That could be pretty terrible."

"How are we going to keep him from doing that?" Axel grumbled.

Petra picked at the cracked skin of her lip. "I think it'll be easy to shift his anger. Axel, you haven't been quiet about fighting for honor. If we approach it from the place where the Sidans wouldn't do the honorable thing by allowing us to take her, perhaps it would redirect his ire. We would have to make sure we stick to our story about being honorable with our bargains after the Sidans did the dishonorable thing. It wouldn't necessarily keep him from doing something nasty, but it could lessen the blow."

Axel snorted. "Except he doesn't care one bit about his bloody honor, so why would he care about ours?"

"Because I'll make sure the kings are telling the same story," Doran said. "This battle is for honor as far as the other kings are concerned. We're all coming to these shores as an effort for survival. They won't be looking to rid themselves of one of their tools of victory. If anything, they'll be looking to get into your good graces to keep you as their shield and will set them up to at least listen when we approach them about turning their backs on Firmin."

Petra's thoughts shot from one to another, connecting lines of speculation and strategy, playing out every scenario. No matter what, they needed to show Firmin they were on Åldras's side. That they were willing to put as much blood into this fight as he was so he wouldn't notice when they went to the kings to convince them to go make the deal with Sida.

A low horn blew over the dark waters.

Petra sat straight up, throwing off the furs and blankets of her bedroll.

Axel was at her side a moment later. "I was hoping he wouldn't arrive until morning."

"Apparently," Doran drawled, "he's making an entrance."

Flickers of light bloomed in the fog, stretching from one edge of the inlet to the other. The lone horn was joined by another, then another, until the whole night was filled with the low drone.

The call of war.

Axel grabbed Petra's hand, holding it tightly in his own. "No matter what happens next," he said, voice low, "I want you to stay beside me."

She looked up at him, one brow raised. *Protective much?*

His lips thinned into a firm line. "The only way we're going to get through this alive is together."

The drowsy fires of the camp took to life, filling Petra's head with their heady song as she held his hand.

Doran began barking orders, collecting his men together and readying the shore for the High King's arrival.

The flickers in the fog took on form, the haze making them look like ships of death as they swept toward the beach.

At the front, loomed *The Sceptre*.

The bear at the stem bared her teeth at the city set upon the hill before her, the promise of violence shining in her lacquered gaze. A shiver ran down Petra's back. If only that bloody boat had sunk into the deeps. At the ship's neck, Firmin stood, a cowl of black fur at his shoulders and a crown of antlers on his head. He looked like the king of the dark elves, a creature of nightmare, an omen of death.

*The Phoenix*'s crew gathered around her. Little Hal tucked himself right between Axel and Petra, breaking their hold on each other. The lad's limbs trembled even as he raised his chin.

"Well," Big Hal said, "I guess our vacation is over."

Ludvig crossed his arms over his chest. "Let's all pray this ends well."

# ᚠᚢᚲᛟᚠᚤᛚ

A LARGE TENT was erected in the middle of the camp, surrounded by hundreds of smaller tents. The banners of the she-bear flicked in the gray light of early dawn. It hadn't taken Firmin even a full night to lay claim to the beach and start making demands of everyone.

Petra followed behind Axel as they made their way through the sea of tents toward the behemoth of canvas built against the sides of *The Sceptre*. She, Axel, and Ulf had answered the High King's summons, leaving the rest of the crew to tend to the ship. The rest of the crew didn't need to help make the spectacle Firmin wanted. Erik hated trekking through the sand anyway.

Eyes tracked their every step, wolves scenting fresh blood.

Four guards stood outside the tent flap to the largest tent, their faces scarred with the runes of the Ekte.

Firmin was taking no chances.

Axel tapped at the side of his leg with his finger.

*Four.*

*Twelve.*

Twelve men inside the tent? Petra settled her hands on the axes at her waist. Most of the kings were still in their tents. She knew because she'd seen Agnar and Gudrun pitch theirs close to Doran's camp and neither of them had come out since.

An Ekte stopped them at the flap.

"You will leave all weapons at the threshold."

Axel's green eyes flicked to Petra then back to the Ekte. "Are we to be treated as criminals then?"

The slight was obvious. Weapons were gathered at the doors when enemies were meeting together or when criminals were brought before their judges.

The Ekte's gray eyes narrowed. "Your weapons."

Axel unbuckled his sword belt, cueing both Petra and Ulf to do the same. Petra gritted her teeth as she tossed her axes next to Axel's sword. Ulf divulged himself of his sword, his bandolier of throwing knives, the long daggers, and at least three other blades he had tucked about his clothing.

Axel pulled forward but paused. "If you decide to touch any of those, I'll allow Lord Petyr to seek his own version of retribution. He's very fond of his weapons, you know."

The Ekte's face paled slightly as he glanced at Petra. She kept her blank mask in place, which seemed only to frighten him further.

Axel didn't wait for a reply and swept into the tent.

Petra followed him, her fingers loose at her side.

Ten more Ekte stood around the room, forming a protective ring.

Firmin sat in his not-a-throne, which he'd hauled all the way from Harligdam, Anders behind him.

"Seize them," Firmin said.

Two Ekte reached for Axel, grabbing his upper arms. Another pair stepped next to Petra, and she pulled the daggers she'd had strapped under her tunic. She placed them at their throats.

The ones holding Axel and Ulf stilled.

Firmin shot up from his chair. "I thought I told you bloody *idiots* to take their *weapons*!"

Petra didn't move, keeping her blades steady against the Ekte's throats. It wouldn't take more than a twitch of her wrist to draw blood.

Axel shrugged out of the grip of his captors, nearly sending them to the ground. "What is the meaning of this?"

Firmin's face mottled with red. "I should be asking *you* that bloody question. I send you to retrieve Anders's little chit, yet I'm instead met with rumors of my best warriors sipping wine and playing servant to our enemies."

"You gave us orders to retrieve Lady Idalia by any means necessary," Axel argued. "You didn't specify the methods."

Firmin spread his arms and looked about the room. "And where is she? No doubt rolling around in the sheets of her marriage bed. Oh yes, I heard about the little ceremony between her and that bloody prince. That little harlot is going to pay for that when we get our hands on her."

Petra's grip on her daggers tightened, but she kept an indifferent expression on her face.

Axel wasn't so unaffected.

His entire body radiated fury.

"You will not besmirch the name of a lady, who has every right to maim your brother after the evidence I was given to how he treated her."

Firmin huffed, glancing back at Anders with annoyance, and waved a flippant hand. "Leave us."

The Ekte holding onto Ulf stepped away, and Petra dropped the daggers only far enough for the pair to back up, keeping them at the ready in case anyone decided they wanted to die today. They filed out of the tent one by one, not even glancing back at them.

Something was not right.

Firmin sank back into his chair. "The failure to retrieve Lady Idalia isn't the only issue I have with you and your crew, Axel. You and I both know I sent you here only to get the council off my bloody back. If I wouldn't have to deal with the headache of getting the other kings to sign off on it, I would already have your entire crew sinking to the bottom of the Vit Sea—you included."

Petra's stomach sank. She glanced at Axel, but he kept himself still, his full attention on the king.

"Why haven't you?" Axel asked, curiosity tinging his voice.

"Because if I did, I would lose half the forces taking over this bloody shore." He glared up at Axel. "Don't look so smug. Don't think for a second I don't know about your plans to turn the kings against me. To lure them to Sida's side with promises of a cure for the plague killing our brothers. I know you've already seduced Doran, not that his disgrace is surprising considering how he mothers the two of you. I may not be able to do much about him, but I'm more than prepared to deal with you two."

*Hel's rocking halls.* Petra glanced back at Ulf, but even he was white with shock. He shook his head, watching the king as if the man were a rabid animal.

Axel took a step forward. "Do you think just because you know now you can stop it from happening? Once the kings hear what we've learned, once they know what we know, there's no way they'll continue with this fool's war."

Firmin stayed staring up at him, his face splitting into a grin so wide it showed his back teeth.

"While I appreciate your guts, Mighty Axel, the only fool in this tent is *you*. There's no way for you to take the kings from me. Not now. Not after you had a hand in King Bjorn's death."

Petra didn't glance at Axel, but she could almost see his entire body stiffen. Could feel the air in the tent take on the chill of Firmin's threat. Her blood sang.

*Get out.*

But she couldn't move. Not when the violent spark in Firmin's eye only grew brighter.

Firmin sighed, getting to his feet. "And especially not once I tell them you've been cavorting with your second. All those kings you're hoping to convince to join the Sidans will turn on you far quicker than they turn on me. Perhaps they could have overlooked some of the atrocities you've committed, but allowing a woman into our ranks? You'll be torn to shreds before I even have to lift one finger."

All the heat in Petra's body fled.

Firmin turned toward her, his steps a prowl as he moved toward her. A sneer spread across his face. "All these years and none of us even saw it."

Axel stepped between them.

Firmin chuckled, circling around them with slow steps. "You both were very convincing. But when your little Häxa disappeared from my clutches, the pieces fell into place. I've only ever seen a handful of warriors who could take down eleven armed men with a dislocated shoulder and nothing but a few garden tools at their disposal. When my men reported the girl had escaped, at first, I imagined it had been Lord Petyr who had gone to fetch her. But the bodies hadn't been killed by a man with access to weapons. The girl had smashed her way out of her prison and used the guards' own blades against them."

Petra's blood roared in her ears.

"If I hadn't fought with her on the way to Harligdam, I may not have thought anything of it. But I've seen Petyr on the battlefield. There's a coldness that comes over him. I saw it in the bedraggled girl in that forest. I knew I was lucky my guards showed up when they did. I know I would have found a blade in my gut that night and the only person I ever would have guessed to get that close was Petyr Mallorysson, the demon. It wasn't until you left that I even pieced it all together and the spies I have in this city confirmed it for me. You weren't here even a week before they sent me word. It was never Mallory's son that had emerged from the ashes of Holmberg. It was his daughter."

"What do you want?" she asked. There was an obvious reason he was rubbing this in their faces. He would have had her stuck on a pyre the moment he stepped onto the shore if he was going to enact revenge on them.

Firmin bared his teeth. "I do like a woman who gets to the point. None of the simpering or begging with you."

Axel actually growled.

Firmin glanced up at him. "I know what a man will do once he's been entrapped in a woman's snare. It's one of the reasons it's been a rocking mess with the Häxa. Our minds are addled with nothing but lust. Even I have been subject to the whims of my wife. It's why we're standing on these bloody shores. For this reason, I'll allow Petyr or whatever your name is to live. I'll allow the two of you to continue the charade and let the kings keep believing that their two best warriors aren't taking turns in the sheets of their tent."

"In exchange for what?" The man honked on and on worse than a bloody flock of geese.

"Your complete support of our efforts on these shores." He leaned forward. "It was worse than pulling teeth trying to get these rocking boats across the sea. None of the kings were keen on leaving their people as the plague spread. I had to practically drag soldiers away from their bloody families. And we still had men fall victim to the illness as we traveled. If we aren't united in the battles ahead, the Sidans will sweep through Åldras."

"You want me to agree to whatever you say," Axel said, "even if I would rather cut out my own tongue."

"Precisely. And if you don't, I'll tell the kings we have all been fooled by both of you. That the names of Mallory the Shield and Asher Redbeard have been dragged through the mud. I'll see her strapped to a pyre and burned for witchcraft. No one will even bat an eye."

Did Firmin know? Did he know what she was? Did he know if he set her skin aflame that everyone would know what she was? The

Ekte wouldn't let her brush the ash from her skin before they killed her.

Axel turned, and Petra met his gaze.

She bit her lips together between her teeth. *Not much of a choice now.*

His brows drew together. *I don't want this.*

"I suggest you make a decision quickly," Firmin drawled. "I have some business to attend to."

"We'll play your bloody games," Axel bit out. "But what happens after the war is over?"

Firmin shrugged. "That depends on who is left standing at the end of it."

The High King pushed himself out of his chair, a sharp smile on his face. "I'm glad this has all come together. Honestly, I'm almost pleased you ended up not having any magic, Petyr, or I would have had to kill you back in Harligdam, and where would we be now? Come along."

He swept past them, even as Petra's ribcage tightened around her lungs. He didn't know. If he did, he wouldn't be threatening her. An ax would already be swinging toward her neck.

Axel came up right next to her, his chest brushing against her shoulder. When she looked back at him, his jaw was clenched so tightly he would have broken teeth if he was susceptible to injury. *This isn't over.*

She gave a short nod. *No, it isn't.*

They followed Firmin out of the tent and toward another tent, where a team of Ekte stood sentinel around one of the smaller tents.

"Get them out!" Firmin commanded.

Several of the Ekte filed into the tent. The first returned, an older woman practically dragged behind him. Blood was caked along her arms where marks had been carved into her skin. Three more women followed the first, each of various ages, but all with blood coating their skin.

*Oh, gods.*

They wore clothing from Åldras, stained and worn from a journey across the sea. Firmin had dragged them all the way here? For what?

Axel grabbed Firmin's shoulder and spun him around. "What the rocks is this?"

Firmin ripped his shoulder away from Axel's grip. "This is your first test. Prove to me you'll do whatever I say. Prove to me you're going to give me your complete support, so I don't have to end a civil war when I finish the war on these shores. Keep your mouth shut and watch or your secrets will be out, and Petyr will be joining them."

The Ekte dragged the women through the camp, the sounds of their weeping rousing others from their tents.

A crowd formed behind them and nearly half of the camp gathered as they reached the trench at the west side of the city.

Guards clad in green skittered about atop the wall. Petra couldn't make out any of their faces, but their attention was obviously drawn to the large crowd of Åldrans coming up to their walls.

But Firmin didn't direct the Ekte to approach the city. He stopped at the edge of the deep trench.

"Line them up."

The Ekte shoved the women to the front, pushing them to their knees at the edge of the steep decline.

Petra lunged forward, but Axel grabbed her arm.

She spun back toward him. *I can stop this.*

His eyes flicked from her to the women, indecision in every line of his face.

One of the Ekte carried a large bucket forward and dumped the contents on the women.

"Oh, gods," Ulf whispered, horror written all over his face.

Åldran fire soaked the ground.

Petra's ears began to ring.

Axel's grip on her arm turned painful.

Firmin held out a hand and another Ekte placed a torch in it.

The magic in Petra's blood screamed and she knew. She knew if she tried to save them, she would be marking her entire crew to the same fate.

Without a word, he pressed the fire into the back of one of the women.

Her entire body went up in flames.

With the torch, he shoved her into the trench.
She fell, screaming.
Then another.
And another.
Until all that was left were their screams.

CHAPTER 31

## MURDERERS

The table flew across Doran's tent, sending maps, parchment, and ink flying.

Axel clenched his jaw, keeping the scream building in his chest from roaring out of him. His body shook so hard he could barely see. Not that he could see anything but the flames that had devoured those women. The sight was burned into his eyes.

He grabbed a chair, and it met the same fate as the table.

"Axel, you have to stop."

He spun around.

Petra stood at the opening to the tent, the crew of *The Phoenix* filing in behind her.

"We should have stopped them!" he roared. "We should have stopped *that*!" Why hadn't he stopped it? Why had he stood there and let those women die? Petra couldn't have stopped them, not with her reactions to fire, but he could have done it. To the rocks with the burns! He could have tried. He could have...

Tears pooled in his eyes, and he didn't wipe them as they fell. As they bled across his face.

Axel crashed to his knees, his chest heaving. "We should have stopped them. But we just stood there and watched."

Petra fell to her knees in front of him, grabbing his shoulders in an iron grip. "Firmin wanted you to fail, Axel. It was all a setup. He

325

practically carved the deal for your silence from your skin, then put you in a position he knew would kill you to keep it. It's all a bloody game to him."

"I don't want to play his rocking games!" Axel shouted. "I should tear his head from his bloody shoulders!"

"We will," she insisted. "We're going to make that rockhead pay for every soul he took today, but we have to survive so we can save others from meeting the same fate. If we take him out now, we'll only be consigning more of our sisters to the same fate."

Axel's chest shuddered. He should have known. He should have expected nothing less. The High King was a bloody monster. This was only the beginning. He could feel it. Firmin would tear away every bit of honor from Axel's bones with his silence.

"We have to get back out there," Petra said. "If anyone thinks you're angry with Firmin, he's going to void the deal. We can't let anyone see how this affects you. You have to bury it until we can meet with Enzo and figure out how to stop this from happening again."

His chest rose and fell in gasps. "I can't do this. I can't be that man's dog."

She shook him. "Then don't be! But we have to wait. We need to get the other kings on your side. We need to push Firmin into a corner until he lashes out. Everything is sitting on the edge of a knife and all we have to do is make Firmin slip and slash his own throat. But you have to keep it together. You have to get back out there and face that bloody rockhead until we can kill him."

Axel looked up, meeting the hard blue steel of her gaze. Her face was lined with the same pain he felt tearing apart his insides. With the same fury burning up his throat.

He rubbed an arm across his face, smearing his tears across his cheeks as thick as any war paint.

"What are we going to do?"

Petra got to her feet, turning back to the crew.

Each of them stood with hardened eyes and thin slashes for lips. Little Hal held a short sword in his hand next to Big Hal with his large hammer. Ulf and Ludvig had donned their armor, and Erik gave Axel a sharp nod. Even Doran's simple brown tunic and broad shoulders felt like a deadly promise. Their anger practically heated the room, their sorrow feeding the fire building between them.

Petra turned back to him and held out her hand.

"We're going to end this bloody war."

ᚠᚢᚲᛟᚠᛦᛚ

THE SIDANS HAD ASKED for a meeting.

Tucked inside the tent Little Hal had put up, Axel buckled the clasp of his leather jerkin over his tunic and threw his green cowl overtop it. The ugly color would remind him of the scrap of humanity he would hold onto, no matter what came next.

Petra slid her axes into the loops at her hips. She'd donned her heaviest vest, the one that could hold at least a dozen blades. The front of her hair was pulled back out of her face, though a few tendrils had already escaped the leather tie. The bruises under her eyes had turned dark purple, though the swelling had gone down.

How would it feel to have a broken nose?

He reached across the space, wrapping an arm around her waist and pulled her toward him. He lifted her face up to meet his and captured her lips with his own. She instantly melted into the kiss, her arms wrapping around his back. Gooseflesh broke out across his shoulders, and he nipped at her bottom lip before pulling away.

"I love you," he insisted. "With Firmin's threats hanging over my head, I feel as if I can't say it enough times. As if I won't fill whatever quota there is of how many times I can tell you."

When she looked up at him, when she placed her hand on his chest, the knots in his stomach eased.

"We're going to make that maggot burn." She traced the buckle of his vest with a finger. "And I love you too."

He chuckled. It took a lot for her to express her feelings so openly. To be that vulnerable with him. He leaned down pressing his lips to the corner of her mouth. Hearing her say it was the best ballad she could have ever written him, but he didn't need the reassurance. Not when he felt it in the press of his skin and the beat of his heart. He'd become vulnerable too, and he wouldn't give it up for one moment if it meant she was his.

"Promise me you'll stay out of harm's way." He rubbed his nose against hers.

Her breath hitched slightly, making him smile.

"This is a meeting," she said, "nothing more. Firmin only wanted all of us armed to the teeth so he could show off his prickles like a bloody porcupine."

"I still don't like it," he said.

"I don't think either of us is going to like any of this for some time, but we're going to do it so we can win." She pulled away from him slightly. "We're going to get Åldras the help it needs. We're going to help our friends."

He pulled her back to him. "And then, I'm going to throw you over my shoulder and run for the hills."

She rolled her eyes and elbowed him in the stomach.

The jab nearly knocked the air from his lungs. Wōden's eye, he still hadn't told her about his magic. His fingers shook. Did he tell her? Was it better for her to know in case something happened?

Something shifted outside the tent.

"Pet—" he choked out.

The flap to the tent opened and Doran swept through as if he ruled the place. He'd even trimmed his glorious beard closer to his face, making him look more regal.

"Are you two ready?" he asked. His eyes narrowed on Axel's hand around Petra's waist.

Axel dropped it. "Aye." Though the bloody man could have given Axel two more minutes to explain what was going on with his magic first.

Doran tilted his head toward the tent flap and slipped back out.

Petra rolled her shoulders back and followed him.

Axel trailed after her.

Fires stretched through the entire Åldran encampment, casting shadows across the hundreds—or perhaps even thousands—of tents stretched across the shore. Men in leather armor embossed with snarling wolves and roaring bears strode through the tents, their eyes turned to the walls of Bellator.

Axel kept Petra between him and Doran, his own gaze scanning the crowds as they went. There was an Ekte for every five soldiers.

Firmin had likely pulled all the bloody heathens from Åldras to fight the Häxa. Hopefully, that meant whatever Häxa were still back home could escape without notice. Perhaps, the people of Ljust Löfte were even now collecting the women and children and taking them to the colony.

The thought brought a sliver of light to Axel's heart.

Doran didn't stop at the back of the crowd, instead pushing through to the front of the throng of Åldrans gathered at the road leading out the northern gate.

Axel could see the green of Sida's uniforms stretch across the road. Their rows were steady, helmets gleaming in the torchlight. They posed as a united front. The Åldrans looked like a pack of lumbering bears staggering up toward them as they poured from all directions.

When they reached the front, Doran gestured for them to stay put and joined the other kings huddled together. A few faces turned to Doran, relief in the sag of their shoulders as he approached. With the cacophony around them, Axel couldn't catch any of the other kings' words, but they were obviously debating something.

Petra's arm brushed his slightly. "What is she bloody doing here?"

He turned to see where her attention had strayed to.

Her attention focused on the top of the wall, the corners of her eyes creasing in sorrow.

Hildi stood next to a cloaked figure.

*Idalia.*

Axel would have applauded the woman's grit if he didn't know that nothing good would come from her watching the meeting tonight. Hell's bloody halls, *he* didn't even want to watch.

A horn blew out over the crowd. The tone buried itself into Axel's spine, making him straighten.

The crowd parted behind them. Firmin's antler crown was the first thing Axel saw as the king made his way toward the front until he reached them, bursting from the crowd like a great whale breaching from the sea. A pair of Ekte broke away from his guard to stand just behind Axel. A threat. Firmin passed by with a smile as if they shared a great secret.

Axel didn't know whether to punch him in the face or throw up onto his boots.

Firmin passed the kings and stood at the very edge of the bridge.

"People of Sida!" he hollered, his voice echoing off the walls of the city. "Your rulers have broken the armistice which bound the hands of my warriors. Your prince has defiled our sacred bonds of matrimony by stealing away one of our precious wives. Your king has rejected the path to peace when I put out my hand in friendship. Where is *your honor?*"

The Åldrans at Axel's back roared.

"Peace!" a voice called over the throng.

The line of Sidan guards at the front parted, revealing Enzo and Roman.

The two princes wore the green guard uniforms, looking every inch the rugged warriors next to their men. No crowns adorned their heads. No horns sounded to announce their entry. In a fight, no one would have been able to tell them apart from any other soldier.

Enzo took the lead, approaching with easy steps down the road. Roman followed behind him, a proud tilt to his chin. They stopped at the middle of the road, and Enzo spread his arms.

"There's no need for all the theatrics, Your Majesty. Let's talk, one man to another."

Firmin scoffed, glancing back at the city walls. "Your king dares to insult me by sending two brats out to treat with me? I haven't come to talk as a man, but as a *king*. If King Leonardo wishes to treat with me, he'll show his face."

*What a bloody idiot.* Weren't the other kings embarrassed to stand behind that squawking buffoon? How anyone could think Firmin was the best option for a representative of their kingdom, Axel couldn't fathom.

The guards behind the princes parted and the king stepped forward. How he'd blended in with the other soldiers was almost a miracle, but just like his sons, he'd stood united with his men. The moment he came into view, every eye drew to him, the huge man commanding attention.

Even Firmin seemed to draw back a bit. *Bloody idiot.* Axel would have cheered for King Leonardo if he wasn't worried about one of the Ekte behind him slitting Petra's throat.

"King Leonardo," Firmin sputtered, "you do your country a disservice by sending your sons to speak for you."

The Sidan king shrugged. "I believe my sons more than capable of dealing with a tantrum. Enzo is most skilled at it, his own child being at the stage where stomping feet and screeching seems to be the order of the day."

No one moved, though everyone's eyes went wide.

Axel almost snorted.

Firmin's face turned purple. "You dare to disrespect a peer, a *king*, in such a way?"

"A true king doesn't need to throw his title about to get what he wants. A true king doesn't arrive at the doorstep of another kingdom stomping about and making threats he has no ability to pay out. Get a grip, Firmin, and comport yourself in a way worth paying respect to. What in the Maker's name do you want?"

Axel nearly burst out laughing. King Leonardo had never been a man to mince words, but this was a new aspect to the king he hadn't seen before. It was about bloody time Firmin got knocked down a peg.

Firmin's mouth was a slash of fury across his face. "I've come to offer you one last chance to accept the terms I sent my emissary with and put an end to this battle before it starts. A chance to save your people, as any *true king* would do."

King Leonardo looked to be holding back copious amounts of exasperation, as an adult would to a churlish child. "And my answer has not changed. A true king does not send thirty-thousand men to their deaths for the sake of one man's greed. I certainly won't. Our city is ready to rebuff whatever attacks your men may bring about. You'll find the walls of our city and the hearts of our people are not so easily besieged."

The king turned away, his sons following suit.

"*Where is my wife?*" Anders burst out of the crowd, his eyes narrowed on the back of Roman's head. "She just waiting back in your bed, princeling? Or has she already moved on to her next conquest?"

Roman tried to spin around, but Enzo grabbed the back of his neck and shoved him forward.

Axel looked up toward where that cloaked figure stood on the walls of the city. She had stepped back from the wall and Hildi had an arm around her.

Anders stepped up next to his brother. "I hope you haven't been too disappointed. I know what an absolute bore she can be in the sheets. It's a good thing she has that pretty face, or she wouldn't be worth much."

*Hel's rocking halls.* Did he really just say that about his own wife? Greater men had died for less. Axel leaned forward, but Petra's hand shot out, grabbing his wrist. She shook her head just slightly, eyes flicking back to where the Ekte stood.

"Don't you dare speak of her!" Roman grappled with his brother, trying to fight his way back down the road.

Firmin grabbed the collar of Anders's breastplate, pulling him back. "What are you doing? This was not what we discussed," Firmin hissed, just loud enough for Axel to hear. "You'll have plenty of opportunity to beat the pup to a bloody pulp once we take his city."

Anders bared his teeth. "Let me kill him. I'll take his head, and you can carry it on the end of a pike as we take Bellator."

Firmin looked back toward the arguing princes, his hold on Anders's breastplate tightening.

The kings gathered behind them muttered back and forth. None looked too pleased as their gazes flicked between the brothers.

Doran stepped away from them and joined Firmin and Anders. "Perhaps we can discuss another route. The prince has already rejected your suit for a duel, Your Majesty. The kings already questioned such a decision. It would be foolhardy to consider it now."

"Shut *up*, Doran," Anders snapped. He leaned closer to Firmin. "Please, brother. Let me regain a bit of my honor. Let me do this for Åldras. For *you*. The kings won't be able to mutter behind your back if I kill him on a dueling field. I'll regain my honor and you'll regain your standing with the kings."

Firmin glanced at the kings gathered at his back.

Axel nearly stepped forward. If Anders faced Roman on the field of battle, there might be a chance for Roman to make it out alive. If they dueled, there was little hope, and if what Anders was saying was true, it would be even harder for them to convince the other kings to join the Sidans.

But if he stepped forward, Firmin would let the ax over Petra's head drop.

Firmin glanced up at his brother and gave a nod.

Axel's stomach sank to the sand under his boots.

A sneer stole over Anders's face, and he stepped toward the princes. "I can speak about *my wife* in whatever way I bloody please. Just because her skirt is light enough to spread her legs for every man with a crown who walks by doesn't mean she doesn't still belong to me."

Roman finally broke away from Enzo. "Shut your filthy mouth!"

"In the eyes of the gods, she is *mine*," Anders continued, "and I have claim to *both* your heads! If you weren't such a bloody coward, you would have accepted my challenge. You would have done the honorable thing and fought for her like a man!"

Axel closed his eyes before Roman even spoke.

"I accept your challenge, King Anders of Oxe!"

The Åldrans burst into a roar, their lust for blood raging in their cry.

Axel glanced down at Petra, her gaze waiting for him. *We knew this would happen.*

*Aye, but I prayed it wouldn't.*

Enzo was at Roman's side, his face twisted in rage, though he said nothing.

Roman ignored him. "Name the time and place."

"Here." Anders's grin stretched wide over his face. "In two sunrises. I want to make sure my sword is nice and sharp when I plunge it into your gut."

Roman's chin lifted, though Axel could see the way his hands shook.

"I will meet you with my sword at the ready."

# CHAPTER 32

## A SUMMONS

*Duels in Åldras are no small thing. They are only used in the direst of circumstances to regain honor. Anders is wise to challenge Prince Roman after what happened with Lady Idalia. If it had been my wife, I would have fought droves of men to win her back. Though, I suppose Anders does not view Lady Idalia in the way I still think of Svala. There is little love lost between the two of them.*

*— FROM THE WRITINGS OF DORAN FINNSSON, THE LAST KING OF GROVÖ*

"He's going to die," Petra said, sitting across the cold fire from Doran. Little Hal had served them the last of the fruit from the ship that morning, so the fires were quiet as the sun stretched high above them.

"Aye," Doran replied. His quill scratched across the parchment on his lap as he scribbled down the story from the night before. He'd been hard at work all night attempting to sow doubt into the kings. Gudrun and Agnar were already willing to speak with the Sidans, but the others had been stirred up by the night's events, their blood-lust triggered by the fight they knew was coming.

Why Enzo hadn't pushed his fool brother off the city wall after he accepted the challenge, Petra would never understand. The idiot would die at the hands of Idalia's tormentor before they'd even had a chance to try to stop Anders from getting anywhere close to her. Hadn't the bloody rockhead taken enough from her already?

"It's too bad you aren't in the palace anymore," Doran muttered. "We might have been able to warn them about our hands being tied. It was clever of King Leonardo to put on a mask of indifference to Firmin. Angering the brute would have encouraged foolishness. However, it hadn't been wise to allow Roman to leave the city walls. Anyone with a pair of eyes in their skull could see he wanted to fight Anders."

Roman certainly hadn't been quiet about his desire to accept the challenge before Firmin had arrived. Petra swiped the whetstone down the blade of her ax. Even she wouldn't have let him anywhere near Anders. And King Leonardo wasn't a fool. So why had he allowed last night to happen?

"It's done now," Petra said, spitting on her stone again to work on the other ax.

Doran continued to scribble on his pages.

Petra shifted her foot in the sand and the tip of her boot caught against something.

She looked down and found the grains had hardened at her boot.

The sands shifted, swirling into the point of an arrow.

She didn't allow anything to shift in her expression as she finished with her ax. "Do you know where Axel is?" She'd promised him she wouldn't go off without him. She certainly wouldn't leave him behind for this.

Doran glanced up from his papers, his brow furrowed. "You two really ought to stop spending so much time together. Your feelings aren't as hidden as you would like everyone to believe and if you hope to discredit Firmin's claims, you need to appear to be nothing but comrades."

She rolled her eyes. "I'm not going to pull him into some random man's tent and ravish him, Doran. Where is he?"

He sighed and tilted his head toward *Sorrow*. "He said something to me earlier about speaking with Harald about repositioning the ship. Harald doesn't like how far it is from the water if we find ourselves in need of a quick escape."

The giant skeid towered over their heads, nearly in line with *The*

*Phoenix* on the beach. It wouldn't take much for *The Phoenix* to push off the shore, but the skeid's hull was nearly twice as wide and a good three times the length.

"You think we're going to have to make a run for it?" she asked, collecting her things.

Doran shrugged. "I think it's better to be safe than sorry. None of this has gone the way I hoped, and I'd rather be wise than prideful."

She stood. "You've always been wiser than everyone else."

"If only that wisdom would be heeded." He gave her a knowing look.

Ignoring his obvious reprimand, she stuck her axes into the loops at her waist and tossed her sharpening kit into her tent. Let him think she was going to track down Axel to find a hidden corner somewhere. He would be so much more concerned if he knew the truth of it.

As she passed by the front of *The Phoenix*, Big Hal stepped out from behind it, a sword in his hand.

Petra reached for her axes. If this idiot was going to fight her again, she was going to cut his rocking arm off.

He paused, meeting her gaze. There were still bruises around his neck from where she'd strangled him. While her magic had banished any sign of their fight, he still bore the evidence of it.

"Pet." He licked his lips. "Do you have a moment?"

She began to shake her head, but he raised a hand.

"Please." He swallowed, running a hand through his loose hair. "Hel's halls, I don't know how we've gotten to this point, you know? When Ulf told me what happened with Firmin, what he did, what he threatened... Hel's halls, I was so angry."

Petra shrugged. "Why? You were right. My secrets are a threat to Axel and the rest of you."

He shook his head, looking down to the ground. "I was an idiot. I see that now. After watching you calm Axel down in the tent, I realized he needs you. *We* need you. Axel is our heart, but you've been our head this whole time and I'm sorry I didn't realize it before. I'm sorry it took those women's deaths to finally help me figure it out."

Petra's hands went slack at her sides. "What?"

He looked back up at her, taking in a deep breath. "I want you to know that I'm with you, Pet. You and Axel. I'll do whatever it takes to protect the crew. To be the heroes Åldras needs us to be."

Without another word, he walked away, leaving her staring after him.

"Well, that was weird," she muttered. Shaking her head, she turned back toward *Sorrow*. There wasn't time to try to figure that whole mess out.

She pulled herself up the rope ladder hanging over the ship's side. The ship wasn't much taller than *The Phoenix*, but she was far longer. Her boots hit the deck, and she found Axel, Harald, and Erik stooped over a stack of parchment.

"Aye, your scale is right," Erik said, poking a thick finger at the page in Harald's hand, "but the current off Död Isles makes this bit of coast run faster than the current closer to Tatawar."

Harald nodded, jotting down notes on another page. "If the Sidans come from Castellum, they'll take the southwest route through the isles."

The three of their heads nodded. As Petra got closer, Axel's eyes strayed to her. The contemplative pull of his brows eased and his green eyes lit. He left Erik and Harald to their discussion and strode toward her. There was a bit of a prowl to his gait that made Petra's stomach flip.

Perhaps Doran had been right to worry.

"Pet," Axel greeted. "You good?"

She stuck a thumb out toward the beach.

It was all the explanation necessary. Axel climbed over the gunwale and stepped off the side of the ship as if water waited for him below. He hit the sand, not even blinking at the drop.

*Show off.*

Petra climbed down the ladder, not willing to break her leg making a jump like that. Not that a broken leg couldn't be healed by the fires sprinkled around the camp. But she couldn't expose her magic to anyone in this bloody place.

"What's happened?" Axel asked.

Petra glanced about. "I got a message from a friend of ours, and I promised not to leave you behind if I went anywhere."

He smiled. "I'm glad you came for me. Erik and Harald have been talking circles around the currents and possible escape routes should we need to make a run for it. I keep telling them it's pointless. Doran suspects the Sidans will raise a sea gate in the inlet any day now."

Petra looked north toward where the edges of land framed the sea. Hildi had talked about that being an option. The stone carvers were trained for such a thing. It would certainly cut off any supply chains running from Åldras to the encampment.

But there likely wouldn't be too many more shipments to block.

Not when there was no one in Åldras to send them. Not with a plague.

The men around them wore hardened expressions, their faces streaked with worry or resentment. Food had already started being rationed from the supplies on the ships and whatever they could catch off the sea. The warm water brought plenty of fish closer inland, but a man could only eat so much fish.

Firmin was planning for a last stand. And it wouldn't be long until he made it.

They broke away from the camp, heading southwest in the direction the arrow had pointed. When they reached the edge of the road around Bellator, another arrow popped up ahead of them.

"That's a neat trick," Axel said.

Petra glanced around. At the top of the city wall, a head of gold hair hovered above the edge of one of the towers. Petra raised a hand in greeting. She'd definitely missed her mornings with Hildi and Idalia.

The arrow led them to the side of the trench.

Axel looked over the edge. "I don't see—"

The ground swallowed him.

Petra blinked at the spot he'd just been standing and took a single step toward where he'd disappeared.

The earth opened under her.

She fell down a tunnel, dust flying up her nose and into her clothing.

The tunnel spit her out into a dimly lit hole, and she rolled to her feet.

"Some warning might have been nice," Axel said, brushing off his clothing.

"You wanted a warning? What about us?" Enzo emerged from another tunnel, a lantern swinging from his hand. "You lot were supposed to be working the kings over to our side, but instead everyone stood there and did nothing as my brother proved himself to be the most idiotic arse to walk the face of the earth!"

Petra glanced behind him, but Hildi must have stayed on the wall to keep watch. No one else followed him through the tunnel.

"Like you weren't the only ones surprised," Axel shot back. "Your father said Roman wasn't going to duel Anders. Why would he let him out of the city when we all knew he was searching for a fight?"

Enzo pinched the bridge of his nose. "I don't know. One moment, Father is telling me to prepare to meet Firmin, the next he's walking out the front of the palace with Roman at his side. It's all a giant mess, and we need to stop it from happening."

Petra glanced at Axel. "Enzo, we need to come up with a new plan."

His head whipped in her direction. "What does that mean?"

"Firmin knew," Axel answered. "The moment he set foot on shore, he knew what our plans were. He knew we were going after the kings and he knew about Petra. We underestimated him, and I'm going to regret it until the end of my days."

Enzo's head fell back, his eyes closed. "Maker take me. This is *not* how I was hoping this little reunion would go."

"We don't have to abandon the plan," Petra said. "We can still draw the kings away, still make them question Firmin's mad scheme. We just need more time."

"We don't have time! My fool of a brother is set to duel Anders *tomorrow*. We need to take them down *now*." Enzo paced a few feet away, lantern swinging from his hand. "How do we get Roman out of the duel?"

"I don't think you can." Petra shook out her tunic and spat the dirt from her mouth. Based on the way Anders and Roman were going at each other the night before, a fight between them was inevitable. Best to get it over with quickly.

Enzo turned to Axel. "You likely have a better appraisal of both Roman's and Anders's fighting techniques. Do you think my brother has a chance?"

Axel's face was impassive, though his eyes were calculating. As if he was pitting Roman against Anders in his own mind. "If he does have a chance, it isn't a very good one."

Enzo cursed—quite colorfully for a prince—and paced back and forth faster. "Is there a way for us to call off the duel?"

Petra snorted. "Not if you don't want Sida's name slandered through the three kingdoms."

"Anders will fight Roman," Axel added, "whether in a dueling ring or on the field of battle. It's his sole objective on these shores. He wants vengeance."

Enzo dragged his fingers down his face and the dirt behind him shifted.

A very angry Roman tumbled out. He cursed nearly as much as his brother had when he finally got to his feet. One glance in Petra and Axel's direction and he went from angry to furious.

"You're meeting with our *enemies*?" he demanded.

Enzo rolled his eyes. "You let these two tag along on your honeymoon not a week ago."

"Does father know about this?" Roman grabbed Enzo's shoulder. "You would risk spilling our plans to the very people who have betrayed us? Don't think I didn't notice how they failed to come to our defense last night."

Enzo shoved him. "If you hadn't made such a mess of all of this, we wouldn't even be here. Axel and Petra would be up there trying to bring their kinsmen to our side, like we planned. But you had to be an absolute imbecile and walk right into King Anders's trap. Now, you're risking your neck for nothing."

"It's for Idalia!"

"You already have her!" Enzo pointed in the direction of the city above them. "You've already won, yet you allowed Anders to beat you by letting him get a rise out of you. Do you think Idalia will be happy when you walk out onto that field tomorrow? Do you think she'll enjoy the sleepless night tonight, not knowing if she'll even get another one with you?"

Roman's chest heaved. "You don't believe I can beat him!"

"*You already did!*" Enzo stepped closer to his brother. "She's all that matters in all this, yet you can't even accept that. Our entire kingdom is willing to go to battle for the both of you to stay together, and you're little temper tantrum last night threw that back in their faces! When will it ever be *enough* for you?"

"When he's dead and she won't ever have to worry about him hurting her again!" Roman bared his teeth. "Then it'll be enough. Then she can sleep through the night without waking up in terror. She can live the rest of her beautiful life without constantly looking over her shoulder, just waiting for him to drag her back to the torment she experienced with that monster. I have to beat him. But I can't do it without you."

Petra swallowed. If Anders died tomorrow, Firmin wouldn't let Sida come out unscathed. Idalia would still be in danger, but Firmin wouldn't be as kind as his brother in doling out punishment.

But if Roman died, it would kill Idalia.

The fight left Enzo in a long exhale. He hung his head, already looking defeated. Petra could feel that same empty hope in her own chest.

"All right, brother. All right." He grabbed Roman. The younger brother looked almost indignant at the manhandling, but he froze when Enzo wrapped him in a hug. "I'll be right beside you. Just don't die."

Roman returned the hug.

Petra glanced at Axel, who hadn't even moved since Roman had arrived.

He stared at the brothers with equal parts frustration and hopelessness. As Enzo said, he knew better than anyone which of the two fighters would come out victorious in the morning.

And it wasn't Roman.

The brothers patted each other on the back hard enough to bruise and separated. Enzo turned to Petra. "Hildi told me to tell you she had something for you. Told me it was some kind of wrap you certainly wouldn't want Axel seeing you try on." He lifted his lantern and pointed it toward a section of the wall that had been shadowed but now revealed a small tunnel.

Petra glanced at Axel, and he gave a small nod. "I'll meet you outside."

Enzo stomped on the ground in a repeated pattern and a set of stairs formed into the dirt behind him.

"Why didn't we get stairs in the first place?" Axel muttered, another set forming behind him.

The men left, and Petra stepped into the small adjoining cavern.

But it wasn't Hildi waiting for her there.

A shuttered lantern opened, revealing the small room only large enough for two people.

"Hello, Petra," Queen Kelda greeted her.

"Your Majesty?" Petra glanced over the queen's shoulder, but no one stood behind her.

"Hildi is still up above with a team of stone carvers. We need to be quick, before my absence is noted."

Petra stepped back toward the opening to the little cavern. "What's going on?"

The queen's hand snaked out and grabbed Petra's wrist.

"I need you to listen to me very carefully. The next few days are going to be pivotal to turn the tides of this war. To save what we love. You play a vital role in our success."

Cold spread from where the queen touched Petra's skin, but it wasn't because of Queen Kelda's magic. The queen's quiet voice sank icy claws into her skin.

> *"A poison flower*
> *'Neath oaken shade.*
> *A deadly power.*
> *A hidden blade.*
> *Yet noble caused,*
> *Her life she gives,*
> *For flower dies*
> *Hence oak tree lives."*

Petra could feel her pulse gallop at her throat. "What does that even mean? Flowers? Trees? It's all just gibberish."

Queen Kelda shook her head. "It's one of the ways of water

prophecy. As with the stone carvers, we are given our own language to interpret our magic and only the one who gives the prophecy can interpret it."

"Then what does it mean?"

The grip around Petra's wrist tightened.

"It means that you are Axel Ashersson's doom, and the only way to save him is to take his place."

Petra ripped her arm away, her heart pounding against her ribcage. "Say it plainly."

The queen's veil rippled with her breath.

"It means that in order to save Axel, you have to die."

Petra shook her head, backing toward the opening. "Axel can't die. It's not even possible." Not unless his magic was failing, which it wasn't. He was still so strong, so reckless. There was no way for him to die. There was still time.

Queen Kelda's hands fell to her sides. "When you're ready to hear how to save him, I'll be waiting."

# CHAPTER 33

## COWARDS

For one split second, Axel allowed himself to pray to the Allfather to take him. For a single moment, he wished he wouldn't have to witness this day.

He'd seen many battlefields over the years. There had been ones with clean lines and fresh grass underfoot. Others in mud made up not only of water, but also from the blood of the fallen. The forces of Åldras and Sida stretched across the land on the west side of the city. The Sidans stood shoulder to shoulder in rows of green, their faces hidden under golden helms. The Åldrans mirrored them, the blues of battle girded about their waists and the steel of their shields shining in the torchlight. There were even a few horses scattered through both sides. The kings of each isle had all been given one. Axel recognized Caeso sitting on a Sidan mount, but he didn't recognize any of the others.

If only they'd had more time. If only they could have won the kings to their side before Anders faced Roman.

Dawn crept toward the horizon. No fog swept over the beach that morning. *Mores the pity.* Everyone would be able to see the battle ahead. The death the day would bring about.

Because one thing was very clear.

Neither side would allow their prince or their king to fall without vengeance.

Thousands of men, ready to die.

All for one man's pride.

Anders sat atop a horse a few ells away, the metal of his armor glittering under the leather jerkin over his chest. He wore a helmet covering the top and sides of his head in a shell of metal. A noseguard perched along the bridge of his overly large nose, a red gem set into the band across his forehead. Beads of every size and material had been woven into his red beard and braided into his shoulder-length hair, a symbol of the honor he fought for in this duel. Many of the men had gone to Firmin's tent to present him with a bead or two, showing their support of their king. Their blessing for this fight.

With the support of his kinsmen, he was a man ready to kill.

"You think the pup will actually come out?" Firmin said from his own mount, beady eyes trained on the open gates of Bellator.

Anders shifted in his saddle. "Oh, he will. And I'll take more than enough pleasure in making him bleed."

Axel's fingers dug into his palm. If only he could pummel the bloody man and finish this.

But Firmin hadn't left Axel forgotten in the crowd.

Everywhere he looked, an Ekte stood a few ells away. None of them met his eye, but all of them kept their attention on him. Even if he had been impervious to their blades, he couldn't risk it.

The back of Petra's hand brushed against his.

Soldiers near the gate shifted. Enzo and Roman rode out, both astride brilliantly white stallions. They looked like the picture of princely virtue. They rode down through the empty houses outside the city walls, followed by a dozen other mounted soldiers.

Axel allowed himself to wrap his littlest finger around Petra's for a split second. Just long enough to ground him. Long enough to get his chest to stop squeezing his lungs so hard he couldn't breathe.

The princes stopped several yards away. Enzo's face was smoothed into a mask of hard steel. His gaze continued to flick over to Roman as the younger prince dismounted, taking a helmet and shield from another rider. Where Anders was all brutish bravado, Roman came in quietly, his head held high even as the Åldrans jeered at him.

Enzo also dismounted and stepped up to his brother. He clasped a hand on his shoulder, his voice low enough that only Axel could likely hear him.

"Wear him down. Just keep him swinging and he'll tire."

Roman glanced over at Anders. "I need you to make sure Idalia's safe. If anything happens to me—"

"Stop." Enzo shook him. "You focus on the end of his blade and the end of yours. Nothing else matters."

Roman gave a quick nod, setting his helmet atop his head.

Anders slid from his own horse, grabbing his sword from where it was sheathed against his saddle. The kings didn't even look at one another as Anders strode forward. He rolled his shoulders, stopping a few yards away.

Roman met him. The prince lifted his shield, his sword poised for attack.

Being the idiot Anders was, he tossed his shield to the side.

Firmin chuckled from his seat on his horse.

But Axel barely spared a glance as the king went after the prince.

Anders didn't hold back his swings, charging forward like a frost giant. The ground vibrated under his feet.

Dodging the first of the swings, Roman skittered to the side.

The Åldrans roared at the first sign of weakness, cheering for their king as he pushed back the enemy prince.

A knot formed in the center of Axel's gut.

Anders jutted his chin out toward the city. "Is my wife watching? I hope she gets to see me skewer you."

Anders's blade met the prince's shield on the fourth swing. The ring of the hit made Axel clench his teeth.

Roman's eyes squinted in pain.

Anders swung again, but Roman spun out of the way. With the prince opening up his front to guard his side, Anders followed and punched the prince square in the face with his free hand.

Roman staggered back, shaking his head from the hit. He spat blood onto the ground at his feet.

But Anders didn't give him a moment to recover. He charged forward, hitting Roman's sword to the side. Roman attempted to twist out of reach, but Anders grabbed the edge of Roman's shield and wrenched it back.

Petra hissed next to Axel.

The shield slipped from Roman's grip and Anders threw it to the side.

Firmin laughed aloud, the sound making the blood under Axel's skin boil.

Anders landed another nasty blow to Roman's gut, making the prince double over. Roman was smart enough to get his sword up between the two of them, stumbling back and falling to his knees.

"Come on," Axel whispered. "Get up."

Anders kicked him in the gut, a laugh bursting from his chest.

Roman kept his grip on his sword, but Anders stepped up and placed the edge of his blade against the prince's throat.

"I truly hope the little chit was worth it."

Rage filled Roman's face and he brought his sword up, knocking Anders's away from his neck. He roared as he got to his feet, blocking another bone-shattering swing from Anders and punched the king in the teeth.

"I'll kill you!" Roman bellowed.

"Yes," Petra whispered.

Anders staggered for only a moment before he rallied and charged forward again. His swings grew more frantic, more aggressive. Roman stumbled back and forth under the onslaught. His own attacks were waning as Anders continued to rain blows down on him.

Roman took another hit.

He twisted too far.

Ander's blade sliced all the way up the back of his thigh.

Roman cried out, falling to his knees as his leg soaked in blood.

"Oh gods," Axel muttered.

The prince was rocked.

Roman scrambled across the ground for his sword, his leg weak under him and eyes wild. Axel could see the tremors of adrenaline and fear shake his entire body.

Axel couldn't tear his eyes away, even as he sent a prayer up to Týr. *Don't let him die at Anders's hand.*

Anders lifted his sword for a final strike.

Roman looked up and rolled away.

Anders kept his sword aloft, but Roman turned around and fled. He dragged himself to Enzo's feet.

"Bloody coward!" Anders hollered, bloody spittle flying from his mouth. "Get back here and face me!"

Enzo's eyes were wide as he stared down at his brother. *Get up*, he mouthed.

"*Is this what you left me for?*" Anders shouted toward the wall. He looked back down at the prince, raising his sword. "It doesn't matter where you die—with a sword in your hand or begging like a mutt at your brother's feet—you die *today*."

Anders stepped forward and swung his sword down, but Enzo's own blade caught it before it could cut down Roman.

The breath Axel had been taking caught in his chest.

Roman's eyes were clenched shut, but he looked up when his brother spoke.

"*Enough*," Enzo snarled, shoving the king back. "You've proven your point."

Anders's face mottled with fury. "Not nearly well enough."

He raised his sword once again.

An arrow sank into his throat.

Axel's attention flew to the castle wall, where a cloaked figure was pulled down by a woman with gold hair.

Anders choked, falling to the ground near Roman's feet.

"No!" Firmin bellowed, running forward. He wrapped his hands around the arrow. He pulled them back, his palms slicked with his brother's blood, and let out an anguished cry.

*Thunder's beard.* Axel pulled his eyes away from the kings. Enzo stood only a step away, his dark eyes wide as he stared down at the brother kings.

"*Murderers!*" Firmin roared. "*Villains!*"

Axel grabbed Petra's hand. He was dead. Anders was truly dead.

"The Sidans have broken the sacred laws of the duel! They have killed our king!" Firmin stood, unsheathing his blade. "*Death! Death to the Sidans!*"

Several of the men around him surged forward, their swords raised in fury.

Enzo fought back one of the first Åldrans to reach him, cutting the man down and grabbing the armor at Roman's shoulder to pull him to his feet.

*To the rocks with the bloody Ekte.* Axel raced toward them, Petra at his side. The princes need to get out of there. Now. If Firmin saw him help them, they could deal with that later. But Axel wouldn't watch them get slaughtered.

The cheer echoed through the Åldran forces at Axel's back. The men surged forward toward the Sidans.

Enzo practically threw Roman onto his own horse, only giving his younger brother enough time to grab hold of the saddle before he slapped the horse's flank, already streaked with red. The Crown Prince turned around, sword swinging as the mounted guards encircled Roman and raced back toward the city gates.

*"Kill them all!"* Firmin bellowed.

Axel slowed and met Enzo's eye.

The Crown Prince's expression grew solemn.

Both of them knew there was no way the kings would join Sida now. Not with Anders's blood staining the ground right in front of them.

All their plans had just fallen to pieces.

Axel drew his sword.

"Run," he whispered.

The two lines finally collided, a crash of green Sidans, blue Åldrans, and the red blood that ran through both sides.

Being at the front line, the Sidans swept toward Axel.

The first man to charge him fell beneath his lysande sword.

Then another.

And another.

Axel slid his sword from the chest of the fifth man to fall at his feet. He kept watch of the blades around him, his ears tuned to the smallest hint of approach. He couldn't let any of these blades touch him. Not if he didn't want Firmin finding out about the shift in his magic.

Ahead of him, Big Hal swung his powerful hammer, smashing it into the bronze helm of the Sidan in front of him. The helmet buckled and the man fell.

Doran charged into the fray, Ulf and Ludvig at his back alongside the other men of his crew. Like the point of an arrow, they pierced the Sidan shield wall, creating a pocket of space for the fighters to push farther into the ranks.

Petra remained at Axel's side, her axes slicked with blood. A guard charged toward her, a sword of ice striking toward her stomach. Petra sidestepped the Häxa's sword and used an ax to cut the blade in half. The other ax sliced open the woman's throat.

Each death carved itself into Axel's chest.

They should have run the moment Firmin had sent them to Bellator.

Three men charged Axel at once, ripping his gaze away from Petra. The Sidan green blurred in his gaze. His sword moved almost against his will, the muscles knowing how to fight while his heart didn't know how he could.

These men didn't deserve to die for this.

Axel tried to dodge the swings, tried to deflect as many hits as he could as he stepped back.

The Sidans kept pushing, as if they could feel his reluctance. As if it gave them an edge.

Axel cut one down.

Then the next.

The third could hold a sword to Axel's. The woman under the helm gritted her teeth. Axel could imagine a Valkyrie looking much the same way as they stormed across a battlefield. She struck at him quick as an adder. Axel's muscles reacted to her movements, his instincts catching holes in her defense and exploiting them.

His sword struck hers, the edge of his blade meeting the flat and breaking the blade in two.

Without so much as a blink, she readjusted her stance and used the broken blade, wielding it more like a long dagger.

In her other hand, a wooden spear grew.

Axel ducked as the magicked spear jabbed at his head. He sliced through the shaft.

Her broken blade struck at his abdomen.

He twisted, but not fast enough.

Pain bloomed through his stomach.

The woman's eyes went wide as she caught a glimpse of the blood along her blade.

She knew who he was.

Her eyes were still wide as the edge of an ax buried itself in her neck.

The Häxa fell, and Petra took her place.

Her own gaze flew to Axel's abdomen.

"Hel's bloody halls," she breathed. She slipped one ax back into its loop at her waist and reached for him with her free hand. She grabbed the shredded fabric and shoved it against the wound.

Axel hissed through his teeth.

"Don't react," she demanded. She pushed him back, away from the worst of the fighting. Her eyes flicked back and forth through the crowd as she shoved her other ax into its loop and reached under his shirt. Her fingers prodded at the slice along his gut.

The edges of his vision spotted with tiny white lights. Nausea climbed up his throat. *Thunder's beard.* Was this how Petra had felt every time she'd been stabbed? He tried to blink away the lights as Petra began spreading his blood over her hands. Her vest. Her neck.

"What are you doing?" he asked.

"Taking any attention away from you." She tucked into his side, putting her arm around him as if he were holding her up when in fact she was the one keeping him from falling over.

She pulled him toward the rear of the Åldran forces.

Axel glanced behind him and found Enzo's dark gaze waiting for him. The prince's eyes drifted down to his abdomen, his brows furrowed.

"Keep moving," Petra barked, dragging him away. "We need to get you out of view."

The farther they retreated, the less men they came across. Warriors were traded for surgeons and the wounded. When one of the surgeons raised their hand to summon them to one of the larger tents, Petra waved him off.

Warmth trickled down Axel's stomach, soaking into his tunic and the waist of his trousers. His fingers felt cold as he gripped Petra's waist. His knees were as stable as blubber, and they kept trying to buckle. The pain had morphed from a sharp ache to a burn that spread through his entire torso. Every step made him want to wince, but Petra's command to keep moving echoed over and over in his head.

*The Phoenix* towered over the tents, still so far away.

He tripped over a stone buried in the sand. A cry yanked from his lips as his entire body revolted at the motion. The bright lights were back with fervor.

"Don't you dare make me drag you all the way," Petra hissed. "Move. Count back from two hundred."

"What?" Axel asked.

"Two hundred. One ninety-nine. One ninety-eight."

Axel's lips counted the numbers alongside her.

They counted back to twenty by the time they reached the tent.

Petra yanked the flap to the side and pushed him through the opening.

He collapsed onto his knees, pain pulsing up his back.

"Little Hal!" Petra hollered. She disappeared out of the tent for only a moment before she returned with a pile of fabric.

The inside of the tent began to spin. Axel swayed to the side, but firm arms wrapped around his shoulders, holding him up. Blood dripped onto the floor of the tent.

Why wasn't the wound healing? All the other ones had healed so quickly.

"Rocks," Petra hissed. "*Little Hal!*"

Axel's head somehow ended up on the ground.

Hands pushed at his clothing.

Something ripped.

Cold air hit his abdomen, sending a shiver through him.

Petra's voice met his ears, but words weren't making any sense.

Something hard slid between his teeth.

A stab of pain pierced him in the side.

He screamed.

The bit of consciousness he'd held onto slipped from his grasp.

# CHAPTER 34

## A CONFESSION

*There have been times during this war when I've questioned which side the gods are on. Do they sit upon their gilded thrones in the branches above us, bickering about which side of this confrontation should be victorious? Does Freyja go to the Three Norns to pluck the strings of fate they weave together to work in her favor? Does Frigg send her blessing on the two lovers who found peace in each other's arms and spurn any who attempt to thwart them? Or do they simply sit above us and laugh?*

*— FROM THE WRITINGS OF DORAN FINNSSON,*
*THE LAST KING OF GROVÖ*

Petra stared down at Axel's bare torso. Little Hal had cleaned most of the blood away after he'd finished the stitching. All that was left were the jagged lines of catgut marring his stomach.

The cut hadn't been too deep, praise the Allfather. According to Little Hal, it had avoided the most vital pieces, which was important. It had simply bled a lot, and the pain had been too much for Axel. As a man who had never truly experienced pain like that, it made sense. Petra recalled the first time she'd had to get that many stitches. She'd been ten and Da had to hold her down while the surgeon had stitched up the slice in her leg from a tumble she'd taken off one of the small cliffs along the edge of their island. She'd been with Gram and Axel, and they'd had to carry her all the way back to the house while she screamed.

Axel's chest rose and fell in sleep, the draught Petra had forced down his throat actually keeping him asleep. That was a first as well. While the rest was a bit fitful, he still hadn't woken.

Frigg's all-seeing eye, how had this happened?

Her fingers dug into her palms, Axel's blood still stuck under her fingernails. She'd let this happen. She'd allowed herself to think fate didn't apply to her. That she could ignore the truth staring her in the face.

She'd known it the day he'd kissed her.

*You are Axel Ashersson's doom.*

Queen Kelda's words stabbed into her chest.

The flap to the tent opened and Doran slipped through. One look at Axel and the man's face nearly crumpled. He fell to his knees beside Petra.

"I never wanted to see this day," he whispered.

She looked over at him. "What day is that?"

Doran met her gaze, his blue eyes hollow. "The beginning of the end. I'd hoped the Valkyries would have ushered me to Valhalla long before this. Yet I am once again expected to watch as everything I love is ripped away from me."

Petra looked back to Axel, not able to witness the sorrow in Doran's face. "How do we get him out of here?"

"I don't think we can. Firmin is already livid the two of you walked away from the battle, no matter that everyone you passed saw you covered in blood. Quick thinking, by the way."

Little Hal had done a good job keeping her apprised of the battle. The skirmish had been quick, ending nearly as suddenly as it started. With the princes' retreat behind the city walls, the Sidans had held off the Åldrans until they'd made it back into the city and locked the gates. Anders's funeral had been a grand affair, according to Ludvig. Petra hadn't left the tent to even check on the crew to see if the rest of them made it out of the battle alive. Surely Little Hal would have told her.

She didn't acknowledge Doran's compliment. "If we tell Firmin the truth, he'll only use it to finally kill Axel and get him out of the way."

"Aye, you're probably right." Doran tugged on the ends of his beard. "But Firmin will chase you down if you try to leave, and I don't think either of you would make it out of that alive."

Petra picked at the skin of her bottom lip.

If Axel stayed and did what Firmin told him to, he'd likely find himself skewered on the end of a sword. If they ran, the Åldrans would bury them in an unmarked grave with the rest of the traitors in their kingdom. If they tried to scale back their involvement, Firmin would tell them they weren't keeping to their agreement and would expose their secret, and Axel would die trying to protect her. If they went to Sida, whatever spies Firmin had in the city would slit their throats in their sleep. They needed to get rid of Firmin first.

"The two of you look like someone died."

Axel's green eyes were finally open, and his brows were pulled low.

A lump formed in the back of Petra's throat, and she glared to cover up the relief pouring into her.

"You bloody idiot," she hissed.

Axel shifted, trying to sit up, but winced. He glanced down at his abdomen, seeing the stitches for the first time.

"Wōden's eye, that's ghastly."

Doran thrust his finger at Axel as if it were a sword. "How long have you been hiding the fact you can be injured? Don't deny you've known for some time." He grabbed Axel's arm, twisting it until Petra could glimpse the thin white line stretching across his skin.

She rubbed at it, making sure the scar was real. Her ribs squeezed together. "When did this happen?"

He licked his lips. "Bjorn."

"That was over a bloody week ago!" she snapped. She rubbed at the skin again. "How is it healed already? Why didn't I see it before?"

Doran shook his head. "Did you tell *anyone*?"

Axel opened his mouth but stopped. He glanced at Petra and she closed her eyes. "Enzo knows. He saw it happen."

Petra cursed harsher than any man who sailed the Vit Sea. Hel's bloody rocking halls, if Enzo knew, Axel was vulnerable. After yesterday, there was no way they would get the kings to work with the Sidans. Not after Roman practically threw his dishonor in all their faces and Idalia killed Anders. With two kings now dead, council would devolve into a panic. They would be ready to tear down the walls of the city. Their backup plan to go to Åldras was rocked, what with Firmin having them watched like criminals.

Axel blew out a breath, grimacing as he tried to sit up.

"Don't rocking move," Petra said, setting her hand on his chest. "Little Hal wanted to wait until you were awake to wrap it. You might get blood everywhere." She hadn't even been able to do the stitching. Her hands shook too much when she helped Little Hal get the supplies. The lad hadn't even offered to let her stitch up Axel before he threaded the catgut through the needle. She'd been nothing but a nuisance, but she would strap Axel to his bloody pallet if he reopened the wound.

But even as Axel shifted, the cut across his stomach didn't reopen. In fact, the skin had already sealed around the catgut.

"What?" Petra said, prodding at the spot.

Axel gasped, snagging her finger. "Don't do that. It still bloody hurts."

Doran leaned closer. "The wound looks like it's days old, not hours."

"I don't think all my magic has disappeared," Axel said, releasing Petra's hand. "The slice on my arm healed in moments, only leaving enough blood to smear. The one on my shoulder took a bit longer, though I'm not sure how long."

"There's *more*?" Petra demanded. "When were you planning on telling me? When I saw a sword slide through your gut? Or when someone slit your throat?"

Axel shook his head. "There was never a good time."

"And you think now is any better?" She shot to her feet. "Axel, if this bloody war doesn't get us killed, I'll kill you myself!"

Doran reached up and grabbed Petra's arm. "Sit back down, Pet."

She ripped her arm away. "Don't try to placate me, Doran."

"I'm not," he said. "I'm trying to keep you from getting loud enough for anyone else besides Little Hal sitting right outside to hear you. We need to come up with a plan to keep this information to ourselves without being suspicious."

Petra plopped back to the floor of the tent. "As I said, there's not much we can do besides move forward and pray we don't all end up dead." She pointed at Axel. "You and I will be doing regular practices from now on. You're going to have to retrain almost all your defense strategies. I'm not going to drag you to the side of a fight and stitch you back up every ten seconds. We'll need to find you a shield big enough to cover your bloody arse."

He gave a solemn nod. At least he was taking this seriously. She would have to test his limits. How fast could he heal? What variables changed that? This was all her fault. If she'd just kept her mouth shut, her traitorous heart silent, none of this would have happened. Axel wouldn't have a bloody scar slashed across his abdomen.

She looked to Doran. "And you need to figure out how we can mitigate the damage Roman caused. If there's *any* way we can get Firmin out of the picture without starting a civil war, we need to do it. Axel and I can't do anything with Firmin's threats hanging over our heads, but you can meet with them and get the other kings to see reason."

"I can try," Doran replied, "but many of them have come to this battle as a last hope. I spoke with King Agnar. He's just received word that a village outside of Skydda has seen the plague. The kings are rallying behind Firmin with the expectation that they'll be able to return to their isles sooner rather than later."

Petra clenched her jaw. "We have to do something." If the kings believed Firmin would get them past that wall, they were rocked. If they could just make the kings see the truth, if they could just get them to see this was a lost cause...

Axel reached out and grabbed her hand. "It's going to be all right."

She snatched her hand away. "Don't say that to me right now."

Axel's eyes flicked to Doran. "Could you give us a minute?"

Doran stood without question. "I'll see if Little Hal has what we need to get that catgut out. I don't think you'll need it for much longer." He fled from the tent as if Fenrir the wolf was nipping at his heels.

"Petra," Axel said, leaning toward her. "I need you to look at me."

She glared at him.

The corners of his mouth twitched and the urge to slap him flashed through her. "I love you," he said.

"Don't you dare try to charm your way out of this!" she growled. "Don't you dare try to distract me from the fact that you're in so much more danger than you were before."

He grabbed her hand once again, pulling it to him. "This isn't your fault."

"Of course it is!" she blurted. He'd pierced through all her bravado straight to her heart. Tears threatened at the corners of her lashes. "I knew this would happen, and I did nothing to stop it. I should've stayed in that bloody cell in Harligdam. Should've stayed in the husk I made of Holmberg and let you leave with Doran. You wouldn't be in this position if it wasn't for me."

He pulled her to him, wrapping his arms around her.

"Don't you dare say that. You are the best thing that ever happened to me. I would give up my magic a hundred times over so long as I got to live the rest of my life with you at my side. I wouldn't understand anything without you. I wouldn't know how to live in a world where you weren't right next to me."

She shuddered. "It's the same for me, you idiot."

He kissed the top of her head. "We're going to be fine. Trust me."

Her fingers dug into his back as she held him tighter.

Because none of it felt fine, and she prayed to whatever gods were listening that his words were prophetic. That the churning in her gut was wrong.

But Queen Kelda's words chose that moment to ring in her ears.

*Yet noble caused,*
*Her life she gives,*
*For flower dies*
*Hence oak tree lives.*

# CHAPTER 35

# HONORS

Axel tied a knot with the strip of linen wrapped around Petra's upper arm. It had been quick thinking on her part to cover herself in his blood in the midst of battle. To make it seem like she'd been the one injured as they'd hobbled back to their tent. But they'd need to keep up the ruse if they didn't want anyone getting suspicious. Not while there were still battles to be won. The fighting had ended the night before, but the aftermath still played out on the other side of the tent flap at his back.

Soldiers with bandaged wounds sang prayers to the gods above.

Crewmates crafted barges out of wood, some already bobbing in the sea to take a fallen warrior to the waters of Valhalla.

Screams echoed down the beach from the surgeon tents a ways off, though it felt like they were staked right next to Axel's.

He pressed his fingers to his side, feeling the bumps of still tender skin. Having Petra pull the bits of catgut from the wound was an experience he didn't think he'd like to live through again. It felt unnatural to have something that wasn't already part of his body under his skin. The wound had already sealed, his magic still healing him faster than any other man. Petra had said the angry red color would fade eventually, but it would never look the same again.

It was an oddly comforting thought.

The reason Petra had mourned the loss of her scars so viscerally made much more sense. To him, scars had always simply been a consequence of someone's mistakes—whether they were created on a battlefield or from an accident. But it wasn't the whole truth of it. They were reminders of horrors lived through. They were a testament to the strength of a body and the fact that while the memory would always be there, bodies could heal as well as souls. Perhaps even better than souls. It had taken him ages to overcome the loss of Father, of Petra's family. That wound had bled for years before the scars set in, and even still it felt tender sometimes.

Would his body finally start reflecting the wounds on his soul?

Little Hal's head popped into the tent. "Doran's here."

*Ah, the escort.* Firmin had sent a summons that morning after Anders's funeral. They were to meet with the other leaders to discuss the battle from the night before and strategize the next steps. Hopefully, it wouldn't just be everyone shouting over one another.

Petra gave the lad a nod, slipping her axes into their loops at her hips. A crease had marred the space between her brows since he'd woken yesterday. A sliver of something violent, something reckless, had taken up residence in her eyes. He couldn't figure out what it was, but it was there.

When she looked up at him, her eyes narrowed the slightest bit.

She was still as angry as a wolverine after winter. But she'd keep it to herself. She'd let herself stew in it until Axel could break through the wall she was trying to build between them.

He stepped up to her, brushing a tendril of her dark hair from her brow. "I can see those wheels spinning in that brilliant head of yours."

Her eyes narrowed to dangerous slits. "Trying to come up with how to kill you, then bring you back so I can do it again."

"Let me know if you figure it out," he said, letting his fingers drop to his side. "I have an extensive list of people I'd love to do the same to."

She turned away from him, but not before he'd seen the smallest bit of mirth in the twitch of her mouth.

Fixing things between them wouldn't be too hard but keeping it fixed would be Axel's life mission. There was something in how she held back from him that felt like she was waiting for an ax to fall and sever the iron ties between them. Like she believed what they had was a fleeting thing she had to guard her heart against. Well, Axel would spend the rest of his life proving this love between them wasn't ever going to break. That the heart in his chest beat for her and only her. He wanted to build a life with her, to have a future together. An eternity.

And he would continue to make mistakes, but he would always fix them with her. He would always fight for her. For the future he wanted to give her.

Before she could brush past him, he snagged her hand.

She looked up at him as he pulled her fingers to his lips. A tinge of pink spread across her cheeks even as she tried to look angry at him.

"Do you think you can use that charm to sway some kings into our favor?" she asked, slipping her hand from his.

He chuckled. "I'm sure some of them would appreciate the attention, though I certainly wouldn't enjoy charming them as much as I enjoy trying to charm you. The rewards are definitely not the same."

She gave him a shove. "Shut up and let's get this over with."

He followed her out of the tent. If he didn't think they'd get dragged out by Firmin's dogs, he would have pulled her back through the tent flap and kissed her senseless.

But Doran's stoic expression kept him from doing just that.

"Come along," the king said. "The others have likely already gathered."

Axel followed Petra as they strode past the tents, many of the men around the camp looking to them in awe. Axel had become a legend, and while he'd likely fought beside many of these men, there was a frantic hope to their eyes now. As if Axel were their salvation.

He took a deep breath. If he could save these men, if he could save all these people from having to live through even more hardship than they'd faced over the last eight years, he would.

Firmin's large tent loomed before them. No Ekte guarded the entrance, but the flaps had been tied open, revealing the many kings and commanders standing about the space. Roughhewn benches had been slapped together and pushed up along the edges of the tent.

Doran strode forward, finding Kings Gudrun and Agnar standing on the other side of the room. Several of the men glanced Axel's way, and there was nothing but respect and curiosity in their expressions.

Axel loosened his shoulders. The gathering wasn't to be a trial then.

Firmin sat in his not-a-throne at the back of the tent, his brow low. There were dark circles under his eyes, and he stared sightlessly into the crowd in front of him. The loss of Anders seemed to be on everyone's mind, including the High King's.

His eyes sharpened when they flicked up, meeting Axel's through the throng.

"Find a seat," he rumbled, straightening in his chair. His voice carried through the tent and the men quickly found places along the edges of the space. Axel pulled Petra into a seat close to the exit. He wouldn't remain in this tent for longer than he absolutely had to.

"Jurgen." Firmin gestured to the commander seated closest to him. "Report."

Commander Jurgen stood from his seat. The man was built like a reed, the muscles of his arms more sinew than meat—which was odd for an Åldran. But the man could keep a war together. Axel had met with him only a couple of times over the years, but he had a knack for knowing where things were and keeping watch over everything. It was the reason Firmin kept him close.

"We sustained heavy losses from our battle yesterday," Jurgen said, his voice far deeper than his frame looked like it could carry. "May the Valkyries ferry the souls of our dead to the waters of Valhalla."

A flood of "ayes" filled the room.

Jurgen held up a slab of clay. "An accounting of our dead has been made. On the field of battle, we lost seven hundred and thirty-two warriors. We have lost another two hundred and forty-seven to mortal injury in the surgeons' care. Five hundred and ninety-two are still being treated for major injuries by the surgeons or their own crewmates. Which brings our remaining number of able fighters to twenty-two thousand, three hundred and twenty-two."

Axel clenched his hands between his knees, the nails of his fingers burying into his skin until it stung. So much death. So much unnecessary pain. What would it take to end this war? How many more men would it take to do it?

"The Sidans also sustained losses," Jurgen continued. "From the battle, the Sidans lost what we estimate to be around a thousand men, though we don't have an accurate accounting. We believe about forty thousand active soldiers have amassed in and around Bellator. We're watching the encampment grow on the west side of the city as well as another collecting near the base of the mountains farther south."

Jurgen gave a short nod and sat, his report having finished. Axel had always appreciated the man's directness.

"Thank you, Commander," Firmin said. "We have chased the Sidans back behind their walls, but the battle is not won yet. Prince Roman dealt our people a great blow by dishonoring the rules of the duel and the Sidans will pay for the murder of King Anders."

Several in the room raised their fists, their faces drawn in stark fury.

Axel bit his tongue. Idalia had taken a huge risk killing Anders the way she did. Hopefully, her involvement would be kept a secret from Firmin. If he found out who had shot his brother, there would be no stopping his retribution.

Firmin pushed up from his seat. "Our blades have tasted of Sidan blood, and they demand more. We will rally our men, and we'll wipe Bellator off the maps of the World Tree. The gods will be at our backs, and we will make the great walls of Bellator crumble under our might!"

Several more men cheered.

Doran stood up. "I don't think it will be a simple matter of charging through their gates. The Sidans outnumber us, not only in men but in resources. We're in their homeland. They're the masters of these beaches, whether we have laid claim to them or not. We're at a serious disadvantage and imagining anything else is foolishness."

King Gudrun nodded beside him. "Aye, this war will not be won by brute strength alone. We must be clever in our strategies and frugal in our planning."

"Gudrun is correct," Doran said, "and to make matters worse, we've pulled our men away from their families who could even now be taken by the plague ravaging our lands. Our word of promise is the only thing keeping these men here, not knowing if they'll have a home to return to. If they kissed their wives and their children for the last time."

And Doran, out of all the men in the room, knew that feeling.

"Whatever path we take forward," King Agnar added, "we must think of our men, not our own vengeance. If there are opportunities presented that will help us move forward without bloodshed, we must use them."

The men's voices flitted about the room, not the uniting cheer of vengeance, but of ideation.

"I'm glad you made that point, Agnar," Firmin said, settling back into his chair. His gaze flicked to Axel for only long enough to give Axel a chance to glare at him. Firmin licked his lips and gestured for one of the attendants at his back. "I have received a missive from Sida."

The voices went silent as the attendant passed Firmin a crinkled square of parchment.

"The Sidans have replied regarding the dishonor Prince Roman paid to our kingdom during the duel. They are prepared to make reparations."

A few of the older kings sagged in relief.

"First, they have offered medicinal supplies for our surgeons to help heal those still in the most critical conditions. Secondly, they've agreed to send three wagons of foodstuffs to help supply our rations."

Axel leaned toward Petra. "Hopefully, there's none of their nasty wine."

She didn't reply, her eyes trained on Firmin as he read.

"And lastly, as Prince Roman did not hold to the rules of the duel and no side was named victor, Crown Prince Enzo has issued a challenge in substitute."

Firmin looked up then, locking gazes with Axel. A smirk tugged at the corner of his mouth.

Axel's stomach dropped.

"He has challenged our own Mighty Axel," Firmin announced,

"to face him in a duel, as Sida is looking to regain the honor tarnished by their second prince."

A roar shook the flimsy canvas of the tent, nearly every man on their feet. Victory shone in their eyes. Several of the men yanked Axel to his feet, slapping him on the back.

But Axel's attention didn't stray from Firmin.

The High King's smirk stretched across his face. "I've already sent back our acceptance. I've even waved the mourning period for Anders's death in order to allow such an honor in his name. At dawn, Mighty Axel will slay the Crown Prince of Sida and avenge our king's murder."

More cheers went up among the men. To them, it was a sure thing. Mighty Axel, the hero of Åldras, would face their enemy and crush him under his heel.

Axel met Doran's gaze across the room. The king's brows sat low over his eyes, his mouth little more than a thin slash across his face.

He knew as well as Axel did. The moment Axel crossed swords with Enzo, everyone would know Mighty Axel could die.

# CHAPTER 36

## A MARTYR

*I never thought I'd see this day. I prayed for it to stay far on the horizon, even though I knew it was futile. There is little a man can do to stop himself from falling for the woman his heart craves. Once I realized who Pet was, I knew there was nothing I could do to keep fate far from this war and protect the two people in the world I thought the gods had given me as recompense for what they'd already taken from me. Yet, once again, my fervent prayers have fallen on deaf ears.*

*— FROM THE WRITINGS OF DORAN FINNSSON,
THE LAST KING OF GROVÖ*

Petra sat back against a large boulder as Axel paced back and forth in the sand. The moment the war council had disbanded, Axel had run from the room, and she'd followed right after him. They hadn't stopped running until they were well away from the encampment. Until she could barely see the tops of the Sidan palace over the hills around them.

Axel didn't speak as he paced. He looked up at her a few times but never spoke. Only considered. The pale skin on her bare forearms had grown slightly pink waiting for him, but she only pulled down the sleeves of her tunic to cover them. He hadn't been this thoughtful in years. Likely since he'd started plans for *The Phoenix.* And even then, he had talked it out.

This silent, worried Axel wasn't something Petra saw often, if ever.

"Are you going to spit it out, or are you hoping your pacing will bury you in the beach and you won't have to make a decision in the end?"

He didn't stop moving, but his eyes trained on her once again. "I can't fight him."

"Enzo?" Petra asked, picking up a stick next to her boot. "Of course you can. All you have to do is show up and stick him in the ribs with the pointy end of your sword. You can even make it quick and painless if you really want to."

He shook his head. "While I usually appreciate your casual morbidity, it's not that simple this time."

"That method has worked thus far." She broke the stick in half. "I don't see what would make this situation any different."

"He doesn't deserve to die, Pet. You and I both know that."

She tossed the stick to the side. "It's a war. Most of the men doing the actual dying don't deserve it."

He finally stopped, rubbing at the shadow of golden hair that had grown along his jaw over the last day. "How am I supposed to kill him? He's a good man who's in the best position to change our world for the better. He has the respect and love of his people. He's the kind of prince men follow blindly into battle because they know he'll be right beside them. Killing him would be a tragedy."

"Whether by your blade or someone else's, his death will be a tragedy. Freyja's tears, the man could drop dead before you even face him because the gods willed it."

His pacing resumed. "What about Hildi? Would you have me take her husband from her? From Aggie? I can't leave a child without a father. How could I?"

Words stalled on Petra's tongue. If anyone didn't deserve Enzo's death, it was Hildi. She had lost so much. Suffered so much and carved out happiness for herself with Enzo. It would kill her if Enzo died. And sweet Aggie. Growing up without even a memory of her father. It was a terrible fate. One Axel understood more than most.

"See?" He ran a hand through his hair. "Even you hesitate because you know the consequences of his death."

She shoved herself to her feet, striding up to him. "There are always consequences for death. There have been since we cut down the first men with our blades. Just because you can see them now doesn't mean they've never existed. It's just been easier to feign ignorance when we can so easily mask it with the honor of the fight."

"And where is the *honor* in this fight?" he snapped. "You saw the kings back there! They clapped each other on the back like Enzo was already dead. Like he didn't even have a chance. How is that honorable? I'm not an executioner."

No, that was her job. She stared up at him. How many people had she killed over the years to save him from having to face that choice? From having to become a monster like her? She knew he hated the death. The destruction. And she'd saved him from it. She'd allowed herself to be the one to kill their enemies in cold blood because it meant Axel got to hold onto that sliver of humanity so many tried to rip from him.

"What other choice do you have, Axel?"

He looked down at her, sorrow creasing the lines in his face.

"No." Cold crept up her spine. She shoved at his chest. "Don't you dare even think of sacrificing yourself. Of allowing Enzo to win that bloody fight."

He caught her hands as she went to shove him again. "He's skilled enough to kill me, has a real reason to see me dead, and I can't kill him. I can't kill my friend. What would that make me?"

The backs of her eyes prickled. "It would make you alive, you idiot!" She tore her hands from his grip. "It would give you a chance to be here, to achieve all the bloody miracles you've been trying to make reality all these rocking years."

He gestured to the palace behind her. "Like what the Sidans have been accomplishing in droves? I've seen the reports. I've seen how many Häxa they've saved. Seen the way the royal family works alongside their people. We would never be able to accomplish what they have. Not while Firmin hangs his ax over our necks. Not while the Ekte continue to slaughter our kind. If we give Firmin this victory, what keeps him from asking for more? What keeps him from telling me to slay Roman after Enzo? King Leonardo? Idalia? The queen? Hildi? Aggie? Because you know if Firmin sets his sights on them, he'll make me kill them and I'll do it because I can't let him kill you. I just can't."

"So instead, you'll let yourself get killed? You'll leave me behind anyway?"

He ran a hand through his hair. "If I die, Firmin has nothing to hold over us. You would be free from this cursed life I've made you live."

"I *chose* this life."

"When has this life ever been a choice?" he countered. "For either of us? From the moment my mother gave her bloody prophecy, our choices have been taken from us. Everyone believes our future is set in stone, that if I fall, so does Åldras. And that has taken every choice from us from the very beginning."

"Allowing yourself to die is going to do exactly that! Åldras will fall to Sida no matter what we do. Why do you have to sacrifice yourself in order to accomplish what we already know is going to happen?"

He straightened. "Because I'll have saved a good man and saved you."

Tears fell to Petra's cheeks, and she swiped them away. "Gods, I'm going to get you killed."

He took her face in his hands. "No, you're going to give me the chance to save so many."

She yanked his hands from her face. "Stop! Just stop! For once, just stop being so bloody heroic! You say you don't want your prophecy to choose for you? Then don't! Choose to take control into your own hands. Choose to cast aside your rocking honor and just survive so we can figure out how to make it out of this alive."

Tears had pooled in his own eyes. "Don't make me choose that. Please. We've fought for so long to make this world better for the people that live in it. Don't make me go back on that."

"What about the *promises* you made to me? Am I not enough to live for? Is the future *you* so wished for us to have together not *worth* living for?"

He reached for her. "Of course you are! I would tear apart this world with my bare hands for you. I would watch both these kingdoms fall under my sword for you. And I would throw myself on Enzo's sword for you. So you can have that future."

"That future means *nothing* without *you*!" she thundered, yanking herself from his grasp.

Her chest heaved as she tried to get air past the burning in her throat. What would there be left for her without him there? No one cared about the demon who haunted the deck of *The Phoenix*. The woman who knew nothing about being anything but a warrior. A killer. He was her compass. Her home.

"And my life would mean nothing without you," he whispered. He fell to his knees in the sand. "There's no right decision here. There's no path forward that doesn't end in tragedy. At least in this choice, there's hope. There's hope for you and the Sidans and Åldras and the Häxa. There is hope for a better future for everyone and I'll gladly die for that."

She stared down at him. He couldn't truly be saying this. He couldn't truly be thinking his death would bring hope. If he wanted hope, then she would burn down every single king standing in their way. She would leave Bellator in ashes. She would purge Åldras of the Ekte. She would let him rebuild everything after she tore it all to the ground.

*In order to save Axel, you have to die.*

Tears ran down her cheeks. Was it really to be one of them or the other? Was that what the gods had willed? Was there to be no hope for their future together? Was all this just some foolish fantasy?

Gently, Axel took her hand in his. She couldn't even stop him. Couldn't think past the crushing end to that beautiful dream.

"I love you, Petra. I love you more than life itself. Please don't let that love be in vain. Please don't make me kill a man who doesn't deserve to die. Please don't make me live the rest of my life hating myself."

She stared down at him, at the resolution in his eyes. He would kill for her if she asked it. He would die for her if she let him.

She slipped her hand from his. "I have to think."

Without another word, she ran.

"Petra!" Axel called after her, but he didn't chase her. He didn't stop her. He'd made his decision, and he would wait for her to come to the same conclusion.

But she wouldn't.

Because he was wrong.

He didn't have to die to stop Firmin.

He didn't have to die to bring hope to the Häxa.

He didn't have to die to save Enzo.

Petra kept close to the sea as she ran, the sun beating down on top of her head and the crash of the waves barely roaring over the tumult in her mind. There was no way she would let him sacrifice himself. She was so tired of watching him be trapped by everyone else's desires. He didn't deserve to die as a loyal pet. It had never been his fate.

When she rounded a bend, she slowed.

There, in a small inlet, stood the veiled queen, her hands folded in front of her. Queen Kelda didn't so much as flinch when Petra appeared. She'd already known Petra would find her there. That fate had other plans.

Petra strode toward her, stopping only when she stood a few ells away.

"Tell me what I need to do."

# GOODBYES

Axel couldn't move. Not until she came back.

Firmin would likely send a pack of Ekte dogs after him if he didn't show back up at the encampment soon, but they would have to drag him back to the city if they wanted him to leave this spot.

The sun had set not too long ago. The smallest strip of purple still kissed the black curtain of night. The day's warmth still radiated from the sand, but the breeze had cooled and sent small shivers across his arms.

But he would wait.

Because he wouldn't leave her until the last possible second. Until there was nothing left for him to do to show his love for her but leave. She didn't understand, but she would. She would see this war to the end, and she would find that happiness, that sense of belonging she had craved for so long. She'd found a piece of it in Sida with Hildi and Idalia. She would find it without him and her world would be better for it.

His chest ached just thinking of abandoning her to this cruel existence. But she deserved a life free from the destruction that always followed him. From the constant attacks. The never-ending expectations to fix everyone else's problems. If it had been anyone else in Holmberg with her, she never would have been dragged into the front lines of this war. Though, if it had been anyone else, they would have died in the fire she created.

He closed his eyes, his head falling back. A single tear slipped down his cheek.

He didn't want to die.

He didn't want to leave her behind.

He wanted to hold her. To kiss her and let the world burn around them.

But he wasn't strong enough to let the world burn. Wasn't strong enough to live with the regret. To constantly be on his guard and watch as those he loved kept falling as he lived the life he abandoned them for. To have to pray every night that the ghosts of the past would stop haunting him.

He was so tired. So bloody tired.

The tide continued to recede, and fog gathered above the water a ways off, slowly creeping toward the shore.

He felt her before he saw her.

Petra's silhouette made its way toward him, shoulders set and stride steady. Of course she would walk toward him as if ready for a battle. She would face this head on. She would survive this because she was so much stronger than him.

It would destroy him if anything happened to her.

She stopped just in front of him, her face shadowed as she looked down at him.

"We should get back to camp."

He nodded and pushed himself to his feet, brushing the sand from his clothing. But before he could take a step toward the ships, she grabbed his hand.

"I won't be angry anymore," she said, dropping his hand to wrap her arms around his neck, "if you promise not to be angry with me. I understand why you think you have to do this. If anyone understands, it's me. But tonight, I don't want either of us to be angry. I want to spend this last night with you as if we have a thousand more tomorrows."

She pulled him toward her, and he could do nothing but comply.

He was powerless against her. He always had been.

His arms came around her, pulling her toward him.

The kiss wasn't the raging inferno that seemed to flare every time his lips touched hers. This kiss was like hot iron, pure and solid but just as scalding. It warmed his chest and spread through his limbs, making his blood pound in his ears. It was a promise and a farewell. A pact between souls and a mourning between hearts.

She pulled away first, her lips slightly swollen. "Come on. We'll get you ready for tomorrow."

He held her hand tightly as they meandered back to the encampment. Neither of them seemed to be in a rush. Axel certainly wasn't. He would stay on that stretch of beach for an eternity if it meant she would keep her hand in his. But soon enough, the lights of the cookfires touched the toes of their boots and her fingers slipped away.

The encampment was in celebration; their faces stretched in wide grins as they cheered at his presence.

Axel could barely push a fake smile onto his face.

Mead splashed into the sand at their feet. Small wooden beads were thrust into his hands until he began leaving a trail of them in his wake. If Axel's chest didn't feel like it had been carved open, he would have been touched by the honors the men bestowed on him. Music sprang up, the song taking form around them.

*"Gather 'round, oh hearty kinsmen.*
*Raise a tankard of honey ale*
*To mighty Axel, son of Asher.*
*Take a seat and hear his tale."*

The words flowed around him, never penetrating the fog that had taken over his mind. He was glad they could celebrate this night, but he couldn't make himself join in their cheer. Not when he knew he brought about their destruction tomorrow.

His kingdom was dying, and he wouldn't be around to watch when the light finally went out.

Firmin swept out of his tent up ahead, his thick arms crossing over his chest. He gave Axel a regal nod, as if bestowing his blessing on Axel's promised victory. They both knew it was a signal for Axel to remember the threats looming over their heads.

The bloody king could rot in Hel's halls.

Axel turned away from him and strode toward *The Phoenix*. It was then that he felt the lump in his throat. The bloody boat was his home. But he saw Doran and the crew seated around the cookfire at her breast. Their faces were more somber than the rest of the camp and when they met Axel's eye, that somberness was replaced with resolution.

Did they know what he was going to do? Did they know what tomorrow would bring?

But it didn't matter if they did. No matter what, they would take care of the ship. Of Petra. They were as much a part of this home as he was. They would see peace brought to Åldras. They would see his sacrifice wasn't made in vain. At least in that, he knew he could trust them.

Little Hal held out a pouch which Axel was able to deposit all his beads into. Ulf took Axel's lysande sword and grabbed a whetstone. Big Hal held up the new helmet he'd bought at Midsummer. Ludvig sat close to the fire, oiling Axel's leather jerkin. Erik dished out two plates of food and passed them to Doran who brought them to Axel and Petra.

"Whatever happens tomorrow," Doran said, "know we are with you. That we'll be the army at your back with the song of victory on our lips."

Axel nodded, taking the plates. He probably wouldn't be able to choke it down, but he took it anyway.

Petra grabbed one of the waterskins near Big Hal and pulled Axel toward their tent. She slipped through first and he couldn't help looking back at the crew.

Each of them met his gaze, their eyes glistening. Even Big Hal wiped at his face.

Axel nodded to them.

While he wished he could give the crew his last night, it wasn't his to give.

He slipped into the tent after Petra.

She'd seated herself between their bedrolls, her plate in front of her. She set the waterskin to her lips, her nose scrunching as the edge touched her lips.

"Thunder's beard, I didn't know it was mead." She lifted it back to her mouth, taking a larger swallow, then lifting it in the air. "A toast. To bloody rocking peace that we'll die trying to achieve."

A chuckle vibrated in Axel's chest. He took the waterskin from her and took his own swig of the stuff. The sweet honey coated his tongue. It was far better than Sidan wine and settled warmly in his stomach.

She stood, coming around to his side and pulling at the hem of his tunic. He pulled it over his head, and she pushed his shoulder back, taking in the wound at his abdomen.

"The scar is already losing the color. I imagine it'll be white by tomorrow."

He didn't even look down, simply watching her.

The steel in her eyes was as sharp as her axes and something in his chest loosened. She was the most beautiful creature he'd ever seen. In that moment, she was a goddess unto herself. The world would quake under her strength. She would strangle the peace she wanted from this world with her own two hands.

She reached into his trunk, shuffling through and pulling out the box of his runed hygiene tools. With careful hands, she trimmed his hair, collecting the curls that fell as if they were actually made of gold. Little Hal would likely appreciate it, as Axel wouldn't be able to give him the strong hairs for his fishing line anymore.

Petra shook the bulging bag of beads he'd collected. "These beads aren't very useful without a beard."

A laugh burst out of him. He shook his head. "No, I suppose not."

She dug through them, picking out a couple and grabbing a spool of thread from his trunk. She braided a few pieces of his hair and wove the beads into the plait, tying it all off with the string.

Petra took both of their untouched plates and set them to the side. She grabbed his face in her hands, looking down at him.

"I love you, Axel Ashersson," she said, her face grave. "This world has seen fit to tear us apart, but I refuse to allow it to take my heart. It is yours and yours alone. You hold my heart in your hands, whether one of us is in this life or the next. Don't you dare forget."

He settled his hands over hers. "I won't forget. I'll never forget."

It wasn't one or the other that pulled them together, but their lips met and that inferno sparked in Axel's chest. He pulled Petra against him, capturing every kiss and tucking them in beside his heart.

Her mouth moved to his jaw, to his neck. She grabbed the water-skin and took another large drink, passing it to him. He did everything she asked. She pulled his mouth to hers again and he could do nothing but obey. In that moment, if she asked him for the moon, he would have reached out and plucked it from the sky. If she asked him not to let Enzo beat him tomorrow, he would listen.

But she didn't ask that of him.

She only asked for his heart. For one moment between them where the world outside their tent didn't exist.

And he could do nothing but give her all of it.

# Chapter 38

## A Duel

Axel's soft breaths filled the tent as Petra pushed herself up from the bedroll. The sleeping tonic she'd slipped into the mead would hopefully keep him asleep long enough for her to be gone before he woke. She grabbed Axel's blue tunic along with three others. She would need to fill his shirt where she was obviously lacking.

She peeked out of the tent flap and found his sword and jerkin set neatly next to the opening. Snatching them up, she slipped back out of view.

Once the jerkin hung on her shoulders, she covered it with his ugly knit cowl. It was soft against her cheek and smelled like leather and pine. Like him. Tears stabbed at the corners of her eyes, but she blinked them back and grabbed the beads and locks of Axel's curls. She'd taken off a couple inches and used the metal beads to attach them to the ends of her own brunette waves. It was tedious beyond comprehension, but she wove the strands into her hair. There was nothing she could do about her height, but hopefully everything else would be convincing enough.

She ran a hand over the beautiful fur cloak Axel had gifted her for her birthday but reached past it for the plain brown one at the bottom of the trunk. She switched out her favorite boots for the bulky extra ones she kept in case she lost her good ones. They were closer to the style Axel preferred.

Her axes lay on the ground at the foot of Axel's bedroll. She touched them gently for a moment and left them there, grabbing Axel's lysande sword and buckling it to her waist. The thing hung heavy against her hip, pulling her slightly off balance, but that wouldn't matter too much once she was wielding it.

She grabbed Big Hal's helmet and set it on her head. It sat a little loose, but she buckled the strap under her chin to keep it in place.

As quietly as she could manage, she slipped out of the tent, pulling the hood of the cloak up over her head to cover the polished metal.

At this early of an hour, most everyone was asleep, their revelry from the night before and the battle before that finally draining them. They all would have gone to sleep with thoughts of Axel's victory to fuel their dreams. But there were still men milling about, patrols and sleepless warriors manning some of the fires.

She pulled the cloak tighter around her shoulders, trying to cover up the sword as much as she could. Sticking to the shadows, she made her way around the circle of *The Phoenix*'s crew. Their regard for Axel had cemented this decision for her. He was worth ten of her. She could never achieve even half of what he could. He spoke about wanting peace between the kingdoms, for the Häxa to be free from persecution. Those were his dreams, and he needed to see them come to fruition.

"Do you think this is the right choice?"

Petra spun, finding Doran leaning against the other side of the ship. He stepped forward until she could see him. His blue eyes were drawn, shadows blooming under them.

She swallowed. "You know why I have to." Doran was likely one of the only people who understood. She couldn't let Axel die. She couldn't let him sacrifice everything he'd worked for to save her. To save Enzo. Both kingdoms needed him. They needed him to end this war.

Doran's eyes lined with tears, but none of them fell.

"Go," he said. "I'll try to buy you as much time as I can."

She gave a sharp nod and spun back toward the city. A few of the men looked up to watch her go, but she ignored them, praying none of the golden hair had slipped out from under her hood.

When she reached the edge of the encampment, she turned west. There was no way she would breach the walls of the city, but she could easily get Enzo to come out.

The moon moved quickly overhead as she traversed through the thickening foliage. The grasses grew up to her waist, tugging at the ends of her cloak until she made it up onto the road.

The trench started a little more than halfway up the eastern side of the city, the hills adding a natural defense in that section. She crested the top of one hill and nearly tripped at the sheer size of the forces gathered outside the gate.

Thousands of tents stretched out before her. She could barely see the end of them. Bowls of fire lined the north perimeter, casting away any shadows someone could use to slip into the camp. Pairs of guards walked the perimeter, their green uniforms dark against the tents.

She untied the cloak and left it on top of the hill. She would need everyone to see the cowl underneath. Only Axel had ever worn the garment. She prayed he wouldn't hate her for taking it from him.

It didn't take much longer after that for the guards to notice her. A pair of them stopped dead in their tracks and stared as she strode down the hill, doing her best to imitate Axel's swagger. She didn't approach them, even as sweat trickled down her back. She walked toward the gate, taking the main road where it curved back toward the city.

More green uniforms began trickling out of the tents, following her progress around the camp. Yet they did nothing. Only watched.

She reached the end of the road not blocked by tents. The bowls of fire sang their greeting to her as she stopped gripping the hilt of Axel's sword at her waist. This section of the road angled downward slightly, giving her a bit of a height advantage over the camp. If she fought from her toes, perhaps she could fool Enzo into thinking she was Axel long enough for him to disregard the height difference. She didn't need to fight him for long. Just long enough.

It made it easy to see Enzo make his way through his soldiers.

He was already clad in his armor, the small metal studs holding the strips of leather together shining in the firelight.

"Axel!" he called. "It's a bit early for the duel isn't it?"

Petra didn't answer, only drew the sword. The sky still held onto the curtain of night, but sunrise was only a half hour away. The Åldrans had likely already stirred, readying for the duel they were so eager to witness.

Hopefully, it would be over before she even realized it.

Enzo's eyes narrowed on her.

Her heart beat frantically against her ribs. Had he already seen through her ruse? Would he call her out for it? Would it all be for nothing?

Enzo turned to one of the men, who went running back toward the tents.

Petra didn't move, even as her entire body fought the tremors rippling through her muscles. Apparently, her body didn't appreciate the thought of dying today. She curled her toes inside her boots to dispel some of the energy. She had to be even more confident than Axel. Had to leave no room for doubt.

The guard returned, carrying a helmet and a sword.

Petra blew out a breath.

Enzo carefully slid the sword from its scabbard and strode toward her.

"I'm sorry it had to come to this, my friend." He set the helmet onto his head. "We both have so much to live for, but more importantly, we both have something worth dying for."

She spun the sword in that flashy way Axel always did. He'd practiced the move in front of her when they were children.

Enzo gave her a short nod and stepped past his men.

Petra didn't give him any more time to discover her. She charged him.

He brought up his sword, his mouth a firm line.

She knocked his sword to the side, using all the force in her arms to make it feel like a strike from Axel. It probably wasn't even close, but Enzo would hopefully think it was only because she was hesitating.

He twisted to the side, keeping his left side closed off to attack. He swung at her torso, but she brought up Axel's sword to block it.

"You've always beaten me," Enzo said under his breath. "You're a better man than I in every aspect. But this needs to end, and the end starts here."

Petra gritted her teeth and shoved him away. Axel's fighting style was more direct than hers, but she couldn't just open herself up. It would be too obvious.

Making him furious would be the best option.

She followed up one of her swings with a fist to Enzo's cheek.

Enzo staggered back, his expression turning hard.

His attacks grew faster.

Petra's arms ached with the vibrations of Axel's sword. It took almost everything she had to keep Enzo from slicing her leg, her arm. If she let him draw blood, he would pause. He would notice.

A sliver of gray touched the sky.

Petra took a deep breath and made her move.

She saw Enzo's feint.

She followed it, opening up her chest.

Enzo twisted just before their swords would have met, and he struck true.

The sword slid right between her ribs. She almost felt it scrape against her bones. She'd been cut by a sword many times over the years. This didn't hurt nearly as much as she thought it would.

Enzo's face hovered next to hers, twisted with emotion, Each one flickered across his face one after another.

Shock.

Understanding.

Triumph.

Those dark brown irises crackled with a fire that pierced Petra's soul. The fire of life and hope. That feeling of living through a miracle. Up until that point, he likely hadn't been sure he would live through that day. There had been the smallest doubt. But relief smoothed away every line in his face.

He looked up, finally meeting her gaze through the helmet.

The fire guttered out.

"P-Petra?" Her name crossed his lips in a stutter.

Her fingers shook as she covered his bloody hands with her own. "I'm sorry, Enzo." Her knees buckled. Numbness spread through her limbs. She couldn't even feel the ground beneath her. Couldn't feel the sword in her chest.

Enzo went to his knees in front of her, her hands holding his in place. Tears gathered at the corners of his eyes. "You've killed me," he whispered. "You've killed me."

Petra's grip loosened a fraction. "I'm sorry." The words weren't enough, but it was all she could offer. Because she knew just as well as he did what she'd done. What this would unleash.

"Why?" he asked. The question was a gasp more than a word.

Petra's hand finally slipped free, the cold spreading through her fingers. "For him." Her own gasps grew wet and sticky in her lungs. "Everything I've...I've ever done has been...for him."

A guttural roar shook the ground beneath her.

Funny. She wasn't numb enough not to feel it.

Enzo's weary face disappeared a moment later.

Axel was there, his arms around her.

"*Someone get me a healer!*" His fingers trembled as he unbuckled the strap under her chin. The helmet clanged on the ground next to her like a death knoll. "Petra, please. *Please*. Open your eyes, love. Please, open your eyes for me."

Petra hadn't realized they'd closed. Her lids felt like they had weights tied to them, but she got them open.

For him.

It was all for him.

Axel's face looked down at hers, tears streaming down his cheeks. "There's my girl. Stay with me, all right? Stay with me."

"Axel—" Enzo's broken voice sounded far away. Petra didn't know if that was because he actually was or because the world was fading around her.

"*No!*" His shout was raw. "You don't get to come *any* closer. You're *dead*, you bloody rocking demon! *Dead!*"

Petra opened her mouth, but the words clogged in her throat along with the air she couldn't get into her lungs.

"*Get me a bloody Häxa healer or I will burn this rocking camp to the ground!*" Axel brushed the hair from her face, leaving trails of something wet. Tears or blood or a mix of the two. "Shh, love. It's fine. You're going to be fine."

Petra shook her head, knowing how this was always going to end. He had to know. She couldn't leave him like this, no matter what Queen Kelda said. He had to know why. She opened her mouth and coughed out whatever had barred her words. The coughs brought black to her vision. She couldn't see.

"Open your eyes, Petra." Axel's voice broke. "Love, please open your eyes."

"Ax...Axel...I..."

# CHAPTER 39

## ASHES

*Why this had to be the end of Petyr Mallorysson feels like asking the sky why it goes dark when Sol sleeps. There was never another option for Pet. She would have watched the World Tree burn to save Axel, and she would have taken a thousand swords for him too. I knew it from the moment she stepped on my ship. From the first lie that fell from her lips.*

*— FROM THE WRITINGS OF DORAN FINNSSON, THE LAST KING OF GROVÖ*

There were no tears in Axel's eyes as he stared down at Petra. Those tears had fallen as he'd carried her body across the Sidan plains, her heart quiet in her chest and her blood staining his hands. They'd fallen as he'd staggered his way to the crew, the grief raw in all their faces.

He should have known. He should have seen it in her eyes. Should have felt it in the way she'd given him her farewells. She never planned on letting him sacrifice himself. And he should have bloody known it.

Enzo should have bloody known it too. How had he not seen Petra under the helmet? How had he not realized who he was facing? How had he killed the one person Axel had wanted him to save?

Little Hal settled a halo of small white flowers around her head.

Axel had changed her out of his bloodied clothing and into her best blues with her favorite boots tied to her feet. The cloak he'd bought her for her birthday spread out beneath her like wings. Big Hal slipped her axes into her hands, gently holding her limp fingers for a moment before letting go.

Erik stood at the tiller, breaking off the pieces of his contraption that allowed him to guide the ship and tossing them into the shallow waters below *The Phoenix*. Axel had told him to in case Erik needed to steer another ship. At least one of them should make it out of this bloody kingdom alive.

A hand settled on Axel's shoulder, and he was too numb to even shrug it off.

"They're ready when you are," Doran whispered. His own cheeks were wet with tears, trailing across the dark bruise along his jaw. He shouldn't have tried to stop Axel from getting to Petra. If Axel had been there even a few seconds sooner, he might have saved her. She might not be lying still in *The Phoenix's* hull.

Axel nodded but didn't move from his post at Petra's feet. He didn't move as Erik finished his work and pulled himself over the gunwale and into the shallows below. Didn't twitch as Little Hal pressed a gentle kiss to Petra's hair and stepped away. Didn't follow as Big Hal carried the last trunk off the ship.

They'd all understood. This ship was no longer their home. Not without the woman who had been its heart.

Axel stood alone on the ship, his empty chest in tatters.

He prayed, just one more time, for the gods to grant him a miracle. For the magic he'd given up to save her. For time to reverse so he could tell her he wouldn't fight Enzo. That he would rather watch the world burn than lose her.

Because now that he knew, he couldn't say anything differently. He never should have asked her to go through this. To watch that future they both wanted be erased. He was the worst sort of hypocrite.

The sun finally set over the horizon, heralding the end to a day that should have never come to pass.

He turned away, finally ripping himself from her side. She deserved the honor of a proper warrior's funeral.

His boots splashed into the shallow water, and he strode through the waves until he reached the stem of the ship.

Every Åldran stood at attention, a sea of stoic faces and honorable blues.

Doran and the crew gathered around the front of the ship, leaving a space in the midst of them. Axel set his hands to the carved feathers of the ship's breast and pushed.

Eric fell back first, the waves crashing into his chest before he pulled away.

Little Hal was next, his tears mingling with the sea.

Ulf gave a roar with his final push.

Ludvig silently slipped away.

Big Hal and Doran were the last to push the ship forward alongside Axel, the three of them giving it the final shove it needed to fly out into the sea.

Axel swam back to shore beside them, shedding his vest when they reached the edge of the water.

Small fires stretched across the edge of the beach, and Axel approached the closest one. King Agnar waited for him, an Åldran fire-soaked arrow and a bow in his hands. He passed them both to Axel with a gravity rarely seen on the old king.

Axel stuck the tip of the arrow in the closest fire, the flames instantly catching on the soaked cloth.

He knocked the arrow and brought the fletching to his cheek.

"I love you," he whispered. "I won't forget."

The arrow soared from his hand, disappearing over the side of *The Phoenix's* gunwale.

More arrows soared over his head. First five. Then twelve. Then hundreds.

The flames glittered like falling stars as they streaked across the sky, bidding their final farewells to the warrior floating on the ship before them.

A low hum started up behind Axel. A song took form, the voices of thousands raw and consuming as the flames devoured the boat. Devoured her.

*"On somber night,*

*Through starlit skies,*
*A lonely, burning arrow flies.*
*It bears its fire*
*To floating pyre*
*Whereon a fallen hero lies.*
*Its flight is true.*
*It finds its mark.*
*A mighty, roaring flame to spark.*
*The ship will burn*
*From stem to stern*
*As well the hero's mortal ties."*

But Axel didn't sing. No words filled his mouth. No warmth of hope and peace filled his chest. He simply watched as the fire consumed everything he'd ever loved one final time.

*"Valhalla calls*
*Each time a worthy warrior falls.*
*Near kindred sing*
*While soul departs 'neath Valkyrie wing."*

Doran stepped up beside him, but Axel didn't take his eyes from the flames licking up toward Valhalla. Had she already reached their gates? Had she met the Valkyries at the foot of Odin's throne?

*"When in the fray*
*True blood is spilled*
*And life's sweet breath by wound is stilled,*
*The noble dead*
*Find life instead*
*In purer self that can't be killed.*
*Immune to pain,*
*No more to toil,*
*Or struggle bound by mortal coil.*
*No blood, no tears,*
*No grief, no fears.*
*A broken heart with rapture filled."*

Doran set a hand on his shoulder, leaning toward him until his whisper could be heard over the voices at their backs.

"I know that look, Axel. What are you going to do?"

> *"Valhalla calls*
> *Each time a worthy warrior falls.*
> *Near kindred sing*
> *While soul departs 'neath Valkyrie wing."*

The wood of the boat finally succumbed to the fire, buckling inward as it all turned to ash.

Axel turned to Doran, whatever was left of his heart crumbling alongside the ship that carried her.

"I'm going to end a war."

# CHAPTER 40

## A MOMENT

*Love, please open your eyes.*

Axel's pleading still rang in Petra's ears, and she finally opened her eyes.

But he wasn't there.

A great hall lay out in front of her. She knelt in the center of the large room, the biggest hall she'd ever seen. Two thick wooden doors stood sentry on the far wall, a pair of snarling wolves carved into the faces of each, so lifelike it wouldn't be surprising if they leaped from the wood and stalked toward Petra. Wooden beams thicker than *The Phoenix*'s mast held up the roof soaring over her head. Instead of a regular thrush roof, this roof had been plastered, the white painted with frescoes of dragons flying through a storm-filled sky, their scales gleaming as they faced down an army of darkness.

Tables lined the walls to either side of her, iron baskets holding flames that looked as if they didn't even use any fuel. She waited for her magic to respond to the fire, but only a warmth bubbled up under her ribs.

In fact, most of her body felt warm. She hadn't felt anything like this since she'd sat around a table with her family. With the twins cracking jokes and Da's booming laugh while Axel beat every single one of her brothers in arm wrestling contests.

Pushing to her feet, she turned around.

At the end of the great hall sat a pair of thrones. They weren't the not-a-throne that King Firmin claimed, or the gaudy thing King Leonardo always sat in. Each boasted a sturdy framed chair, the backs rising high enough for anyone to rest their head against and a single, purple cushion edged with gold covered their seats. They looked comfortable. Seats for rulers who wished to be among others. A place of respect, but not intimidation.

The entire place was familiar to her somehow. As if she'd stepped into her own home after a long journey. She'd never been in this hall, but if she got up, she'd know exactly where she was going. A peace she hadn't felt in years sank into every particle of her being.

She was dead.

She was actually dead.

And it didn't hurt nearly as bad as she thought it would.

She'd died and left everything she'd ever known behind, but the only thing that made her chest ache was the thought of Axel alone. He didn't deserve the sorrow their parting would bring, but the world needed him for a little longer. Åldras and Sida both needed a hero. It was never going to be her. Axel was the only good on either side. With her death, she'd saved him from an early grave. She'd saved him from the fate Queen Kelda had foreseen.

Dying didn't look so bleak knowing the world would be better for it.

The peace suffusing her body hummed, and she slowly trailed over to one of the tables. Breads, meats, and fruits of every size, shape, and color filled bowls of gold and platters of silver. Petra carefully picked up a round, blue fruit, the flesh of the outside like leather while the inside held what looked like beads of jewel.

"Petra."

She turned toward the voice.

A woman stood in front of the double doors. A dark braid hung over her shoulder and a pair of bright blue eyes shone in the light of the fires around the hall.

The fruit fell from Petra's hand. "Mama?"

Tears fell from each side of Mama's face. "Hello, Little Dove."

Petra ran across the great hall, her throat so clogged with tears that she couldn't even speak. She collided with Mama, her arms wrapping around her neck as she cried. She couldn't stop the flow of tears and couldn't decide if she wanted to laugh or sob.

Mama's arms came around her, that fierce warmth encircling her. Mama stood a few inches shorter than Petra remembered. She was soft in the places Petra was hard. Warm in the places Petra was cold. But that warmth mingled with the peace burrowing into Petra's entire being.

"Mama," Petra finally gasped, burying her face in Mama's neck. "Gods, I missed you. I missed you so much."

Mama's hand rubbed her back. "Oh, sweet girl, I missed you too."

Petra finally stepped back, wiping her soggy face against her sleeve. "I'm so sorry. I'm sorry about what happened in Holmberg. I'm sorry I wasn't a better person. That I had to lie about who I was. That I dishonored Da's name. I'm so sorry."

Mama took Petra's face in her hands, wiping away the tears still trailing down her cheeks. "You have nothing to be sorry for. There was no way for you to know. No way I would have ever guessed the fire ran in your veins. If I'd known, that night would have been so different. I'm sorry you've had to live a life fearing the gift you've been given."

Petra shook her head. "I could have made different choices."

"Little Dove, you survived a world trying to put out your spark in any way it could." Her expression hardened. "If anyone is to blame for what has happened to you, it's Constance."

"Constance?" Petra blinked. "Axel's mother? What does she have to do with this?"

Mama drew her toward a bench. "There's much you don't know, but I pray I'll be able to help you understand. Constance has been plotting all of this since the moment Axel was born."

"What?" Petra looked about the room, trying to get her thoughts to match Mama's hard tone. "You mean his prophecy?"

"And yours." Mama blew out a breath. "This is a long story that we really don't have much time for."

Didn't have time for? Petra opened her mouth to ask, but Mama spoke before the words passed her tongue.

"Constance and I grew up in the same small village. We both

came into our gifts during the great Häxa purge under King Vilgot's reign of terror. Our mothers were friends and practiced magic together often, even though it had been outlawed. They were discovered and killed along with Constance's older sisters when Constance and I had traveled with some friends to another town. We learned later that King Vilgot himself came and saw to their execution. We fled, not even returning to our village, and lived on the run for several years.

"We found other Häxa along the way who taught us how to use and hide our gifts. The Great Mother had just begun gathering the others to her to find a new home away from Åldras. But we didn't want to leave. Constance, more than anyone, wanted to fight back against the tyranny of the Åldran king. But the Ekte were growing stronger, and we were running out of options. We finally were preparing to go to Mötesplats to meet with the Great Mother and escape Åldras with her. It was then that Constance met Asher."

Petra shook her head. "Why are you telling me all of this?"

Mama's mouth thinned like it had when the twins were toeing the line with her. Petra's spine straightened, and Mama flicked her braid over her shoulder. "Because if you don't understand the past, you won't be able to change the future. We were in Mötesplats for two months. Constance met Asher and realized she didn't have to leave. She said it was love and that Asher didn't agree with what King Vilgot was doing to the Häxa and wanted to help. Said he also had a friend who had just lost his wife and was looking for a new life for him and his sons."

A tightening took root in Petra's middle. "Da. It was Da."

Mama nodded. "It was the perfect situation. Asher had just been named warlord over Holmberg and was getting ready to take his holding there. He wanted your father to accompany him, as the two of them had fought together throughout the years, but Mallory had lost his wife in childbirth. He needed someone to help him care for his new babe and the four other boys he had."

"You married Da and claimed the boys all as your own."

"Yes, and it was the best decision I ever made." A warm smile bloomed on her lips. "Not only because of the safety it provided, but because of the family he gave me. While none of those boys had come from my womb, they were mine the moment I set eyes on them. Dane was just over six years old and while he remembered his mother, he always treated me like I was his family. The twins and Kol were too young to remember her, and Gram would have never known any better. While I'd learned their mother was a wonderful woman, I was the one the gods allowed to raise them, and I wouldn't trade anything for what they gave me."

Tears pooled in Petra's eyes. She'd wondered. If Mama was a Häxa, how had she had sons? She wiped the tears off her face. "I still don't see what this has to do with anything."

"I'd found my future, and I thought Constance had too. While your da and I took time to truly fall in love with each other, she and Asher had a whirlwind romance. One full of joy and passion. We both found out we were with child within weeks of each other. I was scared out of my mind, but Constance was overjoyed. We debated over girls' names for ages until we'd both come up with ones we liked. Axel was originally supposed to be Astrid, if you can believe it. We were both shocked when only seven weeks after you were born, Axel arrived. It changed everything."

Petra chewed on the inside of her cheek. "I don't understand."

Mama grabbed her hands. "Listen carefully. I was there when Axel was born. I witnessed Constance seeing the prophecy of her son. She saw the destruction of Åldras in the waters of Axel's birth and has been planning to make every bit of that prophecy come to fruition. When she looked to the future, she saw what Axel would become. While I watched her find peace with Asher, her heart had still carried the bitterness of what we'd lost. She saw her chance for revenge against the Åldran kings and their cursed Ekte. Saw how Axel would be blessed with unthinkable power and how that power would help her accomplish her goals. I tried to talk her out of it. Tried to remind her that she had a husband who loved her. Tried to show her that her son was a blessing. The first son born of a Häxa. He was a miracle, but Constance couldn't see it. It was as if her heart had frozen in her chest, colder than the ice she wielded. All she saw was a means to her own revenge against those who had hurt us. Three weeks after Axel was born, she left."

Hel's halls, this was all too much. "To seek her revenge? Where did she go?"

"She killed King Vilgot in his bed. We didn't even know it happened until she arrived at our door, months later. It was the middle of the night, and I had both you and Axel with me." Mama's face grew dark. "She didn't even hold him. Didn't look at him. All she said was that she'd killed the king and her plans were coming to fruition. I begged her to stay, to return to her family. To her babe. But she was beyond reason. She told me she wouldn't be back. That I would never see her again. And instead of brushing the soft, golden hair of her son's head so much like her own, she brushed yours."

The skin of Petra's back began to crawl. "Why?"

Tears gathered in Mama's eyes. "She left me with a prophecy that night, one she hadn't told me before she'd disappeared.

> *"A fearful gift*
> *For ages shrouded.*
> *Oft' in whispers,*
> *By rumor touted.*
> *A blessed curse*
> *For lifetimes hidden.*
> *By fate removed,*
> *By fate forbidden.*
> *Then from the darkness,*
> *A maid emerges*
> *With light that kills*
> *And flame that purges.*
> *Igniting war*
> *'Twixt raptor and bruin,*
> *Laying both eagle*
> *And bear to ruin.*
> *A poison flower*
> *'Neath oaken shade.*
> *A deadly power.*
> *A hidden blade.*
> *Yet noble caused,*
> *Her life she gives,*

*For flower dies*
*Hence oak tree lives.*
*Though with her will*
*The winged beast burns,*
*Once eagle, now phoenix*
*The kingdom returns.*
*Though kingdom not*
*With royal purges,*
*The matrons' power*
*And reign emerges."*

All the warmth in Petra's soul fled.

"She knew you would be the final key to her revenge," Mama continued. "I didn't know it then, but the night the Sidans came to our door, I understood. Through your gift, she could start a war that would destroy the kingdom that had killed her family and abandoned the old ways. It was because of her that the Sidans came to Holmberg that night. It was because she told them to come for you."

Petra shot to her feet. "But if she wanted me so badly, why didn't she ever show herself? You speak as if she's been plotting all of this, but where is she?"

Mama reached out, but her hand passed through Petra's.

"What?" Petra raised her hand up.

"We've run out of time." Mama's eyes grew glassy. "Little Dove, you can't stay here."

Petra stumbled back. "What do you mean? I have to stay. I'm dead."

Mama shook her head. "You were never meant to stay."

"What?" Something tugged at Petra's chest, and she fell to her knees. "What's happening?"

"Fate," Mama said, kneeling down next to her. "I've told you all you need to know. You can't tell Constance what you've learned. You can't tell her you know what she's doing. You can't tell anyone what you know, or she'll see. Her only weakness is that she can't see her own future. Use it against her. You have to save Axel. You have to stop Constance."

Petra gasped. "Please, Mama! I don't want to go!" The flames on the walls flared as she struggled against the pull in her gut. She'd just found Mama. She couldn't go. What about Da? The boys? She didn't want to leave them. Didn't want to go back to the pain and the lies and the heartache.

"I know. I promise you, there's still happiness to be found. Axel needs you. You have to keep Constance away from him. Keep him safe. She can't know what I've told you. Don't forget. Don't lose hope."

The room around Petra was fading, a cold heaviness in her chest replacing the warm peace. "Mama!"

Mama reached out, her hands cupping around Petra's face even though they couldn't touch. Tears tracked down either side of her beautiful face.

"I love you. I love you so much. You're so much more than I ever believed you could be. I'll be waiting for the day it's finally time for our family to be together again."

The room disappeared; Mama's teary blue eyes scarred onto Petra's soul.

# THINGS TO COME

The waters of the Vit Sea crashed against the sandy shore, the waves black under the starless sky. It seemed even the heavens turned their eyes away from the tragedy of the day. From bearing witness to the darkness that had formed with the fall of one little Häxa girl. As if they couldn't even look at her blood still staining the ground.

Queen Kelda, however, didn't give the heavens much heed. She hadn't in years. Not since they'd witnessed the death of her entire family at the hands of monsters.

Instead, she watched the dark waters, letting the very edge of the sea taste the hem of her dark gown. As if kissing her feet in supplication. The queen lifted her hand, and the water wrapped around her fingers like the finest jewels before they dripped back to the sea.

Soon, the sea wouldn't be the only thing bowing to her.

Soon, the entire world would kiss her feet.

The future she'd seen twenty-two years ago was so close she could almost taste it. Like the salt only found in fresh blood and the sea. Addictive. The night she'd killed the monster who slaughtered her family had been her first hit of a drug stronger than anything the underbellies of any kingdom could produce. She'd been chasing it for years now and her entire body trembled with the promised high.

The wind whipped through her hair, the gold curls freed from the headdress she'd worn for so many years as she hid behind the Sidan king until she could be freed. Until she could finally have the vengeance she was so due. She trailed slowly along the coastline, watching, waiting.

It didn't take long until she found where most of *The Phoenix*'s charred remains had swept back toward land. Right where she'd seen they would. The rocks along the coastline here caught much of the debris dumped into the ocean, the currents carrying the sins of Bellator to this particular stretch of beach. She stepped over a ruined plank and used her magic to push the wreckage out of her path.

The bark of a hacking cough caught her ears. She pushed the sea a few steps ahead, allowing her to run quickly through the calf deep water.

Against one of the large rocks, a girl pulled herself up to her knees, her pale, flawless skin glowing as if she'd taken the moon from the sky and stole Màni's light for herself.

The queen stepped closer, and the girl's head whipped in her direction.

Mallory's eyes set in the frame of Mila's face stared up at her.

It was almost enough to make the queen falter. Almost enough to make her dead heart skip in her chest.

The queen unclasped the cloak from around her neck. "Hello, Petra." She wrapped the cloak around Petra's bare shoulders.

But Petra's blue-green eyes didn't leave her face, taking in the runes scarred along her cheekbones, the gold of her hair. Those eyes so like Mallory's darkened enough to see the shadows that lived in this girl. To see destruction surface along with a knowing that likely came from having died, then brought back to the world of the living.

But the last words the queen ever thought she'd hear crossed the girl's lips, as quiet as a lover's promise and sharp as an assassin's blade.

"Hello, Constance."

# Author's Note

Son of Steel was originally the first book I had in mind for Axel and Pet's story. The duel between Pet and Enzo was one of the very first scenes I wrote, knowing that their paths would eventually bring them to the same point Patroclus and Hector found themselves in during Homer's tale.

Now, I do my best to stay close to the core of the story I am taking inspiration from. There are some very obvious differences: Patroclus was never discovered to be a woman, Achilles's abilities have absolutely nothing to do with love, Hector and Achilles never became friends, and so on. I have taken the heart of their story and changed it to feel more intriguing to an audience in today's world. For instance, most readers would have thrown this book in a dumpster if I had allowed Freyja to sweep in during Anders and Roman's duel, cover the shore in a mist, and carry Roman back to his bed in the palace, saving him from an early death. We all would have been like Helen of Sparta to Aphrodite saying, "No; go and sit with him yourself."

So, I studied this story. I read the books and watched the movies. I found the pieces that made this story a legend that has lasted the tests of time. I found where the heart of it is. It was in the honor of Achilles. It was in the love between Hector and Andromache. In the wisdom of Odysseus. In the walls of Troy.

Yes, it was in the death of Patroclus.

This story isn't one about happiness or joy. This is not a story of victory over evil or the end of tyranny. Of happily ever afters.

I think Homer said it best.

"The wrath of Achilles is my theme…"

And I very much plan to do it justice.

# Acknowledgments

I know I say it every single time I write one of these, but writing books is not a one-man show. While my name may be on the cover of this book, there are so many wonderful and amazing people who have helped me bring this story into existence.

First, my family. Eric, I am still in awe that you actually like that I write books. Thank you for loving me enough to keep encouraging me to sit down at my desk and write another one. Thank you for moving our entire house while I edited this book and thank you for making sure one of us picked the kids up from school. Thank you, my darling girls, for being my best cheerleaders. Thank you for not thinking your mom is a crazy person for loving books and for loving them along with me.

Special thanks need to go to Lindsay Hiller. Every time I doubted myself while I was editing this book, I kept repeating in my head, "Lindsay loved this book. You have to finish it because Lindsay loved it." You got me through that *massive* revision. Honestly, you've gotten me through every single one of my books, and I have no idea what I would do without you. Thank you for being my best friend and for writing books with me.

I have to thank my dad. You are the entire reason I'm sitting at this computer. I don't know if I would be where I am today without you. Thank you for always encouraging me and for letting me drag you to all the author things. You're going to be famous one day, and I'll get to rub it in people's faces that you're my dad. Also, thanks need to go to my mom. Honestly, I don't know how you put up with having two authors in the family. Thank you for listening to me talk about books anytime I call and for cheering me on.

A huge thank you to my wonderful cousin Tyleah who always

reads my dumpster fire books and tells me to stop whining about my deadlines because I always finish the dang books on time. Thank you to Kate Ward for telling me Axel and Pet were being stupid and making me do that gigantic revision. You were absolutely right. Thank you, Sally O'Keef, for putting in all those commas I missed. Someday, I will know the difference between "further" and "farther" but today is not that day. I trust you. Thank you to Tanya Anne Crosby and the whole team at OHB for bringing this book to life.

Thank you to all my amazing author friends that continue to inspire me. Thank you to Jeff Wheeler, Kathryn Purdie, Elizabeth Lowham, Jessica Scarlett, and KayLynn Flanders for reading the first book and telling me it was worth writing a second one. I hope you all love this one just as much. Thank you to my horde of writing group friends: Dad, Marci Johnson (x2), Tracy Tyler, Robbie of the Beams of Stuffle, Jared Jensen, David Haynie, Aimee Hall, Ben Bailey, Kelsey Larson, Kayla Tillotson, HR Boyd, Bonnie Jo Pierson, Lindsay Hiller, Sally O'Keef, Amber Mae Weston, Tarry Perry, and my fairy queen Natalie Krause. You all amaze me and I'm so excited for all the good books coming.

And last but never least, thank you to my Heavenly Father. Thank you for being my author and creator. For instilling in me a desire to create and for being there for me all along the way. I know I am never alone.

# About the Author

Allison Anderson lives her best life as a wife, a mom, a dedicated member of The Church of Jesus Christ of Latter-Day Saints, and a fantasy writer. As a lifelong fantasy nerd, she finds it natural to create stories of her own and you can often find her jotting down new story ideas or talking about dragons. She's spent most of her life across the southwestern United States.

https://www.allisonandersonauthor.com/

A small press bound by the belief that every voice matters.

Sign up for our newsletter to learn about new releases and more.

*Buy directly from us to save on ebooks, book bundles, and special editions.*

Follow us on social media:

facebook.com/oliverheberbooks

instagram.com/oliverheberbooks

bsky.app/profile/oliverheberbooks.bsky.social

youtube.com/@OliverHeberBooksPublisher

oliverheberbooks.substack.com

amazon.com/oliverheberbooks

www.ingramcontent.com/pod-product-compliance
Lightning Source LLC
Chambersburg PA
CBHW051129130726
47988CB00005B/1757